Harrow

GALLERIES OF STONE - BOOK TWO

C. J. MILBRANDT

OLEXI

Galleries of Stone, Book 2
Harrow
illustrated edition

Copyright © 2019, 2013, 2012 by C. J. Milbrandt I cjmilbrandt.com
ISBN: 978-1-63123-071-4

Illustrations: Hannah Lavender I studiolavender.com
Jacket design: Elza Kinde I bumblebess.com

*"Doves abide while eagles soar,
but both build nests."*

table of contents

Harrow

1

A Proper Welcome

Tupper sprang lightly from rock to rock, descending from the summit at breakneck speeds, a golden lynx kitten close on his heels. He'd been on the lookout for a carriage for days now, and there was no mistaking the team of blood red bays he'd glimpsed through the yellow-green haze of leaf buds tipping the trees on Morven's southern slope.

His practical mind was already racing through the paltry odds and ends remaining in the pantry after their long winter. Dinner was going to be eggs and biscuits again unless their guest was feeling generous.

The boy hit the cobblestone road with a soft *oof* and lengthened his stride, racing toward home in order to share the momentous news. He burst through the workshop door, exclaiming, "Frey!"

Freydolf didn't react; he was completely caught up detailing a delicate row of feathers on a large brownstone sculpture.

Unsurprised, Tupper placed his hand on the sculptor's arm. "Master Freydolf, did you hear me?"

Dark eyes focused on his upturned face. Relaxing into a smile, Morven's Keeper asked, "What's put stars in your eyes this time, lambkin? Did you finally find what you were so mysteriously looking for the other day?"

A secretive smile flitted across the boy's lips. "*Maybe*, but that's for later. Aurelius is back!"

"Isn't he earlier than usual this year?"

"I think so." Tupper tugged the man's sleeve. "Let's go see why."

"In a hurry?" Freydolf's tone was teasing, but he was already setting aside tools and loosening apron ties.

"Yes. I want to get to him first."

The sculptor straightened. "Aye, that would be best. Where is Graven?"

"Minding the chickens."

"Right across from the stable." Freydolf hurried into his boots.

"Graven will be good," Tupper promised. "He only chases if Aurelius runs."

"Aye, but old habits die hard. One look, and the brat will bolt."

Tupper nodded. "I *could* go on ahead … just in case."

With a knowing look, Freydolf waved him on. "I'll fill the trough and throw down some straw for his horses."

Those were his duties, so he balked. "Shouldn't I …?"

"Nay, lad," his master urged. "Aurelius will be ordering you around soon enough. Get your welcome in while you can."

Tupper seized his chance and rushed off, hoping that the merchant's early arrival meant an extra-long stay. Too excited to wait for the carriage to navigate up the winding road from the quarry, he dove into the woods, skidding down a mossy gully, then dashing through a stand of ferns. Over the last two summers, he'd traipsed all over Morven, so he knew her slopes as well as the contents of his cupboards.

Skirting a blackberry thicket, he paused to check on his little golden shadow. Rimbles sprang playfully through the bracken, keeping up despite her small size. Crouching down, Tupper asked, "Do you want a ride?"

She batted at his outstretched hand, then darted ahead, ever the curious one.

He followed his daytime guardian, taking care not to let his hair get caught in overhanging branches. His last haircut had been near the end of the previous summer, so his white-blond curls were becoming difficult to manage. He often wondered if he could buck Flox tradition and let his hair grow out as long as Freydolf's.

His shortcut led out onto a lower bend in the road, and Tupper turned downhill, jogging along as he strained his ears for the sound of hooves on stone. No telltale *clip-clop* reached him, but when he rounded the next bend, he caught the jingle of harnesses.

To his surprise, the merchant's high-wheeled carriage was parked on a level stretch of the road. The lead stallion greeted him with a soft nicker, and the other horses' ears pricked forward. At first, Tupper was afraid Rimbles might spook them, but Aurelius's team was obviously used to seeing all kinds of odd things.

But something was strange.

The driver's seat was empty, the reins were draped over its back, and the brake lever was engaged. Tupper frowned in confusion. Where was Aurelius? Had he stopped to give the team a rest?

Without warning, arms wrapped around the boy from behind. Claws prickled against Tupper's throat, and a very familiar voice drawled, "How many times do I have to warn you not to let down your guard, sprat?"

"I forgot." Tilting his head back just enough to meet his captor's gaze, he did a terrible job of hiding how happy he was to see the Pred. "Welcome back."

"Leave it to you to smile in the face of danger," Aurelius groused. "Can you call off your ankle-biter. She's scuffing my boots!"

"Rimbles," Tupper gently scolded. "He's not hurting me."

The hand at his throat shifted slightly, and the Pred purred, "By choice, not by inability."

Since it was true, the boy simply shrugged and changed the subject. "Is that a new cloak?"

Dark brows arched over golden eyes, which took on a pleased gleam. "You noticed!"

"It's a pretty color," Tupper explained seriously.

Aurelius released him and stepped back, making a little half-turn while shaking out tiered folds of lustrous fabric. Jeweled daggers glittered in their usual places at the man's thighs, and fangs flashed as he announced, "Aubergine."

"Kind of like purple."

With a vaguely disgruntled glance, the man said, "Aubergine sounds much more elegant."

"So it *is* purple?"

"A distinctive and distinguished shade of purple. It brings out my eyes."

"If you say so."

Folding his arms across his chest, Aurelius commanded, "Let's have a look at you."

Tupper stood a little straighter.

The man prowled around him. "You're all knobby knees and elbows! Are those the longest breeches you own?"

"Yes."

With a disapproving *tsk*, Aurelius said, "You've clearly outgrown them. Which makes sense since you're *almost* big enough to prop an elbow on." He demonstrated, then mussed Tupper's hair. "A little taller, a lot shaggier, and do I detect a bit of a turn in those horns of yours?"

The boy ducked out from under the man's hand and bashfully boasted, "I'm almost thirteen. Flox horns turn then."

"Onset of adolescence, and all that," the Pred mused aloud.

Tupper wasn't sure what he meant, but he nodded anyhow. "Freydolf thinks you're early this year."

"A bit," Aurelius conceded. "How's he faring?"

This time, the glint was in the Flox's eye. "He could do with a rabbit."

"That could be arranged ... on two conditions."

"Name them," Tupper invited, eager to haggle.

Holding up one finger, Aurelius said, "This time around, you will keep that mosaic monstrosity out of the balcony."

The boy winced. "I didn't know he could jump that high."

"Aye, full of surprises, that one."

Nodding, Tupper prompted, "Second?"

With a subtle shift in his expression, Aurelius leaned forward and haughtily replied, "You will welcome me *properly*, sprat."

Tupper had been hoping the Pred wouldn't think him too old for such things. With a small bounce, he threw his arms around the tall man's neck. The Pred returned the embrace, and Tupper squeezed tight, mumbling, "Missed you."

"Naturally," Aurelius replied, sounding excessively smug.

Freydolf unhitched the team and worked his way through the bays, releasing them from their harnesses and rubbing them down as he listened to his idle-handed brother-in-law. Aurelius alternated between gossiping about his winter voyage and giving orders.

"Gruff and young Mister Meadowsweet will arrive tomorrow morning to unload the carriage and take the team down to greener pastures."

"Why didn't you simply drag them up here today?" Freydolf asked. "There's plenty of daylight left."

At that moment, Tupper hopped onto the carriage's step in order to peek through a window. Aurelius scooped the boy up, saying, "No particular reason."

Freydolf eyed the pair with amusement. He suspected that his brother-in-law hadn't wanted to share the lad with Carden.

Tupper looked rather silly cradled in the Pred's arms, for his face was quickly losing the cherubic roundness of childhood. But the lad leaned contentedly against Aurelius's shoulder, not in the least perturbed by the manhandling. They'd definitely missed each other, so Frey held his peace.

Aurelius peered down his nose at his docile burden. "You give up too easily."

"Yes," Tupper agreed.

Freydolf snorted. "Don't underestimate the lad. You've played into his hands."

Scrutinizing the boy, Aurelius said, "Be that as it may, I can still use this to my advantage. Tupper shall be my talisman against gaudy beasts with ready fangs!"

Unable to resist, Freydolf countered, "*You* are a gaudy beast!"

"With fangs," Tupper helpfully added.

Pulling the lad more comfortably into the crook of his arm, Aurelius shot a sour look at the Keeper. "You're still rather puny, sprat. Does Frey feed you enough?"

"I do the cooking," Tupper reminded. Without a trace of artifice, he smoothly added, "I'll eat enough tonight if you hunt for us."

"Aye." Heaving a sigh, Aurelius announced, "I have news."

Freydolf caught the change in mood and slowly straightened. Something must have happened to put such an odd expression on his face. "Go on."

"It sounds worse than it is."

"Bad news, then?"

"Nay." Pursing his lips, Aurelius warned, "*Don't* laugh."

Freydolf relaxed, for if the man found his news embarrassing, it was probably something silly that he'd blown out of proportion. "No promises. What's happened?"

Various emotions flicked across Aurelius's face before settling on what could only be called bewilderment. "I'm a grandfather."

To Aurelius's relief, Frey didn't laugh; indeed, he looked equally stunned.

"Ulrica's a grandmother?" he muttered, rubbing the back of his neck.

Only Tupper was unfazed by this world-tilting revelation. Patting the heavily embroidered vest against which he leaned, he said, "That's really good, Aurelius! Do you have a grandson or a granddaughter?"

"A son." Shaking his head, he corrected, "My eldest son has a son."

The young Flox nodded and said, "I'm an uncle again … probably. Carden's Melina was due mid-winter."

"Aye, I'm an uncle dozens of times over, but *this*."

Tupper studied his face. "You're not happy?"

"Nay, it's not that," sighed the man. "It just makes me sound so deucedly old!"

"Will you grow a beard now?" Tupper inquired. "You're allowed."

Aurelius stared blankly at the boy for several moments, then muttered, "Perish the thought!"

Chuckling, Freydolf explained, "Flox men shave the hair from their chins until the birth of their first grandchild. It's one of their rites of passage. And lambkin, Pred don't *have* beards."

"You're hairy everywhere else." Giving Aurelius's smooth cheek a gentle pat, Tupper said, "This makes you look too young to be a grandfather!"

"Aye!" The man's eyes widened, then took on a joyous shine. "Aye, that's exactly right, sprat!"

Nodding wisely, Tupper went on, "Just like it can be hard to tell if you're a man."

Brows slowly rising, the merchant exclaimed, "You'd have to be an imbecile to call my masculinity into question!" Voice deepening demonstratively, he waved a jewel-bedizened hand, his ruffled cuffs fluttering as he growled, "I'm incensed! I'm insulted! I'm incontestably male!"

Tupper made a soothing gesture and explained, "Farley overheard Aggie asking mother whether to call Freydolf *uncle* or *auntie*, and he tattled to me. I explained that it wasn't a Pred's fault, so it's okay."

Aurelius was even more indignant, but then it dawned on him. Swearing under his breath, he demanded, "Is this about horns?"

"Aye, it seems we're pitied for our lack," Freydolf relayed.

"Preposterous!" Aurelius gave one of Tupper's a flick with his claw. "These will not make a man of you."

The boy's eyes grew thoughtful, and he finally nodded in agreement. "But you're a grandfather because you're a father. That's just how it works."

Recalling his second—and equally mind-bending—piece of news, Aurelius shot his brother-in-law a wary glance and cleared his throat. "Speaking of fatherhood ...."

2

Empty Nest

"Our youngest boy is leaving home, apprenticing out to one of his uncles in the Harrow shipyard," Aurelius began. "He sets sail in a fortnight."

Freydolf frowned. "You should have delayed your visit until afterward!"

"I'm curtailing it instead," the merchant replied, setting Tupper down. At the boy's confused expression, Aurelius put things more simply. "I can't stay long."

"Too bad," the lad murmured, crestfallen.

"I wasn't finished, sprat. There's more to it." Aurelius looked to his brother-in-law. "I came early to warn you. That and to deliver the stones, of course. They take up all the space I'll be needing for luggage."

"Luggage," Freydolf echoed, not following.

"I shall return in a month's time with Ulrica."

"Don't you usually spend summers on Last Continent?"

"Aye, we have a nice place up there, but Ulrica wishes to meet your *lambkin*." Aurelius smirked at the lad. "For that and ... well, for *other* reasons, her mind's made up. Rather than journey abroad, we'll be spending our summer in the interior. How do you feel about long-term guests, Frey?"

"You're welcome, of course. What's it been—ten years?"

"Twelve."

Tupper's fidgeting escalated until he was fairly dancing with excitement. He finally burst out, "You're going to live here?"

"Neatly surmised." Aurelius somehow hid his smile. "As always, you manage to find the crux of a matter."

"All summer?" the boy checked.

Aurelius haughtily warned, "Your workload will undoubtedly triple for the duration."

"I don't mind. I'll work hard." Hurrying to his master's side, Tupper pulled his arm, urgently whispering, "Frey!"

The man knelt to better meet the lad's earnest gaze. "Aye, lambkin?"

"Aren't you glad?"

"To have my bossy sister and bratty brother descend upon my humble home for an entire season?" he deadpanned.

Tupper tentatively answered, "Yes?"

Roughing up the boy's long curls, he admitted, "I'm looking forward to it at least half as much as you."

"So, lots?"

Freydolf grinned. "Aye. Lots."

Once the horses were settled into their stalls, Aurelius sauntered out of the stable only to quick-step back inside. Slipping around behind the others, he graciously invited, "After you."

Tupper nodded and hurried to where a huge tiger crouched beside the hitching posts, tail twitching. Reaching up to scratch Graven under his chin, he sternly ordered, "Be nice."

The statue's gaze never wavered from Aurelius, who glared with ill-concealed hostility from over Freydolf's broad shoulder. The merchant grumbled, "I'll acknowledge that the beast's manners have improved since becoming attached to the boy, but he still brandishes his fangs at me."

"Yours are in plain sight, as well," Frey blandly pointed out. "Come on, I'll guard you against your nemesis until we can stash you in the balcony."

"Stashed!" scoffed Aurelius. "I think not!"

"He's going to hunt," Tupper piped up, already sitting astride the tiger. "I'll keep Graven with me while Aurelius chases rabbits. Otherwise, Graven might chase Aurelius."

Freydolf grunted his acknowledgment. "Shall we? This trunk is *heavy*."

Aurelius held his ground until the tiger bounded off in the direction of the workshop, Tupper bent low over his neck. Falling in step beside the sculptor, Aurelius casually remarked, "You're looking well, Frey."

"I have no complaints ... save your baffling need to over-pack. What's *in* this?" Adjusting his grip, he optimistically guessed, "Rocks?"

"Books, mostly," said Aurelius. "I thought they might interest that boy of yours."

"You spoil him."

Aurelius slyly retorted, "And he spoils you."

Freydolf wasn't sure he could successfully argue that point, so he only said, "Could you at least open the door for me?"

Aurelius breezed through first and exclaimed, "What's this?"

Leaving the trunk in a corner, Freydolf joined his agent, who circled his current sculpture. Unsure why the other man seemed so indignant, Frey answered, "It's the griffin we discussed last autumn. Why? Is something wrong?"

"Aye! It's nearly finished."

"And?"

"This block of brownstone was meant to keep you busy for an entire year." Golden eyes narrowed. "You're getting faster."

"Perhaps." With an easy grin, he suggested, "Maybe you should start bringing me more rocks."

"Idiot!"

A little hurt, Freydolf countered, "I like to stay busy. What's wrong with bringing in more work?"

Aurelius's hands fluttered in frustration. "Think about it!"

"About what?"

"Happier, healthier, cleaner, faster—Tupper's mothering has done wonders for you. You're in your prime, Frey. It's time!"

He shook his head in consternation. "For *what*?"

With a longsuffering sigh, Aurelius said, "You should start your masterpiece."

Aurelius enjoyed watching Freydolf and Tupper communicate, in part because they made such an unlikely pair. The big, rangy sculptor may not have been much of a Pred, but Frey certainly looked the part. The boy seemed little more than a will-o'-the-wisp by comparison, but Aurelius wasn't fooled. Frey's life revolved around the boy, and the servant unobtrusively imposed structure on his master, whose oft erratic lifestyle had long been a source of worry.

As Aurelius prepared for his hunt by shedding finery in the balcony, he spied on the two of them, unabashedly eavesdropping.

"Where will you be?"

"Between fires," Tupper replied with a shrug. "Aurelius will want his bath, and the kitchen embers need to be ready for roasting."

"Do you need help?"

"No."

Frey's face fell. "What should I do?"

Tupper calmly pointed out, "You have a stone waiting."

The sculptor placed his hand on the griffin's back, but he didn't reach for his tools. "I'd rather do something different. Isn't there some way I can lend a hand?"

With a soft snort, Aurelius wondered if his brother-in-law understood that his servant was probably only doing what he always did—tending fires, hauling water, cooking meals. He found a strange satisfaction in seeing Frey taking such things for granted.

"About time," Aurelius muttered under his breath. It was deucedly unfair that someone with a Keeper's prestige had lived for so long without any creature comforts.

After considerable pause for thought, Tupper said, "There's a piece of starstone I was saving. Maybe it wants to be your new grand-nephew's first guardian?"

The sculptor's eyes took on a shine. "How big a piece?"

"Fist," Tupper replied, crossing to a small chest beside his bed. Freydolf trailed after him. "Yours or mine?"

"Yours." Producing a white stone, he held it out. "See? It's good."

"What a beauty." Freydolf's tone as gentle was as his expression.

Aurelius almost laughed as the Keeper succumbed to the blissful absorption that came whenever he handled a new stone. Frey was always bragging about Tupper's knack for picking, and the lad's affinity for stellar finds must still be running true.

With each passing season, the boy grew closer to Frey, and Aurelius wholeheartedly approved of the respectful firmness with which Tupper managed both the man and his household.

"Graven and I are going down to the well," the young Flox announced.

Freydolf hummed distractedly, for he'd wandered over to one of the worktables. His plans for the starstone were already in the sketching phase.

Looking Aurelius's way, Tupper said, "At least four rabbits, please. He barely ate any lunch."

Caught, he executed a short bow, lending a little dignity to his indiscretion. "Aye, sprat. I'll do my part."

The lad nodded and ushered Graven out.

Aurelius gathered his hair, twisting it into a knot as he pondered the subtle sway Tupper held. It was high time the lad learned a few things about Keepers and the duty they owed to their mountain. If Tupper took it into his head that Freydolf needed to produce a masterpiece, it might actually get done. Testing the edge of one of his blades, Aurelius muttered, "Aye, sprat. I'll do my part, and you'll do yours."

"Two baths in one day?" Freydolf slid into steaming water. "Should I accuse you of undue extravagance?"

"The first was much too rushed to count." Selecting a slender bottle from a nearby niche, Aurelius crossed to the sunken tub and poured a generous amount of bath foam into the steaming water. "You didn't even come down to keep me company!"

Knowing he'd been a poor host by Pred standards, Frey dipped his head apologetically. "There was this dainty bit of starstone, and before I knew it, Tupper was calling me to the table."

"Given the circumstances, I shall graciously overlook your rudeness." Aurelius undid the long row of tiny buttons decorating the front of the fitted coat he'd worn to dinner, draping it over Brand's arm and murmuring, "Thank you, my good man."

The red stone warrior smiled pleasantly, but Freydolf grumbled, "He *isn't* your valet."

"From what I've seen, he may as well be Tupper's," Aurelius remarked offhandedly. "How many statues does the sprat have trailing after him these days?"

"Counting Brand? All of them," the Keeper replied. "I'm quite certain he's acquainted with more of Morven's statues than I am."

"Stands to reason." The merchant lowered himself into the bath with a blissful expression, then swished his hands around to encourage more bubbles. "He has time on his hands. Speaking of the boy, will he be joining us?"

"Aye, he'll be here."

"Nay, he'll be *there*," Aurelius corrected, waggling long fingers in the direction of the basket-making station in the corner of the room. "Shy as ever."

"There's nothing wrong with Flox modesty," Freydolf defended, poking at bubbles with the tip of his claw.

"Given his upbringing, Tupper's made a great concession for your sake."

"Mine?"

"Aye, he is," Aurelius agreed, smoothly twisting his brother-in-law's words. Just then, a soft knock heralded Tupper's arrival, and the merchant sharply inquired, "Did you bring that ridiculous pet?"

"Only Olexi," the lad promised, lowering his first guardian to the floor. The little ram trotted back and forth, checking the vicinity for anything unusual.

"You're welcome to join us," Aurelius breezily offered.

"No, thank you."

The Pred inclined his head, not pushing the issue, but he coaxed, "Come a little closer, at least. I've been saving some juicy gossip!"

Freydolf was reminded that his brother-in-law was as calculating as ever. All that extra bath foam hadn't been meant for scent ... but for sensibilities.

Tupper came to sit at the edge of the tub, his feet dangling into the water. "Gossip from where?"

"I'm not entirely certain," Aurelius slowly admitted. "Strange stories have been circulating, and it's difficult to track down the source. There are too many versions to know which one is true, and some are too wild to be believed!"

Freydolf shook his head. "Stories about what?"

"Stones! The closest I could get to firsthand information came from a journeyman sculptor I met on the Songstone Mountain this winter. According to him, three summers ago, the Keeper of the Freshstone Mountain turned away a Grif merchant who was peddling magical stones."

Frey spread his hands wide. "Merchants buy and sell stones all the time. We Keepers rely on our agents in part because there are so many who try to pass off dull rocks for the real thing."

"Aye, but these stones were strange! It's said that they're potent enough, yet no Keeper dares touch them."

"Why not?" Tupper asked.

Aurelius's voice dropped to a whisper. "According to the rumors, they're black as pitch!"

Freydolf snorted. "There are only twelve mountains, and none of them yield black stone."

Holding up one finger, Aurelius solemnly said, "Aye, *everyone* knows that. Which is why the rumor-mongers have begun to whisper that a thirteenth mountain has been discovered!"

3

Family Resemblance

Tupper wasted the first few hours of the next morning muddling over whether or not he was too big to greet his older brother with a hug, but the moment Carden hopped down from Old Gruff's wagon, he opened his arms invitingly. Since that obviously meant it was all right, the boy rushed to greet Carden in the usual fashion. Half-throttling the man, he exclaimed, "You're here!"

"Morning, Tupp," Carden warmly replied. "Looks like you fared well over winter."

"Yes." With an impatient tap of horn against horn, Tupper asked, "Another baby?"

"Another daughter. We named her Yona."

"I like it. Is she big already?"

Carden shook his head. "She's learned to smile, and she's been saving one for you," Stepping back, he asked, "Will you visit soon?"

"Soon."

Gruff called out then, and they hurried to help the old man unload Aurelius's carriage. Tupper was glad to see so many good stones stowed inside, but he was surprised how small most of them were. The others didn't mind, since the hauling was much easier, but Tupper was worried. These pieces wouldn't last long at all, and Frey hated having idle hands.

They were nearly finished when the boy recalled another matter that had been weighing on him, and he asked Carden, "Can you stay extra today?"

"What did you have in mind?"

"I need help moving something from storage."

"Master Freydolf can't manage it?"

Tupper quietly explained, "It's for him. A surprise."

Carden looked to Gruff. "Is there time for some extra lifting if it's for a good cause?"

The old man tugged at his beard. "Tomorrow was your homeward day, anywise. Stay and help your brother, then save some steps by taking the eastern trail into Hayward tomorrow. I'll manage the team."

"Are you sure?" The old man waved aside the question and stumped off in the direction of the stables, so Carden turned to his younger brother. "Where to, Tupp?"

"Down, in, over, and along," he answered, gesturing with his hand.

Carden brightened. "Inside the Statuary?"

Tupper had only taken his eldest brother as far as the storage rooms near the necessary, so he was excited to show Carden more of the Morven's treasures. With a firm nod, he replied, "Into the galleries!"

Of all the Meadowsweet siblings, Tupper was the hardest to describe. He fit in well enough with his looks, for he bore a strong resemblance to their father; however, his personality had always been rather vague. Although no one would have gone so far as to call him weak, Tupper didn't seem to have any strengths. Not like the rest of his clan.

Carden was known as the reliable one, Addy was industrious, and Ewert was shrewd. Edie was their adventurer, and Rachel was prone to motherly bossing. Farley's cleverness and curiosity often led him into trouble, and Aggie was their cuddler.

In every respect, they outshone Tupper, making him seem dim by comparison.

Carden had often worried over the matter, but his wife Melina gently pointed out that their Tupp wasn't truly lacking. According to her, the boy was simply well-rounded, borrowing a little of all their various traits. He might not ever stand out, but his versatility would hold him in good stead.

"You're growing up," Carden remarked.

Tupper paused at a turning and rubbed distractedly at the base of one horn. "Yes. I'm older."

"Do you realize that you're nearly the same age I was when we lost Father?"

His brother's expression became thoughtful. "You seemed bigger."

"You were much smaller." No one had expected much from Tupper, but the boy had come into his nubs with surprising ease. Carden doubted any of his other siblings would have taken to the Statuary's more unusual aspects so quickly or so well.

With a sidelong glance at the fire-bearer walking at his side, Carden asked, "How much farther?"

"A ways." Tupper pointed into the deep darkness ahead as if seeing something Carden couldn't. "The Cavern isn't far, but then we'll follow the crystal gallery to its farthest well. That takes longer."

"Do you often spend time in this maze?"

With a nod, Tupper replied, "I'm still learning my way around."

"So do you know where all these doors lead?"

"Homes."

"People lived *here*?"

His brother's gaze swung to meet his. "I live here."

"True, but you don't live in a tunnel. It's hard to picture people living in the dark."

"They're nice homes." So saying, he pushed through the nearest door, confidently crossing the dark interior to its far corner. With a *whoosh*, he pulled aside heavy drapes.

Carden squinted at the sudden brightness as warm sunlight flooded the room. "I thought we were underground!"

"There are windows. Even window boxes."

Studying the deep stone trough in the wide ledge beyond the glass, Carden remarked, "Those are more like garden beds."

"Yes. The homes on the level below are even larger and have porches."

"Larger than this?" The young man slowly turned to inspect the living quarters, which were more spacious than his house in Hayward. "How long has it been since anyone lived here?"

"More than two hundred years," Tupper replied, pulling the drapes shut and striding past Brand, who waited patiently just inside the door. "These rooms were a home six times."

"How can you tell?"

"Here." Tupper showed him the rows of carvings fanning out on the wall around the door. "These show belonging."

Carden touched the intricate patterns, shaking his head in wonderment. "That's a lot of history."

Tupper nodded and continued along the passage.

"It's a shame they're all empty."

"No one knows about them. Even if they did, no one would come."

Neither of them needed to say why. Morven's Keeper was a Pred.

In all honesty, Carden had been horrified when he first learned that Master Freydolf had chosen their Tupper. Even though Old Gruff didn't take kindly to anyone badmouthing the Keeper in his quarry, there was no denying the dreadful stories about Pred ambition and brutality. Flox from their great-grandparent's era remembered the last invasion.

Finding Tupper safe in Pred clutches had been a welcome surprise; seeing his younger brother's complete trust had opened Carden's eyes. Freydolf was a good man. Sighing, Carden asked, "Do you think it could change?"

"No and yes."

Carden chuckled. "What's that supposed to mean?"

The boy drifted to a standstill, his brow knit in concentration. "From the outside, no. The villagers might always be afraid because they don't know any better. But on the inside, yes. Things are better for Frey, and that's good enough."

Carden rested a hand on his brother's slim shoulder. "I'm glad he has you."

Tupper nodded. "I'm doing my best."

As they continued deeper into the Statuary, Carden decided that Tupper wasn't just older, nor was he simply bigger. He was growing up in ways that were harder to see ... but mattered most.

Maybe it was because he'd been thinking about family traits and resemblances, but Carden was suddenly reminded of their father. For the first time, he realized that Tupper bore more than a passing resemblance to the thoughtful man who'd quietly brought out the best in those around him.

"Say, Tupp. How much do you remember about Father?"

As usual, his brother took his time choosing his words. "Little things. Nice things."

His answer brought a smile to Carden's face, for it neatly summed up their gentle father's way of life. He'd always found little ways to make things better for those he cared about. "You remind me of him."

The boy's glance was puzzled. "I look like him, but so do you."

"Yes, we do. But I wasn't talking about appearances. You do things the same way he did."

Tupper straightened and cautiously asked, "What kinds of things?"

Leaning close to offer an affectionate tap of horns, Carden replied, "Little things. Nice things."

Somewhere in the midst of acquainting himself with the new stones Aurelius had selected, Freydolf realized there were good smells drifting from the direction of the kitchen. Glancing out the windows to check the angle of shadows, he was chagrined to realize that most of the day had already slipped by. No wonder he was hungry.

Wandering into the next room, he found Aurelius warming soup. "Where's Tupper?"

"Off on some errand with his brother."

"He left?"

"Nay, he's still hereabouts," Aurelius assured, waving his hand to indicate the Statuary. "He *said* he wanted to show Carden some of the galleries, but he was lying, of course."

"Not Tupper," Freydolf defended, refusing to believe the lad capable of deception.

"I only meant the lad's up to something. It should be highly entertaining to see what passes for deviousness in his mind!"

Belatedly, Frey checked the center of the kitchen table, where a single chunk of crystal perched in an egg cup. "Did they take Graven along?"

"*That one* is guarding chickens. If you're concerned, Brand is missing from his pedestal, so the sprat has at least one escort along."

"Concerned?" Frey echoed in surprise. "Not at all. There's nothing untoward in the crystal gallery."

The merchant's gaze darted to the stone Tupper had left behind. "I see! You've worked out a way to keep tabs on him!"

"His idea," the man admitted. "I like knowing what direction he's in, at the very least."

Aurelius ladled soup into two bowls and slyly surmised, "Because you're completely *unconcerned*."

Freydolf accepted a spoon and calmly countered, "You've seen how statues respond to him. The lad treats the entire mountain with the same respect. I wouldn't be surprised if Morven herself came to his aid if he were in need."

"I've seen journeymen sculptors with less affinity for stone," Aurelius acknowledged. "Have you given any thought to training him?"

The Keeper's brow furrowed. "Aye, but he's never shown any interest in sculpting."

Aurelius *tsk*-ed. "I sincerely doubt it would occur to him to try."

Freydolf slowly shook his head. "He can feel the potential of a stone, but he cannot see its shape. That's why he brings them to me. Although, to be honest, I'm beginning to suspect that Tupper isn't truly a good picker."

"I thought the stones he brings you are always sublime specimens."

"Aye, every single one, without fail," the sculptor agreed. "But how is it possible that so many excellent stones were overlooked by generations of Keepers?"

"Size?" Aurelius reasoned. "They're often too small to be worth the bother."

Humming skeptically, Freydolf countered, "I think he's changing the stones, influencing them somehow."

The merchant's brows shot up. "Is that even possible?"

"It might be interesting to test the theory," he proposed. "Perhaps over the summer?"

Aurelius's golden eyes glittered. "Aye," he drawled, steepling his fingers together. "Very interesting!"

Not long after Aurelius carelessly heaped their dishes in the sink for Tupper to wash, a rattle came from the direction of the courtyard. The merchant darted to the big double doors with impressive speed and was outside before Freydolf had closed his sketchbook. Moments later, Aurelius reappeared, hands clasped over his heart. "I hope you know that lad is a treasure beyond price!"

With a slow blink, Frey answered, "Aye."

Hurrying over to grasp the other Pred by the shoulders, Aurelius exclaimed, "He is the uppermost of all underlings, a luminary among lackeys!" With a small shake to emphasize each accolade, he continued, "A superlative servant! A magnificent minion! A paragon among peons!"

Chuckling over the man's raptures, Freydolf asked, "What? Did he bring you a keg of spiced ale from Master Platt's private cellars?"

Momentarily distracted, Aurelius whispered, "*Are* there any left? That *would* be a find!"

With a small tap, Tupper peeped around the edge of the door. "Are you helping, Aurelius? We're ready."

"Aye!" the Pred sang out. "I am, and gladly!"

Grinning viciously, he strode to the corner of the workshop where Frey's meager cot was shoved up against the wall. With a dramatic swoop, he pulled it away from the wall, overturning it into the middle of the room.

"I have *never* approved of this unseemly pallet! Good riddance!"

"Here, now!" protested Freydolf. "It's fine. Besides, there's nothing else suited to someone of my ...."

The sculptor trailed off as Carden backed through the door, carefully maneuvering one of the many carts used throughout the Statuary for transporting stone. Tupper followed. Balanced between them was an ornate headboard, its dark wood gleaming from a recent oiling.

Aurelius gestured emphatically at the formidable furnishing. "Look at the color! And that's solid oldwood! An antique bedstead of this quality would fetch almost as much as one of your guardian statues!"

Belatedly stepping forward to assist the Meadowsweets with their burden, Freydolf sought Tupper's gaze. "What's this for?"

The boy shrugged. "I'm in charge of the household, and I decided to move some furniture."

Aurelius snorted. "Don't be dense, Frey. The lad found you a proper bed!"

He'd gathered as much. Or at least that the boy had tried. But he hadn't wanted to disappoint Tupper. None of the beds in the Statuary were big enough. Even Aurelius resorted to sleeping on a mound of cushions in the balcony whenever he visited.

"Do you mind, Mister Harrow?" begged Carden, nodding at the door. "There's the footboard yet."

Freydolf was astonished enough to see his brother-in-law cheerfully accept direction, but his amazement redoubled when they returned with not only a footboard, but long, heavy sideboards and several sturdy crosspieces. The bed wasn't just big enough, it was enormous.

Curiosity brimming, the sculptor prowled until he found a maker's mark. "Aurelius, how's your Skrit?"

"Passable."

His agent peered at the flowing letters and, with a chuckle, read the inscription aloud ... in Skrit. Freydolf only recognized a few words in the sibilant recitation, so he waited for the translation.

Having shown off, the merchant obliged. "Or in plain Verit, the eleventh Keeper was Ursa."

"Their race is big."

"Massive," agreed Aurelius. "He commissioned this from a craftsman brought all the way from his homeland. The carpenter calls this his final extravagance. I hope that means there are more furnishings on this scale."

Both men turned to gaze hopefully at Tupper, who said, "Lots more."

Aurelius sent his brother-in-law a withering glance. "Twenty-odd years of sleeping on the floor."

Frey rubbed the back of his neck. "Since he's a treasure *beyond* price, let's not quibble over the cost."

Tupper wasn't quite sure if Freydolf was happy about trading away his cot, but since Aurelius was ecstatic, the boy decided it was okay to follow his plan right to its end. "Move that workbench," he directed.

The men crossed to inspect its tool-strewn surface, and Carden crouched to see if it was anchored to the wall in any way.

"You want the bed here?" Aurelius asked, eyeing the proposed location. "Why not where the cot was?"

"This is better. It's further from the window." Since his master often grumbled about it, Tupper had hoped to spare him from dawn's insistent light. He confessed, "I couldn't find a bed with curtains."

Aurelius clapped his hands. "You heard him, Frey. Start shifting your assortment of rock tappers and ticklers. They're in the way!"

"Aye," the man murmured, looking a little overwhelmed.

"I'll help," Carden offered.

"Me, too," Tupper quickly added. The workbench wasn't the main one Freydolf used, so he'd assumed the sculptor wouldn't mind if it was moved. Still, he couldn't help checking. "Unless it's bad ...?"

"Nay, lambkin. This can only be called good." Frey ruffled his hair affectionately. "If I seem less than enthusiastic, it's only because Aurelius is carrying on. You've made me *very* happy."

Tupper stood a little taller, pleased and proud that he'd found another way to make the Keeper's life better. It had always bothered him that his bed was so fine while Freydolf's was so meager.

There was an abundance of odds and ends on the workbench, including odd bits of rock that had been saved for one reason or another. Tupper focused on those, quickly filling his arms.

Carden showed more interest in the assorted tools.

Freydolf took notice when the young man expertly tested the weight of a chisel. He asked, "You're a craftsman?"

"Old Gruff is a carpenter, and I've learned a little from him."

Tupper tutted softly. "Not just a little. Carden's good!"

Freydolf chuckled. "No need to be modest."

With an amiable shrug, Carden replied, "You can hardly expect me to brag about making three-legged stools while assembling another man's masterpiece. This bed is a work of art!"

"Aye." Freydolf asked, "These were somewhere along the crystal gallery?"

Tupper nodded. "In the quarters beyond the last well, there's a tricky door with a bear on the knob. A stair leads down to a colonnade with more quarters."

Carden said, "The columns throughout were carved to resemble oldtrees. It was like strolling through a forest."

"I had no idea it was there." Frey said, "I'd like to see it."

"I'd like to *raid* it!" Aurelius interjected. "We can furnish a suite for Ulrica and me and spend the summer in high style!"

"Aye," he readily agreed. "Larger chairs for the balcony would be nice, assuming there are any."

"Lots."

The lad's find had come at a good time. Now Ulrica wouldn't have to sleep on the floor.

Dragging aside the heavy workbench, the men traded opinions on where it should go while waiting for Tupper to sweep the floor and brush down the stone wall. Then with great care, they eased the headboard into place, and Carden quickly set to work fastening the sides and slats.

Aurelius strode back and forth, contemplating the bed from several angles before announcing, "I approve! Now, the only question is where to find a mattress to scale."

"I have one," said Tupper.

Folding his arms over his chest, the merchant pointed out, "Anything in the storerooms here would be decades, if not centuries, old. I shudder to think of sleeping on something that's been moldering in the galleries that long."

The boy patted the footboard. "I ordered one last autumn from Auntie Watercress."

Aurelius's head snapped around. "Did you now? Just when did you find this bed?"

"Last week."

"But you *can't* have known the dimensions."

Tupper shook his head and clarified, "I spoke for enough feathers for three normal beds. All the ladies in Shepley are saving up." With a shrewd glint in his eyes, he added, "If we bring along our empty jars and place a fresh order for sauce, Auntie Watercress promised to have the ticking stitched in two days' time."

Aurelius's eyes narrowed slightly. "How long have you been searching for a bed for Frey?"

"A while."

"How long?" the merchant insisted.

"More than a year."

Carden's expression turned quizzical. "How did you know you'd need the feather bed *this* spring, Tupp?"

"I had a feeling."

In a baffling blend of trans-continental traditions, Aurelius touched his forehead, his lips, and his chest, then bowed low. With careless deference, he intoned, "Sprat, for your foresight, your forays, and your forbearance where this big oaf is concerned, you have earned my gratitude! I shall proclaim it in Verit, Terse, Prose, and Skrit!"

While he waxed eloquent, Tupper listened with interest. Frey knew he loved the different sounds of the many languages Aurelius knew.

But Freydolf wasn't about to let him have the last word.

Pulling Tupper aside, he knelt to better meet the lad's gaze. "I don't have horns, so this will have to do." Emulating a Flox's tap with the flick of his claw, he gruffly said, "Thanks, lambkin. Thanks lots."

4

Talk of the Town

Two days later, Aurelius guided his team up the winding road home while casting sidelong glances at his companion. Tupper was humming nonsense to Rimbles, who'd pitched a feline fit over being closed into the carriage while her charge risked life and limb walking through Shepley without her. Since the locals still looked askance at the boy's usual Pred escort, there was no telling what kind of panic a living statue might invite.

Aurelius had quite enjoyed watching Tupper dicker over everything from homespun to horse manure, but it was still frustrating to be edged out of the proceedings. All he could do was loom ominously at opportune moments, sending otherwise sharp-witted Flox matrons into dithering that tipped the scales in the lad's favor.

At this time of year, there was a brisk business in seeds, cuttings, and livestock, but the day's prize seemed to be Frey's new mattress ... and a neatly folded paper Tupper clutched in one hand.

"Did your gossipy old patroness part with her sauce recipe?" Aurelius inquired.

"No, but these *are* recipes," Tupper replied. "When Auntie Watercress is in a good mood, she shares secrets."

"Was she in a good mood this morning?" asked Aurelius, inviting the boy to brag a little. Personal triumphs were always sweeter when shared.

Tupper turned sideways, tucking up his feet to sit cross-legged on the wide bench as he listed, "Two recipes, three secrets, and a packet of seeds."

"Weren't you learning to cook from your mother?"

Although he nodded, Tupper said, "They say there's nine ways to season sauce, and ninety-nine secrets for making it better. Mother could only teach me three ways."

"So you're raiding Shepley's proverbial pantries, hoping to learn more cooking lore?"

"Yes. Freydolf likes spicy flavors, and so does Auntie Watercress. When I season the sauce her way, he always asks for seconds."

The more Aurelius learned about the Flox, the fonder he grew of the bleaters. Their haggling was conducted with a mercenary streak that was almost Pred-worthy. He had little doubt that Tupper could hold his own in any marketplace around the world. It might be interesting to see how far the boy's skills could carry him. The only hitch seemed to be in the realm of ambition.

Tupper definitely *had* ambitions, but they were deucedly humble ones.

Freydolf was drifting in a pleasant haze, leaden-limbed and heavy-lidded. Given the choice, he would have stayed exactly where he was indefinitely. Unfortunately, someone had other ideas.

"Behold, a Keeper in his natural habitat!" Aurelius declared loftily. "This is a monumental turn of events, for the fool has been living in comparative squalor for nigh unto two decades. You've finally managed to give some dignity to his life, sprat!"

"Do you know all the Keepers?" Tupper asked in a low voice.

"Aye. Comes with the job."

Frey couldn't remember ever being so warm and comfy. He was sure that during his youth, he'd been provided with a similarly opulent bed. If so, the recollection had faded. A feather mattress definitely made sleep worth savoring, but the running commentary made it next to impossible.

The lad asked, "Are they as nice as Frey?"

"Nay, some are stingy, prickly, wily, or otherwise difficult to deal with." With tones that betrayed the smirk on his face, Aurelius declared, "Of all the Keepers, I can say with great authority that Frey is ... tallest."

Tupper giggled, and Freydolf couldn't resist a peek. Cracking an eyelid, he was met by a scene that was as absurd as it was baffling. Two chairs had been borrowed from the kitchen table and placed at his bedside. Aurelius sat on the first, one leg crossed over the other, hands clasped around his knee, and Tupper sat beside him, closely watching his face.

"You're awake!"

"Aye, somehow." With a reproachful look at Aurelius, Freydolf demanded, "Since when do you entertain yourself by watching me sleep?"

His brother-in-law leaned forward. "We placed bets on how long you would indulge in slumber!"

Freydolf snorted. "Who won?"

"Alas, we underestimated you. And the soporific combination of a feather bed and a rainy morning."

Rolling onto his side—but making no move to leave the splendor of his new bed—Frey peered at the gray skies beyond drizzle-dotted windows. "What time is it?"

"An hour past lunch," Tupper reported.

Bunching up his pillow, Freydolf closed his eyes again. "Enjoy the show."

"Told you," Tupper whispered.

Aurelius snidely declared, "You're only partially right on the second round of wagers! I refuse to concede unless *all* the terms are met!"

The sculptor's brow furrowed. Couldn't he be lazy once in a while? Freydolf peered over his shoulder at the two depriving him of his rest. "*Another* bet?"

Tupper nodded. "I said you'd want to stay in bed even if Aurelius woke you up."

"Aye. I do."

"That's half of it," Aurelius interjected.

Suspicious of the sheepish glance Tupper sent his way, Freydolf prompted, "And the other half?"

The boy slid from his chair and propped his elbows on the edge of his master's new bed. With an earnest expression, he confided, "I said you would share."

"And if I do?"

Tupper's eyes took on a calculating shine. "Fresh meat for dinner. It's a good bargain."

"Aye." Patting the bed invitingly, Freydolf met Aurelius's sulky gaze and cheerfully bid, "Happy hunting!"

The other Pred slapped his knees and stood. "The sooner begun, the sooner done."

Once the other man was out the door, Freydolf felt bad for him. Glancing down at the boy who was trying to wriggle himself into a comfortable rut, he asked, "What did Aurelius wager?"

"He said you'd wake up when I made biscuits at lunchtime."

Freydolf's eyes lit up. Even though Tupper had learned to cook other things, they were still a favorite. "You made biscuits?"

"Yes."

With a longing look in the direction of the kitchen, he asked, "Are there any left?"

"Aurelius ate them all."

Suddenly, Freydolf didn't feel so bad for his brat of a brother. Dinner would be served hot, and revenge would be served cold and wet.

Tupper found Aurelius intensely interesting. The Pred was dashing, daring, and just a little bit dangerous. Plus, his arrival always set off a whirlwind of activity. He only had a fortnight to catch up, stock up, take care of business, and take his leave. Endless extra errands livened up Tupper's days, and quiet conversations were traded for grandiose accounts sprinkled with multilingual epithets and enough gossip to last two more seasons.

Nothing could compare to the man, and Tupper had no words to explain him. His big brother understood, but only because Carden had seen for himself. And even he admitted that Aurelius defied description.

This spring was different, though.

Since Aurelius planned to return in a month's time for a much longer stay, the merchant cheerfully tabled all work-related matters. In fact, he and Freydolf let their normal duties slide completely. Instead of piles of work, the merchant plied his brother-in-law with goblets of wine, and long evenings were spent playing strategy games and swapping reminiscences.

During one such lazy evening, Aurelius broached the subject of how best to fritter away his last few days before making the long journey home.

Tupper dared to speak up. "Would tomorrow be a good day to go into Hayward?"

"Planning to buy out the bakery for Frey?"

Tupper hesitated. "That *would* be good ...."

"But ...?"

"But maybe something *else* would be good."

Aurelius asked, "What did you have in mind, sprat?"

Tupper kept his invitation simple. "Would you like to meet my family?"

After due consideration, it was decided that Tupper should have a head start into Hayward. Although Aurelius was eager to meet the Meadowsweets, he insisted on giving their hostess a chance to brace herself before two Pred turned up on her front step.

Tupper wasn't sure it mattered, but Frey deemed it best to bow to the merchant's superior knowledge of social niceties.

That's why he was currently clinging to Graven's back while the tiger slunk through the deep forests skirting Morven's southeastern face.

There were oldtrees here, majestic giants whose fat buds looked ready to burst at any moment, and ground lilies poked their purple heads through last season's moldering leaves, making a pretty carpet.

Twittering birds scattered before Graven, who paid no attention to trails. He dropped into gullies and leapt onto promontories with ease. Some of the tiger's plunges made Tupper's stomach do flip-flops, but Graven seemed to understand the need to be careful of his young passenger. He was a guardian statue, after all.

The varicolored tiger was often grumpy, adored prowling, and demanded pampering whenever his many stones clashed discordantly. Tupper honestly wasn't sure if Graven was his, or if he was Graven's. Either way, he understood both the privilege and the responsibility Freydolf had entrusted to him when he'd used magic to tie him to the tiger. Their bond meant that Tupper had another person to take care of each day.

Before long, the pair reached the brook where Carden had first taught Tupper how to fish.

"Stop," the boy ordered, patting Graven's broad head. "Let me down, please."

Although the tiger obliged, his ears cocked at a peevish angle, as if he didn't want to hear what Tupper was about to say.

"I can't bring you with me." With an apologetic shake of his head, Tupper explained, "Aurelius is too much all by himself. Your turn will wait for another day."

Graven bared his teeth, displeased at being displaced by his favorite prey.

In soothing tones, Tupper reminded, "Rimbles couldn't even come this far!" The little lynx never left his side if she was awake, so she'd been under his pillow since last night.

The tiger's shoulders hunched, but he kept his chin up, pretending he didn't care.

"Go back to the coop and guard Ember's flock," Tupper directed, pointing back up the mountain for emphasis. "There have been more hawks lately."

Graven refused to meet his gaze.

Coaxing was needed.

Tupper dipped his fingers in the brook and reached up to trace the freshstone that outlined the tiger's eyes. This time when he spoke, he had Graven's rapt attention. "I will ask Frey for a day guardian so you can do as you please, but until then, my hens need you."

The tiger blinked, then butted his head against the boy's chest, begging for more petting.

Tupper rubbed every blue stripe within reach, then kissed the big cat's nose. "I need to go, and you need to go back."

His guardian drooped pitifully.

With a small sigh, Tupper whispered, "Thank you for the ride. Wait for me at home."

The statue grudgingly shuffled off toward the Statuary, pausing every so often to see if Tupper was watching. The boy understood the tiger's quandary. Hadn't he been waiting for his maker year-in and year-out? Still, he stood his ground, grateful that no matter how often the tiger dragged his feet, he always did as he was told … eventually.

Graven was doing his best, and Tupper was proud of him.

Freydolf was more than a little surprised when Aurelius didn't complain about walking all the way to Hayward. There could be only one reason why his brother-in-law hadn't disdained the precarious trail that zigzagged down Morven's eastern face. "You must really be looking forward to this."

The merchant hummed noncommittally, then asked, "How many little ones will set to wailing once we're ushered into the sprat's former home?"

"That depends. Tupper has two younger siblings, and Carden's family is likely to be there. But I doubt there'll be so much as a whimper."

"You've tamed them?"

The sculptor chuckled. "I'm fairly certain they believe Tupper's tamed me."

Aurelius looked positively scandalized. "To think, these people base their concept of Pred on *your* example. It falls to me to set them straight with regard to our proud race."

Frey frowned worriedly. "Is that why you refused to leave your daggers at home? I don't want you sending these gentle folk skittering!"

"No Pred travels unarmed," the merchant flatly countered. "And all I want to do is lend the sprat my support."

"I don't follow."

With a superior smile, Aurelius exclaimed, "Think about it. Why do you suppose Tupper wants to introduce me to his family?"

"Because he thinks of you as family?" hazarded Freydolf.

Aurelius's step faltered, but he quickly rallied. "You're not thinking the way a boy his age does," he said in patronizing tones. "Try again."

Freydolf doubted that his brother-in-law understood Tupper any better than he did. "Enlighten me."

Casually inspecting the claws he'd taken care to buff earlier, Aurelius said, "It's patently obvious that he wants to show me off."

"And you mean to be impressive?"

"Devastatingly so! How often has he dragged you home with him?"

The sculptor did a quick mental tally. "Six times."

"Is that all?"

"Aye. He could visit more often if he wished, but ...." Freydolf wasn't sure how to explain the next bit without sounding equally conceited. With a small shrug, he frankly admitted, "Tupper seems happier with me."

"Really?" drawled Aurelius, his gaze sharpening. "What are these Meadowsweets like?

"They seem ordinary enough."

Aurelius snorted. "Do they fall all over themselves in gratitude for the boy's generous wages, all the while hinting that more would be welcome?"

"Nay."

"Do they smile to your face, but sharpen their blades as soon as your back is turned?"

"Nay!" Freydolf repeated, scowling over Aurelius's sly reminders of what passed for normal in many Pred households.

His agent sweetly said, "Then you're going to have to define *ordinary* for me."

The Keeper trudged in silence for a short distance, giving himself time to gather his thoughts. "These Flox—or the Meadowsweets at the very least—they take care of each other just like Tupper takes care of me."

Aurelius's fingers drummed against his thigh as he processed the assessment. Finally, he remarked, "Must be nice."

"Aye. It is. And they are."

There were times when Freydolf wondered if his agent had *any* common sense. Snobbish airs, grandiose words, foppish clothes—Aurelius didn't deviate one bit from his usual presumption as he strode through the streets of Hayward and up to the Meadowsweets' front door.

Merona answered his insistent rap and greeted her guests with a warm smile. "Welcome back, Master Meadowsweet! And you must be Mister Harrow! Please, make yourselves at home!"

Aurelius seized the opening and sashayed through it.

The Meadowsweets never stood a chance.

Frey could hardly keep up as his brother-in-law forged his first impression with aplomb. The crafty Pred knew *exactly* what he was doing. His manners were carefully calculated to put his prey at ease, and his outlandish attire and extreme politeness had Merona and her daughters rallying to meet his courtesy in kind.

Compliments and expressions of gratitude were traded at a dizzying rate, and Frey reached his limit. Clearing his throat, he asked, "Where's Tupper, marm?"

Their hostess glanced about. "Bless me, I forgot! I told him to stay put! He's in the back garden."

"I'll find him," Freydolf quickly offered, only too happy to escape. The genteel gentleman act might serve its purposes, but he honestly preferred an Aurelius who smiled less and spoke with a sharper tongue.

The walled garden showed signs of recent tilling, and nest-building birds pipped and flitted amidst the trees. Stepping with care along the narrow trail that wound between herb and vine, Freydolf rounded the corner of the house and balked.

A young Flox sat on the chopping block near the woodpile, gazing off toward the forest and the mountain beyond.

The Keeper needed several moments to take in what must have happened, for the ground was strewn with white-blond curls. It was a shock when the forgotten boy with newly-cropped hair glanced over his shoulder, for he no longer looked like a child. His lambkin was growing up.

"Hello," Tupper solemnly greeted.

"I hardly recognized you," Frey confessed, ambling over.

The boy's shoulders hunched. "It feels strange."

Freydolf chose to take the remark as an invitation. There weren't many curls left to mess with, but he stroked the bristling hairs and scratched lightly at the base of each horn. "Can't call these nubs any longer. Do Flox keep their hair short to display them better?"

"Maybe."

"Your mother must have thought I was trying to turn you into a Pred," he joked.

Tupper lowered his gaze and mumbled, "She did say that."

Something was wrong. Freydolf crouched before his servant, trying to meet his gaze. "I suppose I do look outlandish."

With a surprisingly wistful expression, Tupper reached for the man, grabbing a handful of his long, wavy hair and pulling his thick ponytail forward. "It's good. I like it."

Freydolf smiled crookedly at the boy's affectionate gesture and staunch approval, but then comprehension struck him upside the head. "You didn't want her to cut your hair."

The boy slowly shook his head.

With a stunned glance at the scattered ringlets, the man felt a stirring of anger. "Didn't you tell your mother?"

"I tried."

No wonder. Freydolf groaned softly and pulled the boy into his arms. "I'm so sorry, Tupper," he whispered, wishing he'd arrived soon enough to prevent the boy's loss.

His servant hid his face against his shoulder, still and silent.

Thinking hard, Freydolf demanded, "At what age is a Flox considered his own man, no longer subject to his mother's wishes?"

Tupper pulled back and, instead of giving a specific age, touched the tip of his horn, then drew a curving line that wrapped partway around his ear.

Freydolf grunted, for it looked as if the lad's independence was still a few years off. "Can you wait until then?"

"No choice."

"Aye, I suppose not," the man sighed. "But when you're of age, I'll back you up."

A hint of sparkle returned to the lad's eyes. "Because that's what brothers do?"

Frey doubted the lad knew it was part of an old Pred proverb, but he nodded. "Aye. Brothers are for back-up. Speaking of which, mine is currently toying with your family. Should we go in and watch?"

With a wan smile, Tupper nodded. "He might need us."

It was a simple statement, but it revealed just how much the lad's loyalties had changed over the last couple years. As much as Tupper loved his family, his strongest ties now linked him to brothers of Pred descent. The boy's support belonged to Aurelius, not Farley.

Grinning broadly, Freydolf agreed, "Aye, we'll back him up."

Freydolf and Tupper rounded the house in time to see Aggie coming along the lane from the direction of Carden and Melina's home, leading her niece by the hand. Little Dulcie caught sight of them and shook free of her minder, running toward them as fast as her tiny feet could carry her. "Unca Tupp! Unca Doff!"

"Good day, Miss Dulcie," Freydolf greeted, swooping Carden's daughter right up onto his shoulders.

"You came!" she exclaimed with a giggle. As usual, she gave the man's head a quick pat-down to see if he'd sprouted horns yet. Dulcie seemed to believe her Unca Doff was a late bloomer, so she was always on the lookout for nubs.

"Aye," he amiably agreed. "And how are you, Miss Aggie?"

Tupper wasted no time in hugging his baby sister, who was already eight. She blinked shyly at the Pred with big, blue eyes and politely replied, "Very well, thank you."

Freydolf marveled at how much taller Tupper was than Aggie, whose devotion to the lad hadn't dimmed despite the long gaps between visits. She leaned into her sibling's side, content to let the others trade pleasantries.

Tilting his head to catch Dulcie's eye, the Keeper innocently inquired, "Has anything interesting happened since last autumn?"

"Yes! Imma big girl now! Imma big sister!"

"Where's your sister, Dulcie?" Tupper asked. "Will you introduce me?"

"Papa has her!"

The lad's eyes brightened, and he looked to Aggie. "Carden's home?"

"Since yesterday."

Freydolf had no difficulty at all seeing how much Tupper wanted to go to his big brother, so he said, "He must have his hands full."

"Maybe I should check ...?"

"Aye. Do that."

The boy dashed down the street, and Aggie gazed longingly after him.

Taking pity, Frey offered, "Dulcie and I will wait here at the gate if you want to follow him."

Aggie flashed him a grateful look, then darted after Tupper.

"Just us," Dulcie declared, sounding pleased with the sudden turn of events.

"Aye," he agreed, sitting upon the ground and perching her on an upraised knee. "May I tell you something?"

"Is it a secret?"

"Nay, but it's something only I know."

She slid off his knee, clambering onto his lap instead. "Tell!"

Nodding obligingly, Freydolf said, "When I was a little boy, my father and mother gave me a baby sister, too."

Dulcie's eyes grew wide with wonder. "You was little?"

"Only for a while," he answered seriously. "Then, I grew."

"Yes. So, *so* big!"

"Aye, and many people came to see my new sister, so ...."

"Was she pretty?" Dulcie interrupted.

"Very pretty."

"Did she have blue eyes or green eyes?" the girl quizzed.

"Brown."

"Like yours?"

"Aye, just like mine." Gently steering the conversation back on track, he reiterated, "All the people who came to meet my baby sister brought nice things for her."

"Presents," Dulcie interjected knowledgeably.

"Now, I was very proud of Ulrica, and I was happy that she was welcomed so generously, but sometimes, I wished that someone would bring *me* a present."

With a soft gasp, the girl confided, "Me, too! But Mama says our Yona is the best present."

"Your Mama is wise," Freydolf said approvingly. "I hope you'll share your Yona with me?"

"'Course!"

"And ... I brought a present just for you."

The girl stared at him in awe. "Just mine?"

"Aye," he replied, chuckling over her surprise. "Something to celebrate your becoming a big sister."

"Can I see?"

Freydolf dipped into his pocket and withdrew a small dawnstone figurine. "Do you like pink?" he asked, placing the wee statue into her open hands.

"Bunny!"

She babbled and cooed over her new toy, leaving the sculptor with a slightly foolish grin on his face. The itty-bitty rabbit didn't bear a master's mark, so he'd never wake with the sunrise, but Dulcie wouldn't know the difference.

It was a shame, really, for the small guardian would have doted on her just as much as his maker.

Shortly thereafter, Carden appeared at the end of the lane, a bundle cradled in one arm and his wife's hand tucked through the other. Dulcie ran to her parents, eager to show off her present, and Freydolf rose and dusted his breeches before bowing his welcome.

As soon as he was in earshot, Carden cheerfully called, "Master Freydolf, I'm so glad your visit fell on one of my home days."

The sculptor was fairly certain the greeting was pitched to carry. The Meadowsweets weren't shy about throwing their support behind Morven's Keeper.

With a small quirk of a smile, Freydolf politely replied, "Good afternoon, Mister Meadowsweet. I hope you're making the most of your rest day?"

Melina piped up, answering for her husband. "His daughters have him by the horns, and that's the truth of it!"

Carden's chagrined expression helped Frey correctly interpret the turn of phrase. "Where I come from, a daughter is said to keep her father's fangs on a ribbon."

The young woman laughed. "Is that where Dulcie keeps yours?"

Rubbing the back of his neck, he said, "Aye, that's the truth of it."

"I hope she thanked you for her new treasure?" Melina inquired.

"Quite enthusiastically."

Carden stepped closer then and smiled up at him. "Care to help me spoil this one, as well?"

"Gladly."

With obvious pride, he said, "Master Freydolf, please meet my second daughter, Yona Meadowsweet." Tickling the little one's fair cheek to wake her, he continued, "Yona, you may as well follow your sister's lead. This is your Uncle Doff."

As the young father transferred his daughter into the Pred's hands, the big man ruefully muttered, "How many neighbors do you suppose are holding their breaths about now?"

"No less than six," Carden wagered in an undertone. "I apologize for their rudeness."

"I'm accustomed to it."

"They'll come around," Melina declared with confidence. "See? Yona's already taken with you!"

Frey looked into a pair of serious gray-green eyes and another corner of his heart melted. Lightly brushing his fingertips across the white-blonde ringlets that formed a halo around the baby's head, he said, "It's a pleasure to finally make your acquaintance, Miss Yona."

To his utter amazement, the baby smiled. And he turned to mush.

Melina giggled. "One by the horns, the other by the fangs!"

Neither man contradicted her. They were too besotted.

Tupper appeared with Dulcie now riding on his shoulders, her hands wrapped tightly around the lad's horns. Aggie followed carrying an enormous basket that smelled of fresh bread.

Melina thanked them for their help, then indicated the house. "Shall we go in? I'm anxious to meet your brother."

"Brother-in-law, actually. He's husband to my younger sister."

Before Frey could share the news of their upcoming visit, the man in question sailed through the Meadowsweets' front door, Farley firmly clamped under his arm. The ten-year-old kicked and complained, but his captor hardly seemed to notice the fuss.

Catching sight of the group lingering at the front gate, Aurelius hastened over and swept into a bow before Carden's wife. "You must be Melina Meadowsweet! Aurelius Harrow, at your service."

"I'm … yes," she faltered, staring openly.

Carden said, "Good day, Mister Harrow. Would you like me to take Farley off your hands?"

"Thank you for your kind offer, but I don't require assistance." Aurelius's smile held a trace of menace. "Your younger brother is an abominable nuisance."

"Farley," groaned Carden. "What have you done this time?"

Waving aside the eldest Meadowsweet's concern, Aurelius smoothly explained, "Young Master Farley has lost a wager and will now pay the penalty. Fear not. Your lovely mother acquiesced to this course of action. I have parental consent to proceed."

"Lemme go!" Farley growled.

Aurelius's voice had an edge to it when he answered, "Based on Tupper's exemplary deportment, I was under the impression that Flox were honest in their dealings. Or is he superior to you in both height and honor?"

"You tricked me!" protested the boy.

"Nay," countered the man. "You were too eager to consider the consequences of a tempting bargain. Be more circumspect, especially when baiting your betters!"

Farley wriggled halfheartedly. "I dunno what half the stuff you say means!"

Tupper nodded sympathetically. "Me, either. Especially when he speaks in Skrit."

Aurelius's eyebrows shot up. "Sprat, you've been shorn!"

"Yes."

"Pity. It was nearly long enough to knot."

The lad's face fell, and Freydolf grimaced.

Fortunately, Aurelius was exceptionally quick on the uptake. Hardly missing a beat, he breezily chose a new gambit. "At least it'll no longer be in the way during our hunts this summer."

Tupper said, "I don't know how to ...."

"Yet!" the Pred cut in. "With an entire season ahead of us, there's time enough to cover the basics. I cannot possibly leave you at the mercy of rabbits!"

"Bunny!" piped up Dulcie, vying for some attention. She held up her dawnstone figurine and smiled at the newcomer.

Aurelius peered intently at the girl, then gave Farley an ungentle nudge in the ribs. "Are you some relation to this bundle of irascibility?"

"That's my Unca Far," Dulcie imparted. "He teases."

Aurelius held up a finger and whispered, "So do I!"

The girl considered that for a moment, then asked, "Are you gonna tease me?"

"Is that any way to treat a lady?" he returned, sounding scandalized.

She shook her head, blonde curls bouncing.

Aurelius inquired, "Is it possible that *you* are the Miss Dulcie that Frey has mentioned with great fondness?"

"I'm Dulcie. He's Unca Doff," she explained, pointing to each in turn. "This is my bunny. And your eyes are pretty."

Aurelius leaned closer to the girl perched on Tupper's shoulders and tapped her pert nose with one finger. "We *must* continue this discussion once I have dealt with your uncle. Hold that thought!"

"What are you planning?" Freydolf asked worriedly.

"I'd *like* to push him off the nearest pier," the Pred muttered. At Melina's disapproving look, he amended, "In a leaky skiff without a paddle. However, the terrain leaves me little choice. A treeing must suffice."

Crossing to the venerable fruit tree that grew against the garden wall, Aurelius hoisted Farley onto a sturdy limb near its trunk. "Consider yourself sequestered here for the duration of my visit."

The boy folded his arms over his chest. "I could climb down easy!"

"*Could* and *shall* are oceans apart," Aurelius countered. Then he dropped both his voice and his syllable count. "Stay put."

Farley's lip jutted, but he sulkily agreed, "I'll do it, but it ain't because I'm nubless. It's only 'cause I don't welch on a deal."

"Excellent policy!" the merchant exclaimed, all smiles again.

As he turned from the tree, the boy called, "Hey, Mister! I want to learn to hunt from a Pred. Take me along!"

Freydolf could tell his brother-in-law's patience was thinning. The man was a good father, in part because he didn't put up with impertinence. Farley must have really overstepped his boundaries for Aurelius to have stepped in.

Pivoting, the man marched back to the tree, drew one of his daggers, gave it a twirl, then buried it in the tree trunk mere inches from Farley's ear. In a dangerously soft voice, Aurelius proposed, "Another bargain, Floxling. If you can wrest my dagger from this tree and return it to me during my departure, I shall consider your request. Agreed?"

The wide-eyed child managed a shaky nod.

"Good," Aurelius drawled. "Now, stay put … and *hush*."

Freydolf shook his head. "And I thought my holding Yona would cause a stir."

"This will definitely be the talk of the town," Melina agreed.

"He does love to be the center of attention," said Frey.

Carden hummed. "He handled Farley beautifully. I'm afraid that boy's more than I can manage."

Aurelius came even with them and offered a wintery smile. "Plenty of practice. I raised four terrors."

"The only reason they were terrors is because they all took after you," Freydolf pointed out.

Carden asked, "Does Farley have any chance of retrieving your blade?"

"Nay, but I shall now have the chance to greet your daughter properly." Holding out his hands to the girl still perched on Tupper's shoulders, Aurelius crooned, "Come, sprite! You were saying something about my eyes?"

The sun was sinking fast when the Statuary's three denizens finally began their ascent. Tupper hung back, shadowing the Preds' steps and listening with great interest to a lively debate that had begun as soon as they'd left Hayward.

"Do not digress!" Freydolf exclaimed. "I make a valid point, and you shall not evade it!"

"I fail to see the validity in your remarks," retorted Aurelius. "Spare me your spurious yammerings."

With a frustrated grumble, the sculptor argued, "Every member of the Meadowsweet family could validate my assessment. You spoiled Dulcie in every way possible."

"I was courteous to the sprite."

"You coddled her, *and* you cuddled Yona. *And* when you

weren't fussing over them, you were flattering Merona and Melina."

"Politeness," corrected Aurelius. "Have you been holed up so long you don't know good manners when you see them?"

Tupper was glad the men didn't ask his opinion, for he thought they were being silly. Both of them had acted just as anyone should. Their behavior hadn't been any different than Carden's ... mother's ... or his own. Hadn't he also let Dulcie, Yona, and even Aggie know how much they were loved?

"Don't even pretend you held onto your fangs today," Freydolf scoffed.

Aurelius sniffed. "As if you behaved any differently!"

"Which is *exactly* my point, you harrowing hypocrite," Frey rejoined, tossing his hands skyward. "If I'm the sad excuse and you're the shining paragon, in what respect did you rectify their opinion of the mighty Pred race?"

Aurelius blinked and looked prepared to belabor the matter further, but Tupper darted forward. Catching at their sleeves, he peered up into the men's faces. "You did your best, and you did some good."

The merchant bemusedly inquired, "In what way, sprat?"

Tupper shrugged. "Pred are tall, dark, and dangerous, but you're the same as Flox when it comes to families."

"The same *how*?" Aurelius prodded.

Both men shortened their steps to make it easier for Tupper to keep up, and he unobtrusively slipped his hands into theirs. "You love babies. You scold naughty boys. You tease girls. And you bicker."

Freydolf chuckled. "Are you implying that Pred are people?"

"A proud people with a long and glorious history," Aurelius countered.

"A proud people who bend their knee the moment a Flox child dubs them Unca Ree," said Frey.

"I was hardly swearing fealty!"

"Yet she ruled over you with every toss of her fair curls!"

Aurelius smirked. "Do I detect a note of envy, Unca Doff?"

"Envy?" Freydolf drew up short and stared hard at his

brother-in-law. "Today might actually be the first time *you've* ever been envious of *me*."

Tupper's gaze shifted to Aurelius's face to see which direction he would next take their banter only to find the Pred peering intently at him. Those golden eyes held the oddest expression as he answered, "Nay. The second."

5

Bows and Bits

The following day, Aurelius propped his elbows on the table. "May I ask some advice, sprat?"

Freydolf glanced up from his sketchbook, and Tupper paused in his sweeping. "Mine?"

"You manage Frey's household, so it's only sensible that I apply to you."

Since this was entirely true, the boy nodded and waited.

"I'll require a furnished suite in a month's time. If possible, I'd like rooms that are close to a necessary."

Tupper mulled over the possibilities, of which there were many. Most of the Statuary's housing was much more convenient than the workshop, with easier access to fresh water and communal bathing facilities.

It was hard to guess what kind of home Frey's sister was used to, but the boy suspected it was fancy. Hoping for some clue, he ventured, "Where did you stay before?"

"We skimped along in a small apartment across the courtyard from here."

Freydolf asked, "It won't do?"

With a grim shake of his head, Aurelius said, "I want something more comfortable for Ulrica, and the lad has the time to find it."

"I know some good places," Tupper assured. "What does she like?"

Aurelius's brows knit. "In what sense?"

"Would she like a balcony, a courtyard, a fountain, a trellis …? Does she have a favorite kind of stone?" Thinking fast, Tupper added, "Do you want high rooms, or would Missus Harrow feel safer inside Morven. And which direction do you want the windows to face?"

When the merchant found his tongue, he demanded, "Are you quite serious?"

Tupper nodded again. "There are plenty of good places, but not all of them are close to where Frey and I live. Is that important?"

"Aye, we're not coming to stay in order to stay away. The closer, the better."

That limited his choices considerably. "I'll show you the three that are closest. If you don't like them, there are lots more."

Aurelius thrust out his hand. "Deal."

Keeping his hands firmly wrapped around the broom handle, Tupper inquired, "Terms?"

The merchant nodded approvingly and proposed, "If you can find a suite that suits my needs, I'll fit you out—tunics, breeches, belts, boots, and the like. All new. Finest quality. My tailor is world class, I assure you!"

Tupper slowly shook his head. "I'm glad to show you rooms, Aurelius. Haggling over common courtesies is too mean."

"Aye," conceded the Pred, who lifted a finger. "But you'll be cleaning my new home from top to bottom, furnishing it from the storerooms, and stocking it for habitation. Not only that, but you'll have a second necessary to scour and supply, assuming the rooms I select are not near the one you and Frey frequent."

Tupper frowned thoughtfully. "Getting ready will take time."

"I warned you that your work load would increase." Aurelius spread his hands wide. "Since these preparations clearly fall outside your usual duties, I planned to compensate you personally. If you prefer coin to clothing, by all means, let's settle a price."

After a lengthy pause, Tupper admitted, "I don't know which is a better deal."

"Take the clothes, sprat."

Frey weighed in. "The new wardrobe will undoubtedly cost more, for Aurelius's extravagances will work in your favor. But I'd push for a no-ruffles clause."

Tupper considered carefully, then countered, "Five gold, with the balance in new clothing, provided they're not too fancy for working."

"I accept your terms," Aurelius swiftly agreed. "Though if I may pry, why do you need coin? I hope you don't plan to squander it on bread."

"No," Tupper assured, glancing at his master. "If it's okay, I was thinking of paying someone to help me."

Frey's eyebrows rose. "Someone?"

"I'm going to ask Carden if he'll let me borrow Melina."

Aurelius steepled his fingers. "Why?"

"They're saving up for lumber. Carden wants to add onto their house before winter."

"I have no objections." Aurelius traded nods with Freydolf. "In fact, I'll put up five more gold in order to bring that brother of yours in to help move whatever furnishings we need from the trove of carpentry in that Ursa Keeper's lair."

Tupper brightened, for the offer was more than fair. "Agreed!"

Aurelius concluded their business by suggesting, "And while their parents are tucking away coins for the future, Miss Dulcie and Miss Yona can stay with their Unca Doff."

The boy sat a little straighter, for the suggestion put a new idea into his head. Reaching for Frey's sleeve, he gave a firm tug. "Would you mind?"

"Nay. If Carden sees fit to bring his family to the Statuary, we'll make them welcome."

The day Aurelius left, Tupper tripped over a stone. Such a paltry thing wouldn't normally be worth noting, but the boy couldn't help wondering if the rock was trying to get his attention. Why else would it be lying someplace he walked several times a day—midway between the well and the fountain?

Rimbles pounced the lump of gray stone, batting it about as if scolding it for causing mischief for her charge. Tupper rescued the rock and carried it closer to the mullioned windows that lined the end of the colonnade.

"You weren't here last night." After some consideration, he amended, "Probably."

His mind had been on other things the previous evening, so he *might* have overlooked the stray.

On the eve of his departure, Aurelius had filled Tupper's arms with wonderful gifts—a small ledger for keeping household accounts, a bound collection of recipes handed down through a family with the surname Rakefang, a Terse syllabary, and a collection of poetry with passages in both Verit and Terse. The merchant often brought him books and maps, pointedly encouraging him to broaden his horizons.

Setting aside his water bucket, Tupper sat on the cool stone floor and crossed his legs, staring at the small conundrum. "When I swept last week, you weren't here," he mused aloud. "Where did you come from?"

He glanced up at the Triad, and even though the ladies weren't awake, he applied to them. "Did one of you see who left him here?" He'd met a few statues who liked to play pranks. Maybe one of them was trying to tease him.

The longer he held onto the stone, the more Tupper wasn't sure what to make of it, for it wasn't quite the same as others he'd picked up. Instead of having what Frey called *aspirations*, the lump seemed hopeful. Or maybe *helpful* was a better word. It wanted to be of use.

Tupper nodded sympathetically, for he felt the same way. Caressing the rock's uneven surface with his fingertips, he said, "Don't worry. I won't leave you here."

Slipping the seemingly insignificant bit of Morven into his

pocket, he hurried to collect his pail, already running through his mental checklist of daily duties. Still, he was conscious of the stone's weight and periodically gave the lump a gentle pat. Tupper was sure that a rock who tried so hard to be found must be extra special. With complete confidence, he promised, "Freydolf will know what to do with you."

Freydolf lounged at the kitchen table with his feet on the hearth, warming them while he puzzled over the new stone Tupper had brought him. It was the first time he'd ever been at a loss over what to do with one of the lad's picks, yet he couldn't bring himself to put it down.

"Maybe I'm looking at this all wrong," he muttered, turning the gray rock on its end. He may as well have stood on his head for all the good it did.

The sculptor was still at a stalemate when Tupper returned from his bath. The boy took one look and asked, "Stuck?"

"Aye," he grumbled. "I'm sorry, lambkin, but I can't see the shape of anything in this one."

With a grave nod, Tupper said, "He's very quiet for one of Morven's get."

Reaching across the table, the lad gave the lump a friendly poke, and magic exploded before Freydolf's eyes, dazzling him. His feet hit the floor as he sat up straight in his chair, demanding, "What did you do?"

His servant blinked. "Nothing."

Frey extended the stone. "Touch it again."

Tupper obeyed without question, and as soon as his fingertips came in contact with the stray bit of his mountain, the Keeper could see it. More accurately, he could tell the shape was there, just out of focus, but clearly present. And it was enough.

The master sculptor's fingers twitched, and a slow smile spread across his face. "Aye, that's done it."

"What?"

"This stone is responding to you," he explained excitedly. "Can't you feel it?"

"No."

"Where did you find it?"

"He found me." At the Keeper's incredulous stare, Tupper expanded. "On the floor near the fountain in the lower colonnade."

Freydolf's interest was caught, and there was nothing for it but to begin. He said, "I'll need your help. Do you mind?"

"No," Tupper assured. "I'll meet you in the balcony."

Frey welcomed the invitation, which signaled a return to their usual evening routine.

On bath nights, the lad generally busied himself with basket-making, and on opposite nights, he buried himself in the books Aurelius gave him. Since Frey was frequently called upon to pronounce or define words, they usually shared space on the rug before the central hearth while he fiddled with small carvings.

He mounted the stairs and selected a few tools from the workbench in the corner, then built up the fire to stave off the early spring chill.

"That's my job," Tupper gently chided, placing a tray on one of the low tables.

"You've had work aplenty for one day," countered the sculptor. "How is the guest suite coming along?"

"Slowly. I want to empty it before I clean it."

"When were you planning to bring in Carden and Melina?"

"Soon." Handing Freydolf a filled goblet, he said, "Next week, if Carden agrees."

Freydolf made himself comfortable on a floor cushion with his back to the wall beside the fireplace in order to take advantage of the light. "Stay close. I'll need you within reach."

Tupper brought over one of his new books and sprawled on the rug.

Extending the stone, the sculptor directed, "Let's see if you can stir him up again."

As before, magic resonated at the lad's touch, and Frey concentrated on the emerging shapes.

"Is that good?"

"Hard to tell, but I've enough to begin." With a wry grin, Freydolf admitted, "I'm a little uneasy about starting when I don't know what the end result will be."

Tupper patted his arm. "Don't worry. He's quiet, but not in a sneaky way. Just in a quiet way."

"Like you?" teased the man.

The boy actually blushed as if he'd been paid a compliment.

Freydolf made a mental note to give better ones more often. Tupper's bashful smile had been rather elusive of late.

Roughing up the Flox's short hair, he said, "You're not near as quiet as you once were. I used to wonder if you knew how to speak in full sentences."

Tupper ducked his head and shyly replied, "I talk more because you listen."

Freydolf might have been surprised that something so simple meant so much to the boy ... if it weren't for the fact that he treasured something very similar. "I like hearing what's on your mind."

After a short break to stretch protesting muscles and stoke the fire, Freydolf returned to his self-appointed task. Tupper had built a nest of cushions and dozed with one hand outstretched, in case the sculptor needed his touch.

Now that Frey knew what direction it wanted to take, he was able to relax into his accustomed role. Excavating miracles was his calling, and long experience lent him the skills needed to bring about even this unexpected one.

While he shaped and smoothed, he pondered several unanswered questions. How had this fragment found its way into Tupper's hands? Surely not without help. But whose? Why did the stone react to the lad? It made sense if Tupper's affinity translated into a sculptor's calling, but the boy was blind to the magical fireworks he set off.

For that matter, why did Frey express his understanding of a stone's heart in terms of sight, while Tupper said he could *hear* them? It could simply be two ways of explaining the same thing, but the Keeper doubted it.

He confided to the stone, "When I chose him, I had no idea what he would become. And I don't think he's anywhere near done becoming what he will be."

Frey was anxious to talk through recent developments with Aurelius, who had journeyed to the other eleven mountains and met all their Keepers. Maybe his agent had heard of stone affinities taking different shapes.

In the meantime, Frey made up his mind to open the archives. There might be a record of another Keeper, apprentice, or journeyman who was able to do whatever it was Tupper was doing.

The sun was close to rising before Freydolf was satisfied with his progress enough to rest. The carving wasn't finished, for its smooth surface begged for embellishment. He looked forward to adding the delicate tracery that would elevate an otherwise commonplace item to a work of art.

"Later," he promised. "Before moonrise."

Snagging a nearby cushion for a pillow, Freydolf stretched out beside Tupper to catch a few winks. However, before shutting his weary eyes, he carefully placed what remained of the gray stone into the boy's outstretched hand.

Magic shimmered briefly across its surface, and Tupper's fingers twitched before closing protectively around the small, stone key.

The following day, Tupper refused to neglect his work, so Freydolf gamely gathered his tools and tagged along. He could finish the key while his servant cleaned, which the boy did with impressive tenacity. Tupper seemed intent on polishing the small necessary next to Aurelius's chosen quarters until it shone ... quite literally.

Whoever had overseen the chamber's construction had incorporated a lavish amount of crystal. When the room's torches were lit, the translucent stones caught and carried the light in enchanting ways.

Frey claimed a bench in one corner, and Brand kept a lantern steady so the sculptor could focus on his fussing. Since there was little doubt that the key would belong to Tupper, he set out to make it a suitable match.

The edges of the key's bow became a three-dimensional set of curling horns, and with excruciating care, he pierced the area between them with a repeating pattern of openwork crescents, an homage to the Moonlit Mountain that was their home. Next, he wreathed the shaft with delicate sprays of meadowsweet, interspersed with the leaves of the lambsquarter Tupper was so fond of feeding him.

He was just sneaking in the tiny whorl of his signature shell on the key's tip when a mug appeared in his periphery, and his stomach greeted it with a rumble.

"Take a break," Tupper urged.

"Lunch already?"

"More like dinner." The lad handed him a spoon for the thick, spicy soup. "We slept late."

Frey was startled when Olexi trotted across the floor. He looked to the row of high windows the lad had been polishing earlier. "Sun's set."

"Yes."

"What's the moon doing?"

Tupper tipped his head to one side. "Low on the horizon, waxing toward full."

The Keeper moved to set aside the soup, exclaiming, "I need to finish the wards and biting, so we can wake him!"

Placing his hand over Frey's much larger one, Tupper said, "That'll be good, but eat first. The sky's clear, so you don't need to hurry."

With a sigh, Freydolf complied, scooting over on the bench to make room for Tupper. "Did you have your dinner already?"

"While I helped Ember with the chickens."

Freydolf frowned. "You shouldn't eat on the run."

The lad shrugged. "There's lots to do. We'll eat at the table again soon." Pointing to the progressing carving, he asked, "Can I see?"

"Aye. Help yourself." While he ate, Freydolf watched carefully out of the corner of his eye, eager for a reaction. He wasn't disappointed. The key sent up a pretty profusion of magical effervescence, as if trying to get the lad's attention. It was a shame Tupper couldn't see this obvious show of preference, but perhaps he sensed something, for his eyes widened.

"This key looks Floxish."

"As well it should. He's as quiet and stubborn as the one he'll be looking to."

"Me?"

"Aye," Frey confirmed, no longer able to hide a pleased grin. He tapped the delicate key. "We'll need to wake him if he's to be any use at all. He's too fragile like this. One twist, and you'd snap him in two."

"But if he's awake ...?"

The sculptor extended his hand to Brand, who obligingly clasped it. "Animated statues are incredibly resilient."

The lad shook his head.

Frey simplified. "They're stronger because they're flexible. Be sure to bathe your key in moonlight before testing him in any locks."

Tupper's brows knit. "What lock does he belong to?"

"No idea," Freydolf admitted, giving the fire-bearer's hand a fond squeeze before releasing it. "Which makes carving these bits as much a puzzle as the key itself."

"If he wakes, can he move?"

"Not in the same way as Olexi here, but aye … somehow."

The lad made a wiggling, twisting motion with his fingers and asked, "Could he change to fit anywhere?"

"A sort of master key?"

"That *would* be useful!" exclaimed Tupper.

Or dangerous. Freydolf's grunt was a grudging acknowledgment, for many of the lower galleries were locked for good reason. What if the lad stumbled across any of the Misbegotten?

For one fleeting moment, dread froze Frey's heart, and he was grateful that the key was still in Tupper's hands. The sculptor had no wish to impress unnecessary fears into his handiwork.

Taking a deep breath, Freydolf firmly declared, "Aye, a guardian key will surely lead you aright."

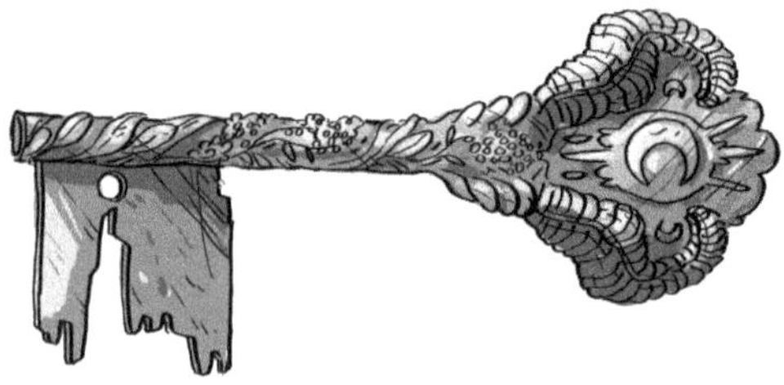

Since he didn't need to worry about fitting any particular lock, Freydolf followed a whim and carefully carved the key's biting into the shape of Morven's silhouette. All the while he scraped and chipped, he silently encouraged this odd little guardian to do his part. Only those doors that led to safe paths and wholesome treasures should be unlocked. Otherwise, the key should do everything in his power to prevent Tupper from straying into dangerous territory.

As a final touch, Frey gently pierced the bit with a tiny, decorative key ward to look like a moon in the sky over the wee mountain. Blowing away a few stray flecks, he scrutinized the addition with satisfaction. "All that's left is my mark."

"Should we go outside?" suggested Tupper.

"Aye, we need moonlight." Standing, the sculptor shook out his tunic, scattering stray bits of stone all over the freshly cleaned floor.

His servant tutted softly.

Freydolf stilled. "I'm sorry, lambkin. I wasn't thinking! Where's the broom?"

"Don't worry. It's my job."

"But it's my mess!" he protested.

"It usually is, and that's why I'm here," Tupper replied as he pocketed Olexi.

Freydolf allowed the lad to lead him to the outer courtyard, where the openness gave them the best view of the moon and stars. Brand trailed after them, his lamp held high, but Graven slunk toward the grove of peach and pear trees.

Choosing a low stone seat, Frey straddled one end of the bench, and Tupper perched on the opposite end. Several statues drifted over to see what the Keeper and his servant were up to, but they politely stayed outside the circle of light cast by Brand's lantern.

A few moments were needed for Frey to cut his inscription into the key's bow. Nodding to himself, he glanced about for a bit of grit. "And last, we'll need tears."

It had always intrigued Freydolf that the White Mountain and Gray Mountain had such similar needs. Many believed that starstone woke to saltwater because it was quarried from seaside slopes, but just about any salted liquid would do—sea water, tears, pickling brine. Aurelius swore that he'd once witnessed the Keeper of the Dazzle Mountain use chicken soup to wake a white guardian.

By contrast, moonstone needed fresh tears. No one was sure why, but nothing else worked to stir a gray guardian. That's why in some places, Morven was referred to as the Melancholy Mountain.

"I know. They're ready," Tupper replied, a slight quaver in his tone.

Freydolf's eyes widened in dismay, for the lad's cheeks were streaked by glistening tracks. "What's wrong, lambkin?"

He waved both hands and promised, "Nothing. I wanted to be ready, so I thought of something sad. It worked."

Using Tupper's own tears would undoubtedly strengthen his tie to the guardian, so Frey set aside his concerns. "Then let's not waste them."

Swiping up a few droplets, he daubed them onto the key and pressed his thumb gently against his mark. Magic stirred, and the Pred quietly called the key by name. "Wake up, Snick."

Nothing happened.

Tupper peered intently at the inert key. "Did it work?"

"Nay."

"Doesn't he like his name?" the lad ventured.

Frey chuckled, for that wasn't the issue at all. Whether it had always been so or his coaching had taken extraordinarily well, this key belonged to Tupper just as surely as Morven belonged to Freydolf. "He wants *you*, Tupper. Give me your hands."

Scooting closer, the lad accepted the key, cupping it protectively between his palms. "Like this?"

"Aye." The Pred placed his own hands over and under, once again pressing his thumb to the mark. "Call him by name."

Tupper coaxed, "Wake up, Snick."

This time, the connection was forged. Freydolf could sense the magical bond, which rivaled the one Tupper had formed with Graven in terms of strength.

The lad shivered from head to toe, then clasped the key to his heart. "So big," he whispered.

Frey thought it an odd remark, considering how small Snick was. Grasping the boy by the shoulders, he gruffly asked, "Why are you still crying?"

"Can't stop," Tupper sniffled.

He'd never seen the lad weep before. "There's no need for tears," he soothed. "Waking statues is cause for joy."

"M'happy."

In a vague attempt to distract him from his tears, Freydolf said, "Didn't you tell me you thought of something sad?"

"Yes," he quavered, fixing him with a heart-wrenching gaze.

"What if you chose someone else, and they didn't take good care of you? What if you were cold … and hungry … with no name … and no baths?"

These tears were for him? Freydolf hardly knew how to respond.

With a hiccupping sob, Tupper went on, "And I … and I …!"

It was no use telling the lad not to cry over might-have-beens. Freydolf had no way of knowing how long these tears had been pent up. They could just as easily be for his lost curls … or for his father. Chances were, Tupper wouldn't even be able to explain himself.

All the man could do was lend a shoulder. Tugging him close, he wrapped his arms around Tupper, letting him soak his favorite red tunic.

Sometimes magic triggered strong emotional responses, especially when moonstone was involved. Old Master Platt used to say Morven was greedy for tears, influencing their ebb and flow as surely as the moon ruled over the tides.

Frey rubbed circles between the boy's shoulder blades and rumbled, "That's the way. Let them go."

Tupper finally sagged against him, snuffling and spent. "Sorry," he whispered, dragging his sleeve across his nose.

"No need for apologies." Freydolf gently scratched at the base of a horn. "Feel better?"

"Some."

"I'd rather hear you say lots."

The lad fidgeted. "I could if …."

"Go on," Frey urged. "What is it?"

"Let me stay always?"

"Aye, if you like."

"Promise?"

Freydolf's arms tightened around Tupper. "I'd fight to keep you."

In a small voice, his servant asked, "You'd fight?"

"Aye, with all my might. Tooth and claw if necessary," he pledged.

Tupper turned his face against the man's shirt, trying to hide emotions he was unaccustomed to putting on full display. Still, his muffled voice reached Frey's ears. "Good."

6

Sun, Wind, and Spice

The very next evening, Tupper waited eagerly for moonrise. Tonight, Freydolf was taking him into the lower galleries to test Snick. They would be going deeper into Morven than he'd ever explored, and he could hardly contain his excitement.

To show his gratitude for the upcoming adventure, Tupper took extra pains with dinner, muddling through one of the recipes in the book Aurelius had given him. He'd picked a fish stew that wasn't too complicated, swapping out stream skimmers for the unfamiliar ocean fish that were called for.

There was no doubt in his mind that the cookbook was Pred in origin, for the broth was heavily spiced. Thanks to Aurelius's thoroughness, all the necessary ingredients were in his cupboard, but the boy had never used several of them. Even stranger were the quantities. Mother would have used seasonings by the pinch, but this cookbook demanded generous handfuls.

With great trepidation, he measured and mixed until he was left with a thick stew whose aroma easily overpowered that of his biscuits. To Tupper, his special dinner looked and tasted odd. "Did I mess up?" he muttered, rechecking the recipe.

Just then, Freydolf skidded into the room, a strange light in his eyes. "This smell!"

Poking at the stew with his ladle, Tupper worriedly explained, "I tried something new."

"*Not* new!" Striding across the kitchen, Frey leaned down to peer into the pot. "Ah, this brings back memories. It smells just like my mother's fish stew!"

"So it's right?" the boy asked dubiously.

"Aye! This was my favorite when I was a boy!"

Tupper looked from the soup to the man to the book in his hands, then flipped to the flyleaf. With a start, he realized something important. "Rakefang?"

The Pred straightened so fast, the boy took a step backward.

Frey seemed to be struggling for words.

Finally, he held out his hand. "May I see?"

Tupper surrendered the book and watched as the Pred slowly leafed through its pages. "These are in my mother's handwriting ... and her mother's ... and her grandmother's. These recipes go back for generations."

"Aurelius brought it."

"My sister must have smuggled it out of the main house." Freydolf reached the last page with writing on it and showed him the final inscription. "Aye, that's Ulrica for you."

Tupper went up on tiptoe to better see her message.

> Frey– What use are gates if you invite your enemy through them? What help are guardians if you let your conqueror tame them? What good are fangs if you yield them to a mere boy?
>
> Boy– My brother is under your heel. Rule over him wisely and well, or I shall tear out your inconstant heart and cast your broken body from Morven's highest height. –U

Once he'd worked out the gist of the words, Tupper paled. "She's going to kill me?"

"Nay!" Freydolf chuckled. Brushing his fingertips over his sister's words with a fond smile. "When Ulrica is pleased, she exaggerates. I'm sure she already likes you."

Rereading the ominous message, the boy blankly asked, "How can you tell?"

"She stole this book for you."

Tupper nodded tentatively, but he wasn't so sure. What kind of person showed affection with sharp criticism, thinly-veiled insults, and death threats? Upon serious consideration, Tupper realized that the answer should have been obvious—a sister.

Freydolf unhooked a cumbersome ring of keys from his belt and sorted through them, filling the chamber with enough *clinks* and *chings* to wake songstone. By his reckoning, it had been six years since he last ventured this low, chasing down a rogue statue foisted upon him by an idiot traveler who'd been tricked into taking it off the hands of a smooth-talking merchant. The only reason Frey had agreed to help was because the troublemaker was carved from moonstone, and its chicanery might damage Morven's reputation.

Since Aurelius was always hounding him to give Tupper the knowledge he needed, Freydolf asked, "Did you know that while there are only twelve Keepers, there are hundreds of talented sculptors?"

"Like journeymen? Aurelius says there aren't enough mountains to go around, so the sculptors go around instead."

"Aye, there's them," Freydolf acknowledged. "And others who set up their own workshops and deal in magical stones."

"Can they wake their statues?"

"Many can, which sometimes causes trouble. Most of the Misbegotten housed in these galleries weren't crafted by Keepers or their apprentices. They're mistakes that had to be hunted down and locked away."

A spark of interest flickered in the boy's wide eyes. "You hunt statues?"

"Once in a great while. Usually, with Graven's help."

"Were they bad?"

He grimaced, for he hated to blame the stones. "In almost every case, the statue is only doing what its maker designed it to do. Sadly, not every sculptor has honorable intentions."

"They tell their statues to do bad things?"

"It varies." Freydolf finally located the key he needed and inserted it into a heavy padlock. With a *creak* and *click*, its shackle lifted. He loosened the chains on an enormous set of double doors. "I know of one sculptor who sold statues that would return to him, so he could resell them to other people."

"Greedy."

"We've a statue here that picks pockets. Another was used by a band of thieves to waylay travelers." Jaw set, he grimly continued, "Worse are the accidents, those that truly earn the label Misbegotten."

"Like what?" Tupper asked, unobtrusively slipping his hand into Brand's as they started down a lengthy colonnade.

Although Freydolf didn't want to frighten the boy, it was important that he understood. "When a sculptor botches a statue, the guardian can quickly become a destroyer. I've seen wrecked buildings, ruined fields, charred forests, ravaged flocks." Freydolf hesitated to go on, but he could tell the boy already knew. Nodding sadly, he finished, "Aye, people have died."

"Then is this a prison?"

"Nay, lad. The Statuary is a haven for those who wish to learn a sculptor's skills from someone trusted by Morven herself. While it's true that dangerous things sleep here, it would be a shame to let a few terrible mistakes rob us of the opportunity to do wonderful things." With a confident grin, Freydolf promised, "I'll show you how I marked the doors I locked, as well as those Master Platt sealed. You'll know what to watch for when you're on your own."

Tupper nodded, but his attention was already caught by a broad door set between two fat columns. "Is this one safe?"

Frey studied the bands radiating around it. "Nothing suggests otherwise. Try and see."

The boy tugged. "Locked."

Rattling his key ring, he said, "I could hunt for one that fits, or you could test yours."

"Let me." Tupper withdrew the cord he always wore around his neck, for he'd added Snick to his small collection of beads and coins. Carefully fitting the key into the lock, he gave it a turn and was rewarded by a soft *snick*. "It worked!"

"Aye," Freydolf acknowledged, just as pleased as the lad over their success. "Now, let Brand go first so that you can see what you're getting into."

The fire-bearer stepped to the fore, and Tupper pulled open the door.

Brand entered, lifted his lantern high, then smiled encouragingly at the lad, gesturing for him to enter.

Tupper asked, "That means it's safe?"

"Brand will know if another statue is stirring."

"How?"

Freydolf pondered that. "Guardians are sensitive to magic on the move. Like calls to like."

The boy accepted that with a nod and walked into the room.

At first glance, the space they entered seemed overly crowded, for it was filled with statues standing in tight formation. Tupper meandered between the rows, pacing up and down, touching and patting various figures in passing.

With a soft sigh, Freydolf placed his hand on the head of the nearest statue, which had probably been some apprentice's first effort—showing potential, clumsily rendered, and abandoned at the midway point. "What a shame," he muttered.

Peeking out from around the beginnings of a bear rising up on its forelegs, Tupper asked, "What is this place?"

"A storeroom. Many of the statues on this level are unfinished. Their makers gave up, lost interest, moved on, or passed away."

"But they're good stones," the lad protested, pressing his ear to a badly-cracked gray column.

"Aye."

Tupper hurried to his side and tugged urgently at his sleeve.

"Did you ever leave a statue unfinished?"

"Not every one of mine is marked and moving, but I always finish what I start."

"Can I see?"

Freydolf shook his head. "See what, lambkin?"

"Your statues from before," he said. "Old ones by a younger you."

Several of the Pred's early efforts were lurking in the Statuary, for they were hardly fit to be seen, let alone sold. Rubbing the back of his neck, Frey hedged, "They're nothing special."

"Aren't they yours?"

Of course they were. Freydolf had poured his heart and soul into each and every one of his statues. The early ones couldn't compare to the level he was now capable of, but they were everything he had once been—awkward, eager, and hopeful.

Freydolf gave in. "There's a door not far from here that's bounded by carvings of shells. If you can find it—and Snick can open it—I'll have little choice but to make introductions!"

Owning up to humble beginnings could be embarrassing, but Frey didn't mind letting Tupper see the truth. What harm could it do? The lad already thought him hopeless!

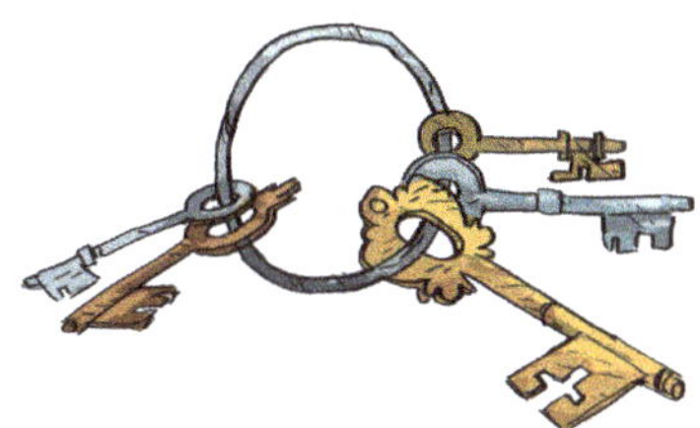

Tupper raced along the passage but slowed when he realized he was causing trouble for Brand. The poor fire-bearer was doing his best to remain at equal distances from both master and servant, for he bore the only lantern.

"Sorry!" Tupper mumbled when the stone guardian caught up. "All together is fine."

The red stone warrior shook his head, refusing the apology; then with a wink, he used his large, hooked nose to subtly indicate a narrow passage off to their right.

Going up on tiptoe, Tupper whispered, "You know the way?"

Brand's small nod was a secret shared.

Tupper snuck a glance in Freydolf's direction. "I would have missed the turning. Thank you for the hint!"

Smiling serenely, the statue offered his hand.

Part of Tupper wanted to prove that he could find the way on his own, but he placed his hand in Brand's. The red stone was cool and smooth to touch, but not hard as rock. Living statues had give—soft skin, flowing cloth, swishy hair, and in the Grif's case, rustling feathers.

Coming alongside, Brand's cape tickled pleasantly across Tupper's shoulders as the fire-bearer tugged him closer and looped an arm around his waist.

This was new. Glancing around, Tupper asked, "Is there danger close by?"

Brand shook his head, and his expression remained expectant.

He stared quizzically at the statue and finally shook his head as well. "I don't understand."

Freydolf ambled up. Circling around, he bent to peer intently into their lantern-bearer's face. "I didn't know this was in your repertoire, Brand."

The statue dipped his head apologetically, and he made a move to step away.

"Nay." Frey placed a hand on the statue's shoulder to forestall retreat. "I'm only surprised. But I suppose I shouldn't be. Your maker was Grif, after all."

Brand inclined his head.

"What?" Tupper begged, looking between their faces.

"Aurelius could explain it better, but I'll give it a go. It's something that's normal for Grif, but not for Flox or for Pred."

"Cultural differences," said Tupper, showing off one of the newer phrases in his vocabulary.

"Aye. When you first met Brand, he led you by the hand. That's normal for most children, no matter their race."

"Yes."

"*Now*, he's offering to walk with you in the fashion of Grif comrades." Mimicking the statue's hold, he went on, "Grif men walk arm in arm, or with their arms looped around each other's waists."

Tupper brightened. "This means we're friends?"

Watching Brand's face carefully, Freydolf gently corrected, "I think he's trying to tell you that you're no longer a child."

The red statue inclined his head once again, then quirked a brow at his young companion.

Rubbing abashedly at his horns, Tupper mumbled, "I think you're too early, Brand."

"You *have* grown, lambkin."

"A little." He could feel the color rising in his cheeks. "But like Aurelius said, I'm not a man just because my horns are coming in."

Freydolf chuckled. "Did it ever occur to you that the opposite is true?"

Tupper shook his head in confusion.

"If longer horns don't make you more of a man, then shorter horns cannot mean you're less of one. Brand believes you've earned a man's place."

Blushing to the tips of his ears, Tupper asked, "Is that what *you* think?"

"Does it matter what I think?" Freydolf countered.

It did. Lots. Tupper nodded.

"I think it's too early, too," his master replied seriously. "You're still a lad in my eyes, but I agree with Brand. There's no longer any need to lead you around by the hand."

"I'm between?"

"Aye." Freydolf came around to Tupper's other side so that he was flanked by Grif and Pred. Indicating the corridor Brand had helped Tupper to find, Frey noted, "And well on your way."

The door at the very end of the narrow corridor was indeed surrounded by carved seashells ... and nothing else. "Just yours?" Tupper asked in surprise.

"Stands to reason, since I'm the one who made this chamber." Freydolf pressed his palm to the intricate border. "Half a lifetime ago."

Tupper was familiar with what it took to build houses above-ground, but he wasn't sure how things worked inside a mountain. "You cut away the stone?"

"None of the potential apprentices who turn up on mountains are simply handed magical stones. One of our first tasks is to hew our own practice blocks. Most newcomers are sent into the quarry to learn the process, but I was ... unwelcome. Gruff was good enough to come down here from time to time and give me pointers." The Pred rapped his knuckles on the sturdy door barring their way. "He even built this for me once I finished smoothing the floor inside to his satisfaction."

"Was it hard?" Tupper asked.

"I'd never done harder work."

"I meant working alone."

"Ah," Frey replied awkwardly. "A little, but I'm glad they stashed me here. Stones quarried from Morven's foothills aren't as powerful as those taken from within."

That certainly explained why the mountain was riddled with rooms and passages.

Pulling Snick from under his tunic, Tupper made short work of the lock, then stepped aside so Brand could precede them.

He'd been expecting lots and lots of statues, but the room echoed slightly. Only a handful were arrayed around the room—a pair of deer, a matched set of mid-sized felines, and two wolves. They were all arranged two-by-two, which made the lone figure standing in their midst stick out even more.

He was mostly made of brownstone, just like the griffin upstairs, and Tupper couldn't resist reaching up to touch the statue's broad chest. Richly hued stone the color of bark suited the man quite well, for there was no mistaking his claws and long, wild hair. "He's Pred!"

"Aye. His name is Haimish."

Circling the brown statue, Tupper paid attention to every detail. Haimish was as tall as Freydolf, but not as broad in the shoulder. In a way, he looked like a younger version of his master, but not quite.

A different nose, downcast eyes, and fancier clothes. What really stood out in the lantern's light were the statue's accessories. Crouching down, Tupper touched one of the smooth, orange circlets decorating Haimish's ankles. "What are these?"

"Titian jade. I was trying to emulate my master's specialty by fusing more than one kind of stone into a single sculpture. I fitted those to his ankles and wrists in the hopes of extending the time he was awake past sunset."

"And earrings." The statue's lobes were pierced by more of the orange stone. Polished rectangles dangled down.

"Aye." Freydolf gave one a flick, sending it swinging. "Creating him was far more difficult than I could have imagined. Master Platt called him a sad waste of valuable resources. I made so many mistakes."

"He looks good to me." True, there wasn't a lot of personality coming from the statue's stance or expression, but the stone itself was wonderful, even better than the griffin's. That had to count for something!

"Nay, my mentor's criticism was just. I put too much of myself into Haimish, so he carries many of the worries I had when I first arrived here." Smiling fondly at his creation, Freydolf admitted, "He's shy, awkward, lonely, and he meant well in spite of all the trouble he caused."

Tupper fitted his hand into the still statue's and peered intently into his downcast eyes. "But why is he here?" The question seemed to take Freydolf aback, and the young Flox pressed, "He should be with you!"

Sadness softened Freydolf's gaze. "Haimish *wanted* to be here."

"Why would he want to be locked away?"

The sculptor sighed. "In making him Pred, I doomed him to the very same shunning I experienced. The servants we hired were as terrified of him as they were of me, and he's so sensitive. He was miserable."

Tupper was quite sure Freydolf had been just as unhappy.

Pointing to the neat rectangle of brownstone on which the

statue stood, Frey continued, "Platt chewed me out for giving Haimish a pedestal small enough for him to carry. Time and again, he picked it up and fled to some far corner."

"He tried to run away?"

"Nay, he would hide. Since it pained him to frighten people, I finally gave up and let him have his way. He's been here ever since."

Tupper latched onto Freydolf's arm and earnestly begged, "Wake him! I want to meet him!"

"I can't, lambkin. Brownstone is only active in daytime," Freydolf reminded.

"I'll wait." Sitting down practically on top of Haimish's feet, Tupper withdrew Olexi from his pocket, setting the small ram on the smooth floor. While the little guardian made his reconnoiter of the chamber, the boy said, "When Olexi sleeps, we'll know the sun is up. Do you have what Haimish needs?"

"Aside from you?"

Tupper nodded once, all business.

Freydolf relented with a grin. Joining him on the floor, he assured, "Aye. Everything he needs is here."

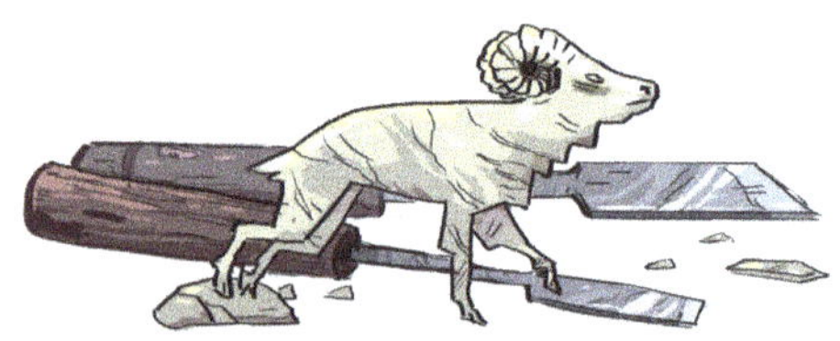

Tupper took a deep breath of the fragrant air and decided that waking brownstone might be his favorite of all. Brand held a taper to cinnabark and star-spice, while Freydolf carefully added strips of thick, dried leaves that gave off a pleasant aroma as they smoldered.

"Scented oils work as well," the Pred said instructionally. "And some kinds of perfume."

"Like Aurelius's?"

Frey chuckled. "Aye, in the early days, all Haimish needed to wake was for Aurelius to come down from the balcony, wafting expensive extracts and essences."

As the warm scent of mingled spices grew stronger, the stone man blinked, then shifted from foot to foot. He glanced hurriedly around the room.

Tupper held his breath in anticipation, eager to introduce himself. However, the moment the tall statue noticed him, he turned to stone.

"Easy there, Haimish," Freydolf soothed. "No need to worry. The lad's not afraid."

Taking his cue, Tupper nodded adamantly. "I waited all night to meet you."

The statue's expression didn't change much, but he blinked a few times, then scanned his surroundings more carefully. This time, he took note of Brand, who smiled and inclined his head. Haimish nodded shyly, then sought his maker's gaze.

Freydolf explained, "Things have changed while you were asleep. Tupper's a brave one, so there's no longer any need to hide."

At first, Tupper took the statue's blank expression for surprise. Haimish's face was plain and pleasant, and the set of his mouth suggested kindness. But there was an odd mismatch between his faint smile and the troubled look in his eyes.

Something clicked into place as he watched Frey talk softly to his statue. While Brand's expressive features suggested that he'd been made by a master, Haimish's maker had been a beginner ... and it showed. Still, there was a soulfulness in his gaze, a testament to the glimmer of talent that Freydolf must have shown at a young age.

Reaching up to touch Haimish's arm, Tupper solemnly announced, "You have nice eyes."

The statue blinked, then placed an upraised hand below his heart and bowed, completely unbalancing himself.

Freydolf quickly grabbed the teetering guardian by the shoulders to steady him and chuckled. "I'd forgotten how clumsy you are!"

Haimish managed to look flustered and grateful all in one glance.

Tupper was relieved that Freydolf didn't seem bothered or

embarrassed by his statue's imperfections.

With a soft grunt, Frey muttered, "Or how heavy! Find your feet, man!"

Once Haimish adjusted his stance, his maker shared, "The first time he stepped off his pedestal, he fell flat on his face. Scared me half out of my wits, and Platt never let me hear the end of it."

"Did you trip?" Tupper asked, his eyes on the statue's face.

Haimish awkwardly rubbed the back of his neck just like Freydolf sometimes did.

"Nay," the sculptor answered for him. "It's my fault, really. I didn't notice until it was too late, but I made his feet too small."

Still addressing the statue directly, the boy asked, "Can you walk?"

Haimish nodded.

Tupper held out his hand. "Good. Come on."

Very slowly, Haimish extended one clawed hand, but he didn't budge.

Ignoring the statue's hesitation, Tupper grabbed hold and leaned backward, trying to get him moving. "This way, so Frey can pick up your pedestal."

Again, those expressive eyes widened, and the statue looked to his maker with easy-to-read confusion.

Freydolf said, "It's time to come home, Haimish."

For the next two days, Freydolf set aside his usual work in order to help Haimish adjust, not that his oversight was needed. Although the sculptor wasn't quite sure why, the statue seemed to be in awe of Tupper. Haimish was either impressed with the lad's fearlessness, or he'd *been* impressed upon waking, in much the same sense that some of Tupper's newest hatchlings believed that Graven was their mother.

Unfortunately, in his eagerness to assist the lad, Haimish often created more work for him.

Freydolf winced when a crash came from the direction of the balcony stairs. "Now what?" he muttered.

He found his well-meaning klutz of a creation sitting on the floor at the foot of the stairs. Tupper knelt in front of him, running his hands over brown stone.

"No cracks," the lad announced, sounding relieved.

"What happened, lambkin?"

"He fell." Turning back to Haimish, he said, "Don't try to carry so much. It makes you tippy."

The statue ducked his head contritely.

Feeling responsible, Freydolf added his own, "Sorry."

Tupper gave him a long look, then asked, "What did you make Haimish want to do?"

Pulling out a kitchen chair, the sculptor sat heavily, hunching slightly to rest his elbows on his knees. He rubbed his chin, thinking back. He'd purchased the block of brownstone from a traveling merchant shortly after being named Master Platt's apprentice. The other potentials and visiting journeymen had called the Keeper's scandalous choice into question, and after many bitter words, they'd left.

Although Aurelius refused to speak about the rumors that were still bandied about, Freydolf suspected that their censure was the main reason why Morven no longer received visits from traveling sculptors and merchants.

"Most of the work I had to do as an apprentice was usually done by a small group of workers, but I was alone. I needed help, so I made myself a helper."

Tupper nodded, then patted Haimish's shoulder. "You want to help?"

The stone Pred offered both his hands to the boy in a show of willingness.

"He's strong enough for all manner of lifting and carrying, but I wouldn't give him anything fragile to tote. Stones, straw, rubble, firewood, water—things like that are best." Recalling one of Haimish's other weaknesses, Frey added, "He's useful, but not very independent. You'll need to give him direction. Constantly."

With a thoughtful nod, Tupper said, "So he's like Graven."

Confused by the comparison, Freydolf asked, "In what way?"

"Graven was made to love Master Platt."

The boy had a knack for cutting to the heart of a matter. Haimish truly had been born out a combination of loneliness and practical necessity. One of the reasons Freydolf had squandered his entire savings on the block of brownstone from which Haimish had been carved was because it had seemed as lonesome as he. Platt had never criticized him for attempting to remedy his solitary existence by crafting a comrade, largely due to the fact that the old Drom had done much the same with Graven.

"Aye, whether I meant to or not, I made Haimish to be a companion. He's happiest when he's keeping someone company—*you*, at the moment."

Tupper gave the brown statue another reassuring pat, then asked, "Can you fix him?

Frey swiftly assessed his statue. "I thought you said there weren't any cracks."

The lad tried again. "If Haimish tips because his feet are too small, can you help him? Maybe give him heavy boots?"

"I see," Freydolf mused.

He'd never augmented one of his own statues before, but it was probably possible. Graven's new bond with Tupper had taken beautifully, and that was vastly more complicated than finding a way to rebalance a top-heavy statue.

Reaching for a sketchbook, Frey said, "Stand up, please, Haimish."

The brownstone statue obeyed, and the sculptor started a rough drawing. With eyes that benefited from another twenty years of experience, he could easily see why his former mentor had been so critical. There were irregularities aplenty, but they were part of Haimish. Frey had no intention of remaking the statue, but if he messed with the magic anchored by his mark, there was a good chance that the statue would be changed.

"I'll have to be very careful," he muttered, pausing to tap his pencil against the sketchbook.

Meanwhile, Tupper collected the scattered blankets Haimish must have been carrying and disappeared outside.

The statue's gaze longingly followed the young Flox, and Frey chuckled. "Don't worry, old friend. Tupper hasn't gone far. You'll just have to make do with me for a bit."

The statue appeared stricken, and he hurried to kneel before the sculptor, offering his hands.

"I was only teasing." Setting aside his sketchbook, Freydolf gripped the Pred's arms. "You help me whenever you're helping him. I have no complaints."

Haimish squared his shoulders and nodded more confidently.

Fixing the statue with a considering look, he asked, "Do you like the lad's suggestion? I could probably find a way to steady you on your feet."

In answer, Haimish took his maker's hands and pressed them to his own cheeks, closing his eyes. For Pred, the gesture was a rare demonstration of utter trust.

"Aye, you can trust me," Freydolf softly promised, smoothing the pads of his thumbs over features he'd shaped with such care. "I'm older and wiser these days. Especially the *older* part. But honestly, I don't know how much my meddling might change you."

Haimish shook his head, and Tupper startled Freydolf by answering, "Haimish is Haimish all the way through. That won't change."

"Aye, I *should* know that better than anyone," he acknowledged, grateful for the reminder.

Sitting back, Frey reclaimed his drawing, and Tupper hurried to his side, asking, "What will you do?"

He hummed. "Boots aren't feasible, and it'd be a shame to add weights to his ankles. They'd cover the jade ... and look like shackles."

"Belt?"

The sculptor penciled in a wide belt, but soon shook his head. "This would be too high to do any good. He'll still overbalance when he tries to carry things."

"Too bad," Tupper sighed.

For a few moments, Freydolf toyed with the idea of taking away some of the excess weight on top—shaving, shaping, hollowing, even a haircut—but all those things made his heart rebel.

Adding was definitely better than detracting, but how? Then, he was hit by a sudden flash of crazy inspiration and barked with laughter.

"You figured it out," Tupper guessed.

"Aye, but I'll need your help, lambkin." The lad's gaze was as expectant as Haimish's, and Freydolf tossed aside his sketchbook and clapped his hands, rubbing them together eagerly. "First, we need to see if we can find anything left over from Haimish's block!"

"What for?"

Freydolf held out his hands. "If I have a chunk of brownstone about *this* long, I can use it and a bit of bosh about Pred to steady Haimish on his feet!"

Tupper was already backing toward the door. "I'll go find it," he offered, earnest in his enthusiasm. "I know it's there."

"Did you see such a piece?" Frey wouldn't really be surprised, given how often Tupper picked over the piles of rubble on the edge of the outer courtyard.

The lad impatiently hopped from foot to foot, but he stayed long enough to answer, "No, but I can hear it!"

"He can hear it," Freydolf echoed in stunned tones. Slowly shaking his head, he looked to Haimish and asked, "How is that even possible?"

No answers were forthcoming.

Graven lounged in the early morning sun, his vividly-striped tail slowly flicking and curling as he pretended to ignore the half-dozen chicks that scratched and pecked between his enormous front paws. Several hens meandered amidst the neatly fenced garden plots scattered here and there along the wide ledge while Tupper tended to his watering.

Stationed on a nearby bench, Freydolf reached for a rasp as he meticulously shaped the edges of the channel he'd prepared in order to add stability to the join between new and old stone.

Morven only knew how Tupper had so easily located a section of Haimish's original block, but Frey wasn't complaining. The piece was *exactly* what he'd needed, and he'd spent all night making sure the new counterbalance would be ready by sunup.

At the moment, Haimish stood at rest, hands at his sides, eyes downcast.

Although Freydolf knew statues didn't feel pain, he'd waited to take a chisel to his old friend until the setting sun had sent him to sleep.

"When you wake, this will all be over."

He and Tupper had moved Haimish's pedestal into the outer courtyard the day before because brownstone needed wind to waken. "Spice for you, wind for the addition, and sun for both," he explained in a low voice. "You'll be the first statue I've ever marked twice."

Haimish's stoic silence endured, but Freydolf kept up his one-sided ramble, hoping to ease any distress he might be causing his old friend with all the gouging.

Finally satisfied with the fit, he called, "I'm ready, lambkin."

"Coming!"

Brownstone was easy enough to wake, but bonding stone to stone was a monumental feat. Freydolf well remembered how much his perception of Master Platt's skills had shifted once he'd wrestled with adding titian jade to Haimish's brownstone. It had taken everything he had to tune the magic of two vastly different stones together.

By comparison, melding two pieces from the same block would be simple.

"What can I do?" Tupper asked, plunking his trusty bucket in front of Haimish and stepping up.

Freydolf handed up a slim vial. "That's the scented oil. Wait to open it until I tell you to."

Tupper nodded solemnly, then reached up to pat Haimish's shoulder. "It looks good. You'll like it," he promised seriously.

This was worlds apart from the first time he'd woken Haimish. Instead of being awash with uncertainties, Frey was on familiar ground—calm, confident, and clear-minded on how the statue's new counterbalance should function. He knelt behind the statue, one hand reaching around to touch the inscription subtly worked into Haimish's belt buckle, the other pressed firmly over the newer seal, proudly wreathed in meadowsweet.

As the magic gathered, its wielder concentrated on blending the new section of brownstone into the whole.

A thrill seemed to run through the stone, and Freydolf smiled in recognition of Haimish's familiar presence. What a difference from the usual waking process. He wasn't reaching into the unknown, searching for the personality that had helped him to shape the rock. This time, Frey was calling to a friend he already knew and cherished, and a wellspring of warm feelings overflowed with the magic. No matter what changed, Haimish was Haimish, just as Tupper had insisted.

A clear, bright, steady bond emerged in his mind's eye, and Freydolf half-expected the statue to turn to Tupper as Graven had done. The boy's soft voice was in the periphery, offering words of encouragement.

Frey wouldn't have minded, but when the magic lashed vigorously before latching firmly onto him, he was startled by a surge of relief. Quickly embracing his ties with the faithful statue, Freydolf could feel the stone's anticipation.

Haimish knew what was about to happen. He was waiting for his maker's call.

Taking a deep breath to steady his voice, the sculptor quietly instructed, "Now, Tupper."

"Yes."

Sun, wind, and spice filled their senses, and Freydolf calmly called, "Wake up, Haimish."

Instantly, brown stone trembled.

The kneeling sculptor sat back on his heels, then ran his hand along the new addition, smiling in satisfaction over the softness of the fur.

Haimish turned slightly to look over his shoulder at Freydolf … and tentatively wagged his new tail.

7

Easing Through

Tupper pressed his cheek to the bare stone against which Freydolf's fruit trees were espaliered before absentmindedly rubbing one horn against the warm rock. They were itching again, and his head ached. Maybe he was getting sick? That wasn't good. There were too many things to do to get ready for Aurelius's return. Although at the moment, he couldn't quite remember what they were.

Rimbles climbed onto his lap, dabbing one paw at his idle hands. He pulled her close.

"Sorry, honey-tufts," he mumbled, using his pet name for the little lynx. "Not sure I can finish the weeding."

She stretched up to butt her head under his chin, and he felt bad for worrying her. "I'll be fine," he promised, managing a wan smile.

Nudging her off his legs, he levered to his feet, steadying himself on a tree limb as he tried to figure out what to do next. Nothing came to mind, and he shook his head, trying to un-muddle it.

A fresh jolt of pain throbbed through his temples, and Tupper slumped against the mountain, sliding back down to the ground.

"Ouch," he moaned, swallowing against a wave of nausea.

Nothing had ever hurt quite like this before, and he was beginning to be frightened. Blinking tears from his eyes, he begged, "I want Frey."

Freydolf was roused from his work by a wild scrabble and repeated *thuds* at the workshop door. He opened it to a wild-eyed kitten. For several moments, he couldn't make head nor tails of Rimbles's histrionics, but the instant he did, his heart slammed into overdrive. "Where is he?"

She hied off along the cobblestones, short tail straight in the air.

Once the Pred realized she was bound for the outer courtyard, he lengthened his stride, easily outdistancing the little statue. "Tupper! Tupper!" he called, scanning the vicinity.

Spying the lad's crumpled form under a blooming pear tree, he muttered a dark oath and sprang up the steps leading to the ledge. Freydolf found no injuries, but the boy's glazed eyes and fever were even more worrisome.

Gathering his servant into his arms, he asked, "Can you hear me, lambkin? What happened? What's wrong?"

Tupper's expression twisted, and he whimpered softly, then vomited all over Freydolf's favorite tunic.

Carden Meadowsweet had just finished adding the names of three newly-nubbed hires to the books when a movement outside caught his eye. It was the oddest sight. Several men were slowly backing up, alarm plain on their faces.

Hurrying from his desk to the window, Carden was baffled to see other quarry workers drop their tools and run for cover, heading in the direction of the bunkhouse or surrounding forest.

Fearing something dire, he turned toward the door just as his younger brother Ewert stuck his head inside. "Better come quick. It's that Pred."

"His *name* is Master Freydolf," Carden sternly corrected.

Jogging in the direction from which many of his men still fled, he soon spotted Morven's Keeper and immediately knew something was *very* wrong. Freydolf wore an outlandish purple tunic trimmed with dozens of silken tassels.

On every side, men and boys muttered nervously.

"It's the monster!"

"Big brute!"

"Lookit those claws!"

Gruff was back in Hayward on a home day, so Carden needed to take charge and quickly. Voice deepening with authority, he snapped, "Show some respect, you nubless scrabblers! I won't have you insulting Master Freydolf on his own mountain!"

Several mouths snapped shut, and most looked relieved ... and quite willing to throw Carden to the wolf. With one last glare for the skittish Flox, Carden hurried to the equally restless man hovering at the edge of the work site.

When Freydolf recognized him, relief washed over his fierce features, and he strode forward to grip Carden's shoulders, causing a ripple of panicky whispers to jump from one knot of onlookers to the next.

With a beleaguered smile, Carden pointedly offered a more polite greeting. "It's rare to see you down here, Master Freydolf. You're most welcome."

"Like a toothache on a feast day," he rejoined in an undertone. Fixing the young man with a pleading look, he quietly asked, "Can you come?"

"Now?"

"Aye. Tupper's in pain, and I don't know what's wrong." Glancing around again, he asked, "Or is it best to find a doctor?"

"Families mostly rely on home remedies," said Carden. "I'll come."

The Pred nodded once and released the man, taking a step back. "Thanks."

"What are brothers for?" he asked lightly. "Let me grab a kit and my cloak."

Wheeling, Carden jogged back toward the office, hollering, "Back to work! Or do you want the one who pays your wages to think you're slacking?"

The quarry workers reclaimed scattered tools and trooped back to their various tasks, giving the Keeper wary glances and a wide berth.

A sole Flox stayed behind, and Frey realized with a start that with his sunny curls and blue eyes, he bore a strong resemblance to Merona Meadowsweet. He searched his memory for a name and came up empty. Shaking his head, he ventured, "Are you one of Tupper's brothers?"

"Yessir. I'm Ewert." He stepped up and extended a hand. "I'm pleased to finally meet you."

Freydolf accepted the Floxish offer of peace. Judging by the length of Ewert's horns, he was just shy of adulthood—perhaps sixteen or seventeen. "Likewise. I suppose I should have made more of an effort to make your acquaintance."

"Why's that?"

The glint in the Meadowsweet lad's eye reminded Frey very much of Farley, and he hardly knew how to answer. Maybe this one didn't think of him as kin? He couldn't blame him.

Carden returned then, a cloak tossed over his arm and a box tucked under it. Cuffing his sibling's shoulder, he asked, "Are you needling Master Freydolf?"

"*And* impressing the ninnies who'll think me braver for standing up to him."

"He's not here to gild your curls!" chided Carden. "Nor

should you serve sauce to your betters!"

Ewert shrugged. "If the Keeper were here on business, I'd snap to, but I figure this is a family emergency. Some brothers *aren't* betters, just biggers."

Latching on to his reference to *family*, Frey gave the young man's hand a grateful squeeze before releasing it. "You can serve all the sauce you like next time we meet, but I need to get back to Tupper." With no further excuse, he hastened back the way he'd come.

Carden caught up and ran alongside, amazingly calm despite Frey's frazzled state. "What exactly happened?"

"Not sure. Found him passed out in the grove. He seemed feverish, and he emptied his stomach."

"Is *that* why you're draped in violet?"

The Pred grunted. "This was the first thing I could lay hands on. So do you know what's wrong?"

"I have a fair idea," Carden admitted. "Relax, Freydolf. I'm sure Tupp will be fine. Let's just focus on the climb."

"No need to climb. We're riding."

"I didn't think you kept a ...."

Carden trailed off when they rounded the first bend in the road and found the path blocked by a crouching stone tiger.

"This is Graven. He's Tupper's," Frey announced, hooking his arm through Carden's and hauling him forward. "Didn't he mention him?"

"When he introduced me to Rimbles, he *did* say something about another cat, but he obviously slighted me on the particulars."

"Aye, let's keep this quick." To Graven, Freydolf growled, "This man is family to Tupper and me. Give him any trouble, and I'll pry out your fangs, then dock your tail." To Carden, he curtly demanded, "Up."

Much to Freydolf's relief, both cooperated.

Tupper woke when the mattress dipped and opened his eyes to find Carden bending over him. It didn't take long for the boy to recall why he was tucked into Freydolf's bed. The moment he tried to lift his head, pain lanced through it.

"Ouch," he complained weakly.

"Let's have a look, Tupp," Carden urged, sitting with his back to the sturdy headboard and easing his younger brother up.

He gratefully hid his face against his brother's vest. "It hurts," he whined, too uncomfortable to be embarrassed about clinging to his sibling.

"I know," Carden murmured, his voice soft with sympathy. "You'll just have to bear it. We all do. Father used to say that our horns test our mettle, making men of us whether we're ready or not."

Freydolf's deep voice came from behind. "This is normal?"

"Completely," Carden assured. "Don't Pred have growing pains?"

"Our rites of passage are a little different and painful in their own way." Tupper could feel the Pred's fingertips lightly touch the top of his head as he gruffly asked, "What can I do for him?"

"There's a tea to take the edge off the pain, and warm cloths feel good."

"Wet or dry?" Freydolf quizzed.

"Either. And don't let him scratch," Carden advised. "I can tell he's been rubbing these against something, and that's a bad habit. He won't want them marred when the time comes for courting."

Tupper butted his brother's chest.

Carden chuckled. "You'll thank me later, Tupp. No more scuffs."

He wasn't in much of a state to protest, so he nodded dully, then whimpered when his brother's fingers brushed against the roots of his horns. To his surprise, the gentle pressure helped.

Carden massaged the taut skin and continued his explanation. "It's the twist. When horns begin to curl, they grow faster, and it aches terribly." As Tupper leaned into his touch, Carden said, "You take over, and I'll start that tea."

Tupper barely had time to comprehend what that meant for him before Freydolf was there, pulling him up and cradling him in strong arms. Tupper felt small and weak and weary. And safe. But he was also horribly embarrassed.

"Sorry," he mumbled.

"For growing up?" Freydolf asked, the teasing tones back in his voice.

Wrinkling his nose, Tupper complained, "It doesn't feel like growing up when you treat me like a baby."

"Aye, I suppose it wouldn't," the Pred conceded, working at the base of one horn with fingers that could coax miracles out of stone. "But this makes it easier for me to reach."

Carden strolled out of the kitchen. "Kettle's on. And don't fret, Tupp. If Father were here, he'd be doing just the same. I know because he helped me ease through when my horns turned. Pay attention because you'll need to do the same for your own sons one day."

That was something to think about. Another day. When thinking hurt less.

Closing his eyes, Tupper turned his face into Freydolf's broad chest and noticed the oddly silky feel of his shirt. As the big man kneaded away the worst of his headache, Tupper quietly pondered the mystery of his master's finery. The last thing he mumbled before dropping into an exhausted sleep was, "... aubergine."

8

Best Intentions

Tupper was gathering eggs when Rimbles came larruping through the door and skidded across the smooth stone floor of the chicken coop. The boy smiled as she turned circles in a mad, attention-grabbing dance. "Are they coming?" he asked, already knowing the answer.

Carden had accepted the offer of work, so he and his family would shortly arrive for a three-day visit during which they'd finalize preparations for Aurelius's return.

Although Tupper knew how to clean, he didn't know how to set up the suite of rooms so that the Harrows would feel at home. Melina's little cottage in Hayward was nice, so he figured his sister-in-law was qualified.

He wouldn't mind holding the baby and getting bossed around for a few days in exchange for a woman's touch.

Tupper was feeling much better today—head clear, feet steady, and heart light. Sharing the next few days with Carden's family was going to be fun, and he had another reason to be glad of their company. Even if it was only in some small, quiet way, his big brother never failed to mark one very special milestone.

Tomorrow was Tupper's birthday.

Freydolf was preoccupied with his sketchbook when Tupper interrupted his train of thought by rushing in. "They're on their way up the eastern trail!"

Glancing at the angle of the sun, the Keeper replied, "Aye. It's nearly the hour your brother said to expect them."

"Shouldn't we go meet them?"

Affecting unconcern, Frey said, "Carden knows the way."

"But ...!" Tupper tugged at the Pred's sleeve. "But Dulcie might be afraid of Itak and Ilam."

Freydolf's lips quirked, for the lad's ploy was well-chosen. There was no way he'd let that little girl fret because of one of his statues. "Aye. I wouldn't want her first impression of my home to be bared teeth and bristling fur."

"*Our* home," Tupper corrected.

On his way out the door, Freydolf paused upon the threshold, looking back. For as long as he'd been Keeper, these rooms had been *his*, and for several generations, they'd been nothing more than a cluttered workshop.

"Ours," he gladly conceded, for without Tupper, that's all they would have remained.

Tupper dashed ahead, but Freydolf strolled after at a slower pace, mindful of his surroundings, for the sprawling stoneworks were ultimately his responsibility. Their familiarity grounded him, their richness inspired him, and their complexity meant there was always a decent chance of spotting something he'd never noticed before.

Without really meaning to, Freydolf systematically picked out the notable contributions of past Keepers, the impressive gifts they'd given to Morven—their masterpieces.

"Daunting legacies," he murmured, knowing he couldn't match them.

Freydolf had no illusions about the towering edifices that surrounded the inner courtyard. They might stand as testament to one man's design, but they'd been accomplished with considerable manpower during times when the Statuary was a city unto itself. A single individual couldn't hope to exceed such grandeur.

Master Platt hadn't even bothered to try. The dour Drom had prided himself on bringing Graven into existence by his own skill and force of will, and Frey supposed he would be confined to a smaller work as well.

"It's not as if I want to spend my doddering years pushing stones into yet another tower," he muttered.

His masterpiece would have to be something else. Something that suited him. Something he hoped would occur to him eventually. The sculptor was still very much at a loss.

Tupper waited at the first bend in the trail with ill-concealed impatience. "Are you coming?"

"You could have gone on ahead."

The lad shook his head. "We'll welcome them together. It's better that way."

Frey grunted his agreement, and they set off down the mountain.

After just two turnings, they met Carden and his family, and Tupper hurried forward to relieve Melina of an enormous basket of bread.

"So much!" he exclaimed, taking the time to tickle the cheek of the baby riding snug in a colorful cloth sling.

Yona burbled a greeting.

"We couldn't come without Master Freydolf's favorites." With a nod at Dulcie, Melina added, "Or yours."

Freydolf was grateful for Melina's baking, which was just as good as any sold at Pennyflax & Quince, but he was more interested by Tupper's reaction to the items Dulcie carried. She brandished two flowering branches, and the boy's cheeks turned pink.

Crouching down in front of his niece, the lad asked, "For me?"

"Surprise!" she cheered, proudly offering them.

"I *am* surprised. These are hard to reach."

"Unca Ewert helped," Dulcie confided in a loud whisper. "He's a good climber!"

Carden, whose arms were occupied with an even larger bouquet of the same branches, casually asked, "Do you have room for these as well?"

While Tupper happily accepted the additional burden, Dulcie rushed to Frey, arms upraised, "Unca Doff! Unca Doff! Carry me!"

He scooped up the youngster, who must have been tuckered out after her long walk. She nestled against his shoulder with a sigh.

"What brings you here?" he inquired as he started back up the trail.

"You live on the mountain," she explained, holding out her hands to show that the answer should be obvious. "And we're comin' to visit you!"

"Aye, your Uncle Tupp told me to expect guests."

"Unca Far says this is *your* mountain."

"That's right."

"The whole thing?" she demanded, eyes wide.

"It's true."

Dulcie thought that over, then said, "It's big!"

"Aye, she is."

"Your mountain is a girl?"

"Last I checked," he replied amiably, slowing his steps so that Melina could keep up.

"How can you tell?" asked Dulcie, who was gazing at the gray stone with new appreciation.

Freydolf tried to think how to answer. "For one thing, Morven loves beautiful things."

"Like pretty dresses?"

"Aye." Pointing toward the foothills below, he said, "Her skirts are a lovely shade of green, and you brought up some of the flowers that she keeps nearby."

"Unca Tupp luffs them," the little girl shared, peeking over his shoulder to where the lad walked with his brother.

Glancing at Melina for help, Freydolf asked, "Are they a Flox custom?"

"A family custom," the young woman corrected. "Thirteen branches for thirteen years."

"Tomorrow's Unca Tupp's birthday!" revealed Dulcie.

This was news to Frey, and he wondered if he'd been remiss over the last couple years. "I had no idea," he admitted.

"Don't Pred celebrate birthdays?" Melina asked.

"Certainly. There are four feasts throughout the year, one during each season," he explained. "Pred mark their age by the festival closest to their birthing."

Dulcie looked crestfallen. "You don't get a special day?"

"I do," he assured. "I simply share it with many."

"And when would that be?" Melina inquired, keen on prying this new tidbit of information.

"Midsummer."

"Unca Doff?" Dulcie asked, clearly ready to move on to more important matters. "Is your house big enough for all of us?"

"Aye, there's room," he promised. "My mountain isn't the only thing that's big."

"What else?" she asked as they rounded another turning.

"The doors, the halls, the windows, the walls, the rooms," he listed, stealing a glance at Melina to see if Carden had warned her about what lay ahead. "And my dogs. Do you like dogs?"

Dulcie's face screwed up in thought before asking, "Do they bark?"

Freydolf chuckled. "My dogs are quiet, but they match my mountain. They're big."

"Very big?"

"Very, very big."

"Mama says that big isn't bad." As if to prove her point, she added, "*You're* big."

"Aye, but Morven isn't just big," her Keeper gently persisted. They'd reached the final bend, and the Apprentice Gate would soon be in view. Freydolf paused, trying to think of anything he could say to prepare his guests. Including Melina with a glance, he cautioned, "She's tall ... and wide ... and long ... and deep ... and touched by magic. You might see strange things while you're visiting."

Small arms wrapped around Frey's neck as his little passenger exclaimed, "I have Unca Doff to keep me safe!"

"Yes, Dulcie." With a small smile at his master, Tupper said, "You'll be fine if you hold on tight. That's how I made it through my first time."

Carden asked, "Do you mean when you were first hired?"

Tupper nodded. "I was scared of Itak and Ilam, but it's a guard dog's job to look scary. It's not their fault."

Rubbing the back of his neck, Freydolf admitted, "I neglected to warn the lad."

Melina looked between master and servant, disbelief warring with amusement in her expression. "Do you mean to say he carried you in?"

Tupper shook his head. "He held my hand."

"Me, too!" begged Dulcie, squirming to be let down. "I'm twice as brave as Unca Tupp!"

"Melina," Carden called, holding out a hand to his wife, who smiled softly as she slipped hers into his.

Freydolf had to stoop slightly just to reach Dulcie's hand, for she was barely taller than his boots.

The little girl frowned and asked, "What about Unca Tupp?"

The lad's shrug lifted his birthday bouquet. "Mine are full."

"Not to worry," Carden swiftly assured.

It only took a few moments to rearrange things so that Tupper stood between Carden and Melina, their arms looped through his.

Hand in hand. Arm in arm. With a show of the Meadowsweet clan's considerable courage, the Statuary's newest guests allowed Freydolf to lead them to safety.

Freydolf knew it was pointless to try to hide Morven's magical properties from their guests, but he'd still asked Tupper to keep contact with the statues to a minimum. The last thing he wanted was to frighten Dulcie. Or Melina, for that matter.

He and Tupper had agreed that Rimbles was as good a place to start as any, so the kitten was waiting on their kitchen table. Assuming she'd stayed put. Freydolf scanned the path ahead, eyes alert for a sunstone puff-ball.

"All of these are yours?" Melina asked, gawking at the innumerable statues arrayed through the inner courtyard.

"My responsibility, but not my workmanship," Frey said. "These have been in place for centuries."

"I had no idea any of this was here!" she exclaimed, staring from turrets to towers.

Dulcie's eyes were just as wide. "Is Unca Doff a king?"

Frey wondered at the reference, for Flox didn't have a ruling class.

Carden solved the mystery with a chuckle. "Is this like the castle in the storybook Mister Harrow gave you?"

The little girl nodded, then peered up at the Pred. "You live in a castle?"

"Nay, Miss Dulcie. Morven is home to Keepers, not kings." Gesturing expansively, he explained, "Men like me serve stone."

"And our Tupp serves you," Melina added warmly. Giving her young brother-in-law's arm a squeeze, she said, "Don't tell me you have to clean *all* these rooms."

"We only use a few," Tupper assured. "More now that Aurelius is going to live here."

"Unca Ree!" cheered Dulcie, tugging at Freydolf's hand. "With Auntie Ree!"

He wondered if the girl had simply assigned Aurelius's name to his wife or if Ree doubled as the shortened form of Ulrica.

Frey grinned and tweaked one of her curls. "Aye, but first ... this is where your Uncle Tupp and I live," he announced, for they'd arrived in front of the workshop's formidable double door.

Dulcie cheered all over again, and Freydolf breathed a sigh of relief. Everything was going even better than he'd hoped.

But all his precautions were brought to nothing the moment Tupper walked through the workshop door and past the brownstone statue quietly standing next to the cloak hooks.

As soon as the spicy-sweet scent of the oldtree blooms he carried filled the entryway, Haimish woke.

Haimish was only trying to be helpful when he stepped off his pedestal, arms extended to take Tupper's burden; however, as soon as the stone man loomed large, Melina screamed. To be fair, it was more of a yip than a shriek, but she frightened Yona, whose small face scrunched before she let loose with a piercing wail.

The poor statue backed himself into the corner, hands upraised in a silent plea for peace. Unfortunately, he also tucked his tail between his legs, throwing off his center of balance.

Freydolf groaned as his creation fell heavily to the floor. He would have put himself between Haimish and his guests, but Dulcie clung to his leg, darting frightened glances between the statue that had moved and her pale-faced mother. The youngster's lower lip trembled, and Frey's mind went blank with dismay.

"It's only Haimish!" Tupper exclaimed. His armful of flowering branches scattered in every direction, and he shoved the bread basket into his older brother's chest in order to reach the cowering statue.

Rimbles chose that moment to add to the confusion, careening into the entryway, her back up as she tried to figure out whom to protect her young master from. Tupper made a grab for her, but she wriggled free and planted herself between him and those she considered strangers.

Melina crowded close to her husband. "What *is* that? What's going on?"

"Rest easy, marm!" Frey begged. "These are some of my statues."

Tupper said, "Please, don't be scared. It'll make Haimish feel bad."

Carden still fumbled with teetering foodstuffs, but he offered hasty support. "It's part of the magic, Melina. The statues move."

"How?" she gasped.

"Somehow," her husband replied lamely. "I'm not clear on all the particulars, but I've seen my share of wonders up here."

Frey quickly apologized. "We meant to take things slowly, Missus Meadowsweet. There's nothing to fear from Haimish."

"Or Rimbles," Carden noted, pointing to the kitten.

"Or Brand," Tupper added with a nod at the door, where the lantern-bearing Grif stood uncertainly.

"We're fine, Brand," Freydolf offered sheepishly. "I'm afraid we startled the ladies."

The redstone warrior took in the scene, then dropped to one knee, making himself less of a threat. Brand smiled encouragingly at Haimish, whose face had become much more expressive since the application of Freydolf's second mark.

The brownstone Pred's answering glance was pained, but far less panicked.

Tupper patted Haimish's shoulder and explained, "Some of my family came to visit. Don't worry. They'll like you fine once you're properly introduced."

"Unca Doff?" Dulcie tugged at the hem of Freydolf's tunic, arms upraised.

He scooped her up. The little girl seemed to be taking her cues from Tupper now, for she no longer looked frightened.

Tupper valiantly took charge. "Melina, this is Haimish. He's a brownstone Pred. Brand is a redstone Grif, and Rimbles is mine. She's made from sunstone."

To Frey's relief, the woman was visibly calmer, probably due to Carden's and Tupper's reassurances.

With shy glances all around, Haimish rolled to his knees and began gathering the fallen oldtree branches.

Melina lifted Yona from her sling and cuddled her baby girl, trying to soothe away her tears.

Wanting to do his part, Freydolf murmured, "You're safe, Miss Dulcie. These statues are gentlemen."

"What 'bout kitty?"

"Rimbles?" he asked, a teasing smile tugging at the corner of his mouth. "A brave girl like you can't possibly be afraid of a bit of fluff like her!"

Dulcie shook her head. "Nuh-uh. *Big* kitty."

Freydolf groaned anew, for at that moment, Graven thrust his broad head through the door and subjected the young family to a baleful glare before zeroing in on little Yona and laying back his ears as if to say, *"Make it stop!"*

Melina contained her surprise more successfully this time, muttering, "They're everywhere!"

"This *is* the Statuary," her husband gently pointed out.

Sparks kindled in her eyes. "I have grasped that much, Carden Meadowsweet."

Dulcie patted Freydolf's head for attention and repeated, "What 'bout kitty?"

The man's eyes widened, for the crotchety guardian had angled one shoulder through the door and looked half-ready to nip at Melina's skirts.

Acting quickly, Tupper threw himself into the beast's maw, wrapping his slender arms around his tiger's muzzle. When Graven's mouth snapped shut, the boy dropped a kiss on his pink nose, then solemnly declared, "He is Master Platt's legacy, a statue made from all twelve stones. Graven is good with chicks, so he should be good with nubbins, too."

Freydolf was almost certain he felt a spark of magic pass between the boy and his tiger, or perhaps it was simply that they reached an understanding. Either way, Graven accepted his young master's charge. Tupper's nieces had been added to the stone guardian's flock, making them safe from the infamous mosaic tiger. And from anyone else, for that matter.

Tupper happily yielded control of his kitchen to Melina. While she ranged between cupboard and hearth, he perched on a nearby stool, cuddling Yona while memorizing his sister-in-law's technique for making a thick custard from some of the milk she'd brought along.

"I wish I had a cow," he said quietly.

"Where would you put a cow in a grand castle like this?" she asked jokingly.

"In the stable. It's right across from the chicken coop."

Melina paused thoughtfully, a pinch of spice poised to add to her pudding. "That makes sense, but do you have pasture?"

"Almost. I found terraces along the western heights. And I think they grazed animals on top of the Cavern. The pastures have dried up, though."

"You could arrange for milk deliveries," she suggested.

Tupper shook his head. "No one wants to come up here."

"Are you so sure?" Melina asked lightly. "I can think of at least two people who'd do just about anything if it put coin in their pocket."

"Like who?"

"Farley, for one." Melina laughed at his wrinkled nose, then offered a more palatable solution. "What about Ewert?"

Tupper considered, and eventually, he nodded. "Thank you. That's a good idea."

If he could work out a deal with his older brother, it would add even more variety to Freydolf's diet, at least until they were snow-stuck again.

Melina's pudding was cooling on the sideboard, and she was carefully toasting thick slices of bread with soft cheese on top when Freydolf ducked through the kitchen door, Dulcie on his broad shoulders. "Whatever you're doing, it smells good!" he exclaimed.

"Mama made her bestest bread," confided his small passenger. "Grampa shares Tremmy with us."

The Pred shook his head in bafflement, and Melina explained, "Tremmy is Dulcie's nickname for my father's oven. It's short for Tremont, the name of the man who built it."

Carden strolled into the kitchen, pausing to kiss his wife atop her head before moving to the basin in the corner to wash his hands. Haimish trailed after him, a basket of fresh greens in his arms. After all the commotion the statue had caused, Carden had offered to keep him busy.

Dulcie wiggled her fingers at the statue in silent greeting, and his tail took on a gentle sway as he smiled back.

"Tremont," Freydolf pressed. "By any chance, is this oven crafted from stone?"

"Yes. It's been in the family for longer than anyone can remember. My grandfather figures it's as old as the hills, or at least as old as Hayward."

"It would be, if it was Master Tremont's workmanship," the sculptor murmured, half to himself. "How big is this oven?"

Green eyes sparkling, Melina replied, "Big enough to feed the whole town!"

Freydolf blinked.

Tupper smothered a smile. To Melina, he said, "Of all the bakeries in all the towns around Morven, Pennyflax & Quince is his favorite."

The young woman's cheeks pinked. "How flattering!"

Feeling out of the loop, Frey asked, "What am I missing?"

"Tupper never mentioned?" Carden looped his arm around his wife's shoulders and revealed, "Melina's maiden name is Pennyflax. I married the baker's daughter!"

Freydolf did his best to look confident and competent, but in truth, he was shaking in his proverbial boots. Maybe he should have seen this coming. Except he hadn't. Rubbing the back of his neck, he ventured, "If you're sure …?"

"You'll be fine," Melina promised. "Yona's clean, fed, and already tucked in, and Dulcie's all worn out. Both girls will be asleep before you know it."

"Aye," he offered lamely, shooting a pleading look at Tupper.

The lad was clearly trying not to smile. "Do your best."

"Aye."

Carden hugged Dulcie one last time. "Listen to your uncle. And save a spot for your mother and me."

The nightgown-clad youngster clambered onto Frey's feather bed, which was spacious enough to accommodate her whole family … and *would* since the Pred planned to sleep in the balcony for the duration of their visit. With a small bounce, she bid, "Night-night!"

Then, they left—Tupper, Carden, Melina, Graven, and even Haimish—leaving Freydolf in a role for which he felt completely unqualified. Babysitter.

"Unca Doff!"

"Hmm?"

The girl clasped her hands together and begged, "Tell me a story?"

Freydolf breathed a sigh of relief. "Aye, I think I can manage that much. Let me get my sketchbook."

"What for?" Dulcie asked.

"Pictures," he replied. "Under covers, miss. I'll join you in a moment."

The girl minded him without complaint, and he tried to decide where to sit. With a shrug, he did what would be most comfortable for all of them. Plucking Yona from the little nest Melina had created for her at the end of the bed, he settled the baby into the crook of his left arm, saying, "It isn't fair to let your Uncle Tupp do all the coddling. It's my turn."

Dulcie beamed. "Yona likes stories, too!"

Frey sat atop the quilts under which the little girl was

tucked, then arranged his sketchbook so she would be able to see. Humming thoughtfully, he began, "In days of old and yore, there was a lad who loved shells, driftwood, and sea glass, but his greatest treasures were pretty stones."

Dulcie wriggled closer as he sketched a scrawny, barefoot boy in a shoreman's belted tunic—dashing through the shallows, picking up sand dollars, and poking at jellyfish with a stick. Frey continued in the sing-song lilt of a storyteller. "He could cast nets while standing in a rowboat, and he learned as many legends of merfolk as he could coax out of sailors. The sea made him feel peaceful, and he knew her tides better than most, for the moon was already pulling at the magic hidden away in his soul."

"Was he good?" asked Dulcie.

"He tried to be."

"Was he happy?"

Freydolf quietly answered, "Not always."

With a concerned expression, the little girl quizzed, "Was he sad?"

Smiling faintly, he repeated, "Not always."

Dulcie blinked up at the man and asked, "Was he *you*, Unca Doff?"

"Aye."

Patting the page, the little girl demanded, "More!"

So he shared some of his fonder childhood memories, sketching his way from one scene to the next until her fair lashes fluttered and fell. Then the sculptor set aside his pencil, stretched out his legs, and glanced down to find a solemn gaze fixed on his face.

He continued, "I was a dreamer in land where fierceness matters most. When the other boys drove me from the shore, I took shelter on the slopes of the White Mountain, where someone finally noticed that I had an affinity for stone."

He stroked Yona's cheek and grinned when she favored him with a smile. Even if the babe didn't understand a word of his history, it felt good to speak it aloud. "There was no place for a peaceable child in the ranks of Rakefangs, but a journeyman sculptor took pity on the Pred without pierced ears. He lent me his castoff tools, gave me a few lessons, then hauled me in to meet his master."

Frey lapsed into silence as he recalled those early days when he'd been little more than a household servant. The sharp-eyed Keeper of the starstone mountain had filled his head with mountain lore while tossing him odd bits of stone.

When it became clear that there was talent lurking within the Pred outcast, Master Cairn had arranged for a languages tutor and put him to work as a journeyman's assistant.

Freydolf Rakefang was elevated from misfit to potential.

Picking up his tale, Frey shared, "Everything changed the day he asked me about my dreams. When I told him they were filled with tears, he smiled and gave me naught but moonstone to work with until I understood for myself that the Gray Mountain was calling for me."

Morven had chosen him, and maybe her acceptance had given Freydolf a little too much hope. He'd spent the next several years learning not to hope for much. Perhaps that's why it was impossible for him to take moments like this for granted. Smiling softly at the tiny Flox in his arms, he was finally able to trade away his hope for something real.

"Between you and me," he whispered to Yona, "It's been worth the wait."

9

Thirteen

Tupper woke a little earlier than usual, probably because of the mild ache at the base of his horns. As soon as his eyes opened, Olexi frisked over and bumped noses with him. Gently stroking his first guardian's bristly back, he wondered if the little ram knew that today was special.

Eager as he was to start the fires and fetch water so he could brew some tea to ease his growing pains, he didn't want to disturb their guests. They'd returned from the galleries very late, so Tupper curled up under his covers to wait for sunrise.

Before long, Yona's waking mewl stirred him from a light doze. Her mother's croon was followed by Carden's murmur, husky with sleep and happy. Melina giggled softly, and Tupper found himself smiling. Family sounds were nice. In some ways, he missed them.

Lifting his head from the pillow, Tupper strained his ears for the sounds he'd grown accustomed to since accepting his place as Freydolf's servant. The chip and tap of stone, the scuff of pencil against paper, the big man's deep breathing—it was strange to have them missing. Either Frey was too far away in the balcony, or he was already gone.

Tupper was thinking about checking on his master when bed curtains ruffled, and his niece clambered up. Dulcie's fair curls stood out around her head in a tangle, and the crease of a pillowcase was pressed into one pink cheek. Scooting over, Tupper lifted the corner of his blankets.

The little girl crawled under and snuggled close before relaying a mumbled message. "Papa says happ' berfday, Unca Tupp."

"Thanks," he whispered back.

The boy—now reckoned a teen by virtue of years—slowly counted up thirteen things for which he was grateful. He blessed each gift, then marveled over the fact that nearly every one had come to him because of Freydolf. Maybe if he was better with words, Tupper could have found a way to explain how he felt, but nothing sounded good enough.

Since *telling* was out, he decided to *show* the man. It was only fair that they make a good trade. Somehow, Tupper would find a way to thank Freydolf for ... well, for everything!

Tupper felt a little like an intruder in his own home. It wasn't that he was unwelcome. He simply wasn't used to being unneeded. Melina ruled over the hearth, and Carden presided over his daughters at the table, burping Yona while listening to Dulcie tell a story about a boy who liked the feel of sand between his toes.

With a final fidget, Tupper blurted, "I'll go find Frey."

Carden studied his younger brother's face. "Do you know where he is?"

"No."

"Where would you even begin to look?"

"I'm not sure," Tupper admitted.

"Breakfast will be ready soon," Melina interjected.

Tupper nodded, but he scooted his chair back. "He shouldn't skip meals."

His sister-in-law's expression softened. "Did you finish your tea?"

"Yes," he assured, rubbing self-consciously at his horns.

She nodded and turned to the stove, casually suggesting, "Bring along some bread, but try to be back for lunch. I have something extra nice planned."

Snagging a few small loaves from the basket on the sideboard, Tupper knotted them into a napkin, then backed out of the room. "I'll find him."

With Rimbles close on his heels, Tupper chose a roundabout way into the galleries, springing lightly down one set of stairs after another as he followed them into the heart of the mountain. He couldn't have explained *why* he knew his master was in the deeper galleries. He just *did*.

Acting upon this certainty, Tupper jogged along a columned passage, lantern held high, key thumping against his chest in time with his heartbeat. Checking to be sure Rimbles was keeping pace, he said, "This way."

He paused at an intersection and studied the notations carved into the wall. He'd never been in this section before, yet he knew which way to turn. Before long, he ended up in front of a large set of double doors with an old inscription— the kind Frey had taught him was used when sealing things away. Only there was no sign of a lock.

Slim fingers traced over the neat rows of letters, but they were in a language he didn't recognize. Tupper hesitated to trespass on a chamber that had clearly belonged to a former Keeper, but the inner tug was even stronger now.

"Go inside?" he asked, his voice echoing slightly off the richly-carved walls.

Yes. That's what he needed to do.

Kneeling down to pet Rimbles, he whispered, "Do you think it's safe?"

The kitten showed no sign of perturbation, so the young Flox took hold of one of the handles and tugged. With a protesting *creak*, the heavy door swung outward, releasing a puff of air that sounded almost like a sigh.

As he strolled inside, Tupper's lantern illuminated a large, circular room. The furnishings amounted to a cluttered workbench, a bare cot, and several cloth-draped lumps arranged here and there around the room. Crossing to the nearest, Tupper uncovered the corner, revealing a gleam of green.

"Songstone." He pressed his ear to its smooth surface, listening closely. What he heard brought a smile to his face. "Good."

Under the next tarps, he discovered blue, red, gold, and white blocks. Every kind of magical stone was represented, some more than once. All were excellent, the very kind of rock Freydolf was sure to love; however, they all had something in common. Someone had started making them into statues, but they'd stopped before finishing. They were incomplete.

Tupper gently patted the flank of a dazzle unicorn half-encased by its uncut block. "Are you still hoping?"

After he'd peeked at each and every draped statue, Tupper sat on the floor in the middle of the chamber, arms folded over his chest as he tried to sort out why he was here. Somehow, he'd mixed things up, because he'd meant to find Frey.

Frowning in concentration, Tupper closed his eyes and searched for that mysterious tug he'd trusted so easily. Had it led him astray? No. This was a good place; he could tell that much. Heavy silence embraced him, giving him a sense of safety. This stillness was peaceful and patient.

"Oh." Tupper felt bad for taking so long to realize what had happened. Hauling himself to his feet, he crossed to the nearest wall. With his palm pressed to stone, he checked to be sure. "This place is mine. A gift."

Although he had no idea how to tell Freydolf, Tupper was quite certain that this room and its contents had been entrusted to him. In a solemn show of gratitude, he kissed the gray rock and whispered, "Thank you very much."

Now he understood what he'd been following all along—the mountain's voice.

Morven's call.

Rimbles capered ahead of Tupper, backtracking every so often to bat at the toes of his boots or twine between his ankles. He knew she was trying to get him to hurry, but his feet still dragged. How could he concentrate on finding Freydolf when the mountain was meddling with his head? Keeping the little sunstone guardian in sight, he shambled along, trusting her to remember the way home.

She led him up stairs and along alleys until he was sure he was lost. But then he heard Frey call his name. His master stood with Brand and Haimish in front of a door surrounded by carved seashells, the storeroom Freydolf had created during his apprentice days.

"It's a wonder you found me," the man said. "Especially since I hardly knew this was where I'd be."

"I didn't ...."

"You've always been good at surprising me," Freydolf countered in gruff tones. "Although this time, I meant to surprise you."

"Me?" Tupper looked between the man and the statues loaded onto his cart. It was the pair of wolves from inside the chamber— one carved from sunstone, the other from moonstone.

"Aye, *you*. You've never mentioned birthdays before this one. I would have marked the anniversary if I'd known it was important to you."

Tupper nodded vaguely, eyes downcast.

"Lambkin?"

"Yes?" he whispered, then started, for the Pred had silently closed the distance and crouched before him.

"What happened?" Freydolf demanded in dark tones. Large hands gripped his shoulders, turning him toward the light of Brand's upraised lantern. "You're pale as moonlight and jumpy as a cricket! Is it your horns again?"

"No." Searching his mind for a good explanation, Tupper finally said, "I can hear her."

"Who?"

"Morven." He nervously searched his master's face. Would the man be upset?

Uttering a soft oath, Freydolf wrapped his arms around Tupper, holding him close. "Did she frighten you?"

"No." Fear wasn't the right word. It was more like the feeling he got when standing next to the biggest oldtree in the forest. Or when the rising moon was the color of copper. Or when magic was stirring.

He'd been brave at the time, but now his knees wanted to wobble. Tupper rested his cheek against the familiar red tunic and wondered if one of the reasons he'd never minded the cool hush of the Statuary was because Freydolf balanced it out. Morven's voice echoed wistfully in his mind, just out of reach, but her Keeper was right here—big, solid, hairy, and not angry in the least.

"No wonder you look so lonely," Frey sympathized. "Our mountain has a sad voice."

"Yes," Tupper agreed, leaning gratefully into the Pred. "Sad, but nice."

"Aye." After a few moments, Freydolf held the boy at arm's length, searching Tupper's face with a mixture of confusion and concern. "But I don't understand. Is there some chance ...? Lambkin, do you want to become a sculptor?"

"No."

Freydolf chuckled. "Nay, I thought not, but I needed to ask. Usually, only potentials can hear a mountain's call." Ruffling the Flox's hair, he playfully accused, "You really do keep finding new ways to surprise me."

"Sorry."

"I *wasn't* complaining." His master made himself more comfortable by sitting cross-legged on the floor. "But what am I supposed to do with you?"

Tupper wasn't sure how to answer, so he settled for pressing a lumpy bundle into Freydolf's hands.

The Pred poked, sniffed, then broke into a wide grin. "For every mystery, there is an epiphany!" he declared broadly, his voice ringing along the corridor. "Haimish! Brand! You stand as witnesses! The answer is clear as crystal, sure as seasons, and welcome as a loaf from Pennyflax & Quince!"

Redstone and brownstone statues traded quizzical glances,

and Tupper asked, "Epiphany?"

"The answer to a question," clarified the sculptor around a mouthful of bread. "Especially when it comes in a flash."

Tupper was amazed. He was beginning to think there was a word for everything in the world, and he despaired of ever learning them all. Still, he wasn't sure what answer Freydolf had discovered.

"Which question?" he checked.

Patting the spot on the floor next to him, the man repeated, "What am I supposed to do with you?"

Tupper accepted the offered place, then the half-loaf Frey thrust upon him. "What will you do?" the boy warily asked.

"Keep you," he cheerfully replied, taking another large bite.

"That's not an epiphany," Tupper gravely pointed out. "You already promised I could stay."

"Aye, lambkin." The man's steady gaze was hard to read, for light and shadow shifted wildly as both Brand and Haimish joined them in sitting upon the floor. Leaning down as if to share a secret, the man quietly added, "You looked like you needed reminding."

"Maybe."

"Only *maybe*?"

"Probably."

Raising one hand, the Pred drawled, "Anyone else leaning toward *definitely*?"

Haimish raised a clawed hand, and Brand's taloned one followed.

Freydolf's fangs flashed in triumph. "You're outnumbered, lad."

No self-respecting Flox let himself be haggled into a corner. He countered, "No, I'm in good company."

"The best," Freydolf agreed.

Tupper couldn't help it. He smiled.

Haimish had the opportunity to demonstrate his considerable strength on the slow journey home. While there were plenty of inclines designed for moving large blocks of stone from one level to the next, the brownstone Pred and his maker still had to lug the two life-sized wolf statues up a few sets of stairs.

A very winded Freydolf sat at the top of one such ascent and muttered, "Now where was the nearest well …?"

"That way." Tupper pointed at the narrow entrance to an offshoot of the colonnade they'd just reached.

"Got this level mapped?"

"I know this part pretty well," he replied modestly. "Do you want me to bring water?"

"Nay," the man replied, mopping his brow. "Give me a few minutes, and we'll go together."

Tupper nodded, wishing he could do more to help than hold the second lantern. He was very glad Haimish was along. Catching the statue's eye, the boy covertly touched his lips and held out his fingers in a Floxish gesture of gratitude.

The brownstone man's eyes widened, then his gaze softened, and his tail began to sway.

Leaning back on his arms and gazing thoughtfully at the pair of statues, Tupper asked, "Do they have names?"

"Aye." The sculptor propped his chin on his hand as he gazed at the wolves. "The sunstone male is named Dag, and the moonstone female is Nott. They were the first set of statues I made according to my own design." Shaking his head, he confessed, "Bit of a disaster, to be honest."

"Why?"

"When I first started out, I mostly sculpted pairs." With a faraway look in his eyes, he mused, "I suppose I didn't want any of them to be lonely."

"Two is better," Tupper agreed.

"I had no trouble with Dag, but when it came to shaping the block of moonstone, I had a terrible time." With a soft sigh, he explained, "My head was too full of my own plans for me to see what should have been obvious. The stone didn't want to be a wolf, and when the time came to add my mark, she didn't answer the call. Nott never woke."

"Too bad."

"Aye, and that was only my first mistake," Freydolf continued. Tapping his forehead, he said, "I always liked stories about wolves, who stay with one partner their whole life long, so I tied them together."

"One for day, one for night," Tupper reasoned. "A good team."

"That was the idea, but when Dag's awake, he stands guard over Nott."

The boy giggled. "He's a good husband."

Frey smiled ruefully. "My master pointed out that it was a mercy Nott never stirred, for if I'd succeeded in waking her, then I'd have doomed *two* statues to a lifetime of never meeting the one they were made to love."

Tupper thought about what that might be like. Finally, he whispered, "That's sad."

"Very," the man sighed. "However, I want to make a present of him."

"You're giving me Dag?"

"For your birthday," Frey replied. "I haven't forgotten that you've been wanting a permanent daytime guardian for your chickens. With a little encouragement, I think Dag can do the job. All we really need to do is place Nott on the porch outside the coop, but if I ...."

That's as far as he got before Tupper tackled him, too excited about his present to be shy. Frey had thought about what he needed and had come up with a useful present that would be good for all of them—Dag, Graven, him, and his chickens. "Thank you!"

"Mind those weapons of yours," grumbled Freydolf, giving the offending horn an affectionate scratch.

"Sorry."

"Nay, I'm the one who's sorry. Is there anything else I should know about how Flox celebrate birthdays?"

Tupper started to shake his head, then straightened and exclaimed, "Yes!"

Bushy brows lifting, Freydolf prompted, "Aye?"

"Melina told us not to be late for lunch!"

They left the statues where they were and ran for it. "Any idea what time it is?" Freydolf asked worriedly.

"No. I wasn't paying attention," Tupper admitted. "How hungry are you?"

"That bread took the edge off," the man replied. "But I could eat."

"We'd better hurry."

"Aye."

Freydolf did his best to keep up with the lad, who bolted up stairs and along narrow alleys. Tupper didn't hesitate at a single turning, and the Keeper finally had to ask, "Where are you taking us?"

"Home. It's a shortcut."

A few alcoves looked vaguely familiar, but they were moving too fast for Freydolf to find his bearings. He was honestly surprised when they emerged from a narrow doorway onto the fountain colonnade, not far from their own necessary. Turning back to stare at the nondescript door, he demanded, "How did you find that?"

Tupper tugged at his sleeve. "I'll show you later. We need to wash up!"

Frey strode toward the white door, but his gaze was on the windows at the far end of the passage. "The sun's not far past its peak. I don't think we're too late."

"Maybe," Tupper muttered, not slowing his steps. He hastily drew a bucket of water from the well. "But we *will* be late."

Once the lad had filled two of the stone basins, Frey stepped up to splash cold water onto his sweaty face before reaching for a towel.

"Soap."

The man sheepishly reached for the bar. It wouldn't hurt to be thorough.

As soon as he'd done a better job of cleaning himself up, Tupper held out a hairbrush. Freydolf gave it a long look, then silently accepted it. The lad was never this fussy about appearances while it was just the two of them, but then it wasn't just the two of them today. Out of the corner of his eye, he watched Tupper wet his hands and pat his own curls into order.

With a sigh, Frey turned his attention to his reflection in the mirror and immediately grimaced. The older he got, the more he looked like his father, and that bothered him more than a little. The man was rigid, even cruel in his dealings.

Like every other Rakefang, Freydolf's cheekbones angled sharply across his broad face, and shaggy brows flared ominously over dark eyes. Lowering his gaze, he groused, "I've never been good at preening. It's more Aurelius's thing."

"I know." Tupper turned his head to check his horns, then shrugged. "Me, too. But Mother always made us wash, so I think Melina would want us to."

"Aye, women are particular about that sort of thing." Dragging the brush through the coarse length of his hair, Freydolf added, "Having a lady around usually forces men to make an effort."

Tupper squared his shoulders, obviously pleased to be counted among men.

Then, a horrible thought occurred to Frey. Ulrica would be spending an entire season in his home. Fixing his servant with a pleading look, he asked, "Are you going to make me bathe every day once my sister moves in?"

The lad solemnly answered, "I'll still only make you bathe every other day, but she might make you wash on the in-between days."

Shoulders sagged in resignation. "Aye, she probably will."

Freydolf and Tupper jostled one another as they opened their front door and held their breaths, listening for some clue as to how much trouble they were in. The Pred hadn't felt like this since he was a boy, late for lessons with his stern languages tutor, but he soon forgot his trepidation.

Melina was singing.

The sweet notes of a nonsensical children's song brought a smile to his face, and he tapped Tupper's head. "Safe?" he asked softly.

"I think so," he whispered back.

Stomping his feet upon the threshold, Freydolf jovially called out, "Something smells good enough to wake brownstone!"

"Unca Doff! Unca Tupp!" Dulcie skipped out of the kitchen and held up most of her fingers. "I found *this* many butterflies on the windows!"

"Are you fond of butterflies?" Frey asked, lifting her.

"Yes! They're pretty!"

"As is this." He gently touched the ruffled hem of Dulcie's tiny apron. "Have you been busy in my kitchen?"

"Come see!" urged the youngster. "We're ready for Unca Tupp's birthday!"

In the next room, Freydolf nodded to Carden, who sat with his feet propped on a second chair, a half-empty cup of tea at his elbow and his baby daughter snoozing upon his chest. The young man looked completely relaxed and comfortable, and Frey's heart squeezed. This was exactly the kind of peaceful cohabitation he'd hoped for amidst these gentle folk.

"Oh!"

At Tupper's soft exclamation, Freydolf turned to see the lad examining the delicacies arrayed on the sideboard. An enormous basin had been employed for the oldtree branches, which overspread several plates of fussy sandwiches, cakes, and tarts.

"But ...!" the boy exclaimed, turning wide eyes on his sister-in-law. "But these are festival cakes!"

"And?" Melina archly inquired.

Pointing to the tiny iced cakes, he said, "They're only sold during midsummer week."

"You're right," the young woman acknowledged, a shrewd light in her eyes. "But I'm not selling them."

"And these are midwinter tarts," Tupper said in awed tones.

Melina giggled. "Carden told me they're your absolute favorites."

"They are, but is this okay?"

Dulcie clapped her hands. "Mama *always* makes them! Itsa seekurt!"

"For birthdays," Melina clarified, looking pleased. "They're family recipes, after all!"

Tupper was clearly impressed, and Freydolf teased, "Perhaps you should marry a Pennyflax, as well, lad."

Melina dimpled and began listing all her younger sisters and cousins, much to the boy's embarrassment.

Once they were gathered around the table, she ladled bowls of hearty soup, and Carden heaped sandwiches on his younger brother's plate, making sure he ate his fill. Conversation drifted from memories of birthdays past to plans for the afternoon, which would be spent cleaning and furnishing the Harrows' rooms.

Good food. Good company. Freydolf couldn't help comparing this quiet celebration to the citywide extravaganzas in his homeland. The quarterly festivals were a matter of pride, with those born during each season doing their best to outdo the rest. Presents were lavish and plentiful, and those who had attained another year dressed all in white. Boys grudgingly submitted to having their claws gilded with copper, and girls proudly added a new coin to jingling headdresses.

Festival days were packed with coming-of-age hunts, showcases of acrobatics or fighting techniques from various schools, and numerous competitions. Nights were illuminated by fireworks, with dancing in the lantern-lit streets and performances by traveling entertainers from around the world.

"Taste!" Dulcie chirped.

Pulled from his memories, Freydolf blinked down at a wee frosted cake presented on a pink paper flower. It was too tiny to make much of a mouthful, but they must have been good, judging by the row of empty papers next to Tupper's plate. Accepting the culinary frippery, the Pred popped it into his mouth. As the sweet melted upon his tongue, he met his servant's expectant gaze and smiled. "We should embrace more of your traditions. They're good."

Tupper asked, "Can I borrow yours, too?"

"Aye, we can share," Freydolf agreed. "I'm fairly certain I have copper leafing in one of my workbenches."

Carden's brows lifted. "What do you use that for?"

"Oh, every so often, a commissioner wants some part of their statue gilded. But it's long been used as an integral part of Pred birth festivals. If Tupper's feeling brave, I'll demonstrate."

Catching the other man's mood, Carden smoothly rejoined, "I'd love to learn more about Pred traditions, wouldn't you, Melina?"

"Certainly. I'm sure our Tupp is brave enough. Right, Dulcie?"

"Yes!" the little girl happily agreed.

Freydolf laughed outright, for good company had turned the tables. Tupper was back to being outnumbered. With a wicked grin, he cheerfully promised, "You'll be fine, lad. It wears off ... eventually."

Tupper finished his nightly routine in his usual roundabout way—draining the bathtub, filling the oil in Brand's lantern, accepting a cold drink from the white lady, and kissing Graven's nose—before slipping into the hushed workshop. Bedtime stories had been underway when it was his turn to wash up, so he wasn't surprised to find Carden, Melina, and the girls already asleep.

Reflected firelight shone high against the tall windows, suggesting that Freydolf was still awake and working in the balcony. It was strange for their home to be so quiet at this hour, and Tupper missed the tap and rattle of creation.

As he stood uncertain which way to turn, the soft glow of a candle beckoned to him from the kitchen. Tiptoeing over, he found Olexi standing guard over a tea tray with a snack all ready. One sniff at the steaming pot was enough to tell it was the medicinal stuff to ward off headaches, and he smiled. Melina was pretty nice ... for a sister.

He'd never had such a fine birthday, and he planned to make it last just a little bit longer. Pocketing the ram, Tupper grabbed the tray and snuck upstairs.

Frey was indeed awake, lounging in one of the new Ursa chairs.

Stealing softly across the thick carpets, Tupper quietly offered, "Want some?"

His master glanced up from the fat book he was perusing. As soon as he spotted the teapot, concern filled his gaze. "Is the ache back?"

Tupper shook his head. "Melina fusses. There's leftover cake."

Indicating his half-full goblet, the man said, "I brought my own refreshment, but make yourself comfortable."

He nodded gladly and lowered both the tray and Olexi to the wide hearth, then poked at the fire. Mindful of his duties, he took the time to arrange his master's makeshift bed, piling cushions and blankets on the hearth rug before choosing a book from his own shelf. Flopping onto the soft heap, he settled gratefully into the companionable silence.

Flipping through pages to find the place where he left off, Tupper was distracted by the glint of firelight on copper and rolled onto his back. He held his hands out and admired the metallic treatment Freydolf had given his blunt nails.

"It probably looks better on claws," Tupper said, his gaze sliding toward the Pred.

The man wiggled deadly-looking fingers. "Aye. It makes no sense to call attention to your lack of weaponry. To properly follow the intent, we should have gilded your horns."

Tupper wrinkled his nose. "That would look silly!"

"Many traditions seem so to outsiders."

With nibbles of sweet cakes and sips of bitter tea, Tupper

stretched his special day long into the night. He didn't realize he was dozing off until he nose-dived into his book, painfully knocking one horn against the hearthstone. Snapping awake, he sat up and gently patted the curling prominence, worried that he'd scuffed it.

Freydolf looked up from his book, his bushy brows lifting.

For a moment, Tupper was afraid the man would send him to bed.

He only crooked his fingers, saying, "Let me see."

The boy meandered over and bent his head, and the Pred ran his fingertips over the finely ridged horn, teasing, "Are they getting heavier?"

"Maybe." After some thought, Tupper suggested, "They probably grow too slow to tell."

"Aye. Sit."

The chair was plenty wide enough for him to squiggle in beside Frey, so he levered himself up onto the high seat and made himself comfortable.

Right away, Freydolf set to massaging the base of one horn just the way Carden had shown him.

Tupper leaned contentedly into his side. "What're you reading?" he asked, his eyes on the book propped on the sculptor's knee.

"This is from the archives. I was looking for information about the different manifestations of stone affinities."

Tupper's brow furrowed. "Say it again."

Rapping the book with a knuckle, Frey said, "Lots of people are good with stone, but in different ways. For instance, you have a way with the stuff, but you show no signs of magic and no interest in sculpting."

"Is that bad?"

"Nay, just different."

"Like Flox and Pred."

"Perhaps." Freydolf switched to the opposite horn. "How do you mean?"

Once more admiring his gilded nails, Tupper said, "Being different means learning something new."

Soon afterward, Freydolf tread softly down the stairs, his arms full of Flox. He felt a little silly prowling through his own workshop, but the lad was sure to rest better in his own bed.

With all the famed stealth of his race, the Pred stole across the room and paused before the lofty bank of windows. Moonlight streamed through stone latticework, bringing its inhabitants to life. Delicate butterflies wafted their wings, and a tiny lizard poked his head out from behind a flower. Tree frogs puffed out their throats, and a nesting bird cocked her head to one side, watching him curiously.

The Statuary truly did have its share of wonders.

Freydolf glanced down at Tupper's peaceful face and felt a pang of envy.

Thirteen. The age when Pred children were permitted to vie for piercing. Old memories tore at him, for his own teen years had been agonizing. Berated by biggers, scorned by youngers, taunted by peers—his mother had run out of excuses for him, and his father had cast him out with an expression of disgust.

"Peace," he murmured, carefully depositing his bond-brother upon his bed. It was all he'd ever wanted, and he'd found it in surprising places. Upon the dawnstone front step of the house he'd disappointed. Along a lonely stretch of shore where land and sea blended. Amidst his stash of cast-off baby toys and colored pebbles. In the company of his fiercely protective younger sister. Atop the melancholy mountain that tugged at his heart. With the extravagant quantities of rock procured from other mountains by his brat of a brother-in-law.

And here. Now. In the care of a Flox boy who was well on his way to becoming a fine young man.

The Pred pulled blankets up to Tupper's chin and lightly tousled hair that looked silver in moonlight.

The lad stirred and opened his eyes, graced his master with a sleepy smile, then curled up on his side and fell back asleep.

Freydolf carefully slid the curtain into place, then turned back to the window. Tranquil moments like this sustained him, and he'd always been able to track down enough to get by. Now that he was blessed with peace in abundance, he meant to enjoy it. Standing straight and tall, he folded his arms over his chest and basked in his contentment.

10

Gentle Nature

Tupper was pretty sure that girls must have a whole different set of rules for living that they never explained to boys, complete with tips for alternately bossing and baffling their brothers. Even though he very clearly explained to his sister-in-law that he'd already cleaned the Harrows' rooms, Melina rolled up her sleeves and did it all over again.

It made no sense, but Carden pulled him aside and said, "Let her do things in her own way."

"I cleaned it so she wouldn't have to," Tupper protested.

"Thank you for your consideration," his big brother warmly replied. "I'm sure that'll make things easier for her even while she's making things hard on herself."

"But ...!"

Carden gripped his shoulder. "Let us keep our end of the bargain, Tupp. We have a wage to earn."

Nodding reluctantly, Tupper gave his attention to Yona, his only "task" for the afternoon. He'd planned to help out more, but his brother had pointed out that the girls would enjoy spending as much time as possible with their uncles. That went both ways.

Tickling the baby's cheek, Tupper suggested, "Let's go find

your sister and your Uncle Doff. He has a special surprise in the long hall."

Brand was waiting in the six-sided chamber, lantern ready.

Since no one had bothered yet, Tupper took the time to make introductions. "Brand, this is my niece, Yona Meadowsweet. Yona, this is my friend Brand."

A slow smile spread across the redstone warrior's face, and he offered a taloned finger to the little one. She gripped living stone with both hands and tried to pull it into her mouth, but Brand gently extracted himself from her grip, then brushed his knuckles against her cheek

Since he'd just done almost the same thing, Tupper gazed intently at the statue. "You know about babies?"

The statue smiled warmly. Obviously, he did.

"Was the man who made you a father?"

Brand's smile deepened, and he nodded.

"Is that why you're good with children?"

The Grif tipped his head to one side as if considering the question, but he answered with a small shake of his head and a helpless shrug. Even though Brand seemed smarter than most, statues had their limits. They weren't very good at answering *why*.

"That's okay. I'm not sure why I do everything I do either," Tupper confided. "Would you like to hold her?"

Lifting his lantern and its open flame, the fire-bearer shook his head.

"It *would* be tricky with one hand," the boy gravely agreed. "I guess we'll wait until she can walk, and you can hold her hand."

Brand was clearly pleased by this suggestion. Unusually so.

When he eagerly waved for the boy to follow him downstairs, Tupper accepted the fire-bearer's help, but his steps slowed along the colonnade as he puzzled over his friend's enthusiastic reaction. Then it occurred to him. "Brand?"

The Grif warrior turned.

"We can't keep them," he announced apologetically. "They're only visiting."

Brand peered down his hooked nose at the boy and baby.

This time, there was a wistfulness in his expression as he nodded his understanding.

Tupper felt bad for disappointing his friend. Reaching for the Grif's hand, he gave it a sympathetic squeeze. "I wish they could stay, too."

It was a nice idea, but he didn't see how it could work out. After all, the reason Carden and Melina were here was to earn enough money to add onto their house in the village.

"If I ever have my own little girl, you can guard her," he gravely offered.

The red statue's brows lifted in surprise, and then his shoulders shook with silent laughter. Smiling much more broadly now, he slipped his arm around Tupper back, sheltering him and Yona with his feathered cape.

This was new. "I didn't know you could laugh."

Brand shrugged, then drew him along.

Tupper had the feeling the statue was laughing at him. "Did I say something strange?"

The Grif shook his head, then gave his shoulders a friendly squeeze.

It wasn't until they reached the first turning that Tupper realized what his offer actually meant. To keep his end of such a bargain, he'd need a wife. A very brave wife.

Tupper took Melina along the hall, opening one door after the next. "These are only used for storage right now. Everything inside belongs to Frey, so you can take what you need for the Harrows' rooms. Pick anything."

"How many rooms are there?"

"I'm not sure," he admitted. "Lots, but these are closest. If this stuff doesn't work, I can take you to one of the other sections."

"Unbelievable," she whispered, roaming through the cluttered rooms with wide eyes.

Bracing little Yona against his shoulder, Tupper pulled aside the heavy drapes, flooding the room with sunlight. "When you find something you want to use, have Haimish carry it out to the cart. Carden is bringing a second one, so you can just point."

The brownstone Pred executed a small bow, eager as ever to be of service.

After the fourth storeroom, Melina got over her awe and got down to business. "Thank you, Tupp. Haimish and I can handle it from here."

So Tupper carried his precious cargo across the hall to where Freydolf and the blue bear cub were busy delighting Dulcie. The Pred knelt before the statue of a red dog, a taper in his hand. Lighting some internal wick, he sat back on his heels, saying, "And now, he'll wake!"

Right on cue, the puppy's mouth snapped shut, and he shook thoroughly before bounding off his pedestal and running in circles, chasing his own tail.

Dulcie clapped her hands appreciatively. "Another, Unca Doff! Do another!"

Tupper had played with the Statuary's pets many times, and Yona was looking sleepy, so he took her further along the hall and sat with his back to a dry fountain. Cradling the baby close, he hummed the tune to a folk dance, then told her some of the things he'd learned about oceans, continents, and the other mountains scattered around the world.

Yona winked and blinked, then drifted off.

Carden returned with Brand, pushing a rattling cart and paused to speak with Freydolf, who gestured broadly as he answered some question. Now that Tupper was paying attention, he realized that ten additional doors stood open, allowing sunlight to stream into the corridor.

Busy women, talking men, laughing children, scampering pets—for the first time, he could picture what it would be like if more people lived in the Statuary.

Noisy.

Tupper hunched his shoulders, but Freydolf looked happy about having more people to talk to. It occurred to him that the Keeper was almost a chatterbox. How long had it been since he'd seen Frey smiling so much? Tupper sighed and wished he was better at saying interesting things.

Suddenly, Dulcie interrupted her father, and Tupper could tell that she was begging for a cart ride. Giving in with a calm smile, Carden sedately wheeled his daughter over to where Tupper sat, Freydolf and Brand trailing in their wake.

"Sleeping?" Carden asked, nodding toward Yona.

"Yes."

The Flox man gazed up and down the hall. "Quite the runway you have here."

"Aye." Freydolf's dark eyes took on a mischievous sparkle. "This stretch has seen its fair share of races."

Tupper could tell they were subtly bargaining and perked up. He'd ridden through these halls on Graven's back enough times to know it was a good place to go fast, but attempting it on a cart sounded *really* fun.

"Go faster?" asked Dulcie.

Carden hummed. "It's probably not wise. This doesn't have sides or straps for hanging on."

Freydolf suggested, "What if you held onto her?"

"I'd ride?"

"Aye."

Carden lowered his voice conspiratorially. "Let's try it!"

In a matter of moments, the hallway was filled with a roar like thunder as Freydolf dug in, building speed, pushing the cart and its passengers down the hall. As they sailed along, Dulcie's excited shrieks and Carden's hearty laughter echoed off the walls. Tupper could tell he was missing out.

Yona woke with a whimper, and he crooned reassuringly. Standing, he headed over to the last of the open doors just as Melina appeared, wiping her hands on her dusty apron.

"What's all this?" she asked exasperatedly.

The boy shrugged. "Frey's giving rides."

Shaking her head at the echoing din, Melina waved him

closer. "Give me Yona. I'll feed and change her while you boys play with Dulcie."

"Are you sure?"

"You want to, don't you?"

"Yes, please!" Tupper flashed a shy grin, then took off down the hall, calling back, "... and thank you!"

Melina sent four cartloads of crockery and furnishings ahead to the suite of rooms they were readying for Aurelius. As Haimish trundled her latest selections along the hall, she sighed deeply and said, "It's a good start."

"You'll need more?" Tupper asked incredulously. It seemed to him that she'd chosen enough things for two houses.

"Those rooms are big, and their cupboards are bare. Setting up housekeeping takes more than you might realize."

"Maybe," he admitted as they followed Brand along the wide corridor. Carden and Freydolf had taken the girls back to the workshop for their nap, so he and the two statues were acting as Melina's assistants. He hesitantly asked, "But wouldn't it be bad if the rooms were crowded with fancy stuff?"

Melina nodded. "We'll pick and choose, then put back anything we don't use. Can you give me some idea of what this new lady likes?"

Tupper thought hard. If they went by Aurelius's tastes, only the finest, but that didn't really answer Melina's question. With a slow shake of his head, he tried to explain what he knew. "She travels with her husband, so she's used to changing scenery. I don't think she'll expect this home to be just like her own, but Aurelius said he wants Missus Ulrica to be comfortable."

Melina smiled. "Even a grand lady who's seen the world will need the same things everyone needs. We'll cover the basics, and later, you could invite her to explore for herself. Women like doing their own choosing, after all."

Tupper wondered why he hadn't thought of that.

At the top of the curving staircase, they caught up to Haimish, who was conscientiously transferring items from the cart on the fountain colonnade level to one out in the courtyard. They lent him a hand, then walked with him to the Harrows' guest house, making sure none of the housewares toppled during the last leg of their journey.

Just as Aurelius had requested, their house wasn't far—a short walk with no stairs.

Tupper's favorite part of this particular set of quarters was its private garden, complete with a fountain graced by a beautiful mermaid. The freshstone statue had been thrilled when Tupper filled the dry basin and Freydolf set the fountain's inner workings into motion. Now, during daylight hours, she lounged upon her pedestal, flicking water up onto her scales with her fanning tail.

To Tupper's surprise, his master was already in the sunlit courtyard, standing calf-deep in sparkling water as he talked to the blue statue.

"Making friends?" he asked.

The man grinned. "Aye, after a fashion. I wanted to see if she could tell me who used to occupy that niche." Frey pointed to an elevated alcove opposite the fountain. "It's ideal to have both a day and a night guardian watching over a home."

"I thought statues couldn't talk," Melina interjected.

"Nay, not with words," acknowledged the sculptor. "But she can make herself understood. Definitely a master's work."

With a playful flip of her fins, the mermaid sprinkled the Keeper with cold water, then blew a kiss at Melina.

The Flox woman blinked, then smiled tentatively at the statue. "I'm sorry, miss. I didn't mean to be rude."

The fishtailed lady winked.

Getting back to the subject at hand, Freydolf explained, "As far as I can figure, she's glad to be rid of whatever statue used to stand there, so we've been discussing the merits of a replacement. Ulrica has always favored titian jade, but this courtyard doesn't face west. I was just saying that a starstone guardian would be my second choice."

"Titian jade?" Melina pounced on the tidbit of personal information. "Your sister likes orange?"

"Aye, it's her favorite color."

The young woman tossed up her hands. "And you're only mentioning this now?"

Freydolf shot a worried look at Tupper. "Was it important?"

Shaking her head in exasperation, Melina called, "Haimish!"

The brownstone statue appeared in the doorway, a blue water pitcher in his hands and a quizzical expression on his face.

"One more trip into the galleries, please," Melina briskly directed. "I passed up some things I shouldn't have, and I want to gather them up!"

"I'll help," Tupper quickly offered.

"Aye," Freydolf added, all chagrin. "Me, too."

"Thank you," the woman primly accepted. "And while we're going, you can tell me anything else that might be useful in making your sister feel welcome."

Tupper felt bad for his master, but he was glad Melina wasn't afraid to take charge. She'd make sure the job was done right, even if it meant bossing around a full-grown Pred.

Maybe ... just maybe ... he should check to see if there were any other Pennyflax girls as brave as she.

The following morning, Freydolf woke Tupper. It was usually the other way around. No, it was always the other way around! What was going on? The big man's eyes were laughing at him as he held a clawed finger to his lips, then beckoned for the boy to follow.

Grabbing his breeches from atop the chest beside his bed,

Tupper hurried after, hopping for several steps as he tried to pull up his pants. Once they were safely out the door, he whispered, "What is it?"

Freydolf smirked. "I thought you were a morning person."

Tupper frowned in confusion. "I suppose."

Chuckling, the Pred said, "You're not very convincing today. That hair of yours is wild enough to strike fear into the hearts of lesser men."

"I'm scary?"

"Not in the least, but it's nice to know you can look a mess."

Still baffled by the predawn wake-up call, he patted at his unkempt curls. "It's always like this," he muttered. "You just sleep through it. Why are you up? It's early."

"It's hard for me to settle down when I can't sculpt." The man shrugged, saying, "I was restless, so I went for a wander."

Tupper nodded. He'd noticed the fidgeting and had slipped the sculptor a bit of songstone the evening before. Apparently, it hadn't been enough to hold his interest.

"You woke me to tease me about my hair?"

"Nay. Come on, lambkin. There's someone waiting on you."

The boy obediently followed his master out the Apprentice Gate, then gasped. "Dag!"

"Aye." Freydolf led the way over to the sunstone wolf and his moonstone mate. "Daybreak will reach him here."

The boy knelt before the golden wolf and patted his rough fur. It was time to give the stone guardian a new purpose. A thought snuck into Tupper's head, and he asked, "If Dag is loyal for life, won't he want you? Not me?"

"We'll know soon enough," the man replied, for the sky was lightening.

Impulsively flinging his arms around the wolf's neck, Tupper whispered, "Give me a chance?"

Moments later, the sun crested the eastern horizon, and the light worked its magic. Fur softened, ears flickered, and Tupper sat back on his heels, eager to introduce himself. However, Dag stood and walked over to Nott. Clearly, *she* was his first priority.

Tupper did the only thing he could think of. He crawled

over to the gray wolf and slipped his arms around her neck instead, pressing his ear to her chest. The stone was good, but its voice was barely a whisper. Still, the longer he listened, the stronger it became. "Hello," he murmured. "Don't be shy."

Freydolf surprised him by gripping his shoulder. "What are you doing?"

"Listening."

Frey's gaze darted between Dag and Nott. "That's not all you're doing. Can you feel that?"

Tupper shook his head, then tried to explain. "She's sleepy, so I wanted to wake her up. Otherwise, her voice will be too quiet to reach you."

The man's brow furrowed. "Sit over there," he directed, an odd tension in his voice.

Taking a seat a few paces away, the boy watched Freydolf inspect the female wolf.

Almost immediately, Dag settled beside Tupper, head in his lap. With a faint smile, Tupper scratched the big canine behind his ears. Making friends hadn't been so hard after all.

Wonderment dawned on Frey's face, and he muttered, "She's changed."

"Nott?"

"Aye." With a slow shake of his head, Freydolf announced, "I want to move her into the workshop. Or better yet, the kitchen."

"Not the hen house?"

"Not yet." Resting his hand atop her head, he said, "We'll keep her close for a while and see what happens."

Tupper didn't mind. He smoothed his hand over Dag's rough fur and invited, "You and your lady can stand guard over my hearth."

The sunstone wolf's tail thumped against the ground.

It looked as if Dag would be giving him that chance.

Freydolf sat straight in his chair, arms folded defensively over his chest, not that the stern veneer did him any good. His heart wasn't in it, and it was patently obvious that Dulcie could tell. Her wide eyes watched him from across the room, waiting for him to fold.

"You're no match for her," the girl's father remarked in a low voice.

He glanced at Carden, who'd joined him on the sofa in the balcony. "Aye, and she knows it."

"She's taking no chances, though." With a tilt of his head, he pointed with his horns to where Dulcie had sidled up to her young uncle. "My girl's rallying support from Tupp."

"Divide and conquer?"

"Exactly." Carden's lips quirked. "If she sways Tupper, nothing will save you."

Frey's soft grunt acknowledged the possibility, but he doubted the lad would actually side with Dulcie against him. Of course, that didn't preclude the possibility that he'd take sides with the stone.

"I'll back you up," Carden offered, a teasing light in his eyes. "Assuming you can make up your mind on the matter."

The last few days had changed the shape of Freydolf's acquaintance with Tupper's oldest brother. It was already established that this mild-mannered Flox would succeed Old Gruff as manager of Morven's quarry, a fact for which the Keeper was enormously grateful. However, Carden had resolutely overstepped the usual boundary between employer and employee.

Freydolf was heartened to be counted as a Meadowsweet ... and humbled that Carden and Melina allowed him to dote on their precious daughters. But now, he was realizing that he'd also gained a like-minded friend.

Gratitude for all these things was part of why Frey was having a hard time refusing Dulcie's plea. She was one smart little girl, wanting to know why all the statues around Morven moved when her pink bunny couldn't.

"It's such a small thing," Freydolf muttered, lacing his fingers together. "But waking her guardian could lead to trouble."

"*Or* it might be the first step toward reconnecting this mountain with its valleys," reasoned Carden. He set aside his goblet and picked up one of the twelve stone balls resting on a nearby table. Idly inspecting its dappled surface, he pointed out, "Fear of you shouldn't have to mean fear of Morven. Or any of the other mountains, for that matter."

The Pred's brows knit. "What are you suggesting?"

Carden chose another sphere, turning it this way and that. "May I be blunt?"

"Aye."

Nodding, the man quietly advised, "Give up on what you can't change. Focus on the future. Most villagers will never fully trust you, but you can foster friendly feelings toward Morven. Remind them why *she's* special ... and worthy of respect."

The younger man's words rang true, and Freydolf's heart leapt. Wasn't it his duty as Keeper to preserve his mountain's honor, even if his came to nothing? Clenching his hands into tight fists, he begged, "But *how*?"

Reaching for a different stone sphere, Carden rolled it between his palms. "You told us that Pred children grow up with toys like Dulcie's rabbit and Tupper's ram."

"Aye, they're commonplace."

"If Flox children had their own little guardians, wouldn't they grow up thinking that their magic was the most natural thing in the world?" Nodding in his daughter's direction, he said, "Dulcie doesn't question things that still boggle my mind."

Freydolf slowly shook his head. "But the best guardians are bonded to their charges."

"And how do you do that?"

Tapping the dawnstone sphere in Carden's hands, Frey said, "I'll show you when we wake that bitty rabbit at sunrise."

Freydolf kept half an eye on the eastern horizon, mindful of the time as he added his mark to Dulcie's pink rabbit. "The mountain where dawnstone is quarried is on Far Continent, so it's rare here," he explained in a low voice. "It's not often used for guardians, but many choose it for ornamental pieces. The soft color matches its gentle nature, and it's rumored to heighten happiness."

Carden held the lantern steady for Freydolf, peering interestedly while the sculptor made deft incisions. "I didn't know stone could have so much personality."

"Up until now, all you've known is local rock," he pointed out. "And only those with an affinity for stone would notice variations from one chunk of gray to the next."

"I like the dapple," Carden remarked.

Over the last few days, Frey had noticed that the younger man often touched things crafted from that particular stone. "Why's that?" he invited conversationally.

"Oh, I don't know. I suppose I find the mottling pretty—all those pinks and browns."

"Aye, it's eye-catching," agreed the sculptor.

"It reminds me a little of dawnstone."

The Pred smoothed his thumb over the finished mark decorating the wee rabbit's paw. "Because of the splashes of pink?"

Humming softly, Carden said, "I suppose it feels like morning."

Freydolf's dark eyes snapped to the Flox's face. "Does it?"

With a shrug, the younger man asked, "Doesn't it?"

"It does."

Carden's brows lifted. "And ...?"

"How did you know?"

"Know what?"

The sculptor scrutinized the Flox's open countenance. "Has anyone ever told you what wakes dapple?"

"I don't believe it's ever come up. Why?"

Freydolf knew he was probably reading too much into a chance remark. "Dapple also wakes at dawn, but only if its covered in dew."

"That's very specific. It's a wonder anyone discovered what was needed."

The Pred frowned thoughtfully. "Magic has a way of leading us along, and nowadays, the lore is passed down."

Carden nodded, but just then Tupper's voice interrupted.

"Frey, it's almost time." The lad stood in front of the window, Dulcie propped on his hip, her curly head resting on his shoulder. Addressing his niece, he asked, "Do you have a name ready for your guardian?"

"Yes." She happily revealed, "Bunny."

Tupper tipped his head to one side. "You're naming your bunny ... Bunny?"

Dulcie's chin tilted stubbornly. "It's his name!"

"Then I'm sure he'll listen when you call," said her young uncle, setting her on her feet.

Freydolf had decided that the most natural place to catch the early morning light was the room in which Master Tremont's dawnstone Triad stood poised to greet the day. Moving to the window, he knelt in front of Dulcie and asked, "Shall we wake up your friend?"

"Yes, please!"

"This doesn't seem nearly as complicated as waking that blue dragon," commented Carden.

"Aye. All we need is daybreak and physical contact, preferably with the one to whom the stone belongs."

The little girl piped up, "Me!"

Keeping his thumb over the rabbit's new mark, he held the bunny out to Dulcie. "Any touch will do, but a kiss is traditional."

Carden chuckled. "Is *that* why I caught Tupper kissing Graven on the nose before bedtime last night?"

Freydolf cocked a brow at his servant, who blushed to the roots of his fair hair. With a faint smirk, the sculptor said, "The lad spoils that tiger, and I hope Miss Dulcie will do the same for Bunny."

"Promise!" pledged the youngster.

"Aye. When it's time, I want you to call, 'Wake up, Bunny.' If you say it like you mean it, he'll hear you and wake up."

Dulcie nodded eagerly, and all eyes swung to the east. Day broke, spilling light through the window, waking the Triad, and mingling with the magic already woven through the master sculptor's mark.

"Now, Miss Dulcie."

The child took a deep breath, then bossily exclaimed, "Wake up, Bunny!"

Delighted by the eager tug of magic taking hold, Freydolf prompted, "And a kiss."

At Dulcie's hearty smack, the little figure wriggled so excitedly, Frey quickly closed his fingers around her pet lest he leap to the floor.

The girl looked up at him worriedly. "Is he 'wake?"

"Hold out your hands," the Keeper prompted.

She obeyed, and he carefully dropped Bunny into them. Dulcie's reaction was adorable, and Frey had to swallow past the emotions thickening his throat.

This really was his favorite part.

The pink statue's ears quivered as Bunny gazed raptly into the face of the little girl who'd called his name. It was like love at first sight all over again … for both of them.

"Bunny!" Dulcie cooed. Then, with a soft giggle, she kissed his tiny, twitching nose.

"Dawnstone brings happiness," murmured Carden, a lopsided smile on his face.

The sculptor was about to agree, but Tupper quietly corrected, "No. Freydolf does."

11

Making Peace

And suddenly, it was just the two of them again.

The Statuary felt much emptier without Carden's family, but Freydolf filled the gap with as much noise as possible. As soon as their guests disappeared from view, the sculptor had fallen upon the brownstone griffin like a starved man, and for three days and nights, the crack and rattle of chunks and chippings had echoed through the workshop.

By now, Tupper knew when to let his master have his way.

He was very glad the Harrows would have their own rooms for the summer. Freydolf needed to sculpt, not because his commissions were coming due, but because he couldn't do without stone. Holding back had left him feverish.

Once the Keeper exhausted the build-up of creative passion, there would be a mighty crash, and Tupper could pick up the pieces. Only then would life settle down to normal again.

In the meantime, the young Flox had things of his own to attend to.

Thanks to Melina's efforts, the Harrows' suite fairly sparkled, but their new home lacked one important detail. His master may have forgotten about the empty niche in their small courtyard, but Tupper couldn't. Not when Morven whispered to him about starstone knights, gypsies, and panthers who longed for a glimpse of the stars.

Late though it was, Tupper slung a pack over his shoulder and slipped out the front door. Lifting Snick toward the pale moon that shone against the brightly-spangled sky, he woke his master key, then clambered onto Graven's broad shoulders. The big cat sprang away, swiftly carrying his boy down into darkness.

Until sunrise called him back to Frey's side, Tupper planned to search for a good guardian, someone he could trust. It might not be easy. The new statue would need to be beautiful enough for refined tastes, deferential enough for haughty attitudes, and clever enough to keep Graven away from Aurelius.

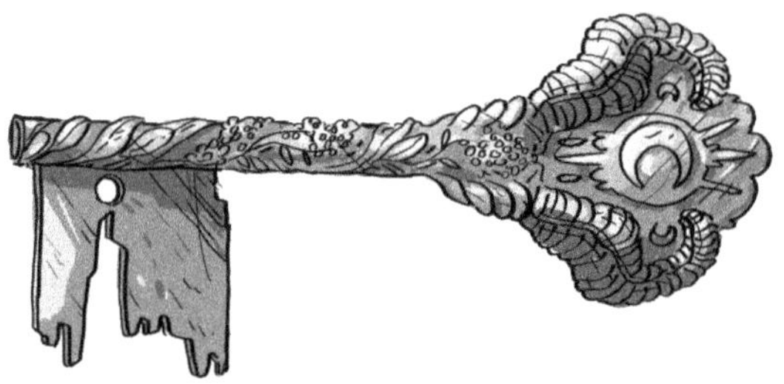

Tupper's eyelids were heavy when he snuck back into his home. Predawn silence pervaded the workshop, and he hesitated on the threshold, listening. It was good that Freydolf had stopped work for the night, but shouldn't there be snoring?

Quietly closing the door, the boy tiptoed further into the room. To his surprise, the sculptor's bed stood empty. After a moment's thought, he padded upstairs, but the balcony was similarly vacant. What could have happened?

Skipping back downstairs, Tupper checked the kitchen table for a message, but it was as clear as he'd left it.

With a start, he murmured, "I didn't leave a note."

Maybe his master was searching for him? He'd been so certain Freydolf wouldn't notice he was gone, but then ... the Pred usually did pay attention to him. Hunching his shoulders, the boy wondered how much trouble he would be in.

Should he search? Stay? With a weary shake of his head, Tupper decided to wait for his scolding in bed.

The last thing he expected to find when he pulled aside the tapestry curtain was Freydolf.

Tupper's bed was a fine thing, carved as it was into the very mountainside, but the niche wasn't long enough for the Pred. The man didn't look particularly comfortable. Actually, he looked sort of sulky, his dark eyes fixed on Tupper from under the arm flung across his face.

"Here you are!" the boy exclaimed, relieved.

"I could say the same."

Bare feet scuffed the floorboards. "Were you worried?"

"Aye."

He ducked his head, whispering, "Sorry."

Freydolf collared him, hauling him up into the niche. "This isn't like you, lambkin."

Tupper rebelled against the accusation. "I always do my job."

With a snort, the Pred demanded, "Which of your duties led to your vanishing for an entire night?"

"You wanted a white statue for Aurelius's courtyard," he replied staunchly. Wasn't he servant to the Keeper of Morven? He'd only been taking care of things for his master.

"But I never asked *you* to find one!"

"Who else is there?"

Frey looked so taken aback, Tupper was nervous that he'd actually displeased his master. If so, this was the first time, and his stomach knotted uncomfortably.

The Pred grumbled, "You could have waited for me."

"You were busy," he stubbornly reminded. "Besides, I know my way around."

"But why in the middle of the night?" pressed Freydolf.

Tupper fidgeted. "I needed Snick."

Heavy brows drew together. "You opened locked doors?"

In a very small voice, he answered, "A few."

Silence stretched ominously between them, but finally, Frey sighed and asked, "Were you careful?"

"Yes."

The man pulled a pillow from the pile in the corner and plunked it down, patting it. Tupper gratefully accepted the invitation, which felt like a peace offering.

In softer tones, the sculptor asked, "Did you find many starstone statues?"

"Lots."

"I know of an archer."

Tupper nodded, for that was one of the first he'd tried. "He wasn't very friendly."

"And there was a dancer," the Keeper mused.

"She's too silly."

Freydolf messed up his hair, then asked, "How many starstone guardians did you find?"

"Twenty-eight."

"So many! And did any of them meet your lofty standards?"

Tupper was caught mid-yawn but answered as soon as he could. "I found a prince brave enough to stare down a tiger."

"I don't recall any princes, but I assume the tiger is Graven?"

The boy hummed his agreement as he burrowed more deeply into his pillow. "Graven is grumpy, too. *He's* sulking in the stable."

Frey kneaded at the base of one of the young Flox's horns. "I'm *not* grumpy."

Already more than half asleep, Tupper mumbled, "Not anymore."

They were early. Only one more week passed before Freydolf and Tupper were startled by the clatter of hooves and the jangle of harnesses outside.

"Already?" gasped the boy, vaulting toward the door.

"Aye," his master replied, doing a much better job at hiding his excitement.

Ulrica had been closer to him than any of his agemates, and he harbored vast amounts of affection for the fierce girl, now a grown woman and a grandmother. Frey tossed aside his work apron and followed Tupper just in time to see Aurelius alight from the carriage.

The latest fashion back home must have called for excessive tailoring, for his ever-dapper brother-in-law sported a form-fitting vest in shades of orange reminiscent of titian jade. By contrast, his creamy white shirtsleeves exhibited an excess of fabric and poofed ridiculously. Tupper wasted no time in flinging himself at the Pred, who caught him neatly and tossed him over one shoulder before strolling over to the sculptor.

"I scraped up a couple of smaller commissions to tide you through the summer, Frey!" Aurelius announced without preamble.

"What sort of stone?"

"Redstone for one, crystal for the other," his agent proudly revealed.

Tupper patted Aurelius between the shoulder blades for attention. "Did you remember a mattress?"

"Naturally," drawled the Pred. "Is the rest ready?"

"Yes." With a fidget and a glance toward the carriage, Tupper whispered, "Where is she?"

Amusement sparkled in the merchant's eyes. "Be a gentleman and open the door for my lady, sprat."

Tupper clambered onto the bottom step of the carriage, stretching to reach the handle. He poked his head through the door, softly calling, "Missus Harrow?"

Then, the boy yelped vanishing inside with a *whoosh* and firm *click* as the door locked behind him.

Aurelius sighed. "The lad may *never* learn! How often do I have to warn him to keep his guard up?"

Frey grimaced. "Is it safe to assume that Ulrica wished to introduce herself?"

"Aye." Fluttering his fingers unconcernedly, he added, "In her own inimitable way."

"Should I be worried?"

"Nay," Aurelius replied, smirking faintly. "There's a decent chance he'll survive."

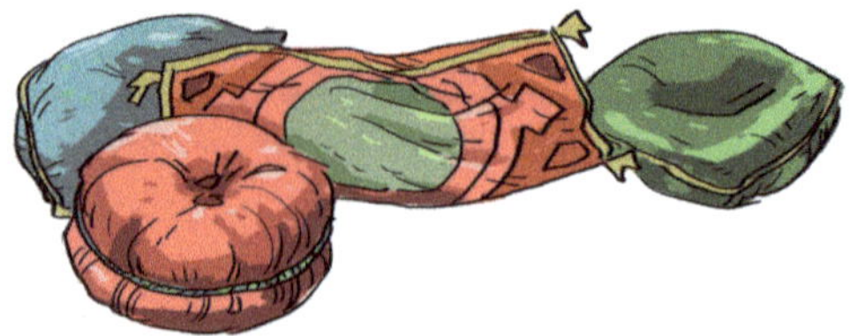

The interior of Aurelius's large carriage was dim, but Tupper didn't need much light to recognize the merchant's cramped traveling quarters or to realize what had happened. Slowly, he reached up to rub at the base of one of the horns Ulrica had misused to drag him inside.

He tipped his head back, hoping for a glimpse of Freydolf's sister. No luck. She was directly behind him.

Heart still hammering in his chest, he stared up at the ceiling and wondered if all Pred introduced themselves by attacking, or if the Harrows were just … special.

"Hello. I'm Tupper."

"There's not much to you," the lady remarked. Her voice was low and rich, but hard at the edges.

"No," he acknowledged. "Flox are lots smaller than Pred."

His first impressions of Ulrica were of soft fabric, spicy perfume, and the sting of claws at his throat. The woman had him expertly pinned, and he couldn't have gotten away if he wanted. Which he didn't. He'd been looking forward to this moment for weeks.

There was a rustle of cloth, then the faint tinkling of tiny bells as she adjusted her grip. "Are you calling me large?" she inquired sweetly.

Oops. Tupper knew enough about womenfolk to know he was going to have to haggle hard to stay in her good graces.

"I know you're strong, and your hands are bigger than mine," he reasoned, slim fingers brushing lightly against those encircling his neck. "Are you as tall as Freydolf?"

"Not quite." Humming close to his ear, Ulrica inquired, "Aren't you afraid, Floxling? The villagers scattered like prey when they caught sight of our carriage."

Afraid? No, not when this woman's husband was so fond of

catching him at knife point. It was strange how used to it he'd grown. Besides, if this woman was truly a threat, Aurelius and Freydolf would have battered in the door by now.

Tupper patiently explained, "Aurelius makes the villagers nervous, but I think he *likes* making them nervous. He teases."

The woman started playing with his curly hair. "Aye. He does."

"Are you teasing me, too?" Tupper checked.

"Aye." There was a smirk in her tone this time.

Relaxing in her grasp, he offered, "Thank you for the book of recipes. Frey's eating better."

"I'm pleased to hear that you had the sense to put it to use," she replied, releasing him and sitting back.

Tupper turned. Aurelius seemed to have created a seat for his wife using the mattress he'd procured for their bed, and the soft mound was strewn with numerous silken pillows. Tupper sat cross-legged on the floor before Ulrica, who looked very much like a grand lady.

Jeweled slippers peeped out from under skirts made from layers of filmy fabrics. He noticed lots of fancy details— bracelets around her ankles, amber droplets dangling from her earlobes, jeweled combs tucked into thick, dark hair, and lips painted the same deep orange as her bodice.

Those lips turned down in an unhappy frown, and Tupper asked, "Is there anything you need, Missus Harrow?"

"What would someone like you have to offer someone like me?" she asked haughtily.

"A drink of water?" he tried. After some thought, he continued, "If you're hungry, I can fix dinner early, or if you're tired, I can get your bed ready. Aurelius picked a really good place for you to live while you're here."

"So he keeps telling me," she muttered darkly.

"He wants you to be comfortable," Tupper defended. Now that he could see Ulrica for himself, he understood why. With a shy smile, he added, "I'm glad you're safely here, Missus."

This was Tupper's first time seeing a lady Pred, and he was having a hard time not staring.

Ulrica was tall and curvaceous, and her skin had the same

bronzy cast as her husband's and brother's. He searched her face for signs of a family resemblance. Her kohl-rimmed eyes might have been the same shade of brown, and he thought perhaps the shape of her chin was similar, though hers had a cockier tilt. Tupper decided that she was much prettier than Freydolf, but not quite as pretty as Aurelius. Not that he was foolish enough to say so.

Ulrica had been studying him just as closely. "You look like a doll—dainty and delicate. My brother's pet."

"Servant," he firmly corrected.

"And brother?"

"Yes. Frey's a Meadowsweet now, same as me," Tupper confirmed.

The woman's dark brows drew together in a scowl. "Let's set some things straight."

Tupper nodded and waited expectantly.

"My husband says you're remarkably obedient."

"Yes, Missus."

She wrinkled her nose at him. "Nay, that won't do. Since you call my brother and husband with excessive familiarity, I'll permit you to call me Ulrica, but you'll *not* look down on me."

"I'm pretty sure you're taller."

The woman's brows arched. Then, she chuckled.

It was a warm sound, and Tupper scooted forward, putting his hands on her knee. "You *are* Freydolf's sister. I can tell when you smile."

Her expression hardened. "Aye. I'm Freydolf's sister, and he's my brother. Nothing ... *no one* can change that! Not even you."

Tupper wasn't sure what to make of her remark. Was she upset that Freydolf wasn't a Rakefang anymore? But that wasn't his fault. Or was it? He *had* given his master a new name. "Ulrica, are you angry with me?"

"I'm furious enough rend stubborn flesh from rigid bone—and mad enough to try it—but no, child. *You* are the one I've chosen."

From amidst the gory threats, one thing made sense to Tupper. "You picked me? For what?"

Placing her hand atop his head, she murmured, "My husband says the oddest things about you."

She caressed his hair and patted his cheek, gestures that reminded him that this woman was a mother.

With a bitter smile, Ulrica announced, "I've run away from home."

Tupper remembered the story of how she'd chased after Freydolf. "You did once before."

"Aye, and this time, I won't let Aurelius woo me back."

"So why do you need me?" he pressed. He was a little worried what she might be expecting, because his first duty would always be to Freydolf.

"Hold out your hands," she demanded.

When he obeyed, she reached behind her back and withdrew a sheathed blade. It was much larger and heavier than his own little knife, and much more elegant. He admired the inset stones decorating the handle—gray, white, and orange.

"This is yours," he guessed.

"Aye, and I've placed it in your hands."

Tupper could tell she'd done something important by giving him her knife, but he was lost. Shaking his head, he asked, "What does this mean, Ulrica. I don't understand many Pred traditions."

"I am forging a necessary alliance," she announced. "You shall be my advocate in this place. My peacekeeper."

"What does a peacekeeper do?"

"Mostly, you'll make sure I don't kill anyone in a fit of temper," she nonchalantly revealed.

His eyes widened, and he hoped she was teasing. "How would I do that?"

She tapped the blade in his hands with the tip of a claw. "This is my promise to listen to you. Your counsel shall be my guide."

He thought he understood what she needed. Someone to show her around. Someone to teach her the local customs. Tupper hugged her knife to his chest. "A guide," he softly echoed. "I can do that."

Ulrica shifted restlessly, then grudgingly announced, "My husband set one condition for this journey. He made me swear."

"If Aurelius thinks it's for the best, it probably is," Tupper encouraged.

Rebellion glinted in her eyes. "It's utterly ridiculous!"

"But you promised?"

She growled softly, and Tupper decided that Aurelius was a very brave man.

He stuck her knife into his belt and took one of her hands into his, patting it soothingly. "Maybe it won't be so bad."

She bared her fangs at him, then sighed morosely.

It was amazing how quickly this lady changed her mood. The promise must have been truly terrible. "Tell me?" he coaxed.

"I could break you like a reed!" Ulrica exclaimed, pulling away to snap her fingers demonstratively.

"I know."

"You're nothing but a wispy boy!" she raged.

Tupper found it interesting that Aurelius's lady used her hands when she spoke, so much so that the bells on her bracelets jangled urgently. Bold colors, bold words, bold gestures—he kept his voice soft, as if talking to a wild animal. "Yes. I'm growing, though."

"Do you have any idea how humiliating this is?"

"Not really," he admitted. "Maybe you should explain."

Ulrica muttered, "Fine. I shall keep my word, but it shall be in my own way!"

He nodded, grateful that she was finally getting to the point.

"Tupper Meadowsweet," she began, all haughty formality. "I wish to be mothered."

He blinked. "By me?"

"Aye. And *only* you," she warned. "If you allow those two worrywarts to coddle me, I'll flay you alive!"

He was impressed, for Ulrica had found a way to keep her promise *and* her pride. In a sense, she'd outwitted Aurelius by making Tupper her ally before tacking on the mothering clause. With a nod of approval, he said, "It's only natural for your peacekeeper to look after your well-being."

The lady smirked. "Aye. We have reached an understanding."

"I'll do my best," Tupper promised, then set to his task with a soft *tut*. "And you shouldn't growl at Aurelius. Of course he would fuss!"

She huffed but didn't argue the point.

"How soon?" Tupper asked.

"Not soon enough," she grumbled.

"Can I?" he asked, holding out one slender hand.

Ulrica frowned at him. "Are all Flox boys so bold?"

Tupper thought about it. "Usually only with relatives."

"And I'm to be counted as family?"

"If you don't mind."

Her dark eyes searched his upturned face, and with a bemused expression, she replied, "I'll permit it."

Flashing a bright smile, Tupper let his palm rest lightly upon the prominent swell of her belly. Wouldn't Freydolf be surprised? Mindful of his horns, he leaned down to press his ear to Ulrica's stomach, listening intently.

When his gentle pressure was met with a sharp prod from within, his heart leapt for gladness, and he softly called, "Hello, little one! I'm your Uncle Tupp!"

12

Last to Know

While they returned from the stable, where the freshly-watered horses had been made comfortable, Freydolf eyed his brother-in-law, trying to figure out what was off. Finally, he said, "Something's wrong."

Aurelius shook his head. "Nay. The journey came off without a hitch. All's well."

"You're distracted," Frey accused. "Or are you hiding something?"

Aurelius smirked faintly. "Does it have to be one or the other?"

"Both?" The sculptor's eyes narrowed. "For that matter, you haven't demanded a bath yet! What's gotten into you?"

"The prospect of a bath thrills me to my toes, but it shall wait until Ulrica is settled." Just then, the man nodded toward the spot where they'd left the carriage. "Looks as if she's done with him."

Freydolf's gaze shot to the fore in time to see Tupper jump out, then grab a squat stool from within, setting it down as a step. The lad offered his hand, and a woman followed more slowly.

Aurelius lengthened his strides, but Frey faltered.

Ulrica *was* older, but the years hadn't diminished any of her beauty. She looked settled, confident, and mildly exasperated when her husband solicitously slipped his arm around her waist.

"I can walk!" she snapped.

"Mind the cobbles," Aurelius murmured, stubbornly keeping his place at her side.

"Wretch," she muttered, though there was affection underlying the insult. "I'm not doddering yet."

"Perish the thought. Although I'm shocked to see that the sprat managed to disarm you. Did he slip in under your guard?"

"Be grateful my blade is in his keeping," she retorted. "Else it would be at your throat!"

"Aye, my gratitude knows no bounds."

"They haven't changed a bit." Freydolf shook his head over the swift exchange of barbs that were the hallmark of the couple's conversations.

Tupper rushed over and grabbed his sleeve, tugging him toward their guests. "Come see!"

"Aye, and gladly." With a crooked smile, he asked, "What do you think of my baby sister?"

"She's tall!"

There was no denying that. Ulrica was taller than most women from their country, just shy of her husband's height and as strong as she was fearless. Frey sometimes envied her for being everything a Pred should be. Everything he was not.

"Welcome ba–"

The rest of his greeting faded on his lips. Was it possible that she was …?

As if the gleam in Aurelius's eye wasn't enough, Tupper was right there, guiding the sculptor's callused hand to Ulrica's stomach. Freydolf was shocked she allowed his claws near her young, for Pred were not usually so trusting. But his sister placed her hands over his, her eyes flashing challengingly.

His gaze softened. "Ulrica, you shouldn't have risked a journey."

Her chin lifted proudly, and she swore, "This child shall know my brother."

Freydolf searched his sister's face. Despite the severance of family ties, she insisted on calling him brother, but even her stubbornness wasn't enough to mend this rift. Shaking his head, he said, "Father wouldn't allow it."

She didn't even flinch. "I've done my duty by the family.

Four sons—tall, proud, strong, and clever. The line is secure." Ulrica's hands tightened over his, pressing his palm against the swell of her stomach. "This time, I shall fly in the face of duty and scratch out its eyes. My son *will* know my brother!"

Tupper piped up. "What if your baby is a girl?"

The woman arched her brows at the young Flox. "Then she shall wear his fangs upon a ribbon."

He nodded wisely, then tugged at Frey's sleeve, happily relaying, "I'll be an uncle, too!"

"Her very favorite one," Ulrica indulgently confirmed.

"Even if she's a *he*?" checked Tupper, sneaking his hand back onto her belly.

"Then he shall dog your heels and sharpen his first teeth upon your horns."

Tupper rubbed uncertainly at one's base. "Girls sound easier."

Ulrica's fangs flashed in a wicked grin. "Oh, we are far, *far* worse!"

Something clicked in Freydolf's head, and his stomach flip-flopped. The Rakefang legacy would pass to his sister's surfeit of sons. Ulrica had made up for his lack by providing their father with heirs more to his liking. The gap left by his banishment had been filled, and a new generation was poised to take control of the family's holdings. Looking to Aurelius, the sculptor asked, "Your eldest has been named heir?"

"Aye." With ill-concealed pride, Aurelius revealed, "His son's the first Rakefang with eyes of Harrow gold."

Frey grunted in surprise when the child his sister carried shifted under his hand, a sensation he'd never experienced. Without thinking, he knelt before her and brought up his other hand, spreading both palms in hopes of a repeat performance. "I never expected ...." he murmured in awe.

"You and me both," muttered Aurelius, earning a sharp elbow to the ribs.

"Brand will be so happy," said Tupper. "He loves babies, too."

And another belated epiphany filtered through the haze of Freydolf's surprise. Gazing into his sister's dark eyes, he asked, "You're planning to have your baby here?"

"Aye."

He was staggered. This went against longstanding Pred tradition, for a woman gave birth at home, attended by her mother and surrounded by her sisters. "I can't believe Mother let you leave."

Ulrica sniffed. "Who says she did?"

Tupper patted Freydolf's shoulder and helpfully explained, "She ran away from home."

"But you should be at home," he argued weakly.

His sister gently touched his cheek, but her tone left no room for refusal. "Then you'd best show me the way to the purportedly magnificent rooms my husband selected."

As Tupper eagerly led Ulrica in the direction of the waiting suite, Freydolf sat back on his heels, still reeling.

Aurelius crouched in front of him. "You took that well."

"Another baby," Frey whispered.

"Aye. Caught me by surprise, too." Aurelius checked to see if his wife was in earshot. "As you well know, large families aren't the fashion. Four sons was already pushing the boundaries of propriety."

It was true. In old, influential families, two children was the norm. Large numbers of offspring were equated with the working classes—to which the Harrows belonged. Aurelius might have been pegged as a gallant gold-digger if his attachment to Ulrica hadn't been so obvious.

"Fancy *you* committing such a glaring social faux pas,"

Freydolf teased.

Aurelius scowled. "I'll not apologize for any of my children!"

Offering his hands in a peaceable gesture, the Keeper said, "Nor would I criticize. I've seen you with your boys. They're a tribute to you and Ulrica both."

Somewhat mollified, the merchant admitted, "Still, she hid this pregnancy as long as she could."

Frowning deeply, Frey asked, "Because of the social stigma?"

"Nay." Aurelius fiddled with his cufflinks, eyes downcast.

"Then why?"

He made a fluttering wave of his hand. "For me. For you."

Frey shook his head. "Us?"

"It's deucedly hard to make sense of her rationale, but aye, she chose this course for our sakes as well as her own." With a solemn expression, he explained, "The babe she carries will be a Harrow instead of a Rakefang. This child won't have to admire the accomplishments of their uncle, the world-renowned master sculptor, in secret."

The first part was news to Frey. "*All* your sons are Rakefangs? Not Harrows?"

"Your father made it a condition of my acceptability," Aurelius grudgingly admitted. "None of my children bear my family name."

"I didn't know!"

His brother-in-law shrugged. "They wear the prestige of their mother's heritage well. I have no regrets."

"Yet she is abandoning that heritage?"

"Aye, you heard her. Ulrica's had enough of familial obligation." Aurelius explained, "This past winter's voyage was the last on which our youngest could accompany us. The boys are making their own way in the world. She wishes to do the same."

"No one knows about the baby?"

"Nay, not even our sons. The whole family is under the impression that Ulrica and I are traveling to Far Continent, so we won't be missed for months. I'll have letters delivered just before the snow flies to reassure them that we've found safe harbor, but I don't think Ulrica means to return."

"But you have a grandchild now! And your sons ...!"

"I'll eventually put a word in their ear," Aurelius calmly replied. "They know how to be discreet, and they know which roads lead to Morven."

He'd obviously thought it all through before carrying out his wife's wild plan. Freydolf propped his fists upon his thighs. "What about your business travels?"

Aurelius chuckled. "Fear not! I mean to continue as your agent. This summer, I'll stay on-continent. It's been a while since I visited the Sunstone Mountain."

"Very reasonable." Slowly getting to his feet, the sculptor asked, "And the winter voyage?"

"Postponed," the merchant said with finality. He rose gracefully and straightened his vest. "We'll overwinter here with the baby."

Freydolf wasn't even remotely upset by these plans, but he couldn't resist a gruff retort. "Didn't you imply you would stay through summertime?"

"Aye," Aurelius sweetly acknowledged. "I just didn't specify how many summers!"

Ulrica wandered through her new home, making no comment, but touching this and that as she prowled from room to room. Tupper shadowed her steps, watching closely. There was a graceful sway to the way she walked, and he liked the way the tiny bells at her ankles tinkled. He'd never seen such a tall woman, and he was frankly fascinated. At thirteen, he was easily as tall as his own mother, but Ulrica towered over him, making him feel very young. Tupper touched his horns to reassure himself that he hadn't actually regressed.

Eventually, she declared, "It will suffice."

"Is that good?"

The woman's gaze rested on him for a few moments, calm and calculating. "Aye, boy. I'm pleased."

He nodded, relieved to have passed muster.

She inclined her head, then broached a new subject. "What are your usual duties?"

"I manage Frey's household," Tupper reported matter-of-factly.

Ulrica's lips quirked. "And him as well?"

"Him I mother."

With a low chuckle, she inquired, "Does he ever lift a finger?"

"Sometimes, but the others usually help if I need it."

"What others?"

Tupper listed, "Graven, Ember, Brand, Haimish ...."

"The statues?" Ulrica asked dubiously.

"Yes."

She hummed thoughtfully. "While I shall submit to your mothering, I came prepared to barter for my rights and responsibilities."

He was pretty sure he understood what she meant. "You want chores?"

Her dark eyes flashed. "I refuse to wallow in boredom! Let me fend for my family!"

"We can trade favors," Tupper quickly assured. "What terms?"

The Pred woman's chin lifted. "I wish to hunt," she announced.

Tupper's gaze drifted uncertainly to her stomach, but he only asked, "That's all?"

"Nay," Ulrica rejoined brusquely. "I am fond of the fruit trees."

"You're the one who planted the first ones," he recalled.

"Aye. I enjoy gardening."

"We have lots of gardens. Do you know anything about pastures?"

"A bit, and I can cook."

Tupper kept his expression neutral, but his heart leapt. It would be wonderful to have help in the kitchen. He casually replied, "Your peppers are Frey's favorite."

"Aye, which is why I brought seeds."

Oh, she was *good*.

She hummed again, a pleased sound, almost like a purr. Then, from within the folds of her voluminous skirts, she withdrew a pouch that looked as if it was mostly constructed from loosely woven rope—part net, part basket. She passed it along, and Tupper found that it was warm. Bits of straw and shreds of silk poked through the mesh, and he studied the weaving, trying to unravel the secret of its pattern.

"Those are just the wrappings. Look inside," she prompted.

Slipping its catch, he lifted the carrier's lid and gently extracted the topmost silken bundle. "Oh," he gasped, for this was precious cargo indeed. By the time he reached the bottom of the makeshift nest, he had ten eggs, their pink shells liberally speckled with brown.

"Do you have a brood hen?" Ulrica inquired.

"Yes."

Nodding, the woman proposed, "Let her mind them, and you may very well add ten hatchlings to your flock."

"These are big eggs," he mused aloud. "Are they chickens?"

"Aye. This variety is raised by Grif for their feathers, their eggs, and their flavor." With a smug smile, she added, "If you can foster them here, in the future, these fowl may prove valuable for trade in the valleys."

Tupper knew full well it was chancy to count on a flock that was still in the shell, but the risk was definitely worth it. These eggs were more priceless than jade in his eyes, and he cupped one in his hands. His decision was easy. He wouldn't stymie Ulrica's desire to lend her support to their family.

The tricky part was making sure the bargain had the right balance of give and take in order to uphold dignity on all sides. Choosing his words with great care, he began, "If you and Aurelius can hunt for us, I'd be glad for the meat ... and for lessons. I only know how to fish."

"You shall be taught," she promised.

"As for the garden, tending is one thing, toting water is another," he continued. "Until your baby comes, leave the heavy buckets to me or Haimish."

"Agreed."

"And I'll share my kitchen. We can help each other."

"I accept your terms."

Tupper rewrapped the eggs and pushed the carrier under his shirt, anxious to keep the eggs warm, but before he could run off with them to the hen house, Ulrica stopped him.

"I have something else for you." Reaching into another hidden pocket, she withdrew a small, cloth pouch and held it out. When she dropped the bundle into his upraised palms, it chinked softly.

Tupper fiddled with the ribbon ties, then gasped in delight. "Shells!"

"Aurelius said you love stories about the sea," she said with a faint smile.

"I do!" He knew it was bad business to show how much he wanted them, but he couldn't hide his hopefulness. "What will you trade for these?"

"Those?" she scoffed. "They're mere trinkets I found on the ground the day before we departed."

Brimming with happiness, Tupper set aside both the eggs and shells in order to fold his hands over his heart, then flung them wide in his people's most exuberant show of gratitude.

"So much fuss over such a paltry gift?"

"Yes!" he insisted, barely containing his enthusiasm. He could almost imagine this grand lady walking barefoot along the beach, looking for the same kind of shells Frey had loved as a boy.

The blade meant alliance. The eggs were for barter. But the shells were a present, plain and simple.

"And why's that?" Ulrica inquired lightly.

Unable to hold back a smile, Tupper said, "Because you picked them for me."

Somehow, Haimish managed to sidle up to Aurelius without the Pred noticing. Freydolf huffed in amusement when his brother-in-law whirled, blade flashing, only to come up short.

"Oh, it's you," Aurelius grumbled, adding a few choice oaths in Terse and Prose. Looking the abjectly apologetic statue up and down, he drawled, "Frey, why does Haimish have a tail?"

"Fashion statement."

The brownstone Pred's tail swayed tentatively, and he held out his arms, offering to carry things.

"Aye, I'll put you to work," Aurelius agreed, sheathing his dagger and half-disappearing into the carriage. When he reappeared, he thrust a bundled mattress upon Haimish, saying, "Bring this to Tupper—he'll know what to do with it—then bring a cart."

"He can't even see where he's going," Frey protested.

"Nay, but he probably doesn't need to." Aurelius watched the statue stride up the cobblestone road. "Now, where was I?"

"On the starstone mountain."

"Aye, where I read every tractate and tome in the old bounder's archive." Beckoning for the sculptor to join him, he set off in the direction of the outer courtyard.

Freydolf followed without complaint, but jibed, "*All* of them?"

"All the pertinent ones," Aurelius countered haughtily. "And I've devised a plan."

The Keeper hurried his steps, coming alongside his brother-in-law. "You found out more about stone affinities? Were there records of people like Tupper, who seem to interact with stone differently than sculptors?"

"Not specifically," Aurelius hedged.

"What *did* you find?"

The other Pred drew up short and faced him squarely. "To put a fine point on it—nothing."

"Yet you have a plan?" Freydolf asked suspiciously.

"Aye, one I'm sure will shed light on the sprat's little quirk."

Freydolf hardly considered shifting the nature of stone and hearing Morven's voice a *little quirk*, but he was willing to hear Aurelius out. Trailing after the man, who was aiming for the rock piles at the far edge of the courtyard, he asked, "What's your plan based on?"

Fingers fluttered gracefully. "Common sense!"

"Do you possess any?" At Aurelius's glare, Frey relented. "Tell me about your grand scheme."

"For starters, find me a rock."

Gesturing broadly at the jumble of cast-off stones, Frey generously offered, "Take your pick."

"Nay. You choose, and make sure it's a dud—one with nothing to recommend it to a Keeper of your abilities."

"That's most of them. The Barrens are a scrap heap!"

"Humor me," drawled the merchant.

Freydolf stepped down to wander amidst mounds loosely sorted by color. "As you wish ... Grandpa."

"I heard that!"

There were stones aplenty, and most truly were useless. Oh, Aurelius could sell them by the basketful to crafters who made beads and baubles, but their magic was dim or dead. Tupper still brought him odd bits for slow times, but it was a wonder to Freydolf that the lad found any at all amidst the rubble.

"Color preference?"

Aurelius shrugged. "I don't care. What's your least favorite?"

Freydolf straightened and gaped over his shoulder at the man. "What kind of *ridiculous* question is that?"

"What? You don't play favorites?"

"Nay!"

"Of all the ... *fine*! They're all splendid stones, each special in their own way. It would be a terrible, *terrible* thing for you to slight any of the magical mountains," he droned sarcastically. "Now pick up a lackluster lump so I can proceed with the next stage of my brilliant plan."

But how could he? Now that Aurelius had insinuated favoritism, the Keeper felt that choosing any stone was tantamount to insult. Rubbing the back of his neck, he muttered, "I can't!"

"For pity's sake, Frey!" Aurelius groaned. "Dapple, then."

The sculptor frowned. "What do you have against dapple?"

"*Nothing*. Just choose!"

Growling irritably, Freydolf stalked over to the tumble of mottled stones. It had been picked over innumerable times, so nothing at the top showed any promise whatsoever. Finding a piece that fit nicely into the palm of his hand, he tossed it at his brother-in-law, who caught it neatly.

"Happy?" he grumped.

"Too soon to tell," Aurelius replied briskly. "Come on. Time for stage two!"

Freydolf trailed after the man all the way back to the workshop. "So, what does this next part involve?"

"Mostly observation. No need to rush into things when there are entire seasons ahead of us."

"Aye, I suppose not." He allowed Aurelius to precede him inside.

When the man made a point of creeping past the threshold and listening for signs of Tupper's return, Freydolf rolled his eyes. There were times when Aurelius's love for showmanship went way over the top. "He's obviously still with Ulrica."

Aurelius ignored him in favor of stealing across the room on cat-light feet.

Suddenly, Freydolf realized what his brother-in-law intended to do with that forlorn chunk of dapple. "Are you actually planning to ...?"

"Aye."

"*That's* your brilliant plan?"

The merchant's brows lifted challengingly. "Do you have a better one?"

"Nay."

Freydolf rubbed at his chin to hide his amusement while Aurelius stealthily hid the stone under Tupper's pillow, then slunk away.

13

Staying

Freydolf carefully lowered the side of Aurelius's carriage to make it easier to get at the rest of the luggage. Crates, boxes, and trunks were packed right to the compartment ceiling. "How long did it take you to maneuver all this into place?"

"Repacked the thing several times before I was satisfied," Aurelius admitted.

"Your whole life, reduced to one wagon load?"

"I own estates on all four continents," the merchant reminded with a sniff. "However, I was forced to economize. Leaving with three carriages would have raised suspicions."

"Were you able to bring all your shoes?" Frey teased.

"Don't be ridiculous," scoffed Aurelius. "I emptied my wine cellar."

Freydolf didn't doubt that most of the crates represented the little luxuries his brother-in-law couldn't bear to live without, but he hadn't been entirely selfish. Running his hand along the polished side of a fine block of crystal, the sculptor murmured, "I'm glad you made room for this beauty!" The superlative clarity of the green-blue column reminded him of the sea.

"Aye. Some sacrifices are worth making."

"What, your shoes?"

"On the contrary! I left behind my entire winter wardrobe for your sake," Aurelius revealed.

Frey's brows lifted in surprise. "How noble."

"Not really," the other man replied breezily. "I'll order replacements while I'm in the Drom capital later this summer."

The Keeper tapped the crystal. "So this is actually just an excuse to buy new clothes?"

"Nooo." A smirk playing across Aurelius's lips. "But the slab of redstone taking up the lower compartment probably is."

"Nice to see your mercenary streak is still intact."

Aurelius didn't deny it. With a philosophical air, he said, "Stones last, but fashions come and go. This way, we're *both* happy."

While they strolled toward Freydolf's workshop, Ulrica inquired, "Will I offend you if I ask to take your hand."

Tupper wasn't sure if she was treating him like a child or a gentleman, but either way it was a peaceable gesture. Still, he was curious. "How old do I look to you?"

She studied his upturned face, then pronounced. "You're about the size of a weedy eight-year-old."

He goggled at her, for eight was nubless, and he was more than half-grown. "I'm thirteen," he carefully informed her. Taking her hand, he also took the lead, firmly guiding her toward his kitchen while he sorted his priorities. He planned to make this lady some tea, then fill the cauldrons. Aurelius would be wanting his bath.

"*Have* I offended you?"

"No."

After a few more steps, she remarked, "You're a quiet one."

"Yes."

"I've raised sons, so I know my fair share about boys," she announced.

Tupper wondered if Pred boys and Flox boys were the same on the inside even though they were different on the outside. It might be interesting to trade places with a Pred and grow up handling knives instead of reeds. Then, he could have long hair and pierced ears, but almost immediately, he felt bad for the Pred boy, who would be made fun of for his lack of horns and feared for his claws and fangs. With a small sigh, he mentally switched back to his rightful spot in the world.

Ulrica gave his hand a small squeeze. "In my experience, even talkative boys keep most of what they think inside their heads."

"Probably." Maybe Ulrica was going to turn out to be as chatty as Frey.

"Will you tell me the truth if I ask for it?" she inquired lightly.

"Yes."

"Do you love my brother?"

Tupper was honestly surprised, for the wary expression on Ulrica's face suggested that she was asking an intensely personal question. Maybe Pred were shy with their feelings the way Flox were shy about baths? She clearly cared about his answer, so he gave her hand a reassuring pat. "Lots."

"And my husband?"

"Aurelius, too," he freely admitted.

"And what about me?"

That was harder to answer, since he'd only met her a few hours ago. "Do you want me to love you?"

"Aye," she replied with equal solemnity.

With a small shrug, Tupper said, "Then, that's probably the way it'll end up."

They reached the men in time to prevent a small catastrophe. Thrusting his precious egg basket into Ulrica's hands, Tupper said, "Excuse me, please," then trotted forward. Taking a deep breath, the boy bellowed, "Graven! *NO!*"

With an oath, Aurelius dropped into a crouch. "I thought that mosaic monstrosity stayed in the hen house at this hour!"

"I'm late to bring feed and check the eggs. Leg up, please?" Tupper begged of Frey, who laced his fingers together for a foothold, tossing his servant onto the low roof of a pretty little portico. The boy skittered up sloped tiles, angling toward the next tier of masonry where his tiger crouched, varicolored tail twitching.

"Call him off!" demanded the merchant peevishly.

Keeping a wary eye on the statue, Aurelius backed to his wife's side and slipped a protective arm around her. Either that, or he was hiding behind her. It was kind of hard to tell.

Freydolf soothed, "Graven's never turned on Ulrica."

"Aye, he wouldn't dare," the woman retorted.

Tupper hugged the big tiger's muzzle and gazed straight into blue-rimmed eyes. "Aurelius brought Ulrica—them *and* their baby," he sternly shared. "I already told you they're staying, which means they're ours now. Be good."

Graven blinked lazily and sprawled onto his side, hooking one paw around the boy and pulling him closer. With a small smile, Tupper accepted the invitation, marveling anew over the way stone could be ruffled like real fur. Master Platt had done a very good job in making Graven real. Lavishing the big cat with affection, he crooned, "You did well to find me. I'm sorry if you worried. Are your chicks hungry?"

From below, Ulrica inquired, "Smitten?"

"Mutually," Freydolf replied.

Tupper made sure to give Graven a good scratching all the way around his fancy collar before clambering aboard. "Down, please," he urged, tangling his fingers through thick fur as his sleek mount rose and padded along the high ledge, then flowed gracefully to the ground.

"Can you imagine hunting astride a tiger?" Ulrica asked in awed tones.

"Nay, but I can tell you what it's like being hunted by one," Aurelius rejoined sourly.

"We could try," Tupper offered. "Graven is much quieter than I am in the woods. Very sneaky."

"I'll take it under advisement," the merchant replied with wary interest. "But now is not the time for games. Banish the beast so we can finish unloading."

The boy slipped off the tiger's back and patted his shoulder. "I'll come as soon as I'm done filling cauldrons."

As Graven slunk away, Ulrica lifted the woven egg basket, saying, "We should go with him and settle these."

"No." Tupper hurried to her side and took her hand. "Tea first, and after you've rested a little, I'll take you to the gardens."

"I don't need to rest," she grumbled.

Ignoring the rebellious glint in her eyes, Tupper went on. "I'll show you which parts I changed, and you can visit the grove."

"We can do that *now*."

Tupper shook his head, calmly repeating, "Tea first. Then you can pick a good place to plant your pepper seeds."

The woman sighed and submitted with gracious amusement. "Aye, little mother."

Aurelius gave his wife a squeeze. "Smitten?"

"That *was* your goal, was it not?"

"Aye." The man's lips quirked as he gazed at Tupper with a mixture of gratitude and smugness. "Taming tigers seems to be the sprat's specialty."

Tupper's nightshirt flapped around his knees as he wearily pulled himself into his niche. The bed was carved directly into the mountain, something he hadn't truly appreciated until Morven made herself known. Now, whenever he tucked himself in at night, there was a sense of being cradled by the mountain. She kept him safe, whispering little secrets as she watched over his dreams.

"He's happy," the boy reported, giving the wall a pat. "I can tell."

She seemed to laugh at him. Or maybe she was just happy, too. Tupper didn't understand much about magic and mountains, but that didn't seem to matter to Morven. Her concerns aligned with his, for they both wanted the best for Freydolf, who needed them both. In so many ways, the man was hopeless without them, but that was okay. They relied on him, too.

Being needed *mattered* to Tupper, but tonight, he was stretched thin. Huddling under his blankets, he tried to relax, for tomorrow was sure to be just as busy. Common sense demanded that he rest, yet his thoughts whirled ahead—pepper seeds to plant, eggs to turn, messages to send, meals to plan, tigers to soothe, stones to seek, fires to tend, water to draw ….

"Oh!" he gasped, sitting up fast and shimmying to the edge of the bed.

Tupper froze, half-in and half-out of his covers, for Freydolf barred his way, arms folded over his chest. "Where do you think you're going?" the man inquired.

"I forgot to visit the white lady."

The Pred's bushy brows lifted. "What for?"

"A drink."

Frey jerked a thumb toward the corner. "If you're thirsty, the pitcher is full."

"But she'll be waiting," Tupper explained.

His master sighed. "I think you've done enough for one day, lambkin. Sleep."

Stubbornly, he started to slip to the floor. "It'll only take a minute. She needs me."

"Tupper."

The warning note in Freydolf's voice was new and a little frightening, but mostly frustrating. Of all times to exert his rightful authority, did it have to be now? Tupper knew he'd never get to sleep knowing the white lady was waiting in the inner courtyard. "Please?" be begged. "Let me go?"

"Nay."

Tupper stared at the sculptor in frank dismay. What was he supposed to do now?

"I'll not let you set foot to stone." Hoisting the startled boy into his arms, Freydolf gruffly explained, "Not with my mountain clamoring at me from all sides. You're worrying her, and she's blaming me."

Tupper maneuvered around so he could ride piggyback, wrapping his arms snugly around Freydolf's neck. "Morven?"

"Aye, so let me tend to whatever remains for today."

The mountain had tattled on him, not that he really minded. Going limp, Tupper whispered, "Thank you."

"Do you think with them staying on ..." Frey hesitantly began. "Do you think you'll need help?"

"You have your own work."

"Nay, not me. I meant hiring another servant. We could bring in someone to help you with the extra work."

The boy's hold tightened. He didn't want to share his bond-brother, but he had to consider the needs of their whole household. Most Flox mothers hired in a helper for right after a newborn's arrival, so he should consider that much. Tupper doubted he could keep up with the laundry once there were diapers to wash.

Reluctantly, he said, "I'll need help."

Freydolf nodded, then asked, "Can we put it off a while?"

"Why?"

"Because I like the way things are."

Patting the Pred's shoulder, Tupper reminded, "You like people. You'll make a new friend."

They reached the courtyard before the sculptor pointed out, "They'll work with you, lambkin. You're the one who'll have a new friend."

He shook his head. "People mostly don't bother with me. Except you."

The Pred reached up and tousled his hair, and Tupper smiled.

Even if their home got busier, it would always be theirs.

Perhaps they could find someone who needed a kind master as much as he had. Wouldn't that make the sharing easier?

When the white lady brought them water, Frey thanked her and drank deeply, then waited for the starstone statue to refill her cup for Tupper. Treating the boy to a sidelong glance, he asked, "Do you want to try to make do without someone else?"

"Yes, but that's not best for Ulrica. We'll need someone by the time her baby comes."

The Pred gazed at the stars overhead. "I'll work on getting used to the idea, and you work on finding someone suitable."

"Me?"

Freydolf took the refilled cup from the white lady and passed it up. "Aye, I'll leave the choosing to you. Find someone you can get along with. Preferably someone brave enough to deal with three Pred, a cantankerous tiger, and assorted statues."

Tupper nearly choked on his first swallow, for these criteria sounded very familiar. Maybe he could make one pear do for two tarts. With a light cough, he asked, "Would a girl be all right?"

Aurelius wafted into the kitchen on a cloud of spicy perfume, and Tupper blinked in surprise. "You woke Haimish!" he exclaimed, for the brownstone Pred hovered just inside the door, a hopeful expression on his face.

"Aye, he seems to prefer the smell of me to that of your mush. Is that *all* there is for breakfast?"

The boy glanced out the window, gauging the hour. It was still early. "I could check the fish traps," he admitted, though it would throw off his routine a little.

"*Or,*" countered the man. "*I* could."

And he was out the door again, already knotting his hair.

Tupper slowly stirred the mush as he contemplated this turn of events. Was it possible that a visiting Aurelius was different than a resident Aurelius? A slow smile crept into place. If the Pred took over hunting and fishing duties, it would help tremendously.

Within the hour, the man was crouched between Dag and Nott, turning fish over glowing embers. "I remember these wolves," he remarked. "Why did Frey dredge them up out of deep storage?"

Tupper bashfully shared, "For my birthday. Dag will be the hen house's new day guardian."

By the time the young Flox had finished explaining birthday traditions, Aurelius was grinning wolfishly. "I'd surrender coin to see you with gilded horns."

"I'd rather not."

The Pred chuckled ominously. "Then don't sleep too deeply!"

Deeming it wise to change the subject, Tupper said, "I need to wake Frey. Is Ulrica coming?"

"Nay," Aurelius replied, his tone even despite his lips' downturn. "Can you fix a tray for her?"

"Is she sick?"

"Indisposed," he corrected.

Tupper knew this game. "Unwell?" he tried.

Aurelius smirked and said, "It's more of a malaise. A few days in the airy courtyards of these halcyon heights will work wonders."

The boy shook his head, for no matter how you fancied up the words, being sick felt miserable. Filling the kettle and adding it to the crowded space over the fire, he proposed, "I'll make tea. Is there anything she likes to eat?"

"She ate most of a jar of peppers last night before bed."

Pausing in the act of sliding a generous serving of fish onto the woman's plate, Tupper started to ask if that might be the reason she was sick; however, the question felt rude. So he changed the subject. "Will you be going down the mountain soon?"

"Aye, later today. The horses need greener pastures."

"May I go along?"

"Do you need a ride into one of the villages?"

"No. I need to talk to my brother," Tupper explained.

"Carden?"

"Ewert. He works at the quarry, too."

"Aye, I recall seeing other Meadowsweets on the payroll. You have business with him?"

Tupper fixed Aurelius with a solemn gaze. "I'm going to barter with him."

"I take it you find the prospect daunting?"

Nodding once, the boy said, "If the bargaining goes well, we'll have fresh milk every other day for a fair price."

Aurelius's brow quirked. "And if it doesn't?"

Sighing softly, Tupper admitted, "I'm going to ask you to buy me a cow."

While Aurelius oversaw the settling of his horses into the quarry stables, Tupper asked around for Ewert. He was a little surprised to discover that his quick-witted, fast-talking brother's horns had taken a turn toward adulthood over winter, and he couldn't help staring. "Are you taller than Carden now?"

Ewert glanced over his shoulder. "Hello, little brother. Yep, I've got the edge on him."

Tupper nodded, then said, "Thanks for climbing trees."

His brother's blue eyes narrowed shrewdly. "As grateful as I am for your gratitude, that *can't* be why you're down here."

"No." Keeping his expression carefully neutral, Tupper proposed, "Let's trade."

By the time they clasped hands, Tupper was wrung out.

Ewert drove a hard bargain, but Tupper had managed to whittle down the cost by changing the delivery point from the Statuary to the stream closest to the quarry. His brother would leave the bottles inside the fish trap below the falls, which would keep the milk cool. In addition to coin, Tupper had grudgingly offered to let Ewert take as many fish as he wanted from the cache. That little perk had sealed the deal, and it was a good one, especially since Tupper maintained two other traps. Ewert didn't have to know that.

The young man pocketed the initial payment, promising, "There'll be milk waiting tomorrow morning."

"Please, watch for a good cow, too," Tupper urged. "I think we'll need milk in winter this year."

"I can do that," Ewert agreed. "But why the change?"

The boy smiled. "We're having a baby."

For a fleeting moment, his brother's expression blanked, but Ewert quickly put the pieces together. "Missus Harrow?"

"Yes."

He gazed toward the mountaintop but only said, "Interesting."

In the silence that followed, Tupper surprised himself by blurting, "Do you have a girl?"

With a bemused expression, his brother challenged, "Have you *ever* known me to drag my feet and let someone else get the better deal?"

"No," he admitted. "But you can't haggle for a girl."

"It's more like haggling *with* her in hopes of establishing a mutually beneficial partnership."

Tupper's brow furrowed, for he'd been under the impression that marriage was more about ... other things. "Are you sure?"

Ewert rolled his eyes. "Quite sure. I picked someone two years ago, little brother."

"Does *she* know it?" he checked.

His brother burst out laughing. Dropping his hand onto Tupper's shoulder, he assured, "Yes, we have an understanding. That's part of the reason why I'm so keen on earning your coin. I'll be needing a house."

"When are you getting married?"

"Too many weddings already this year. We'll wait for next spring."

It certainly was shaping up to be a busy summer for the Meadowsweets. Two of Tupper's older sisters had made matches. Addy's wedding was set for midsummer, and then Edie would marry right after harvest.

Giving Tupper's shoulder a poke, Ewert asked, "Aren't you a little short in the horn to be interested in girls?"

"Probably," Tupper sighed. "But it might take me a while to find the one I need."

Plainly amused, Ewert asked, "What's your hurry? You'll have an easier time of it once you finish working up top."

"No. I won't leave Freydolf."

Ewert's brows shot up. "You're planning to stay on permanently?"

"Yes."

Taking another, longer gander at Morven, Ewert shook his head. "I hate to say it, little brother, but you're going to need some serious leverage—and a whole lot of luck—to come out ahead in that haggle."

There was no denying that luck might help when it came to finding the right girl, but leverage sounded all wrong. Tupper blushed, for his own vague plans hinged on something else entirely. Love.

14

Asking for Trouble

A few days later, Tupper was checking on the eggs Ulrica had given him when Graven did something new. The big cat reared up on his hind legs, forepaws splayed against the steep rock face over the hen house door. Poking his head between the network of crisscrossing vines overhead, he stared intently to the northeast.

"Is there a hawk?" Tupper asked, scanning the clear blue sky.

Ears pricked. Tail switched. Even more ominous, the fur on Graven's back went up.

The young Flox pushed close, placing a calming hand on his tiger's flank. "Can you hear something?"

Starstone fangs flashed as the stone guardian dropped to all fours and bounded away. Assuming he'd caught wind of Aurelius, who might already be back from hunting, Tupper gave chase.

Scrambling up the narrow flight of stairs, he looked both ways and spotted Graven's striped behind disappearing along the cobbled road toward home. The tiger loped right on past the entrance to the Harrows' residence, continuing straight through the inner courtyard and out the Apprentice Gate.

"Not good," he muttered. What if someone had come up from the valley? If so, Graven was sure to cause trouble, and Tupper poured on the speed.

He skidded past the towering doors, only to be met by the sight of an all-too-familiar trouble-maker standing atop Ilam's back, desperately fending off the snarling stone tiger with a walking stick.

Tupper stifled a groan. "Graven, enough!" Folding his arms over his chest, he sternly demanded, "What are you doing here, Farley?"

As his younger brother slowly lowered his weapon, Tupper noticed that the boy wore a small pack on his back, and he carried his hunting knife at his belt. Farley had taken the time to prepare for his hike up Morven, so he wasn't relaying any urgent messages.

"Are you snooping?" Tupper asked in edged tones.

"There's a gate up here!"

"Yes."

"And these dogs are huge!"

"Yes."

"And that tiger listens to you!" Farley continued, still wide-eyed in the face of so many discoveries.

With a sigh, Tupper said, "Mostly."

"How come Carden never told us there's a whole fortress on the mountain?" the boy demanded.

It was Tupper's private opinion that their eldest brother had shown considerable wisdom in keeping such details from their inquisitive sibling, but the cat was out of the bag.

Farley goggled, demanding, "What's *that*?"

Tupper checked in the direction his brother was pointing. Make that two cats. "Rimbles."

"Is it made of stone?"

"Yes, *she* is," he confirmed. "Sunstone."

"Then how come it's moving?"

"*She*'s moving because the sun's shining. Now, get off Ilam."

Prodding the hound's back with his toe, the impertinent boy asked, "Do you name all the rocks around here?"

"Mostly. Get *down*, Farley."

With a nervous glance at Graven, who crouched nearby, the boy checked, "Is it safe?"

He simply pointed to the ground, and Farley nimbly descended the hulking redstone dog. With a short nod, Tupper repeated, "Why are you here?"

Farley lowered his head, then shot him a sulky look. "Because."

"Because why?"

"Because there's only girls left in the house," he muttered. "Carden and Ewert are at the quarry, and you're closer."

"Is something wrong at home?"

Making a face, Farley accused, "You sure are dense."

That was hardly fair, but Tupper was terrible at guessing games. "Yes, I am. So explain."

With his blue eyes flashing warnings, Farley marched right up and grabbed his brother's hand, moving it to the top of his head.

Realization hit Tupper like a bolt from above. His little brother had come to *him* for his first tap.

When a Flox's nubs first showed, his father or brothers were called upon to confirm their emergence. This was by far the most important rite of passage in every boy's life. In the absence of their father, Carden had confirmed the appearance of Tupper's budding horns, then taken him and Ewert on a for-men-only camping trip to celebrate.

Farley was eleven already, a late-budder and understandably anxious to be recognized.

Easily recalling how proud he'd been to earn his nubs, Tupper didn't hold back. Pulling his little brother into a fierce hug, he asked, "They broke through?"

"Yeah, I think so," Farley mumbled.

"Let me see."

The boy stood a little taller, and Tupper sifted slim fingers through white-blond curls, gently probing until he found two protuberances. While it would be a while before they'd show past his hair, the proof was there. Tupper leaned in and very carefully touched the tips of his horns to each tiny nub in turn, delivering the gentle taps that made Farley's first step toward manhood official.

"You have horns," he confirmed.

The boy puffed out his chest. "Bet they'll be even bigger than yours."

"Maybe." Tupper checked the nubs again, scratching lightly around them. "Do they hurt any?"

"A little, but I can stand it. I might be the youngest boy, but I'll be strongest."

Boastful as ever. Snatching his brother's hand, Tupper pulled Farley straight through the gate and along the cobbled road toward the workshop. There was a lot to do, and he was going to need help.

"Where are we going?" Farley asked as he gawked at the mountain haven's grandeur.

"First, we're going to show Frey. He's a brother, too."

"And then?"

Tupper had never particularly liked Farley, but this was no time to be miserly. Giving his younger brother's hand a small squeeze, he replied, "We'll celebrate."

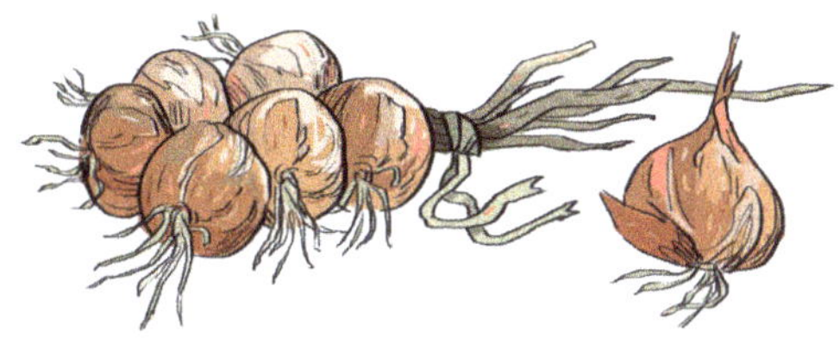

Farley refused to let on how nervous he was as his older brother hauled him past one unbelievable sight after another. Could someplace this incredible have been practically in his backyard all along? Obviously. Yet mind-boggling. It was like finding hidden treasure in the turnip patch. "Stingy!" he muttered.

Tupper glanced back sharply. "What?"

Thrusting out his lip, Farley accused, "You've been hogging all this to yourself! It's not fair!"

As usual, his slow-witted brother took forever figuring out how to answer, but finally, Tupper asked, "What would happen if we told?"

It took mere moments for Farley to reach the obvious conclusion. "Nothing," he sighed. "Everyone's too nubless to face the Pred."

"That's what I thought, too."

Farley searched his mind for some way to use this new knowledge to his advantage, but he couldn't even fall back on bragging rights. "So I'm in on a secret that no one wants," he mourned.

Tupper shook his head. "I want it."

"Maybe I should take it away," proposed Farley. "I have nubs now. Master Freydolf could hire me instead."

His brother actually smiled at him. "This isn't something you can take from me, but it's something I can share. For today."

Farley made a face, but at the same time, he was really glad he'd come. At least, he was until he followed his brother over a threshold, through a huge room with tall windows, and into a kitchen that smelled like blood.

He goggled at the enormous woman who lifted a red-streaked hand, using its back to push hair out of her dark eyes. Farley was alarmed, but Tupper exclaimed, "Aurelius's hunt went well! Good. We'll need the extra today."

"I was *hungry*," the Pred woman replied, giving the carcass she'd been trussing a satisfied slap. When she caught sight of him lurking in the doorway, her brows arched. "Who's your fluffy little friend?"

"Ulrica, this is my brother Farley Meadowsweet. Farley, this is Ulrica Harrow—Aurelius's wife and Freydolf's sister."

A smirk spread across the woman's face, revealing the tip of one fang. "Farley, is it?" she drawled. "My husband has mentioned you."

Farley gulped.

"I need Frey," Tupper announced. "Where is he?"

"Roped into hauling water for Aurelius's bath." Pointing to Farley, she asked, "Can I keep him?"

Tupper took way too long to say *no*, and then ruined everything by saying, "For now. I need to do some stuff, so he can help you until I get back."

Ulrica chuckled darkly, and Farley shot his brother a panicky look.

Tupper met his gaze steadily, then leaned close to whisper, "Show some nub, and be nice. I'll try to hurry."

Farley shook his head, but it was no use. Tupper was already gone.

A few hours later, Farley no longer feared for his life. Kitchen work was too ordinary to foster any illusions to the contrary. Ulrica had him peeling vegetables, stirring pots, scouring pans, and turning the big spit of meat over the hearth fire. He was good and grumpy that Tupper had skipped out on all his chores. It wasn't fair to make him work his fingers to nubs instead of celebrating them!

Finally, the front door creaked and slammed, and Farley caught the sound of Tupper's voice. "This way. He's probably still in the kitchen."

"Smells good," replied a familiar voice.

When Carden followed Tupper into the room, Ewert close on his heels, Farley tripped over his own feet in his haste to get to them. His oldest brother was the only father he could remember, and he'd wanted him more keenly than he could tell. Falling into Carden's open arms, he quavered, "You came?"

"Of course," the eldest Meadowsweet said. "Tupp tells us that you have important news."

"Yeah."

Carden asked, "So this is it? All the Meadowsweet men have come into their own?"

"Except for Freydolf," Farley sassed. "But there's no hope for him!"

"Picking a fight in a Pred's lair?" drawled Ulrica from her post by the hearth. "You're even more foolhardy than I was led to believe."

"I apologize, missus," Carden quickly offered. "He meant no offense."

"None taken," Freydolf said, shouldering into the crowded room. "Is Aurelius back yet?"

"Nay," Ulrica answered.

While the Pred conferred, Carden coaxed, "Let me see, Farley."

He stood to his full height, blushing and beaming as his biggest brother confirmed his budding horns with a congratulatory tap.

Ewert left off ogling every mote and mullion long enough to pull his brother into a headlock and check for nubs. The young man's eyes sparkled as he whispered, "Were you starting to worry if they would ever show?"

"Course not!" Farley lied.

"My turn?" inquired a deep voice, and Farley looked way up into Freydolf's face. The master sculptor's gaze was cautious, as if he wasn't sure of his welcome.

"Sure," the boy casually agreed.

Farley hadn't expected to be swooped up into the Pred's strong arms, but it was kind of fun to be able to look down on all his older brothers. Maybe someday, he'd be the tallest! He squirmed when Freydolf kneaded the tip of each new horn.

Delivering a sharp flick with a claw, the big man rumbled, "Congratulations, Farley."

Tupper stood off by himself in the corner, watching everyone lavish their attention on him without any trace of jealousy. Looking his serious-faced brother in the eye, Farley wrinkled his nose, then mouthed, "Thank you."

Like always, his brother took his time figuring out how to react, and when he did, it was only with a nod.

Tupper might be woefully dense, but he was a decent brother.

While they washed dishes together, Tupper scrutinized Ulrica's face. "You should rest."

"Don't fuss, little mother," she countered in an undertone. "I promise to excuse myself soon so you boys can wreak manly havoc for the remains of the day."

"Manly ... havoc?" he echoed uncertainly.

"I can remember when my boys first lunged into manhood," she eagerly shared. "The howls, the brawls, the bloodshed!"

Tupper's eyes widened. Ewert would probably dare Farley to do increasingly stupid things, and Carden was bound to give him the growing-up talk. They would make tonight as fun as possible for their little brother, but clearly not Pred-style fun.

He explained, "We'll play games and let Farley stay up late."

Ulrica casually warned, "Aurelius won't be able to resist adding spice to the mix. He wants to toy with the lad."

She was probably right.

While Tupper and Freydolf had hurried down into the quarry to find Carden and Ewert, Aurelius had hiked into Hayward to let Merona Meadowsweet know what had become of her son. Judging by the size of the pack he'd returned with, the merchant had requisitioned more than just the fresh bread that had accompanied their dinner, but he'd been very mysterious about the remaining contents.

Tupper shot a glance at the crowded table, where Farley and Ewert took turns coddling Rimbles. Aurelius looked on with an odd little half-smile, then leaned over to make a soft remark to Freydolf, who smirked conspiratorially.

"They're up to something," Ulrica whispered.

"I think so, too." Tupper didn't mind if Freydolf and Aurelius wanted to blend a few Pred traditions into today's celebration.

He just hoped their plans didn't extend to howls, brawls, or bloodshed.

Aurelius excused himself in order to escort his wife to their home. Freydolf invited the Flox to explore the balcony, leading the way to more comfortable quarters. Tupper hung back, looking on as his brothers slowly relaxed enough to act normally with one another.

Carden's calm acceptance.

Ewert's shrewd inquisition.

Farley's insatiable curiosity.

The trio monopolized Freydolf's time and attention, but Tupper didn't really mind. He couldn't. Not when his master's lively expression made one thing glaringly obvious.

"He's happy," Tupper whispered to the wall he leaned against.

His master might live in solitude, but he flourished in a crowd. His deep voice took on a teasing lilt as he debunked the rumors Ewert had heard being passed around between quarry workers.

Tupper mumbled, "Frey likes people."

He felt bad that he wasn't very good at talking. Maybe he should try to ask more questions? That had worked once before.

Plucking at the hem of his shirt, he tried to think of something interesting to say. Nothing much came to mind.

It was probably a very good thing Aurelius and Ulrica were here now. They weren't dull company.

"Tupper?"

He glanced up guiltily. Had he missed something important?

Hurrying to Freydolf's side, he asked, "Did you need something?"

"Aye," he replied easily. "You were too far away."

"Woolgathering?" asked Carden.

"Maybe." Tupper rubbed uncertainly at the base of one horn. Frey lightly tousled his curls, and he could feel his cheeks flame. "Probably."

His master said, "Your elder brother is about to make a Floxish speech, and unless my ears deceive me, Aurelius is skulking in the kitchen. See if he needs a hand, and tell him to hurry. I'm sure he'll want to hand down some words of Pred wisdom to young Farley."

With a quick nod, Tupper slipped downstairs.

Halfway there, he picked up the soft clatter of dishes, and as soon as he reached the bottom step, he caught a whiff of citrus. What was Aurelius doing in his kitchen?

"There you are, sprat."

"Frey wants you," Tupper reported.

Aurelius nodded toward the tray on the table, which was

already crowded with bottles and goblets. "Aye, but he wants *this*, as well!"

Tupper sidled up to see what he was doing. Various fruits lined the board, most already reduced to neat slices, although several rinds looked as though they'd been wrung dry. A pile of red, jewel-like berries glistened in the slanting sunlight, and steam rose from a bowl of amber liquid. Tapping its lip, Tupper whispered, "What's this?"

"Sweetwater. They make this beverage on First Continent for festive occasions. It's not difficult to make, but the ingredients are deucedly hard to procure on this continent ... unless you happen to have excellent connections."

Tupper wasn't sure why they were whispering, but he kept his voice low. "Which you do?"

"Aye. Shipped them in myself!"

"Is it good?"

Shaking back his ruffled sleeve, Aurelius dipped his pinky into the cooling concoction and popped it into his mouth. With a satisfied smile, he urged, "See for yourself."

Following the man's lead, Tupper dipped and licked. "It's sweet."

Aurelius hummed in agreement, then pulled their biggest pitcher close. Tupper propped his elbows on the counter and watched intently as the merchant confidently followed an unwritten recipe—muddling the berries, adding tart juices, pouring in the sweetwater, and finally adding fresh, cold water right to the brim.

After a quick stir, Aurelius dribbled a little into a teacup and passed it along. "Test."

The taste was like fruit and honey, tangy and sweet, and unlike anything in Tupper's admittedly narrow realm of experience. "It's even better than cider!"

Aurelius was positively beaming as he shoved a wine bottle into each of his coat pockets, then hefted the brimming pitcher. Whisking toward the stairs, he called, "Bring the goblets!"

Carden kept his remarks brief, probably more because of Farley's attention span than the presence of the Pred. Then Aurelius made a great show of filling everyone's cup and toasting the rascal's nubs. It wasn't until the second round that the Pred pulled something.

Tupper was the only Meadowsweet to witness Aurelius's sleight of hand as he dropped something into Farley's cup. He frowned in concern, but Freydolf caught his eye and raised a finger to his lips.

They were in on it together. All Tupper could do was watch.

Farley had chosen the tallest chair in the room for his perch, and it was easy to tell he was pleased with the party. He was already boasting that his celebration was better than any Flox's had ever been or would be.

Both Pred stole silently up behind him, but Aurelius simply passed him his goblet, "For you, young Master Meadowsweet," he purred.

Ewert caught the man's tone and stilled expectantly, which clued in Carden. The hush came too late to warn the victim, though.

Farley raised the cup to his lips and drank. An instant later, he yelped and tossed the goblet away.

Aurelius was ready and caught it, and Frey lunged to rescue the tumbling bit of blue stone that had been lurking within.

"Is that any way to treat carpeting," scolded the merchant. "It's a mercy it was only water this time."

Farley spluttered, "It ... it moved!"

"Naturally," Aurelius retorted. "Blue stone calls for fresh water."

Farley's wide eyes took on a shine. "For me?" he exclaimed, looking at Freydolf. "I didn't even see it! Where'd it go?"

"Hold out your hands," Frey directed.

Farley eagerly thrust out both, and Freydolf dropped a small, freshstone figure into them. It took a moment for the statue to find his balance, but once he did, he shook his mane at the boy, then pawed his palm with one tiny hoof.

"A horse!" gasped Farley. "Can I keep it?"

"That depends," drawled Aurelius.

"On?"

"On whether you have the nubs to visit the Cavern with me. Tonight."

"Where's that? What is it?" Farley asked suspiciously.

"Here." Tupper said. "It's a room as big as a town that's full of statues."

Carden suggested, "It would be a good place to play hide-and-seek!"

Aurelius rubbed his hands together. "I *excel* at hunting games!"

"I should mention ..." Freydolf interjected. "The sun's low, and the moon will soon be on the rise."

"Aye?" his brother-in-law returned innocently.

"Thrall will be waking soon."

Aurelius simply repeated, "Aye?"

Oh. Tupper caught on. This was perfect. Tests of bravery were often part of first tap festivities. Farley was in for one *very* memorable night!

15

A Different Path

At daybreak, Ulrica glided into Frey's home, catching him with one hip propped upon the window ledge, lost in thought as he gazed out at the sky. He turned, and bushy brows lifted in surprise. "It's early," he murmured.

She joined him in contemplating the view before quietly answering, "Aurelius was quite full of himself when he came swaggering home an hour ago. He regaled me with a full account of last night's escapades."

Her complaint really wasn't one. "You adore gossip."

"Aye, but I'd like to hear your version."

"I doubt he exaggerated," Freydolf said with a grin. "Aurelius was in fine form."

Ulrica chuckled. "He's *always* in fine form, but I'm more interested in knowing if you had as much fun as he did."

"More. I didn't want the night to end."

"Is that why you're still up?" Facing her brother's extravagantly-large bed, she folded her hands over her stomach. "Or is it their fault?"

"Nay. I couldn't sleep, so I insisted."

Her dark eyes studied the slumbering Flox. "They're nothing like my four sons. Too adorable!"

Freydolf huffed. "They're men, Ulrica. Don't trample their pride."

His sister flicked her fingers at the brothers. "Adorable *men*, then. Just look at them!"

All four Meadowsweets were sleeping off their night of carousing through the galleries. Farley nestled between Carden and Tupper, with Ewert snugged up close behind his younger sibling. Biggers protecting their littlers, though they all looked helpless by Pred standards, even with the various sets of horns curling against fair hair. Tupper slept with a small smile on his face.

Frey murmured, "He's happy."

"Aye," Ulrica agreed. "And with good reason."

"When I chose him, I thought he was all alone in the world. I was naïve enough to think his family didn't want him." The sculptor sighed. "They're at home together."

His sister waved off his words as if they were pests. "That boy *looks* as if he belongs with them, but he stays with you. Your lambkin has chosen a different path than the rest of his people, just as you did."

"He's changed my whole life."

"Aye," she returned evenly. "He's changed theirs, too."

The sculptor glanced at her in surprise. "His brothers?"

"Think about it," Ulrica said, keeping her tones light. "They followed that little lamb here and glimpsed a beguiling new world. When they go back to their valley, it will have changed. They'll be wanting more of what they found here. It'll lure them back."

Freydolf shook his head. "You make it sound like I'm trapping Flox."

She smiled indulgently. "They *would* make cute pets."

"You're even worse than Aurelius!" he grumbled.

"I'm right, though." Ulrica's expression grew more serious. "It's probably easier for me to see because you and your mountain caught me, too."

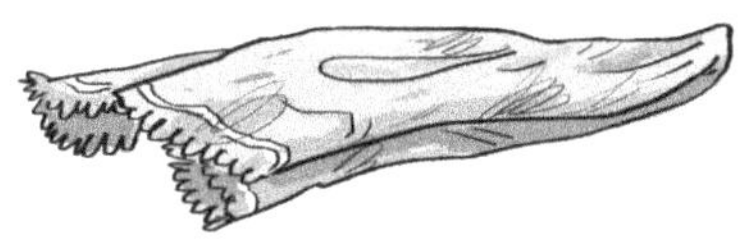

"Can I stay?"

"No." Carden and Ewert had excused themselves shortly after breakfast, but Tupper was beginning to doubt that Farley would ever leave. The sun was sinking fast, yet the boy lingered, clearly hoping to stay another night.

"I wouldn't mind," his little brother wheedled.

"No."

The newly-nubbed Flox was nothing if tenacious. "Master Freydolf can spare the room. Probably the coin, too."

That was entirely beside the point. "Go home, Farley."

"But it's only girls left there!"

"Which is why Mother relies on you more than ever."

His brother thrust out his lower lip. "It's more fun with all guys."

Tupper asked, "I wonder what Ulrica would think of that?"

Farley twitched noticeably, then announced, "I better get going!"

Finally. Tupper waved and called, "Do your best."

"Always do! Thanks, Tupp."

As soon as his younger brother disappeared around a bend in the trail, Tupper turned wearily toward his own home. His horns ached, his eyes burned, and all he wanted was sleep. Maybe Freydolf would forgive him for slacking off this once.

When he reached the workshop, he realized that Frey probably wouldn't even notice. The sculptor only had eyes for the brownstone griffin right now.

Boosting Rimbles up ahead of him, Tupper crept into bed for a much-needed nap.

Persistent scraping with a rough tool gradually pulled Tupper from a heavy sleep. Light glowed beyond his bed curtains, and he tried to get his bearings. Was it morning already? There was a soft rustle amidst the blankets, and Rimbles popped up to bat at his cheek. No, the sun hadn't set. Tupper tickled his kitten under her chin, then stretched, seriously considering just going back to sleep, but his fingers encountered something unexpected.

A rock?

Sitting up, he cradled the lump in both hands. It took a few minutes, but Tupper finally gave up trying to guess why the silent stone had been under his pillow.

He pulled aside the curtain and called, "Frey?"

Somewhat to his surprise, the man heard him.

"There you are!" Freydolf set aside his tools. "How are you feeling, lambkin?"

Ignoring the question, Tupper held up the chunk of dapple. "I found this."

"Ah. I wondered when you would."

"Is it yours?"

Freydolf shook his head. "Aurelius put it there, so we'll call it *his*."

"It's for me?" Tupper checked.

"Aye. What do you think of it?"

He trailed fingertips over rough edges as he searched for something polite to say, but nary a platitude came into his head. Finally, he said, "Aurelius isn't very good at picking."

"Nay," Frey agreed. "Is there any hope for it?"

Tupper blinked. "Do you need a piece of dapple?"

"Not in particular."

"What should I do with it?"

Freydolf sighed. "I'm not sure what to make of Aurelius's reasoning, but keep it close," he urged. "Let's see what happens."

"I can do that." Giving the stone a small pat, he pushed it back under his pillow and moved on to more important matters. With a rueful smile, he asked, "Is bread okay for dinner?"

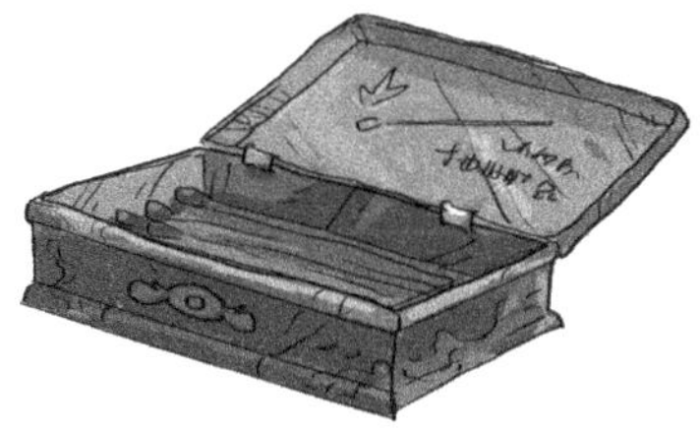

Tupper usually frittered away his free time with Graven down by the hen house, but dark clouds rolled in during the afternoon, and fitful rains kept him cloistered in the workshop. He could have escaped into the galleries—indeed, he was anxious to return to the room Morven had entrusted to him—but he chose to stay in the kitchen because Dag looked as if he needed the company.

Propping his back against Nott's still, gray form, Tupper stretched his legs across the wide hearth and scratched her golden' mate's ears. There had been enough daylight to wake Dag that morning, but the sunstone guardian was moping over its disappearance.

"The sun's still there," Tupper informed him. "Shining behind the clouds."

The wolf's tail wagged halfheartedly, and he pushed his nose against the boy's hand, begging for more attention.

Tupper was happy to oblige, for Dag's bristling fur was funny and rather fun to play with. It stood out in clumps around his body, like a bad haircut. No matter how much he petted and patted, the wolf's rough coat couldn't be smoothed. It was so different from Rimbles's fuzz, proof that Dag had been made before Freydolf had learned how to get fur to behave. The Keeper's early statues might not be perfect, but they had admirable qualities—friendliness, gentleness, and unfailing loyalty. Wild hair just gave Dag extra character.

As interesting as it was to think about a time when his master wasn't one, Tupper continued with the wolf's lesson. He was coaching the guardian on his future duties.

"There are eight hens and six chicks, but if all of Ulrica's eggs hatch, that's ten more peeps. Ember watches over the hen house at night, but during the day, the chickens like to wander. The best scratching is in the stable, which is safe, but they also like the gardens in the outer courtyard." Tapping Dag's muzzle for attention, Tupper solemnly warned, "Wide open sky is where the hawks wait."

Freydolf shambled into the kitchen, his arms weighed down with a stack for reading. "Light the lanterns in the balcony, lambkin?" he requested. "Rain always drives me to books."

"I'll start a fire, too," Tupper offered.

"Aye, that would be welcome. We may as well while away the rest of the day in comfort."

Tupper hesitated. "Can Dag come up with us?"

The sculptor's gaze rested for a moment on the golden wolf lolling before the hearth. With an expression of exasperated affection, he answered, "Aye. Let me put these upstairs, and I'll come back for Nott."

Smiling to himself, Tupper turned to the gray wolf. Gently folding his arms around her neck, he explained, "Frey was very young when he tried to find you. Maybe you're the reason he learned to listen better? That's good, isn't it?"

Her mate's tail wagged faster, and he bumped noses with her.

Before Freydolf came for them, Tupper begged Nott's forgiveness with a kiss, whispering, "Dag isn't the only one who loves you."

Maybe—just maybe—he heard a tiny sigh come from the silvery stone ... and an answering whine of encouragement from the gold.

The afternoon dimmed quietly toward evening, and Tupper basked in the relative silence. Peace was accentuated—rather than interrupted—by the crackle of their fire and the rustle of pages. As much as he cherished his family, their noise made it hard to hear the quieter voices of mountain and statue.

For several minutes, Tupper worried that he might come to dislike having visitors, but he shook his head. If he needed quiet, there was plenty in the galleries. He could find all he liked in Morven's winding passages.

"I found something!" Frey exclaimed, tilting his book toward the lantern as he quickly reread a passage.

Tupper stood and drifted closer. "What are you reading?"

"Old records from the archives," the sculptor replied distractedly. "I was looking for something else entirely, but I've found an entry about that room of yours. The one filled with unfinished statues."

"That's good." He knelt beside his master on the big couch and tried to read over his shoulder, but the text wasn't in Verit. "What does it say?"

Freydolf tapped the pertinent passage. "One of my predecessors took it upon himself to gather all the best unfinished sculptures from the galleries into one place. He calls them the Orphans."

"Why did he pick them?"

"He used them for training his apprentices. They're all excellent stones, master-quality choices."

"They have strong voices."

"Aye, and since all twelve mountains are represented in the collection, his potentials were exposed to all the subtle variations that exist between the magics, attuning themselves to their many nuances, gaining the best sense of ...."

His master might have waxed into further eloquence, but Tupper tugged at his sleeve. "What does that mean?"

Freydolf simplified. "His students learned to listen by spending time with the orphaned stones."

"That wasn't very nice."

The sculptor blinked. "I don't follow, lambkin."

"How long have the Orphans been in that chamber?" Tupper asked, frowning at the printed page.

Flipping to the front flap, then thumbing through the nearest entries, Freydolf replied, "Eight hundred years, give or take."

Indignation welled up in Tupper's heart. "That's a long time to listen and not answer."

Freydolf seemed confused, but then a glimmer of understanding shone in his eyes. The man actually paled. "Do you mean to say ...?"

"The stones keep asking, and no one listens." Shaking his head, he amended, "The students learned to listen, but their masters still left them unfinished."

The Pred opened and closed his mouth, then explained, "Each of those pieces is an unfinished masterwork. They were begun by great men, all Keepers. No one would have dared to touch the stones their masters claimed."

It was incredibly sad, knowing how many desolated hopes resided in that chamber. Tupper urgently met his master's gaze. "They whispered to me, wanting to know where their creators had gone. Stones don't understand time until they're marked."

Freydolf stared at him in frank astonishment. "What gave you that idea?"

"You tie them to the sun, the moon, and the stars with magic," Tupper reasoned. "Once they're wakened, day and night matter to them. Otherwise, they're only stones."

The Keeper grunted, then grunted again. "You're the first person I've *ever* heard speak from the stone's point of view."

Tupper was pretty sure Frey meant that as a compliment, but there were more important things to consider. Now that the boy understood about the Orphans entrusted to him, he needed to do something.

Latching onto his master's arm, he said, "*You* could finish them."

Freydolf winced. "Weren't you listening, lambkin? They're not mine to touch."

"No," he agreed. "They're *mine*."

Turning to face him more fully, he asked, "Do you realize how long it would take?"

"Bring them here. Give them a place. They'll be so glad!" Tupper blushed and bared his heart, softly adding, "I was."

With a soft growl, Frey gave in, and Tupper flung his arms around his bond-brother's neck.

Sighing softly, Freydolf begged, "Could we not tell Aurelius about this?"

"Our secret," Tupper pledged.

"Come see!" Tupper exclaimed, pulling at the Pred's hand as he led her through the hen house door. He'd finished clearing out the past week's litter and was scattering fresh straw on stone floors when he caught the soft peeping coming from under his broody hen.

Eager to share his news with someone, he'd sought out Ulrica. "They're hatching!"

"Aye," the woman replied in amused tones. "It's begun."

She lowered herself onto a clean bale of straw in the corner, rearranging her abundant skirts until they formed a nest. Crooking her fingers, she urged, "Bring me a puffball or two. I love their tiny perfection."

Tupper knelt beside the straw-filled basket, and the presiding hen fluffed her feathers and clucked at him. "Let me check," he coaxed, slipping his fingers under her breast and encountering the warm shells of her clutch. Locating a fuzzy lump, he carefully extracted it.

"They're black," he announced excitedly.

Village chicks were always yellow. He hadn't even known they could come in any other color. Of course, before meeting his master, Tupper hadn't known that men could have wild, dark hair and brown skin. Maybe people and chickens came in *other* colors too, depending on where they were from.

"Aye, this variety has richly-hued feathers," Ulrica replied. "You'll see for yourself, by and by. How many have broken shell?"

Tupper ferried over three chicks, and it was funny to watch the fierce woman coo over them like ... well, like a girl.

"Three is a good start," he said as she rubbed her cheek against one wee hatchling's down. "More are cracked."

Ulrica flashed a pleased smile, then commanded, "Get my brother."

"Really?"

"Aye, he might not admit it, but he always did dote on puffballs!" Fluttering her fingers at the door, she ordered, "Shoo! I'll mind things here until you return!"

Freydolf admired Tupper's ingenuity when it came to getting his attention. One moment, he was lost in a world where nothing existed save griffin feathers, and the next, he was staring cross-eyed at half a biscuit smeared with peach preserves.

"Bribery?" he inquired, relieving the boy of his offering.

"A break," the lad countered. "Ulrica says you might like to see what's happening in the hen house."

Frey chewed thoughtfully. "Is it those eggs of yours?"

"Yes."

"Perchance, are they hatching?"

"Yes." Tupper answered, eyes taking on a hopeful shine.

"Aye, I suppose I can spare some time." He set aside his tools and loosed apron ties. "Having eggs hatch is probably as monumental an event as waking stone around here."

"Then you should hurry," Tupper urged, tugging him along.

In the hen house, Freydolf found his sister crooning over a lapful of peeping chicks. Dropping to the floor beside her, he asked, "Nesting instincts on the rise?"

Her heel found his hip. "*You're* the nurturing one, big brother. Shall I tell this boy how many unwanted stone guardians you clucked over like a mother hen?"

Freydolf ducked his head. "I doubt he'd be interested in old stories like tha–"

"Yes!" Tupper interrupted. Returning to his master's side, he knelt and held out an egg in both hands. "Tell me?"

The man accepted the egg, cupping it to his chest to keep it warm. It twitched, and he turned it slightly, finding a tiny pip missing and a series of fine cracks fanning out from it. Freydolf blinked. "Will it hatch while I'm holding it?"

"Yes." Tupper patted his shoulder. "If you're patient enough."

"Aye," he breathed, awed by the prospect. He'd never

experienced something like this before, so he hardly noticed when Ulrica launched into a tale, laying bare his embarrassing past as only a sister could do.

Her voice faded into the background as he gave all his attention to the small life struggling to begin. Wasn't this, too, a kind of magic? The end of a tiny beak poked through the speckled barrier, and he touched it, setting off a round of urgent peeping.

It was tempting to hook the tip of one claw into the opening and tug, but Ulrica reached over and stayed his hand. "Let young ones find their own strength," she chided. "They must fight for the right to stand in this world with the rest of us."

Tupper pressed close to Freydolf's side. "But it's okay to let them know you'll be glad to see them. Do your best," he urged the struggling chick. "When you make it out, you'll be home!"

"Aye, we're right here," the sculptor called in a low voice.

Ulrica's rich laugh rippled through the shadowy hen house. "While you're at it, warn the bit of fluff to steer clear of Aurelius, whose interest won't be piqued until they're plump enough to grace the dinner table."

At Tupper's insistence, the woman returned to stories of Freydolf's youth, and the sculptor watched and waited until, with a sudden *crack*, a damp chick tumbled from its shell, sprawling limply onto his palm.

"Welcome to a wider world," he whispered.

They lingered in the hen house until Aurelius hunted them down, lantern in hand. All ten of Tupper's eggs hatched—three of them directly into Freydolf's hands. The sculptor found the afternoon nothing less than inspiring. He could hardly wait to get back to the workshop and his sketchbooks.

16

Baby Steps

Tupper's first hunting lesson didn't involve much hunting. Nor did it involve Aurelius. It didn't even take place outside. He sat on the kitchen table while Ulrica tied pretty green ribbons around his ankles. With such tight knots, he knew his new accessories wouldn't be coming off unless he took his knife to them.

"Aye, this brings back memories," Ulrica said. "I haven't played this game in at least a decade."

He did the math and cringed. "Is this a *baby* lesson?"

Her smile widened until fangs flashed. "If I were to back up any further, it'd be potty training."

Struggling with mortification, he asked, "Am I *that* bad?"

"Worse," Ulrica assured. "Which is why my husband won't take you into the woods until you've learned how to walk."

Tupper extended one leg and gave it a shake. Tiny bells twinkled brightly. "Won't these make me *more* noisy?"

"Not if I can teach you to think before you step. Try it."

He hopped down from the table, making a cascade of musical notes. Immediately, he was hit in the forehead with a small, green pea. Rubbing the spot, he stared at her in confusion. "What was that for?"

"Noise." Ulrica smiled serenely as she placed a bowl beside

her teacup. It held more peas ... and several pebbles. He gaped at her incredulously, and she smirked. "Aye. Those *will* sting, my lad, so think before you step. And do the dishes."

Tupper slowly lifted his foot. Bells jingled. Another tiny projectile bounced off his cheek, and he froze, eyeing her warily. She was a good shot.

"Be mindful how you move," she coached.

He took it slower this time, but the moment his hands were busy, he forgot about his feet.

Zing. *Ping*!

"Ouch!" he complained as the deadly-accurate missile clattered to the floor. That one had been a stone.

"Don't give yourself away lest the hunter become the prey."

Turning back to his task, Tupper asked, "Did your sons like this game?"

Another pea zipped across the room, colliding harmlessly with his horn. "Nay," Ulrica drawled. "But I did!"

Three days later, Tupper reached his limit and ran for it. His resources were few, but he meant to make the most of them. He found Aurelius in the upper loggia, taking in the view while going over some ledger books.

Doubling over, Tupper planted his hands on his knees and tried to catch his breath enough to speak. To his utter embarrassment, the green statue came to see what he was up to.

The merchant took one look and shook his head. "If you're walking musically enough to wake songstone, you're doing it wrong."

"I know," he said glumly. "Just don't throw something at me."

Aurelius set aside his book and laced his fingers together. "How are your lessons going?"

Tupper shook his head. "She's not teaching me. She's teasing me."

"And you came to whine?"

"No. I came to see if you can do a better job."

Aurelius's eyes lit up, and he leaned forward, elbows on knees. "Interesting."

This was exactly the reaction Tupper had been hoping for, and it must have showed.

"Don't look so relieved, sprat. If you're proposing what I think you are, you'd only be trading one tormentor for another."

"Yes, but when you explain things, I can understand." He shuffled his feet, setting off a soft twinkle of bells. Grimacing, he admitted, "I don't think I have what it takes to be a Pred."

The man waved his hand. "Close your eyes."

He obeyed, and in two heartbeats, he felt claws at his throat. No warning. No escape. "Aye, you're a poor excuse for a Pred, but so is Frey ... and he's an excellent tracker. Do you *want* to learn?"

"Yes."

"Will you submit to whatever rigors I deem best to surpass this monumental hurdle?" he inquired silkily.

Tupper might have been desperate, but he wasn't stupid. "Are you more interested in my success than in your own entertainment?"

"Nay," the man conceded. "But I'll enjoy Ulrica's mystification when your improvement robs her of her prey."

That was good enough for him. "When can we start?"

Late that very evening, Aurelius led the way down into the galleries. Tupper walked along under the shelter of Brand's feathered cape, jingling softly with every step.

Pausing at the turning into the long hall that led to the Cavern, Aurelius asked, "Are you even trying?"

It wasn't a mean question, but Tupper ducked his head. "Not really. Should I?"

"Aye. Show us what you can do."

Painfully conscious of Freydolf's and Aurelius's scrutiny, he took a few cautious steps, doing his very best to keep the bells at his ankles still. Even after three days' practice, Tupper couldn't manage it.

"Too stiff," sighed Frey.

"Too slow," Aurelius added.

Tupper squirmed under the criticism. "If I walk normally, they ring," he explained.

Tossing up his hands, the merchant exclaimed, "Exactly!"

He shook his head. Did that mean he was supposed to walk abnormally? After so many failed attempts, all he *wanted* to do was stand still. That seemed to be the only way to keep the little bells from tattling on his every move.

Freydolf hummed. "Maybe if we show him?"

"Aye, I came prepared for that." Aurelius set down his lantern and divested himself of boots and stockings. To Tupper's dismay, he also shed his shirt and knotted his hair. This was going to be a hunt? That didn't bode well.

The sculptor, who'd been barefoot all along, settled beside his brother-in-law, who produced four more ribbons strung with bells. He shook the strands, setting off their tiny peals. "Just like yours," Aurelius assured, and the two men knotted them around their ankles.

Tupper watched with interest as Freydolf levered to his feet, giving off the faintest tinkling. Aurelius snickered at him, and the big Pred rolled his eyes before picking up his lantern and walking off. It took a second for the boy to realize that he did so soundlessly.

Impressed beyond words, Tupper only managed a questioning look.

Aurelius's eyes were especially eerie by lantern-light, aglow with anticipation. He was definitely amused, or perhaps *entertained* was a better word. In any case, he wasn't making fun. "Take your time. Watch us," he invited. "See if you can imitate the way he moves. Or if you want more grace than lumber, watch *me*."

So saying, Aurelius lifted a finger to his lips, rolled to his feet with an exaggerated flourish, and sauntered after his brother-in-law. Silently.

Thankfully, it was a very long hall. If Tupper was lucky, he'd have time to catch on.

Freydolf and Aurelius strolled ahead of him, chatting about the agent's upcoming trip into Drom territory. Tupper jingled along behind them, face burning. He was the only one making any noise, but he couldn't figure out what he was doing wrong.

His master glanced back and nudged his companion. The two of them subtly exaggerated their steps, encouraging Tupper to steal the secret of their stealth.

Tupper rubbed at his horns and glanced up at Brand, who was similarly silent. The redstone warrior smiled sympathetically and made a rippling movement with his free hand.

Yes. That's how it was. Lithe. Limber. Loose. Aurelius's slow strides were as graceful as a dance, and Freydolf was just as perfect.

He blinked. He backed up. He thought it through again.

What if walking were a dance? Tupper loved to dance during the midsummer festival. Floxish steps involved springing, kicking, twirling, and stomping. But being nimble was different than being sneaky.

With this new frame of mind, Tupper stopped trying to figure out what was wrong with how he walked, and instead bent his concentration on learning the steps to a dance that all Pred seemed to know by heart.

The Cavern was even darker than usual, for the night was overcast. Neither star nor moon could stir the chamber's guardians, but Freydolf and Brand woke dozens of fire-bearers, who fanned out in a wide circle around Thrall. Their torches and lanterns defined the center, casting long shadows into the collection of statues.

Tupper shrugged out of his shirt and shivered, more from excitement than cold. The mountain's interior was cool, but not uncomfortably so. He could hear a faint crackling as fire consumed old wood, tinging the air with the acrid smell of smoke and pitch. A sneeze took him by surprise.

"Warm enough?" Frey asked, handing off his lantern to Aurelius while he shed his shirt and dropped it beside Tupper's.

"I'm fine." He touched his horns, then folded his arms across his chest, then rubbed his palms against his pant legs. Finally, he blurted, "Are you going to chase me?"

"What good would that do?" Aurelius scoffed. "You're the one who wants to become a hunter. Therefore, you'll have to do the hunting!"

Tupper thought back to the wild game of hunt-and-hide they'd played while his three brothers were staying over. Both these Pred were highly competitive, incredibly strong, and long of leg. He doubted he could keep up with them, let alone catch them. "But you're faster," he pointed out.

"That won't matter." Aurelius dropped to one knee, and Freydolf followed suit. Holding Tupper's gaze, Aurelius explained the rules of this new game. "We are your prey, and our ears are sharp. If you want to catch us, you'll need to move softly. Every so often, we'll ring our bells so you can track us through this maze."

Freydolf lifted his heel and struck the stone floor twice, ringing the bells at his ankle. "If your ears are sharp, they'll lead you straight to us."

"Mind each step," Aurelius warned, pointing with one clawed finger at Tupper's ankles, "If we hear you coming, we're free to move to a new hiding place. However, if you're silent, we cannot escape."

"Any questions?" prompted Freydolf.

Tupper thought it over. "You're going to let me catch you, but only if I can walk like a Pred?"

"Aye," Aurelius confirmed.

"Is this another baby game?"

"It's the sort of game fathers play with their children in

order to hone their skills," said Aurelius. "The rules grow vastly more complicated as a young hunter improves. Do your best to keep up!"

This sounded much more dignified than being pelted with peas.

Tupper nodded, and the men melted into the shadows. Moments later, their bells shook. Time to hunt.

He'd been a little frightened by the prospect of being turned into prey, mostly because he knew he couldn't elude Aurelius, even *without* bells on his ankles. But this was a game he could play at his own speed. Plus, it made sense. If he was noisy in the woods, the rabbits would bound away. He needed to learn how to sneak up on something if he was going to catch it.

They started easy, staying close but springing away every time Tupper messed up. Which happened a lot. He sighed in frustration as a long series of peals marked Aurelius's escape. Was he going all the way around to Thrall's other side? That meant a long walk.

Just then, two sharp jangles sounded, and Tupper held very still. That was Frey, and he was *close*. The boy rounded the bulky statue of a standing bear and nearly jumped. His master crouched against its pedestal, poised to flee at the smallest sound.

Tupper fought to steady his breathing and eased forward. Careful steps. A fluid dance. A dangerous game?

Freydolf looked wild, too ferocious a prey for his slender stalker. Tupper's heart skipped faster as he stole closer to the cornered man. His quarry's gaze bore into his, and he bared his fangs. It was an unnerving sight, but Frey was only pretending. Right?

The way Tupper's pulse raced, it was hard to be sure. Anyone else would have fled, but he determinedly closed the remaining distance, ignoring his master's low growl, stretching out his hand until cold fingers brushed hot skin.

"Caught you!" he muttered breathlessly.

"Aye," Frey acknowledged. "But can you keep me?"

Tupper's first triumph slipped from his grasp as the man roughed up his curls, then silently vanished into the deeper darkness toward the Cavern walls. He would have liked to hold onto victory a little longer, but Freydolf had boosted his confidence. This was a game he could win.

Ringing sounded somewhere nearer the circle of torches, and Tupper had his bearing. This time, he was going to catch Aurelius. With a grim smile, he quietly promised, "Here I come."

17

Night and Day

Tupper basked in a sunny patch down by the stream, his face tilted to catch the occasional breezes that found their way through the trees. Training had made for several short nights over the last few weeks, so dozing came easily. He sprawled on Graven's broad back while Rimbles draped herself across his chest, playing with his fingers. Tempting as it was to sleep, Tupper was expecting company.

Ewert had left word with his last milk delivery that he wanted to meet up during his lunch break.

Near noon, Tupper caught a faint change in the forest sounds and opened his eyes. Blinking at the clear, blue sky, he wondered if he would have noticed it before Aurelius's oft-baffling lessons. Lately, he was so focused on how much noise he made that his ears strained for the smallest sounds.

Turning his head just as Ewert emerged from the forest, he quietly called, "Hello."

"Tupp," the young man replied, his blue eyes taking on a speculative sheen. "Will he let me up?"

Reaching down to smooth his hand over the tiger's bristling fur, Tupper coaxed, "Ewert can pet you, right Graven?"

His guardian answered by turning his head away with a moody clicking of teeth.

"Good, good," he softly praised.

Ewert first strode to the edge of the stream, bending to dip in his fingers. He trailed them over a few blue stripes, murmuring, "Thanks, big fella."

"You remembered," Tupper said, sitting up to make room for his older brother.

"I'm not likely to forget something that keeps me on Graven's good side," Ewert replied with a wink. "So what's with the ankle decorations? Trying to adopt Haimish's fashion sense?"

"Not really." Tupper lifted a leg and gave it a shake. His green ribbon had worn out, so Ulrica had traded it for an orange one.

"Sleigh bells are out of season," Ewert prodded.

Knowing his brother wouldn't give up until he got more specifics, Tupper explained, "This is part of my training. Aurelius and the others are teaching me how to hunt."

"Oh? How's that working out?"

Tupper blushed and said, "They're very patient."

His brother didn't tease him as Farley might have. He only hummed and asked, "Do you like these lessons?"

"Yes."

Ewert unslung the small pack from his back. "Then you'll definitely learn a useful skill."

Rather flustered by his brother's near-compliment, Tupper changed the subject. "What's that?"

The young man withdrew a squat disk wrapped in cloths and offered it to him. "Does your master like cheese?"

Tupper straightened. He didn't really know if Freydolf liked it, but it was one of *his* personal favorites. "Maybe."

Ewert smirked knowingly. "The family who makes this cheese is willing to trade more for pears."

"Cuttings or fruit?"

"Fruit," said Ewert. "And they might be willing to part with one of their older cows by summer's end."

"How do they know we have pears?"

"I might have mentioned it," his brother replied nonchalantly.

Ewert had always been the family's best haggler. Even though he worked at the quarry, he still wove his share of baskets for the family business, and he had a knack for sniffing out good trades. This for that. Ewert's quick wits and keen eye had often benefited their family—and kept his own pockets lined with modest finder's fees.

"This round is a gift to entice the Keeper's interest. How many pears can you spare?"

"Some are already spoken for, but this is a good year so far."

"Interested?"

"Yes."

Ewert nodded. "Do you want me to handle things or make an introduction?"

"Who wants them?"

"The Quinces," he revealed, eyes sparkling. "They want to sell pear tarts during the harvest festival."

Tupper didn't know the Quinces well, so he shook his head. "You handle it."

"Usual terms?"

"Yes."

"Done." Rubbing his hands together, Ewert announced, "And at Carden's request, I have *another* offer to share. This comes courtesy of Melina, who's been talking you up to the Pennyflaxes. The front step of her father's bakery cracked over-winter, so he ordered a new stone from the quarry to replace it. Our Melina suggested having the mountain's Keeper carve the sides with their family's emblem.

"They asked for Frey?" Tupper asked wonderingly.

"Not exactly," Ewert admitted. "Carden says Melina hinted that a master's touch would bring them as much prosperity as their old oven has. They think it'll be good for business."

"Frey will probably want to do it."

His brother nodded. "If people see him working in town, they might not be so skittish in the future. Try to time his work day to match Carden's or my home day so we can lend a hand."

"Yes," the boy mused, scratching Rimbles behind her tufted ears. "Yes, that's best. Do you share a home day soon?"

"Two days."

As far as Tupper was concerned, it was a plan. Nodding firmly, he accepted on his master's behalf. "Two days."

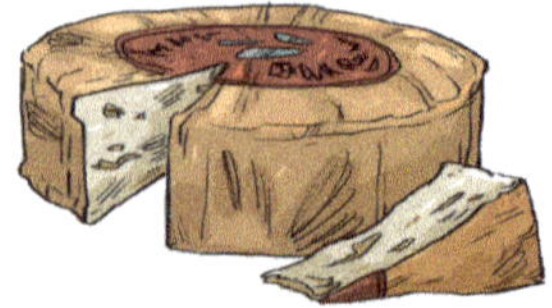

After Tupper returned from the stream and stashed the round of cheese in the kitchen, he thought it best to check on Ulrica. It wasn't that the woman couldn't take care of herself. Her husband certainly didn't hover and fuss—at least, not *all* the time. But Tupper thought maybe the reason Aurelius didn't worry was because he was relying on Ulrica's "little mother" to make sure she didn't overdo.

Now that he could move more softly, Tupper could check more discreetly. Depending on Ulrica's mood, he would either let her be or gently intrude. Today, he was surprised to catch the sound of her voice coming from the Harrows' small courtyard.

"I can't fault your taste. He's royalty," she said brightly. "And he has beautiful manners."

Tupper didn't catch any kind of response, but Ulrica kept right on talking.

"The scales are a little too exotic for my tastes, but I can understand why they'd appeal to you!"

The woman laughed lightly, and Tupper poked his head around the corner, curious who she was gossiping with.

"Aurelius checked his heel," Ulrica continued. "I wonder why he was never shipped overseas. My husband suggested several dull reasons, but I think it's much more romantic to think the noble was slain. Cut off in the prime of life, yet living on in starlight—an eternal prince, cast in starstone."

Tupper didn't see how dying could be romantic. Maybe it was a Pred thing.

Ulrica caught him peeking. "Don't loiter at the gate, my lad. Join us!"

"Sorry." Quickly—and silently—he crossed to stand before

the woman seated on the fountain's edge. Glancing at the freshstone mermaid, Tupper said, "I didn't know you and she were friends."

"Aye. We enjoy our little chats."

"That's good."

The water guardian lay in the shallow pool, her arms folded on the fountain's edge. Fluttering her lashes at him, she blew a kiss.

Poking abashedly at the base of one horn, Tupper asked, "Are you talking about your night guardian?"

Ulrica's painted lips curved coyly. "Naturally, since my day guardian is head over tail for the Basq prince!"

Water droplets spattered Ulrica's bare arm as the mermaid silently protested.

"You cannot deny it!" Ulrica laughed and lowered her voice conspiratorially. "From what I can tell, the last statue in that niche was a boorish Tisk who did nothing but sneer all day. Prince Phineas is vastly superior in every way!"

"I didn't know his name." Tupper gazed up at the starstone guardian he'd chosen from deep within the lower vaults. He'd assumed Phineas was some kind of mythical creature. "Are there people like him somewhere across the sea?"

"Aye, the Basq are real enough, and he's a fine figure of one," Ulrica confirmed.

The statue was dressed in strange clothes. A vest hung in long sections from his shoulders while leaving Phineas's broad chest bare, and loose pants were tucked into the tops of fancy boots with pointed toes. Patterned cloths had been twisted and tied into an elaborate headdress just above ears that came to long, slender points. What's more, the statue's skin wasn't entirely smooth. In several places, there were patches of reptilian scales, and his slanted eyes showed slit pupils.

"Basq," Tupper whispered, awed by this new tidbit of information.

These ladies were acting like the girls who clustered on the edges of the dance meadow during festivals, giggling together as they waited to be chosen as a partner. Tupper never would have expected a woman as fierce as Ulrica to be the same. Maybe all girls were silly about love?

That put a new idea into his head, and he blurted, "Did you see Aurelius first, or did he see you?"

Ulrica's brows shot up, but her dark eyes took on a soft shine. "*He* saw *me*," she confided. "But that's another story for another day."

"Which day?" he asked, suspecting the tale was a good one.

She waved off his question with a flutter of fingers. "Right now, I'm more interested in helping these two. Isn't there anything that can be done?"

Tupper wasn't sure what she meant. "Why do they need help?"

"Isn't it obvious?" Ulrica demanded in exasperation. "They're in love!"

Could that really be true? Guardian statues were usually meant to protect something, but that wasn't the same as loving someone. Of course, Dag protected Nott, and his devotion certainly seemed like love. But Freydolf had made them that way. Could two statues form such a bond on their own? The mermaid seemed attached, but she flirted with everyone.

"Maybe. And I don't think Frey would mind."

Ulrica heaved a sigh. "*Think*, boy. My brother's hardly an insurmountable obstacle."

It would have been so much easier if Ulrica just told him, but Tupper did as he was told, wriggling his toes as he gazed between the white prince and the blue mermaid. Was it because they were different species? Maybe the prince didn't like the mermaid, so it was a one-sided affection? But if Phineas got to know her, maybe they could ... oh.

These two were just like Dag and Nott. Freshstone only stirred by day, and starstone only woke at night. His heart sank for their sakes. "They've never met."

"And never shall," Ulrica confirmed. "At least, not left to their own devices."

It was then that Tupper realized something new about Freydolf's sister. She was a first-class meddler.

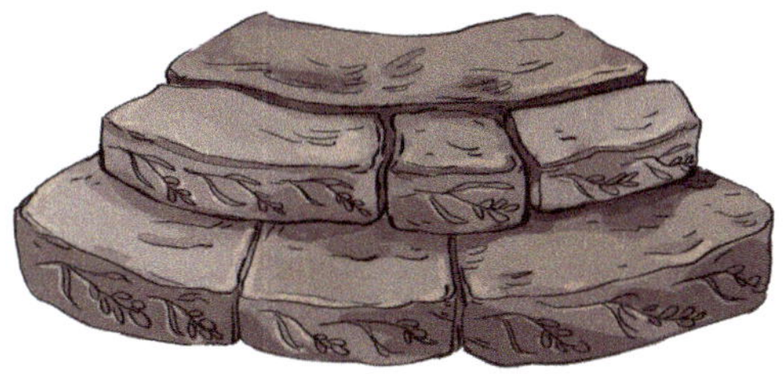

"Hey, mister! Is that heavy?"

"Aye, Farley. Stone usually is."

"Do you want help?"

"Nay," Freydolf patiently replied. "Let me take care of this part."

He was still a little awed that his favorite bakery had hired him. Aurelius had pointed out that a world-renowned master sculptor shouldn't be trading away his rare talent for paltry fees, but the merchant couldn't argue the benefits of making further inroads with the villagers.

The Meadowsweets were doing their utmost to smooth the way, but Farley's technique was definitely drawing the most attention. The lad seemed to have dared half a dozen of his agemates to come watch Freydolf work. Either that, or he'd bribed them.

"You sure, mister? 'Cause I'm pretty strong."

"I don't doubt that, lad. I'm only seeing to my own responsibilities."

"And I'm not scared," Farley boasted.

Freydolf feigned astonishment. "Of a rock? I should hope not."

Farley snickered. "Of *you*!"

"Aye, you've an impressive set of nubs," the sculptor agreed, carefully easing a long slab of gray stone away from the bakery's foundation.

"*See*," the boy said, his loud whisper pitched to carry. "Tupp's got himself a good place up top with Master Freydolf."

"But he's not from here," whispered one of the other boys.

"So?" Farley challenged. "He's lived here longer than you have!"

With a sidelong look at the knot of youngsters, Freydolf wryly reckoned he'd lived on Morven longer than some of their parents had been alive.

"He's scary," whispered a little girl with silvery curls.

"Naw. Watch me!"

That was all the warning Freydolf received before the irascible boy took advantage of his bent stance to launch himself right up onto the Pred's back.

"I thought you wanted to help me," he gruffly scolded.

"You were done, werntcha?"

"With the heavy lifting, aye. But there's much to do before sunset." Slowly straightening, he turned to face Farley's awed friends and offered, "You're welcome to watch, but it's a one-man job. I've no need for extra workers today."

Farley's arms tightened around Freydolf's neck. "Hey, mister ... if you *had* work, would you pay us in gold?"

"Aren't you forgetting something?" the Keeper said with a small smile. "I have Tupper."

"Tupp's *so* lucky," grumbled the younger boy.

He was rather touched to realize that Farley really meant it. Roughing up the lad's curls, he said, "Him and me both."

Freydolf found it ironic that his people were famous for making off with the threshold stones of conquered cities, symbolically placing those they defeated under their heel, yet he knelt on the ground outside Pennyflax & Quince in order to add decoration to their front step.

"Is this part of your mountain?" Farley asked.

"Nay, it's the bakery's front step."

"But it *used* to be yours?"

Freydolf glanced up from the sketch he'd made of the embellishments on the vast oven around which the bakery must have been built. "It used to be a part of Morven, and I'm Morven's Keeper. However, I don't make a habit of claiming every pebble and cobble in the vicinity."

"Could you?"

"What would be the point?" the sculptor asked, curious if the boy was going anywhere with this newest line of questioning.

The youngster knew how to twist words in interesting ways. "In the book that had a castle, there were people who had to give stuff to the king because the land was his."

Freydolf rubbed the back of his neck uneasily. "Aye. Taxes."

"But you don't take stuff."

"Nay."

"You could," Farley insisted. "But you pay us instead. Three of my brothers take wage from you, and my papa did, too."

The Pred relaxed somewhat, for this was apparently another of the boy's defense tactics. "Aye, the quarry offers good wages for those willing to learn stone-crafting skills."

"My papa works in the quarry," one of Farley's friends announced.

A little girl shyly said, "Mine, too."

"And mine," offered a boy who wasn't to be outdone. "*And my brother!*"

"Aye, that's good. Old Gruff and Carden tell me fine things about the men who work for me."

The kids elbowed each other and traded smug looks.

Thankfully, that satisfied Farley for the moment, and Freydolf was able to give his full attention to the stone. It was a good one, and the quarrymen had clearly taken care in dressing it. The sculptor caressed its smooth surface, envisioning the Pennyflax family's emblem, which would make a fine border. The rock didn't protest his plans, but it had been cut from Morven's foothills, too far from her heart to have much stubbornness. Still, its magic resonated faintly, enough to support Melina's claim that their mountain's blessing rested upon it.

If nothing else, Pennyflax & Quince had the Keeper's hearty approval. Melina's father had been pleased when Freydolf asked to be paid in bread.

With a bit of chalk, he sketched rough shapes in a repeating pattern along the face of the step, twining sheaves of wheat with the blossoms of both flax and quince. In no time at all, he lost track of the angle of the sun, his audience, and everything but his hammer and chisels. It wasn't until a hunk of bread was thrust under his nose that he looked up into his servant's smiling face.

Frey thought the lad seemed especially pleased with himself.

"Did you make a fine trade, lambkin?" he inquired lightly.

Tupper shook his head. "You make a fine centerpiece, Master Freydolf."

The subtle emphasis on his title was enough to make the man take notice of his surroundings. Or rather, to notice that he was surrounded. Blankets spread across the ground, along with an abundant picnic feast. All the Meadowsweets in Frey's acquaintance were accounted for, each prepared to tease him for his inattentiveness.

"We snuck up on you!" Dulcie cheered.

Ewert grinned. "I think this counts as capture! What shall we do with him?"

"Feed him, of course," tutted Merona.

Freydolf sat upon the stone slab and muttered, "How long have you all been here?"

"Ages!" claimed Farley.

"More like minutes," Carden countered.

"*Several* minutes," Tupper added. "And they weren't even quiet."

"Were you?"

His servant joined him upon the step. "No jingles."

Taking a large bite of bread, Freydolf mumbled, "At this rate, you'll be a better Pred than I ever was."

Tupper patted his arm. "If it weren't for the horns, you'd make a fair Flox."

"He's far from *fair*, little brother!" Ewert exclaimed, only to be shushed by Rachel.

"Not all wool is white," quoted Merona as she passed a filled plate to Dulcie, who carefully carried it to her Uncle Doff.

Edie volunteered, "There's a family in the village where I've been working with *brown* hair. They call the color cinnamon!"

"You don't say," said Merona. "How strange!"

Melina giggled softly. "I thought you were trying to assure Master Freydolf that he's *not* strange!"

Tupper's mother tutted at herself. "So I was."

"Hey, mister. Should we call *your* color molasses?" suggested Farley.

"Sounds tastier than pitch," Ewert said.

Melina patted little Yona's back. "How about pumpernickel rye?"

"Mud!" exclaimed Dulcie.

"That's hardly appetizing," Carden said. "What about coffee?"

"Too bitter," complained Farley. "I still say molasses!"

As more suggestions were offered, Freydolf ate his way through the first plate of food, then accepted a second from Tupper. All the while, he darted glances up and down the street, for their impromptu gathering beside the bakery was the object of village-wide interest.

Eavesdroppers loitered in gardens and doorways or found reasons to stroll past. It was the first time he'd seen more curiosity than alarm from these people.

"At this rate, I'll be taking a turn at the midsummer festival," Freydolf murmured to Tupper.

The boy beamed. "That's the plan. You can dance at Addy's wedding."

Freydolf shook his head in wonderment at the Meadowsweets' audacity. He may have been cast out as the black sheep of his own family, but he quite enjoyed being accepted as the brown sheep in theirs.

18

Put Right

The hour grew late, and Freydolf doused the lanterns, but not before lighting a single candle and setting it up next to his bed. Sleep would find him eventually, but in the meantime, he meant to spend a quiet hour or two on the little experiment he'd been fiddling with whenever time allowed. He weighed the golden egg in his palm before resuming the slow, patient task of polishing its matte surface. Sunstone didn't always cooperate with those who wanted to add a sheen to its surface, but Frey knew how to sweet-talk the stuff.

"You're getting sand in your sheets." Tupper's soft voice carried through the darkness.

Freydolf smirked but didn't bother glancing up. "Nay. At this stage, there's naught but dust."

There was a rustle and the pad of bare feet as his servant hopped up onto the big bed and crawled over to pat the blankets. "Crumbs," he accused.

"Aye, but you can't blame this rock for those," Frey argued. "They're from the bread I ate earlier."

Tupper held one of the larger grains up to the meager light, then sighed. "This is the third time this week I've had to take out your bedding."

Frey looked at him out of the corner of his eye. "Fussy."

"Messy," he accused.

"Just leave it," the man urged. "I can work on this side and sleep on the other."

The lad tutted disapprovingly. "You shouldn't sleep with pebbles in your bed!"

"Odd complaint from someone who sleeps with rocks."

"That's different," said Tupper, showing off the small chunk of dapple he'd carried along. "He's with me because you told me to keep him close."

Freydolf's heavy brows drew together. "Since when?"

Tupper scooted closer. "You forgot? But you're the one who told me Aurelius ...."

"Nay, nay." Reaching over to tap the dapple with the tip of one claw, Frey asked, "How long has *it* been a *he*?"

"Oh." Tupper cupped the rock in two hands and frowned thoughtfully. "Not long."

"Since when?"

The lad gazed at him solemnly, then shrugged. "Just now."

Tupper's fidgeting increased the moment Freydolf lifted Nott onto his workbench. The man must have noticed, for big hands slipped under his arms, hauling him up onto the high table next to the gray wolf.

"You're as bad as Dag," the sculptor teased.

"Are you going to break her?" Tupper asked worriedly. "Change her into something else?"

"Nay, I won't undo what's been done. But I think I've figured out how I can give her mate a little more range."

As Freydolf picked up hammer and chisel, Tupper asked, "Will it hurt?"

"She can't feel pain, but I don't want to distress her. I'll be gentle, lambkin." With a sympathetic smile, he said, "Since you're here, fussing in her mate's place, you can help me keep her calm."

"Where *is* Dag?"

"I closed him into a cupboard late last night and draped him with a tarp for good measure. I don't think he'd take kindly to what I'm about to do."

"Which is ...?"

Freydolf leaned past him and snagged his sketchbook, placing it in his hands. "Something simple. And stylish, since the design is Aurelius's."

It took a few moments to catch on, but when Tupper did, he brightened. "You're giving Dag a collar?"

"Aye, made from some of Nott's stone. If he carries a piece of her with him, he'll be freer."

Tupper stroked the gray statue's back. "That will be good for him, don't you think?" he whispered to her.

"I'll not leave her out," Freydolf said, tapping the open page. "She'll wear his sunstone."

"Even though she can't move?"

"Aye. Otherwise, she might miss him while he's chasing your chickens."

"Will he be awake at night, then?"

Freydolf hummed. "Only if I reapply my mark. I wasn't planning to, though. Ember has the night shift."

"But *could* you?"

"Aye, I suppose so."

Tupper thought hard, then shyly asked, "Do you think statues can be in love?"

Dark eyes warily studied his face. "I know of coupled statues. Did you find a pair in the galleries, because I should warn you ..."

"No." Tupper wasn't sure why the color was rising in his face, but he forged ahead. "No, I meant two statues who see each other for the first time."

Freydolf rubbed the back of his neck. "Should I go get Aurelius? If you're curious about girls, he has much more experience with the kinds of questions you might have."

Tupper blinked at his master. "Not *me*. I told you—a statue!"

"Really?" Freydolf asked, looking very relieved. "I thought you'd found your own twist to the hypothetical friend scenario."

"What's that?"

"Some lads are too embarrassed to ask delicate questions, so they pretend to be asking on behalf of a friend."

Tupper nodded. "I really *do* know a statue who might be in love with another statue."

Freydolf chuckled and said, "Then let's distract Nott with the latest household gossip. Tell me about these statues."

So Tupper told his master the unlikely story of a Basq prince and a blue mermaid, stroking unbending gray fur all the while. Between sharp taps and rasping, Freydolf asked several questions of his own, grumbled about his sister's matchmaking tendencies, and finally agreed to speak to the purportedly lovelorn statues.

Tupper was satisfied, but also a little curious. Tugging the Pred's sleeve, he whispered, "Are you embarrassed about girls?"

The man grimaced and whispered back, "Aren't you?"

He had a point. The boy hugged his knees to his chest and candidly said, "For now. I figure I'll get over it once I'm married."

"Tupper, I may have lied," Freydolf whispered.

The master sculptor hadn't expected to *find* anything while harvesting moonstone from Nott's underside, but many of the best discoveries take you by surprise.

When upright, the gray wolf sat on her haunches, her tail curving gracefully toward her front paws atop her pedestal. He'd been making careful progress right up through the stone when a shy burst of magic took him by surprise. A greeting. A bright personality he'd foolishly dismissed in the days of his apprenticeship. A shape he'd never seen clearly, for his mind had already been made up.

"Is it Nott?"

"Aye." Freydolf was enormously grateful that he'd had so much practice carving out eggs lately. "I'm going to take away a larger piece. It'll leave a hollow, but the wolf will look the same from the outside."

"Can you see her?"

"Probably as clearly as you can hear her." What a mess he'd made of this fragment of his mountain. It's a wonder Morven had trusted him with her keeping, given his early mistakes. "She was upside down and backwards all this time. Must have been confusing."

"Is she whole?"

"Mercifully," the man murmured. "She's just a tiny thing."

While the sculptor resumed his task, Tupper kept right on stroking the wolf's head and ears. "It's almost like she's having a baby."

Freydolf chuckled. "In a way, but she won't look much like her mother. This isn't a wolf cub."

"Won't Dag be surprised?"

"I know I am."

The boy's expression flickered, and he whispered, "She's nervous."

"I suppose anyone would be." Frey began crooning to the stone. "Let me bring you out into the moonlight, little one."

Tupper nodded. "I want to see you, too."

Freydolf went on, "Dag is sure to love you, no matter your shape. Your bond's stone-deep, so it'll hold."

"But they're still day and night."

"I'll mark them both," their creator said decisively. "I may not be able to bond twelve stones at once, but I'm master enough to manage two. So long as the sun or moon is shining, they'll be together."

What had started out as a simple project took much longer than Freydolf had anticipated, but that was mostly his own fault. He spent days crafting the rescued stone into its rightful form, lavishing the little female with all his accumulated knowledge and skill. After such a long wait, she deserved perfection.

Words could not express the enormity of his emotions, but he poured them into the stone. No more sorrow. Only joy.

She responded beautifully, and several nights later, Freydolf sent Tupper out to check the sky. The lad rushed back, practically skipping in his excitement. "The moon's high, and the stars are bright!"

"Aye." He hauled Dag into his arms, taking a moment to check the gold wolf's fancy new collar. "We'll come back for Nott, then wake her first."

"Does she still need the wolf?"

Freydolf nodded. "I'll not take her away from Dag, not after he's spent so long guarding her."

"Is that why you gave her a collar, too?"

The man grunted, a little embarrassed to have done something so sentimental. For all practical purposes, he'd stolen the she-wolf's heart and given it a form of its own. "Think of her wolf form as an elaborate pedestal. Nott will return to her whenever she needs to sleep."

"That's good," said Tupper. "Will Dag know the difference?"

"Aye, he'll know."

In the outer courtyard, Freydolf set the pair of wolves side by side, then called upon the magic that would wake Nott. Teardrops and starlight. Magic and mending. Bonds and blessing. He whispered her name, and she sprang to life, capering up his arm and across the back of his shoulders before reaching around to grab his nose.

"Excitable little thing," he laughed.

Tupper was smiling, too. "She's cute. Especially her tiny hands."

The monkey wrapped her tail around Freydolf's neck, then leaned way down to steal a pencil from his apron pocket. He rescued it, only to have her loosen the tie holding back his hair, and while he gathered it back up, she tested her teeth on one of his buttons.

"She's more mischief than I would have expected from such a wistful stone."

"She's happy," Tupper reasoned, holding out his hands. "Come, say hello."

Nott paused in her antics to stare at the lad with a solemn face, then leapt to his palms, using them for a springboard to launch herself onto his head. Perched amidst his curls, she wrapped her tail around one of Tupper's horns and busied herself with rearranging his fair hair until it stood up.

Freydolf chuckled again. "We'll show her to Dag as soon as the sun's up."

Tupper nodded very carefully so as not to unseat his passenger.

Nott pointed to the sunstone wolf, and Freydolf warmly said, "Aye, little one. He's yours, and you're his. Same as ever."

The gray monkey blinked a few times, then bounded straight from Tupper's head onto Dag's. She clambered all over the sleeping male, poking at his rough fur and peeking into his alert ears before paying special attention to the new moonstone collar he wore.

"Not much longer," Tupper promised.

Grinning broadly, Freydolf said, "Something tells me it'll be love at first sight."

They were more than halfway through one of Aurelius's better bottles when Freydolf recalled his promise. Glancing up from the egg he was polishing, he looked toward the darkened windows. Their latticed lengths mostly reflected firelight from where they'd gathered in the balcony, so he asked, "Clear skies tonight?"

"Yes." Tupper searched his face. "No moon, though."

"The heavens have taken pity!" said Aurelius. "I needed a respite from your wee shoulder imp."

"Nott isn't *that* bad," the lad defended.

"Nott should be renamed Naughty," groused the merchant. "She's far too fond of shiny objects."

"Meaning yourself?" inquired Freydolf innocently.

The man snorted into his goblet.

"It's too quiet without her," Tupper murmured, stroking Olexi's back with one finger.

Aurelius breezily said, "There are more than enough statues rambling about if you find present company lacking."

"I didn't mean that." The lad closed his book and hurried to the merchant's side.

Freydolf was proud to note that Tupper managed it without a single jingle. The bells had done their work, and Ulrica would soon be releasing him from his musical fetters.

Setting aside his assorted tools, the sculptor said, "I've been meaning to talk with that Basq in your courtyard. Do you mind?"

"Ulrica's dragged you into their little love affair?"

"Aye, in a roundabout way." Freydolf folded his arms over his chest. "There's no harm in seeing what that fellow might want."

"Oh, I could tell you," Aurelius said, draining his goblet. "But it'll be more fun to show you."

A minute later, they strolled across the deeply shadowed courtyard, aiming for the light Ulrica had hung in the niche beside the Harrow's gate to guide her husband home.

Aurelius kept one hand on Tupper's shoulder, placing the lad between him and Graven. Despite all attempts to get the two to make peace, mistrust lingered between man and tiger.

Halfway to their destination, Aurelius signaled a halt and soberly addressed the sculptor. "I do appreciate your provision of a night guardian for our domicile, especially in light of my upcoming absence. The Basq is a noble fellow and most courteous, but I don't believe his priorities are entirely straight."

"How do you mean?" asked Freydolf.

Aurelius struck a dramatic pose. "I shall demonstrate! You attack from the front, I'll come at him from over the back wall."

Freydolf's brows furrowed. "You expect me to *attack* one of my statues? I'm their Keeper!"

"It's for show," the other Pred soothed. "And the results will be telling."

"How many goblets did it take to inspire this plan?"

"I'm *not* inebriated," Aurelius retorted. "Merely invigorated. Let's see if this guardian's mettle is made of as stern a stuff as his visage." And with that, he darted up the closest set of stairs, dropped down onto the roof of an adjacent portico, and ran over the top of a wall toward his courtyard.

Graven surged forward, eager to pursue, but Tupper managed to grab the tiger's collar. "Is this a Pred game?"

"Aye. One that never gets old. For some."

"For you?"

Freydolf shook his head. "I never *asked* to be included in games of this nature."

"You were the prey."

"Always."

Tupper said, "We should hurry, or Aurelius will have no one to show off for."

The lad certainly had his moments, for the insight into Aurelius's foibles was spot on. "Softly, or he'll hide us for spoiling his hunt."

Silent as the shadows they slipped through, the two and their tiger approached the gate, cautious of the lantern-light spilling across the threshold. Frey leaned around the corner just enough to ascertain the guardian's position.

The starstone statue was no longer in his elevated niche. Phineas stood gazing at the beautiful mermaid perched at the fountain's pinnacle, one of her hands upraised in a graceful stretch. She looked as if she was trying to pluck a star from the sky. If his sister's stories were true, it was probably so she could give it to her prince.

Phineas's stance was relaxed, though his hand rested on the pommel of one saber. He hadn't noticed them, which was unusual. At the very least, he should have responded to Graven. Aurelius must have been waiting on them, for the merchant dropped into the far corner of the courtyard, going for the Basq with both blades drawn. Raising his stone sword, Phineas blocked one blow after then next, fending off his attacker with admirable ease.

And in so doing, he betrayed himself.

"Enough, brat." Freydolf strolled into the open. "You've made your point."

Aurelius sprang backward, gave his daggers a showy twirl, then sheathed them. "Brilliantly," he boasted.

Phineas stood uncertainly, his gaze darting from face to face in ill-concealed bewilderment.

Tupper hurried to the Basq's side and patted his arm. "Don't worry. It's just us."

The lad might have said more, but Graven slunk through the gate, crossing a line he wasn't supposed to, so Tupper hurried to chase him out of Harrow territory.

Meanwhile, Freydolf placed his hand on Phineas's shoulder, gripping it in a friendly way. "You are a capable swordsman, but I have a complaint."

Stiffening to accept the Keeper's criticism, the stone guardian bravely met his gaze.

In kind tones, Freydolf explained, "You should be defending the door that leads to my sister, not the lovely lady who graces this fountain."

By keeping the fountain at his back, Phineas had allowed his would-be attacker to get between him and the one he was meant to protect. The statue dropped to his knees so quickly, Frey's toes curled protectively inward.

"Nay, there's no need for that," soothed the master sculptor. "Your actions actually make this easier to ask. Do you want to meet her?"

The prince's reptilian eyes slanted toward the mermaid.

"Aye. If you don't mind more meddling, I can make that

happen." With a rueful grin, he said, "I seem to have developed a knack for bringing opposites together."

Phineas covered his face and abased himself, and Aurelius snidely remarked, "That would be yes. So what's his lady's name?"

"I've never checked," Freydolf admitted, promptly stepping into the fountain and wading closer to the freshstone guardian. "Bring a lantern, lambkin? It's too dark to see." Tupper ran for a light, and the sculptor glanced at the prince, who'd risen to his feet and hovered at the pool's edge. "A moment, sir. I'm sure you want to know even more than we do."

After a pause, the white statue offered a curt nod.

"Ah." Aurelius's tone took on petulant strains. "Ulrica will be deucedly hard to live with once she learns she's getting her way."

"My balcony is always available to you," Freydolf offered magnanimously.

Aurelius wrinkled his nose. "I refuse to go back to sleeping on the floor!"

"Best stay on my sister's good side, then!"

Tupper brought the lantern, and the sculptor held it aloft, poring over pedestal, fin, and scale in his search for a maker's mark. "It must be higher up. Have a look, Tupper?"

He clambered onto his master's shoulders, and they circled the freshstone statue once more. Finally, the lad exclaimed, "Found it!"

"Well?" Aurelius asked impatiently. "What does it say?"

"I can't read these letters."

Tossing his hands toward the starry sky, the merchant commanded, "Trade places."

With much grumbling and growling, Aurelius climbed onto Freydolf's shoulders, then snapped his fingers impatiently for the lantern to be handed up. Suspense mounted as he located the foreign letters. "Aye, it's here."

"We *knew* that." Freydolf tightened his grip around Aurelius's ankles, pushing up slightly to keep his heels from biting any further into his shoulders. "Skip to the important part."

Aurelius deigned to offer his brother-in-law a withering look, then peered down his nose at the Basq. With a grand sweep of one arm, he graciously revealed, "Your lady's name is Nerine."

19

Looking to the Future

Freydolf was used to Morven's mood swings. There were seasons of silence when all she did was sleep in the sun and soak in the moonlight, but more often than not, she made little bids for his attention. The mountain filled his days with fleeting impressions, and while Frey didn't exactly tune them out, neither did he pay them much heed. His former master had warned him to keep his wits where she was concerned. Balance was required to keep both self and sanity intact. That's likely why it took so long for Freydolf to realize that his mountain's whispers were important this time.

She could roar when it suited.

His bones still remembered the cry that had rattled through them on the night Master Platt died. The man might have been a cantankerous old Drom, but he had been Morven's choice, and her grief at his passing had been so keen, the very memory could still bring tears to Frey's eyes.

However, sadness wasn't what stirred her right now. There was an excitable quality to the frissons vibrating against his awareness. "What has you in such a state?" he murmured, setting aside his tools.

Her answer riveted his attention, then lent him speed.

The Keeper charged through the Harrows' front door, bellowing, "Aurelius!"

"In here," his brother-in-law sang out.

Following the sound of his voice into the sleeping chamber, he found the man packing for his trip.

Holding up two vests in slightly different shades of brown, he asked, "Chestnut or nutmeg?"

"Aurelius," he growled, voice deep with authority.

His expression sharpened, and clothing slipped from his fingers. "Well?"

"A poacher. Poachers," Freydolf corrected. Then he shook his head. "I'm not sure."

"You have rabbits aplenty," Aurelius blandly pointed out. "Those hunters are likely doing you a favor."

"Nay. Someone's tampering with stone."

"Can you tell where?"

"Aye."

Aurelius was already knotting his hair as he strode out the door. "Life here might be more exciting than I expected. Do you often entertain thieves?"

Freydolf hurried his steps, catching up to the other Pred in the courtyard. "We had to deal with them several times during my apprenticeship. They were actually part of the reason Platt created Graven." Leading the way, he jogged toward the summit and the slope beyond. "Since then, even legitimate traders have avoided coming here."

"Why hasn't Graven tended to this one?"

It was a very good question.

Morven's excitable promptings led her Keeper unerringly into the old quarry. Fern and root softened the otherwise angular surfaces on this side of the mountain, and the two Pred paused to listen.

"If they were here, they've fled," Aurelius whispered.

Freydolf nodded and led the way across green-carpeted stones to a place where one weathered wall had been scraped free of moss and lichen. Carvings that had no business being there were etched into the gray surface. He traced his hand over a rough band that must have been several days in the making.

"Interesting choice in motifs," Aurelius remarked.

Oldtree blooms blended with honeybees and doves. This wasn't vandalism. Freydolf could feel the sentimentality, the determination, the shy exploration of stone. Reaching the end of the line, where the work was the freshest, he could tell that the carver had settled into a kind of rhythm, as if they'd worked out how to get the look they wanted.

"Obviously local," Aurelius said.

"Aye." The Keeper was stunned. "This is very Floxish."

"Good?"

Frey pressed his palm to the stone. "There's enough potential here to have Morven in a furor."

Aurelius's eyes flashed. "They're still close enough to catch."

Was it possible that someone from the villages might have an interest in stone? Whoever it was, Morven wanted them. Gazing along the path their intruder had followed, Freydolf tried to remember which villages were closest. "Aye, they haven't gotten far."

"Kill or capture?"

Freydolf frowned. "I'll need to *talk* to them. They're a potential, and Morven is looking to her future."

"Then let's see what the future holds." Aurelius disappeared along the trail.

Following more slowly, the sculptor wished he'd thought to bring Tupper along. Interaction with the locals went so much more smoothly when the lad mediated, and this was a matter of towering importance.

Ever since the moonlit mountain had selected a Pred for her Keeper, their isolation had been nearly complete. If he could take on an apprentice from amidst the Flox ...!

With a jolt, he hastened his steps. Aurelius mustn't scare off the one who might very well be his successor.

Just then, his brother-in-law's voice rang out. "Frey! Come see what I found!"

"Don't be too zealous!" he pleaded, rounding a bend in the trail. "Please, I need to ...."

His voice trailed off at the sight of Aurelius's dagger resting against the throat of a wide-eyed Flox.

Aurelius prompted, "Didn't you have *words* for the one audacious enough to mark up your mountain?"

Relief turned Freydolf's knees to mush. As he sat amidst the bracken, he did manage to stammer out *one* word. "Y-you?"

"What happened to all that delicious righteous indignation?" Aurelius sighed gustily and asked, "Are you actually crying?"

He was. How could he not?

Morven liked tears in general, but especially from him. The mountain's magic swirled with delight over every salty splash. Many believed the Moonlit Mountain fostered sorrow, but in truth, she loved tears of joy best.

"Sorry," Freydolf said gruffly. "And for pity's sake, put away your dagger."

"If you insist." They were the right words, but Aurelius made no move to release his captive.

Frey frowned. "Aye. I do."

His agent didn't budge. "You have more leverage if the blade stays."

"I'm not going to force the issue!"

"Do you even plan to *broach* the issue?"

And so while his brother-in-law kept a deadly hold on his catch, Freydolf sheepishly met a bemused, gray-green gaze and muttered, "I apologize."

"I'm getting used to Mister Harrow's ... enthusiasm," Carden replied evenly. "But *I'm* the one who should be apologizing. I knew I was trespassing, but once I started ...." The young man spread his hands wide in a helpless gesture.

"You couldn't keep away," Frey finished for him.

This was actually happening. Morven had found someone to answer her call. He glowered at Aurelius. "Let him go!"

This time, the Pred's arms fell to his sides. Carden turned to the merchant and met his unrepentant smirk with an unoffended smile. Then, the Flox knelt beside Freydolf, offering a clean square of cloth. "I'm very sorry, sir."

Frey waved the handkerchief off, saying, "No need. She likes them, but more to the point, she likes *you*."

"The mountain?" Carden asked thoughtfully. "I've been wondering about that. I keep dreaming about the dragon in the Cavern."

Dreams, too? Freydolf could hardly believe it. Tupper's own brother, a man Frey already counted as a friend, was poised to become his first student. *If* he was willing.

"Let me test you," he begged. "It's mostly a formality, for the affinity is there ... and getting stronger."

"What does that mean?"

Frey gently gripped the young man's shoulder and announced, "You've the makings of a sculptor, Mister Meadowsweet, and I'm in need of an apprentice."

They hauled Carden home and dispatched Tupper with a message for Gruff, excusing the eldest Meadowsweet from his usual duties for the rest of the day.

"Stay over," Aurelius insisted. "There's much to discuss."

Freydolf was sure his brother-in-law would put a grandiose spin on the work of sculptors and the role of Keepers, but the merchant stuck to more basic things. The initial lecture reminded Freydolf of when Tupper was only ten—innocent and ignorant of the rest of the world. Carden may have been older, but he was no wiser. Aurelius began with tales of the sea and far-off lands where other mountains were also touched by magic.

The day passed in a blur that left Carden looking dazed, but dinner revived him somewhat.

"You went fishing, Tupp?" he asked as Ulrica slid more fillets onto his plate.

"Yes."

"It's good."

His younger brother simply nodded and passed a bowl of pickled vegetables. "Ulrica makes these. They're good, too."

Conversation moved on, but Freydolf's gaze lingered. He and Carden weren't the only ones left reeling by the day's events. Tupper was quieter than usual—pensive and withdrawn.

The evening became less of a lecture and more of a review. Tupper crawled across the balcony floor, rearranging carpet balls in a rough approximation of a world map. "The dazzle is too close to the dapple, boy," Ulrica directed. "That mountain is much farther up the coast and would be unbearably cold if not for their hot springs."

"It's always winter there?" Carden asked.

Aurelius said, "Nay, but their summers are deucedly short."

"And pleasant," said Ulrica. "Which is why we bought a house there."

"I thought you were from a Pred city."

"We were." The woman smiled serenely. "But we cut our moorings and left bloodied stumps where each grasping tentacle once writhed."

"And with *that* delightful mental image firmly in place, let's turn our attention back to Far Continent," Aurelius suggested.

As the informal lessons continued, Tupper played quietly with Olexi, who discovered that he could push the smooth stone balls across the floor.

Although the eldest Meadowsweet sibling was putting a brave face on it, Carden looked more than a little overwhelmed, but Freydolf didn't have the heart to interrupt. This was how it should be. Potentials needed to be plunged into a world beyond their imagination, for this awe would sustain them through the tedium of training.

Many lads loved the *idea* of sculpting magical guardians, but few willingly endured the long years of hard work required to attain mastery.

Carden would. Frey was certain that Morven had chosen well.

The Flox would hew to the sculptor's traditions, flourish in his role as apprentice, and spend the rest of his life impressing peaceful memories, noble ideals, and loving ways upon stone, turning them into something immortal. The very idea settled Freydolf's heart, and he wondered if Platt had felt the same when a gangling young Pred showed up unannounced at the Statuary's gate. The future seemed brighter with Morven's continued happiness secured.

"Frey!" Aurelius called, yanking the sculptor from his musings. "Is that acceptable to you?"

Both he and Carden were looking at him, but Freydolf had no idea what was going on. "What?"

The Flox patiently repeated, "Our midsummer festival is less than a week away. Can you wait until then for my answer? I'd like time to get Melina used to the idea."

"Aye," Freydolf agreed. "Take whatever time you need."

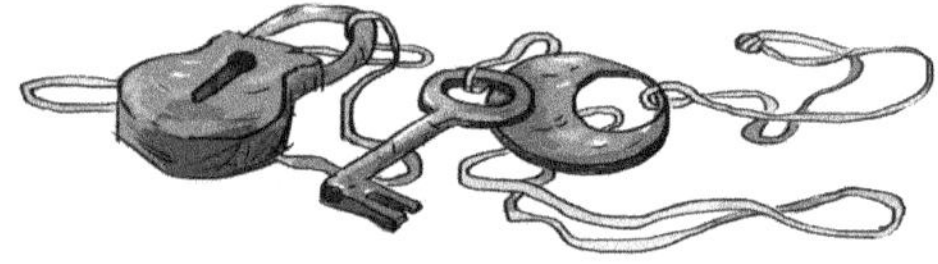

Late that night, Freydolf woke to a telltale patter and pounce, and he soon had a small, gray monkey turning his loosened hair into a nest. With a sigh, he eased over to make room for Tupper. He'd assumed the boy would need to talk, but he couldn't resist voicing his usual complaint. "Your bed is over there, lambkin."

Tupper wriggled down under the covers anyhow and whispered, "Frey?"

"Aye?"

"You're going to be Carden's master?"

"Aye."

Tupper hesitantly asked, "Are you glad?"

"Aye." Frey couldn't lie. Giving the lad's shoulder a poke, he asked, "Do you mind?"

"Maybe." Tupper fidgeted a little, then owned up. "Probably."

Even with nothing but starlight to see by, Freydolf could tell that the boy was struggling to sort out his feelings. It took little imagination to guess where this was headed, but he let Tupper find his own words.

"Will he live here?" the boy asked.

"Nay, not in the workshop."

"In one of your houses?"

"Aye, if he's willing. It would be best if he moved his family to the Statuary. An apprentice's hours are long, and he'll want his loved ones close."

"Melina can cook better than me. And she's a real mother."

"Aye, that's so."

Finally, Tupper spoke his fear. "Does that mean you don't need me anymore?"

Freydolf was proud of the lad for asking straight out. It couldn't have been easy. "I'm not trading you for Carden, lambkin."

"Oh," he breathed, the single syllable a sigh of relief.

"Did you trade me for Aurelius when he barged in on us?"

"No."

"But you're glad *he* came?"

"Yes."

"This will be a little like that, except now the Flox will outnumber the Pred."

"Unless Ulrica has twins."

Frey chuckled. "Aye, that would even us up. But this workshop will remain our bachelors' quarters. I fully expect you to manage my household until the day you run off to wed that wife you've mentioned."

"No, I'll bring her here."

"Will you now?"

"Well, not to the workshop," Tupper corrected. "We should probably get a house of our own."

"Aye, that's a sensible plan."

"Otherwise, the babies might wake you up when they cry."

Freydolf grinned. "Already planning for children?"

"Lots."

Then the full weight of Tupper's plans hit him. "You want to raise your family here?"

"Yes. This is home."

Old memories and feelings meshed, and the Pred suddenly understood how much power he had over this boy. He'd once trembled at his father's voice, listening in as his banishment was formalized and his name was struck from the family ledger.

Tupper was essentially asking not to be cast out.

With a soft groan of sympathy, Freydolf found the boy's slim hand and guided it to his own chest. Holding it over his heart, the Pred swore, "I will never send you away. This is *our* home. No matter what happens in the future, that will not change."

"Is this for promises?" Tupper asked, pressing.

Freydolf nodded. "It's used for the most solemn of oaths. If I break my word, you're allowed to carve out my heart."

The lad tutted softly, but said, "Good." Then, he snuggled down, taking up half the pillow.

"When I said you could stay, I meant in the workshop," Freydolf grumbled, transplanting one clingy monkey onto the bedpost, only to be butted in the shoulder by a wee ram. "Your bed's still over there."

But Tupper was already asleep or—more likely—feigning it in order to keep close.

Frey had never been able to deny the lad anything, least of all comfort, so he surrendered, stroking bright curls and kneading at the base of each horn until he was sure Tupper really had dropped off.

Olexi patrolled.

Nott returned to nest-building.

Freydolf's dozy thoughts took an interesting turn. What if Carden's newfound affinity for stone was just another manifestation of Tupper's? Could a boy capable of calling magic into dull stones also coax it into the souls of those who were near or dear? Assuming this was even possible, had Frey been affected?

The man closed his eyes with a smile. Aye. His life had taken on the shape Tupper deemed best.

If this was magic, Freydolf was quite willing to embrace it.

Shortly after sunrise the following morning, Aurelius stealthily entered the workshop and took note of all the signs of mischief. Freydolf slept with one arm flung across his eyes, the other curled around Tupper's slender shoulders.

Most of the time, the lad acted like Frey's mother, but this was one of those instances when his brother-in-law might be mistaken for Tupper's father. With a nostalgic smile, Aurelius reminded himself that he'd soon be back to having his beauty sleep interrupted by a tiny bed-invader.

A small, gray monkey leapt from the nearest bedpost, and Aurelius caught her. "Was this some form of protest for keeping you away from your mate?" he softly inquired as she frisked up onto his shoulder.

Nott must have spent half the night ferrying figurines from the balcony, for master and servant were surrounded by a confetti of colorful stones. The pair slept on despite the mess, or perhaps the rocks were the reason behind their peaceful expressions.

"Frey would sleep sweetly on a bed of rubble, and the sprat's been chipped from the same block."

Nott poked at Aurelius's earring, sending the green gem swaying.

He spared her a warning glance. "I've bigger business than *you* to tend to this morning, so none of your guff. Go find your chicken-hound."

Aurelius turned her out, then strode to the kitchen, making a mental note to ban monkey guardians as baby gifts.

Carden sat alone at the table, stroking Rimbles's tufted ears as he gazed out the window. "Good morning, Mister Harrow," the young man offered, his voice low and drowsy.

"Did you sleep?"

"Yes, thank you."

Dispensing with further niceties, he asked, "Any questions?"

Smiling wryly, he said, "More than I can keep straight."

"Understandable. Make lists if necessary, since I won't be able to answer most of them until I return."

"The trip to Drom?"

"Aye. I leave for the capital tomorrow, so we'll have to settle up afterward, but I want to make a few things clear so you can make an informed decision."

"Like?" Carden prompted.

"First and foremost, we're prepared to pay you during your years of apprenticeship."

"Would my wage be comparable to what I earn at the quarry?"

"Nay." Aurelius withdrew a slip of paper from inside his breast pocket and slid it across the table. "*This* will be your wage."

Carden took one look and said, "This is too much."

Taking the seat across the table, Aurelius chided, "I thought Flox were more business savvy than that, Mister Meadowsweet."

"This is three times my current wage," he rejoined, still polite but showing signs of ruffled pride. "Is this meant for a bribe? I don't need one."

Aurelius folded his hands together and patiently explained, "This isn't coercion. Nor is the sum inflated in order to soften the blow of a housing allowance. You and your wife can have your pick of residences."

The Flox shook his head in confusion. "Even more reason to refuse such a ridiculous sum. I don't need it."

"Ah, but you *will*," Aurelius countered.

"For what?"

"For starters, magical stone isn't cheap. When the time comes, you'll be expected to purchase your own practice blocks. An average upstart would also be accumulating books and arranging for tutors, but you're fortunate on both these counts. Frey will give you access to the Statuary's archives, and my wife and I are fluent in all the trade languages. Speak with Ulrica. She's already teaching your younger brother the basics of Terse."

Carden sat up straighter in his chair. "I need to learn languages?"

"This isn't a simple trade, Mister Meadowsweet. You're entering a worldwide community with a long history. Frey will have you studying the lives and works of your predecessors, and you'll need to learn all you can about the other eleven mountains. There are the business aspects, too, but I can make myself available to you for a modest fee."

"Aren't we getting ahead of ourselves?" Carden asked warily. "I don't even know if I *can* sculpt stone."

"Didn't you say you are a wood-carver? You were modest, but your brother seemed to indicate your skills are better than average."

"I've always enjoyed working with my hands."

Aurelius smirked. "If you still enjoy it after your master has you embellishing cobblestones with daisy chains until your back aches and your knuckles bleed, we'll call it destiny!"

"Why would anyone decorate cobbles?"

"Look around more carefully," the merchant recommended. "The Statuary has been the proving ground for countless apprentices. Anytime you see a repeating pattern, chances are it was assigned as practice for a promising young potential like yourself."

Carden gazed around the room, which had carved borders around window and doors, along the baseboards, and even an elaborate medallion on the ceiling. "Not exactly glorious work, but neither were their efforts wasted. This place is beautiful."

Aurelius was pleased that the Flox showed sense. Too many apprentices complained over endless and seemingly pointless projects. Of course, most potentials were snapped up at a much younger age. Carden's temperament was a good match for Freydolf, who would probably have been too soft to push a lazy boy. "Morven must know what she's doing."

"Excuse me?"

He waved off his musings and reiterated, "Save up for stone.

And there's also the possibility of travel expenses. At the very least, you should visit the other two mountains on this continent. More if Frey will spare you."

"This is still hard to take in," Carden murmured. "The quarry is the farthest I've ever traveled from home."

"There's another thing to consider. If you accept Frey's offer, you'll be consorting with Pred. You, your wife, your daughters—there's a decent chance you'll be shunned. Also, you won't be able to visit your families as often as you once did, and winter means total isolation."

Carden nodded to acknowledge the possibility.

"If you'll permit it, I can promise that your children will be well-educated and well-traveled. However, these benefits may make it difficult for them to find suitable marriage partners when they're of age."

The Flox searched his face. "You considered these same things for your wife and child before moving here?"

"Aye."

"And you chose to come despite the drawbacks."

"Clearly."

Carden said, "I'll admit there would be difficulties, but we wouldn't be facing them alone."

Aurelius was pleased. This man might have questions, but he didn't have any doubts. Carden *would* accept. "Aye, Ulrica would enjoy another woman's company, and with three children ...."

"Four," the Flox corrected. He cleared his throat and bashfully admitted. "Melina's expecting again."

Aurelius offered his palm. "Congratulations."

Carden's clasp was firm. With a small smile, he said, "You called this isolation, but the way I see it, we're well on our way to starting our own village."

Tupper hurried through his usual duties to free up his afternoon, then plunged down through the thick forest on Morven's southwestern slopes. With Aurelius gone, he needed to collect their milk delivery and empty the fish traps, but he had his heart set on something else as well.

Today was one of those bright and burning summer days that drew a boy unerringly to water. Tupper wanted a dip.

Dense foliage and vines overhung the narrow deer-track that was the quickest route to his farthest trap. He and his cats slunk through the greenish half-light, making no sound until he caught the sharp splash of the waterfall just ahead.

Turning to scratch the soft fur under Graven's chin, he coyly asked, "Wanna get wet?"

The tiger's head lifted. His ears flicked forward, but he pretended not to care.

"Race you," the boy coaxed, taking a few backward steps.

It was a silly challenge, but Graven liked to show off almost as much as Aurelius did. The big cat's broad forehead butted Tupper's chest, knocking the boy onto his rump, and with a bunching of sinewy muscles, the tiger sprang right over Tupper's head.

He laughed, scrambled to his feet, and dashed after Graven, reaching the edge of the creek in time to see the hurtling guardian plunge into the deepest part of the pool beneath the falls. Chill water splashed in every direction, spattering Tupper's face and arms. It felt good.

Shimmying out of his sweaty clothes, he called, "Leave some for me!" Their private swimming hole wasn't very big, so it was mostly full of tiger. Tupper waded in to where Graven's striped haunches jutted above the rippling surface, his colors even brighter now that they were wet. Dunking himself, Tupper shook water from his curls, then worked his way around the tiger, scooping water over all the exposed bands of blue stone.

"That's better, isn't it?"

The tiger went back to ignoring him, but no one was fooled. Glancing toward the shore, Tupper smiled at the sight

Rimbles made. His kitten paced unhappily along the edge of the stream, lifting one paw and then the other, trying to shake off the water. Even though the water couldn't hurt her, the little sunstone lynx always avoided getting wet.

"It's okay, honey-tufts," he promised. "I won't stay in for long."

He truly meant it at the time, but it was almost a lie. It had been so long since he'd simply played. Noisy leaps and splashes were great fun, but then it occurred to him that Pred probably swam as quietly as they walked. Needing to see for himself how it might be done, he moved more stealthily, sneaking up on crayfish in the shallows and chasing a frog downstream. There, he found a pool of still water filled with tadpoles and lay in the warm mud, watching them dart back and forth.

Now that he was doing something as sensible as soaking in the sun, Rimbles joined him, curling up between his shoulder blades for a nap.

Eventually, Tupper noticed how much of the day had gone, so he washed off under the waterfall, gasping for breath in the rarefied spring water. Sprawling on a sun-warmed stone to dry, he hummed a little tune for Graven's songstone stripes, luring the tiger from the water. Dropping a kiss on his pink nose, Tupper pulled on his clothes, then led his stone friends downstream to fetch the milk and fill a stringer for the evening meal.

The refreshed young Flox's hair was still wet when he ambled through the kitchen door and found Freydolf lashed to one of the chairs with rope. Tupper almost dropped all the fish on the floor. "What happened?" he gasped.

Freydolf growled, "*Ulrica* happened."

The woman whisked into the room with a saucy jingle of bells that meant she wanted to be seen and heard, a small, wooden box in her hands. "Found it!" she exclaimed. To Tupper she offered a wide smile and purred, "You're *just* in time."

"What are you doing to Frey?"

With a swirl of full skirts, Ulrica sat across from her brother and haughtily replied, "Only what's good for him!"

Tupper was at a loss. He should probably try to help his master, but he was no match for the Pred. Choosing his words with care, he asked, "Is that for you to decide?"

"Aye, listen to mother," grumbled Freydolf.

"It's no use trying to hide behind him. Our little mother will side with me." Extracting some small bottles and brushes from her box, Ulrica added, "Now, hold still, or I'll cut off your fingers to get at your claws."

Tupper tossed the fish into a basin and set the milk bottles in the sink, fully prepared to throw himself between the siblings if necessary. In stern tones, he reminded, "Frey is a sculptor. He *needs* his fingers."

"Aye, but tomorrow is his birth festival, so he needs them gilded."

The boy's shoulders sagged with relief. Treating his master to a look of sheer exasperation, he asked, "Is *that* all?"

"Nay. That's only the half of it! Look at the ridiculous clothes she wants me to wear!"

"Please, do," she sweetly invited.

One look at the fine clothes hanging from the orange door was enough to drive Tupper to the sink where he washed his hands twice, just to be extra clean before touching.

Freydolf's new tunic was sewn from a light fabric that slipped across the boy's fingers. The white shirt was edged with extravagant copper trim that would look nice with the gilding. "Fancy," he murmured, giving the tunic an approving pat.

"Yours is hanging behind his," Ulrica said.

Startled, Tupper folded back the pristine cloth to find a much smaller version. His tunic looked just the same, but it was cut from green cloth. Aurelius knew it was his favorite color ... and never teased him for liking nice things. Glancing hopefully at Freydolf, Tupper said, "These would be very good for a wedding. And the edges will shine with the torches during the festival dances."

Freydolf's gaze softened. "Aye, weddings and finery do go together. You'll do your sister proud."

"As will you," Ulrica jibed.

While stealthily untying the man, Tupper told Ulrica about Flox wedding traditions. Freydolf stayed put and admitted to learning some local dances from the dawnstone Triad. Ulrica brushed off Tupper's wheedling to have his own nails gilded to match his master's, for it was *only* for birthdays. And thus, harmony between siblings was restored.

20

Well Met

"Lend a hand, Tupp?" Ewert wheedled.

"With what?" Even though it was only mid-morning, he and his older brother has been to nearly every garden in and around Hayward, collecting contributions of flowers for the festival bower in the town's square.

"Missus Butternut needs her lettuces brought in."

Tupper fidgeted. He'd come down the mountain extra early in his work clothes to lend Mother a hand, and she'd turned him over to Ewert. Gathering armloads of blossoms was one thing, but why should he pick a neighbor's lettuce?

Only one answer made sense. Tillie Butternut was Ewert's bride-to-be, and he was trying to impress her parents. With a small sigh, Tupper squatted beside the long row of greens and started picking. It would be quicker to simply do the work than argue the matter.

They were nearly finished when three girls minced out the Butternuts' front door in bright, new dresses. Ewert stood and dipped his head, casting sheep eyes at Tillie. Tupper had noticed that for all his talk of marriage as barter, his older brother was definitely sweet on the girl with silvery curls and a saucy smile.

"You remember Tupper?" Ewert asked, kicking his leg.

Tupper slowly stood to say hello and was immediately distracted by how much taller he was than Pearlie and Luce. Tillie's sisters were about the same age as he and Farley, but they looked sorta small and dainty. After living with Pred, it was strange to be looking down on people for a change.

The girls blushed and giggled. Pearlie swished her skirts and coyly said, "Hello!"

Luce dimpled and offered a shy wave.

Tupper nodded.

An awkward little silence hung over them, but then the sisters traded a look, shrugged, and flounced off, Tillie trailing after them.

As soon as they were gone, Ewert elbowed him. "You should have told them they looked pretty!"

"Did they?"

His older brother rolled his eyes. "I thought you wanted to meet some girls."

"But I know Pearlie and Luce. We grew up together."

Ewert shook his head and grumbled something about late bloomers. "I gave you an opening! You could have at least asked them to save you a dance tonight."

"Maybe. But there's usually lots of girls who want to dance."

"One's as good as another?"

Tupper caught a glimmer of what his brother was getting at and nodded. "So far."

"When that changes, so will you," Ewert said wisely. "I'll just go in and give all this to the missus. Wait here."

He nodded again, peering off in the direction the Butternut sisters had disappeared. Hard as it was to imagine, maybe Ewert was right. Maybe someday he'd change his mind, but right now, Tupper knew one thing for sure. He didn't want a girl who didn't pick her own lettuces.

When Ewert finally ran out of odd jobs to delegate to his younger brother, Tupper rushed back to the Meadowsweet home. Dulcie and her father had posted themselves beside the garden gate, and Carden scolded, "You're nearly late."

"Sorry," Tupper mumbled, giving one of his niece's long curls a playful tug. "Are those flowers for the bower?"

Dulcie held out a lopsided bouquet. "I picked dem for Auntie Ree!"

"You did a good job finding her favorite colors."

The little girl beamed happily, and Carden urged, "If you're going to change, do it now, Tupp."

"I'll hurry," Tupper promised.

Grabbing a partial bucket of water and clean towel from the kitchen, he ran up the rungs of the ladder into the loft that had always been the boys' room. Since Farley was the only brother left at home, their mother had started storing more of her basket-weaving supplies and garden produce up here. Sheaves of rushes and drying herbs smelled nice.

Stripping off his shabby shirt, Tupper squatted beside the pail, quickly and carefully rinsing off. He let the water cool his skin as he ran damp fingers through curls that had already grown too shaggy for his mother's standards. Thankfully, Merona Meadowsweet was far too busy with wedding preparations to take her shears to them. He'd been treading stealthily as a Pred, avoiding her notice so he could keep them.

Patting dry, he slipped into his new finery. The green cloth felt good against his skin, and the tunic did all the luxurious draping and fluttering things Aurelius's clothes tended to do. Tupper wished the merchant had been there to thank, but he understood why the man was in a hurry to get his trip into Drom over with. It would be sad if he missed his baby's birth.

Aurelius's hasty departure might *also* have had something to do with his wife's graphic descriptions of what she'd do to him if he delayed his return for anything more frivolous than dismemberment, evisceration, or personal fatality.

Ulrica certainly had a way with words.

Tupper peeked out the widow, which faced the mountain. He

loved everything about this festival—the gathering, laughter, games, cakes, music, and especially the dancing. But he was standing in his old home feeling homesick for Morven.

Rimbles was safe under his pillow, but would Nott behave? And what about Graven? It might be a problem if he followed Freydolf and Ulrica down to the village.

This would be the first time his master attended the midsummer festival, and Tupper wanted to make sure the Pred and his sister were welcomed. The last few years, Frey had simply given his servant the day off and waited up for him late into the night at the Apprentice Gate.

"This is better," Tupper earnestly declared.

Eager to include his bond-brother in all the fun, he sneaked quietly downstairs, replacing the bucket in the corner of the kitchen and his towel on the drying rack before easing out the door.

Merona turned and her voice carried out into the garden, "Is that you, Tupper?"

But he was already as good as gone. And his curls were safe.

Pred training was paying off in surprising ways.

Carden's whole family strolled along the road out of town in order to meet their honored guests, who soon rounded a bend in the forest. Tupper's heart swelled with pride, for the Pred were resplendent in their festival attire.

Ulrica walked with her head high, bells tinkling at both ankle and wrist. Now that Tupper had been through her training, he understood that the woman's musical accessories were a promise of peace. If she'd been attacking, no one would have heard her coming.

Tupper was a little awed by the sight of his bond-brother. Ulrica had done something to his hair, so it was less bushy than usual, its fullness falling in loose waves behind his shoulders. The fancy white tunic made him look even darker than usual, and his claws flashed copper. Frey looked elegant ... and entirely ill-at-ease with himself.

Carden stepped forward. "Welcome to Hayward, Master Freydolf." To Ulrica, he said, "I'd like you to meet my wife, Melina."

The women stared interestedly at each other, but Dulcie wriggled excitedly into the spotlight, holding high a bunch of orange and white flowers. "For you, Auntie Ree!"

Ulrica blinked several times, then muttered several things to her brother in a language no one else understood.

Frey sighed and answered in kind. Holding out his hands, he invited, "Come up here where your Auntie can see you better!"

"Ah!" Dulcie's eyes rounded. "You're shiny!"

Freydolf balled his hands into fists, trying to hide the gilding on his claws.

Carden's eyes lit up. "That's right, it's your birthday."

"Aye."

"Up, up!" cried Dulcie, hopping impatiently. He obliged, and she carefully extracted an orange flower from amidst the rest in her bouquet and tucked it behind Freydolf's ear, then kissed him noisily on the cheek. "Happy birthday, Unca Doff!"

"Thank you, Miss Dulcie," he murmured. Clearing his throat, he turned to Ulrica. "This is my sister, your Uncle Ree's wife. Her name is Ulrica Harrow."

"Auntie Ree is bee-yoo-tee-ful!" Dulcie exclaimed in admiring tones. "Can I put flowers in your hair?"

Tupper had been watching Ulrica closely, for it wasn't like her to be so quiet. He wasn't sure why she was holding back, but the little girl's question was the Pred's undoing.

She melted, but did her best to hide it by sharply asking, "You're not afraid of me?"

"Nuh-uh."

Ulrica's lips quirked, and she demanded, "How old are you?"

Dulcie struggled for a moment but managed to get three fingers free from the rest. "Dis many!"

With a muttered oath, the woman turned to Melina. "I dearly hope you and I can reach an accord, for I wish to keep her."

Melina giggled, and Freydolf groaned. "She's not a pet, Ulrica."

"Nonsense. I've never seen anything more adorable!"

Carden winked at Tupper, then casually announced, "And this is Yona."

Ulrica slapped her hands over her mouth, dark eyes wide with want.

Tupper plucked at Melina's sleeve and slyly said, "You don't mind if she holds the baby, do you?"

"Of course not," she replied with a light laugh. "Yona should meet her aunt."

The Pred expertly gathered the curly-topped youngster into her arms, bracing her against one shoulder. Yona reached for the woman's earrings, which swayed temptingly. Ulrica captured her hand and crooned nonsense in several languages. "Now, I understand why my brother is a toothless old fool."

"Unca Doff has teef!" Dulcie argued, poking her finger into the man's mouth. He obligingly curled his lip to show off a gleaming fang. "See?"

"Aye, you're right," Ulrica agreed, boldly flashing her own. "Tell your auntie what she should do. She's never been to a Flox village before."

"Do what I do," the child suggested. "It's easy!"

So they strolled into Hayward together. Dulcie perched on her uncle's broad shoulders, and Yona played contentedly with the tiny bells on Ulrica's bracelet. Carden and Melina took one side, and Tupper sidled up to the other, escorting their guests to the family's garden. Maybe it was silly to try to defend Pred from a village full of skittish Flox, but the Meadowsweets had always been protective of their own.

Freydolf nudged his sister and murmured, "You're being surprisingly polite. I expected you to have the entire village cowering by now."

Ulrica's brows arched. "I've visited more cultures then you have toes, and every one of them trembles at the sight of our race. My husband overcame many obstacles and became an accomplished diplomat for your sake. Fear is bad for business."

"So you learned politeness from Aurelius?"

Her eyes narrowed. "Did you think me incapable of restraint?"

Freydolf was spared from placing his foot in her waiting snare by Tupper, who only left their side to procure refreshments. He trotted back to their shady niche balancing a fresh round of delicacies. This time, there were tall glasses of water in which cucumbers and herbs floated and a plate of festival cakes.

"These are good," he promised, whisking Yona away from Ulrica in order to free the woman's hands. He plopped down in the grass at their feet and told his niece, "Aggie's bringing you something nice, too. See? There comes your auntie."

A blue-eyed girl in a new dress with a yellow sash hurried over. Tupper's little sister was still shy, but she no longer feared Freydolf. Indeed, he was rather pleased that she seemed to prefer him to Aurelius. "Good day, Miss Aggie."

"Hello, Master Freydolf," she replied, peeping under her fair lashes at his companion.

"Please, meet my sister, Ulrica Harrow," he introduced.

The girl dropped a small curtsey and politely said, "Missus Harrow."

She inclined her head, asking, "*Another* sister? Just how many Meadowsweets *are* there?"

"Lots," Tupper replied, turning over the baby to his little sister. Aggie tied a bib around Yona's neck before patiently feeding the girl sips of the same flavored water Tupper had brought for them. "It's hot," he explained. "So it's Aggie's job to water the babies."

"Sensible," Ulrica replied, giving the girl an approving nod.

Aggie was patting the little one's pink cheeks with a damp cloth when Carden strolled over, escorting his mother.

Merona Meadowsweet tutted over the Pred woman and bluntly asked, "When's your baby due?"

"Early next season," Ulrica stiffly replied.

Merona nodded and explained, "Your husband shared the news back when Farley ran to Tupper for his first tap. He invited me to attend your child's birth." When Ulrica didn't immediately respond, the Flox woman gently pried, "If you're Master Freydolf's younger sister, we're probably agemates. Have you been through this before?"

Ulrica's chin came up defensively. "I am not ashamed to say I have four sons, all grown."

Tupper's mother blinked at her words, then looked to Freydolf. "Have I said something offensive?"

He gave his sister's arm a poke with one gleaming claw. "Nay, marm. Our relatives favor small families, so she's sensitive about bearing a fifth." Ulrica's elbow caught him in the ribs, and he winced. "Leave off, little sister. Didn't you come here to be free of mother's ridiculous censure?"

"Aye."

"Then don't be embarrassed. Least of all with these good people. Or has it escaped your notice that Tupper has even more siblings than Aurelius?"

Merona frowned slightly, then tapped her eldest's arm. "Carden, be a dear and fetch Wynn and Lilia."

Tupper smiled in a manner most suspicious, and Freydolf flicked one of his horns. "What's this about?"

The lad scooted close enough to lean against his master's leg. "Just more Meadowsweets," he replied innocently.

Carden returned leading two children with telltale gray-green eyes, and asked, "Shall I?"

"By all means," Merona replied, giving the boy and girl an encouraging nod.

"Master Freydolf, Missus Harrow, I'd like you to meet my uncle, Wynn Meadowsweet. He's twelve."

Ulrica's eyes slowly widened, and then she narrowed them at Merona. "Your sibling?"

"My late husband's, actually."

Placing his hands on the little girl's shoulders, Carden continued, "And this is my Aunt Lilia. She's nine, the same as Aggie."

"Siblings the same age as your children," Ulrica murmured.

"And this is usual?"

"Common as curls," Merona assured.

Ulrica sat a little taller. "My first grandchild will mark his first year this coming winter."

"Congratulations!" Merona gestured between the girls, cheerfully sharing, "The whole family had bets on whether my mother-in-law or I would deliver first."

"The whole *village* laid wagers," Carden interjected. Winking at Aggie, he added, "And we won!"

Tupper patted Freydolf's knee. "Aggie's five days older than Lilia."

"Children come when they come, and we're glad for each one." Boldly resting her fingertips on Ulrica's stomach, Merona said, "This one will have more aunts, uncles, and cousins than he or she can count."

"Don't underestimate this babe," the Pred retorted. "I'm sure my child will have an excellent head for numbers."

"Like their father?" Freydolf teased.

"Aye, like a true Harrow," Ulrica declared proudly.

Carden whispered his thanks and turned loose his aunt and uncle.

Merona knelt before Ulrica, gazing up into the woman's dark eyes. "Send for me when you know your time is close. I've been helping with birthings since I was Aggie's age, and I've a sure hand and a strong voice, should you need shouting at. Also, I hear there's a fair chance that Melina will be there as well." She took the Pred's hand in both of hers and kindly promised, "You won't travail alone."

Ulrica placed an upraised palm beneath her heart and bowed her head. "That puts my mind at ease, Missus Meadowsweet."

"Call me Merona."

"And I am Ulrica."

Freydolf breathed a sigh of relief. Another accord had been reached, and even better, Merona had let slip a tantalizing tidbit. Catching Carden's gaze, the sculptor softly inquired, "A fair chance?"

The young man took a moment to realize what he meant, but then a slow smile spread across his face. "Fair as Flox."

Judging by Tupper's glad smile, that mean yes. Carden would accept the apprenticeship. It was by far the finest birthday present Freydolf had ever received.

Tree climbing. Treasure hunts. Footraces across a fallow field. Ball games in the meadow. Tupper didn't bother to participate in any of the many games and competitions organized for the afternoon. He cheered on Farley instead ... and watched girls.

Some helped their mothers serve food or sell treats, industrious in the midst of the fun. Others led along younger siblings or kept their grandparents' glasses filled. Those who were freed from such responsibilities clustered together in giggling groups.

Silvery curls, soft as moonlight. Creamy hues that reminded him of dazzle. Glossy gold, like wet sunstone. Buttery blondes with endless ringlets. There were plenty to choose from, but as the day progressed, the pickings grew slim. One by one, he dropped each girl from consideration, and all it took was a glance. From them. At him.

It surprised Tupper how much a person could say with a glance. For just an instant, their eyes gave them away. He could understand their fascination. He didn't mind their curiosity. But he refused to allow certain things into the precious haven that was his home. Dismay. Pity. Scorn. Fear.

Freydolf deserved better, and Tupper wanted ... more.

With a soft sigh, he squared his shoulders, comforting himself with knowledge he hadn't had before his master chose him. Once upon a time, Hayward was the whole world, but there were other villages, each with their fair share of girls. It wouldn't be easy finding someone good enough in the weeks that remained before Ulrica's baby was due, but Freydolf was trusting him to pick a good servant. He'd do his best.

Farley dropped down beside him, cheeks pink from exertion. "Didja see me?"

"Yes."

"Whatcha lookin' for?" his younger brother asked curiously.

Tupper shrugged. "Just looking."

"I heard Mother saying you're taking Carden and his."

There was no sense denying it, so he nodded.

"That's mean," Farley grumbled.

His brother's tone surprised him, and Tupper searched his brother's face. "Why?"

"On account of Aggie!"

He glanced around and spotted his little sister sitting in the grass beside Melina, showing Dulcie how to braid flowers into a crown. "Aggie?"

"She cried when you left. But she stuck with Dulcie 'cause you asked her to. Now, you're taking her babies away." With a surly glare, Farley said, "She's been crying again."

He gasped, "Aggie!"

"You're probably the worst brother in the whole world."

Tupper leapt to his feet but paused long enough to flick one of Farley's nubs. "But you're the best."

"Glad someone noticed!" the boy shouted after him.

It took three tries to locate Mother, who'd been chased out of the kitchen by Edie and a couple of Meadowsweet aunties. He found her leaning her elbows on the low garden wall behind the house, gazing off toward the oldtree forest. She smiled at him, but then her gaze drifted to his hair and sharpened.

Before she could send him for the shears, he blurted, "I want to barter!"

"For what?"

Tupper knew it was poor technique to let someone know how much you wanted something, but he plucked at his mother's sleeve until she turned, opening her arms wide. He had to bend down to fit into her embrace, and she held him close. Would she hear him out?

"Well, then?" she prompted.

"It's a good bargain. Please, say yes," he begged.

"Gracious, child! What could you possibly ...?"

"Aggie," he interrupted, his voice cracking with adolescent earnestness. "Let me have Aggie."

21

Blades and Bells

With the setting of the sun, the Flox migrated to the village center, where bearded old-timers lit numerous torches and four small pyres. Assorted musicians clustered under the bower, tuning their instruments in preparation for the evening's entertainment.

"Will you dance?" Ulrica sweetly inquired.

"Not if I can help it," Freydolf muttered.

He unobtrusively steadied her as she lowered herself onto the long bench Carden and Ewert had shifted from the Meadowsweet's garden. The sturdy seat was newly made and clearly designed for persons of Pred proportions, so Dulcie needed a boost up from her young uncle.

"Is this good?" Tupper asked.

"Aye, very defensible," she automatically replied. With Pennyflax & Quince at their backs and the entire square in full view, she could rest easy.

Freydolf chuckled. "Expecting an invasion?"

She pinched his arm. Only a fool dropped their guard. Every Pred knew that much. Or should.

Tupper's fingers tapped in time to the sprightly tune that opened the first set, and Ulrica smirked. If what Aurelius had shared was true, Frey's lambkin possessed hidden depths, but she had no idea where they might be lurking. "Do you like to dance, boy?"

He nodded, then invited, "Watch me!"

"Aye."

While the boy hurried over to one of his many sisters, Ulrica turned to her new pet for distraction. Dulcie chatted about light, sweet, insubstantial things. The bakery was her grandfather's, and its step was her Uncle Doff's. Her ringlets bounced beguilingly as she showed off a dawnstone bunny and prattled on about kisses and her Uncle Farley's very best bath toy.

It was all so deucedly *cute*.

Catching Freydolf's eye, she drawled, "Was I ever this adorable?"

"Never," he promised.

The man's dark eyes gleamed softly in the firelight. He'd always been a terrible liar. And a doting brother.

With a moody huff, she searched for Tupper amidst the dancers. After much sifting through too many fair curls, she caught the glint of the trim on his new tunic. Aye, he looked very fine. He was also enjoying himself. His bearing gave him away rather than his expression, for he was as serious as ever. Still, he seemed a cut above the rest.

"He surpasses his agemates," she smugly remarked.

"Aye. He reminds me of you."

Ulrica's gaze gradually slipped out of focus. She'd relished street festivals when she was young, whirling gracefully through the complicated choreography of a traditional dagger dance, where a misstep could end in bloodshed and humiliation. Lovely times.

One song led to another, and Tupper chose a hopeful-looking girl from those clustered on the edge of the square. At first, Ulrica thought he might have an interest in the dainty lass, but with every dance, their boy traded partners. It wasn't the company he craved; it was the music and movement, and the more complicated the dance steps, the more his eyes sparkled.

Carden strolled over, bringing chilled glasses of something

sweet and fruity. "Tupper asked me to tend to you since he'll be occupied for the remainder of the evening." The young man cut a small bow. "I'm at your service."

Freydolf snorted lightly. "Do we require a minder?"

"A mediator, perhaps," Carden suggested. Nodding toward Tupper, he said, "He'd dance all night if the music lasted."

"I may need to carry him home," Frey joked.

Carden hummed. "He's gotten better since last year. I've never seen him so light on his feet."

This sibling wasn't the only one to notice. A small buzz had begun among the girls closest to Tupper's age.

"A Pred's grace is a power unto itself," Ulrica intoned. "If he had bells on, they'd be silent as stone."

"Dance with me, Papa!" Dulcie interrupted, holding up her arms.

"Gladly." Carden lifted his daughter and twirled her around. Catching Freydolf's eye, he warned, "Once Melina has Yona settled, she means to ask you to dance."

"Me?"

"Yessir. I heard her plotting with Merona and Edie. They intend to show you off."

Ulrica laughed at her brother's expression and linked her arm through his. "I'll ensure that Master Meadowsweet doesn't escape before the ladies arrive."

"Thank you. Now, if you'll excuse me," Carden said, carrying Dulcie to the edge of the square and joining the dance.

With a soft sigh, Ulrica leaned against her brother's shoulder. "Aurelius would have loved this."

"Aye."

She keenly missed her favorite dance partner and lifted her gaze to the stars. Her hand smoothed over her skirts, then cradled her unborn child, and she drifted off into precious memories. Aurelius was as fine a dancer as he was a huntsman ... and father ... and husband. Despite heavy criticism over the match, she knew she'd chosen very well indeed.

"Ulrica?"

She started, reaching for her missing blade and berating herself for losing sight of her surroundings. Tupper had caught her off guard, and judging by his small smile, he knew it. However, he didn't mock her. Bowing, he held out his hand and invited, "Dance with me."

"Me?" She cringed. If Freydolf commented on the similarity of her reaction to his, he'd be nursing a seeping wound during the walk home.

"*Your* turn to be shown off," Freydolf murmured. He smiled in the face of her scowl. "Go on, little sister. You *love* dancing."

"I'm too cumbersome these days," she groused.

"Not for this dance. It's easier than walking." Tupper quietly added, "I can teach you the steps, and I won't throw things at you if you get it wrong."

Ulrica laughed, soft and low. "Aye, I'll permit it. But *only* if you don't make a spectacle of me."

Tupper nodded and led her away from the glow of bonfires. Starlight and moonlight were enough to see by as he taught Ulrica the steps of a childishly simple Flox dance. The promenade took them further from the music and laughter, which is why they were the first to catch the rattle and creak of an approaching carriage.

Ulrica didn't recognize the sound made by the harnesses, and she moved to push Tupper behind her.

Her little mother beat her to it, though, stepping protectively in front of her and firmly ordering, "Get Frey."

"Why?" she demanded, eyes warily fixed on the oncoming rig. Tupper radiated tension, which set her fangs on edge.

Finally, the boy answered, "I can hear a stone."

"Did you bring my dagger?" Ulrica hissed.

"To a festival?" Tupper flinched at her dark look, then blushed when she hoisted her skirts to reach a set of smaller blades strapped to her thigh. "You had more?"

"Aye, but I relinquished my favorite." She growled, "Which you *will* carry at all times from now on."

Tupper contritely ducked his head. "Sorry."

"No time for regrets," she murmured, giving two blades a deft twirl.

He was impressed. "Did you learn that from Aurelius?"

Ulrica snorted delicately. "Don't be ridiculous. I taught *him*."

The rig rolled to a halt a short distance away, and two horses tossed their manes, jingling their harnesses. A lone driver casually kicked the brake into place, looped the reins over the back of his seat, and lifted down one of a pair of small lanterns hanging from the vehicle's high sides.

Springing down, he swaggered over, lantern low, shoulders hunched, and eyes fixed on Ulrica. "Is a wolf tending the lambs?" he asked, his clipped tones heavily accented. "Are you belonging to the great and terrible Pred who keeps Morven to himself?"

"Who asks?" Ulrica demanded.

He bowed at the waist, arms spread wide. "A humble merchant. Peace, good lady."

The man's fluid grace unsettled Tupper. He moved too much like a predator to be anything but. Plus, there was a confusing chatter coming from beneath the lumpy tarp on the back of his wagon. Tupper knew stones were actually silent, but that didn't stop him from "hearing" their disjointed babble. Something felt wrong about it.

Ulrica's short laugh was filled with mockery. "You ask a Pred for peace? A merchant should know better than to haggle for something that is beyond price."

Tupper wondered if he should get Frey. But that would mean leaving Ulrica with the stranger. Torn, he stood his ground.

"I heard this mountain was guarded by a tiger," the man rejoined, sounding wholly unconcerned. "They said nothing of a tigress."

She snarled something in Terse, and he answered in kind. Switching back to Verit, she ordered, "Lift your lantern! Let me see how many lies are reflected in your eyes!"

He immediately obliged, and Tupper had his first good look at the traveler. Ragged clothes that must have been fine once. Dusty boots that had traveled far. Blue eyes with an audacious glint. A broad-brimmed hat adorned with a fluttering cascade of black feathers, gleaming green, purple, and gold in the lamplight. Curving talons at each fingertip. A prominent, beaky nose.

The clues and cues took several moments to add up, but when they did, Tupper reached a dazzling epiphany. *Real* Grif weren't red.

"Your wife made it official," Freydolf shared. "You're accepting an apprenticeship."

"Melina didn't need long to make up her mind," said Carden. "The books may have helped."

"Books?" he echoed quizzically.

"The Harrows gave me an entire stack to read. Histories, mostly," the Flox explained. "With this and that, I've never had much time for schooling, but books are precious to Melina. Every evening I'm home, she reads them aloud while I'm carving."

"You're already shaping stone?"

"Wood." Carden smiled and explained, "We'll be needing a second cradle."

"Aye. Your wife may have mentioned *that* as well." Freydolf dropped to the bench outside the bakery. Melina had made good on her threat and dragged him into a dance. "I can hardly keep up."

Carden laughed. "I'll bring something to drink."

"Something strong," the sculptor begged.

"I believe Old Gruff is guarding a barrel that can accommodate your needs. I'll bring two mugs."

Hoping the mugs were of a decent size, Freydolf kept his eyes lowered, avoiding the villagers' frank stares. Thanks to Tupper's fondness for the dawnstone Triad, the Pred hadn't made a complete fool of himself, but he envied his sister. "Spectacle, indeed," he grumbled.

Suddenly, Tupper bolted into the square and rushed over, wide-eyed as he whispered, "Ulrica wants you."

Freydolf's brows drew together. "Is she all right?"

"I think so," he replied, jouncing from foot to foot. "But there's a Grif."

"Brand is here?" the Keeper asked, his gaze flying toward the mountain. "That doesn't ...."

"A *real* one!" Tupper interrupted, tugging at his sleeve and pointing in the direction he'd come. "Ulrica has her daggers out. I don't think she likes him."

The Pred didn't wait to hear more. He sprinted into the darkness, ears straining for the sound of his sister's bells, but they were silent as stone. If the Grif was a fool, he was already dead, but if he was circumspect, *maybe* Frey could save his life.

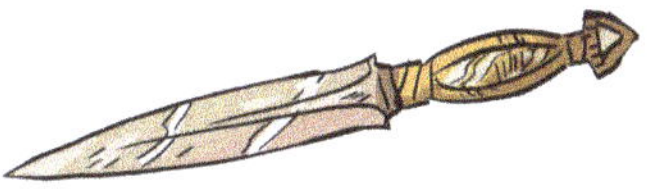

Even in his hurry to get back to Freydolf's side, Tupper noticed that the dance underway was one of his favorites. He was missing out, but at the same time ... a real, live Grif! Aurelius had told many stories about the various races that were scattered across the world, but Tupper had never expected someone from Far Continent to show up in Hayward.

Just then, Carden called his name. His older brother carried two foam-topped mugs—Old Gruff's special reserve, no doubt.

"You're not dancing, Tupp?"

"I *was*, but a merchant came."

"Odd timing. Villagers generally return to their homes for midsummer festivals. It's not one of the tinkers, is it?"

"No. He's not from around here." Eager to show Carden, he pointed toward the road, and urged, "I'll show you!"

He lifted the brimming libations and asked, "Is that where Master Freydolf disappeared to?"

Tupper nodded.

"Then, lead on!"

Once away from the bonfires, their eyes adjusted enough to spot the rig standing near the village's edge. Two lanterns. Three figures. Low voices carried through the darkness, a clipped conversation that Tupper couldn't follow.

His brother paused to listen and asked, "What is that?"

"They're speaking in Terse."

Carden's eyebrows slowly lifted. "How far has this merchant come?"

"All the way from Far Continent," Tupper whispered. "He's Grif."

For several long moments, they hung back, simply listening to the foreign gibberish. Ulrica sounded annoyed, and Freydolf's deep voice was pitched to soothe. The Grif spoke freely, gesturing broadly with one taloned hand.

Carden murmured, "Well, he's certainly not Flox. If I didn't know better, I would have mistaken him for a Pred."

There *were* similarities. The merchant was tall, but not nearly as broad as his companions. He seemed to be of a darker complexion than Flox, but lighter than Pred. "He moves like one," Tupper commented, staring at the animated newcomer.

"He has talons like Brand," Carden whispered.

Tupper nodded. "I like his feathers."

His older brother hummed. "I'm not sure they're *his*. Isn't that hair gathered behind his neck?"

They stared hard, heads together. With a sigh, Tupper acknowledged the death of another fond wish. Pred didn't have tails. Grif didn't have feathers. Determined to look on the bright side, he confided, "I hope he likes to tell stories about the places he's been."

"Would you even understand them?" Carden asked. "I can't make any sense of what's been said."

The merchant switched to Verit then, including the Flox eavesdroppers as he announced, "I accept this master's offer, and gladly! Now, who are these? *Do* say one of those tankards is for me!"

At Freydolf's nod, Carden hurried forward with the refreshment. "Welcome to Hayward, sir."

Tupper wasn't about to be left out, so he sidled up beside Freydolf, leaning bashfully into his master's side. Frey gave him a pleased smile and ruffled his hair. "This is my servant Tupper," he offered by way of introduction. "And his elder brother Carden is my apprentice."

"It is my honor to meet you both," the Grif said with a small flourish of one hand. "I am a trader of goods and good fortune, a merchant of magic and magical stones, and yet a beggar upon your doorstep. Thank you for extending hospitality to a wanderer such as myself. You may call me Torio!"

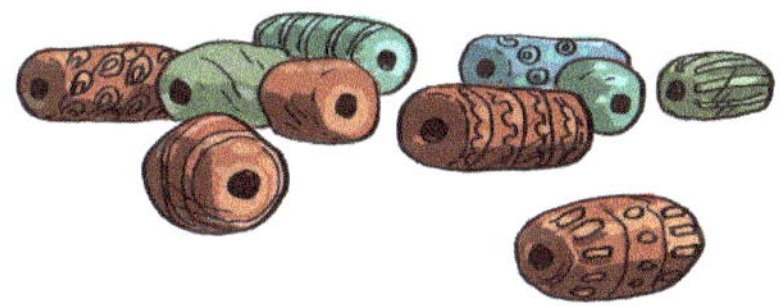

Despite the lateness of the hour and the Meadowsweets' offer to put them up overnight, Freydolf begged off and undertook the long trek home. One of the most basic principles that governed the lives of Keepers was their need to stay with their mountain. They couldn't stray far or for long. Morven wanted him home, and Tupper knew his master had no desire to resist her tug. Home called to both of them.

Tupper sort of wished that Torio was joining them, but at Ulrica's insistence, Freydolf had slightly postponed his hospitality. The Grif merchant was in Old Gruff's keeping, to be escorted to the summit on the morrow along the quarry road.

"Look," said Tupper. A sleek shape emerged from the deep shadows at the base of the eastern trail. "Graven came to meet us."

"If he'll cooperate, he could spare us the worst of the walk," Freydolf hinted.

"Yes." He hurried forward and patted his varicolored guardian. "May we ride?"

The tiger lowered his belly to the ground and rested his chin on his front paws in a longsuffering manner, and Freydolf tried to help Ulrica onto the big cat's back. The woman swatted away his hands, hiked up her skirts, and ascended on her own. Her brother followed, and Tupper smiled when Frey was just as insistent in wrapping her safely in the circle of his arms.

With a kiss for *thank you* upon the tiger's nose, the boy clambered up behind them and hooked his fingers through Frey's belt.

"I don't trust that Grif," Ulrica said sulkily as Graven ferried them along the steep, winding trail.

"I know," Frey soothed.

"He's not telling the whole truth."

"Merchants rarely do. Bad for business."

"I wish Aurelius was here."

"Aye. I'd prefer that myself. I've never had to handle stone trade."

"Then send that feathered fiasco packing!"

"If need be," Freydolf promised. "We'll see how it goes."

Graven glided through the Apprentice Gate and along the cobbled road to the Harrows' residence. Once Freydolf had seen Ulrica to her door and made certain that Phineas was on guard, he rejoined Tupper and sighed, "Finally."

The boy knew what he meant and nodded. Their day had been busy, noisy, and even a little wild. "But today was good?"

"Aye."

Tupper was taken completely off guard when Freydolf swept him off his feet and tossed him into the air. It was a little embarrassing to still be small enough that the Pred had no trouble flinging him about. As soon as Tupper caught his breath, he had to smother a giggle. Frey grinned and threw him higher, then draped him across his shoulders and strutted toward home.

Not wanting to be treated like game, Tupper scooted around

for a piggyback ride and locked his arms around the man's neck, hugging him tight. Frey was happy, and that made him happy. Hiding his smile against the man's broad shoulder, Tupper thought about the exciting day they'd shared ... then recalled one thing he'd been saving back.

"Brother," he whispered, testing the title.

"Hmm?" Frey replied, accepting it without a trace of surprise.

"I have a present for you. For your birthday."

That brought him to a standstill. "Oh?"

"Yes." Pointing along the passage, he said, "It's that way. Unless you're too tired."

"Nay." He turned in the direction Tupper indicated, asking, "Is it far?"

"Maybe."

"Are you sure you know where we're going?"

"Probably."

Freydolf chuckled softly, then lapsed into a contented silence. As they slipped along moonlit streets and alleys, Tupper marveled that the Pred could still move soundlessly, even with the addition of a spring to his step.

As they wended their way through a short maze of back streets, Freydolf hummed and asked, "Will we need a light?"

"No," replied his young navigator, who pointed to a narrow set of stairs. "We're staying above ground, and there are windows."

From a wide veranda two flights up, the Keeper took in a moonlit view, getting his bearings. "We're not far from the summit," he murmured.

Tupper nodded.

"In fact, those are the stairs down to the hen house," he said, pointing.

The lad nodded again, then patted Frey's head for attention. "Through this door."

Freydolf could tell that some preparations had been made for this birthday surprise, for the door swung smoothly on oiled hinges, and the wide room within had been swept and dusted. It was mostly empty of furnishings, save an enormous wooden table that smelled freshly polished.

Rows of tall, narrow windows lined both sides of the room, suggesting that this would be an airy, sunny space by day. They let in sufficient moonlight for Frey to see what Tupper obviously meant for his gift. "Is that what I think it is?" he whispered.

"Yes."

He swung Tupper off his shoulders and strode forward to touch the bands of possession surrounding its opening. "It's almost as big as the one at Pennyflax & Quince!"

"Yes."

Several generations of bakers had laid claim to it over the years, and it must have fed most of the mountain. Shaking his head in awe, Freydolf murmured, "I have a bread oven?"

"Yes." Tupper tugged at his sleeve. "And Melina is coming. She could make you lots of bread."

With a soft grunt, Freydolf ambled over to the wall and sat under the windows, leaning back as he gazed at his gift. When Tupper was close enough to catch, he pulled the lad onto his lap and wrapped his arms around him, resting his chin atop his curly head.

"Are you magical?" Frey asked.

"Me?"

"Aye." He tightened his hold on Tupper, who relaxed into the embrace. "You defy reasonable explanations, so I'm resorting to the miraculous."

Tupper peered at him, a sleepy smile on his upturned face. "That sounds nice."

Freydolf chuckled and switched to things the lad was more likely to understand. "We'll need extra firewood this year."

"And flour."

Minutes slipped softly by, and Frey murmured, "Tupper?"

"Yes?"

"Earlier ... should I have introduced you as my brother instead of as my servant?"

After some thought, the lad replied, "No."

"Why not?"

Tupper shrugged. "Because this is hard to explain."

"That a Pred and a Flox swore an oath to become bond-brothers?"

"Oh," he murmured. "You said it really good."

"How else *would* you explain it?" Freydolf asked curiously.

In a small voice, Tupper admitted, "I mostly get mixed up at the part with the pepper."

22

Heart of a Lion

In the light of day, Torio seemed much more ordinary, but Tupper wasn't disappointed. Shouldn't men from Far Continent still be men? He liked knowing that someone with curved talons and a fantastical hat could have scuffed boots and frayed cuffs. The normal parts helped balance out the strange ones.

"And this is our home," Freydolf announced, swinging wide the door. "It doubles as my workshop."

Torio strolled inside, eyes bright with curiosity. "I can see you're the sort who lives for stones—waking and sleeping, working and dreaming! This space is at once inspired and inspiring!"

"Insipid thing," muttered Ulrica in another caustic aside. She'd been at it since the Grif arrived earlier, still suspicious of the merchant's intentions.

Tupper tweaked her little finger and whispered, "Be nice."

"I cannot bear his simpering," she hissed. "And despite all my warnings, my brother is letting this tattered interloper in under his guard."

"Torio is our guest." Tupper couldn't quite figure out why she found the merchant's grand way of speaking so annoying since Aurelius wasn't much different. Maybe it was because his clothes were less fine?

She inclined her head and lapsed into stony silence, but her eyes never left the visiting Grif's face.

The man doffed his feathered hat, revealing sandy blond hair. Noticing the boy's frank stare, Torio's brows lifted. "Do you wish to remark upon my nose? Most do."

Tupper shook his head. "Your hair. It's like a mane."

Torio pulled around the long hank of his hair and stared at it in puzzlement. "The Grif have the heart of a lion, but this makes a meager mane."

Tupper sidled closer and gave the sleek hair a tentative pat. "Not a lion's. A horse's."

Ulrica muttered, "Horse is too good a comparison for one who brays like a mule."

Freydolf firmly escorted his sister into the kitchen, leaving Tupper with their guest. The boy tried again. "Your hair is straight."

Bright blue eyes took on a shine of understanding. "Hardly a novelty where I come from, but your folk *are* all done up in ringlets."

"All Grif have straight hair?"

"Straight as sticks," he replied, tapping the side of his nose.

Tupper touched the crown of his head and said, "Common as curls."

When Freydolf returned, Torio was nose-to-beak with the completed griffin statue. "I call this auspicious! My people's namesake!"

"Aye," the sculptor acknowledged, affectionately resting his hand on the statue's shoulder. "If I remember correctly, this statue was commissioned by a Grif."

"Do you favor brownstone?" Torio asked, strolling over to where Haimish stood.

"Not especially."

The merchant rattled off something in Terse, then switched back to Verit to inquire, "Brownstone with titian jade accents? Is he one of yours?"

"Aye."

"Is the jade just for show, or did you manage to bond the two?"

"If Haimish catches the sunset, he'll remain awake until dawn," Freydolf shared, a touch of pride in the tilt of his chin.

Torio whistled. "Not many can link the magic of two such diverse stones. Of course, you *did* train under Master Platt. I really must get a look at that tiger of his!"

Freydolf chuckled. "Aye, that's easily arranged. Turn around."

The lean man straightened, then glanced toward the door, where Graven was doing his best to force his way through. Muttering an incomprehensible oath, the Grif strode to the tiger, wholly unruffled by the big cat's baleful glare. "Feather my cap! He has redstone eyes!"

"Oh, aye. Well-spotted," drawled Ulrica from the kitchen doorway.

Both Freydolf and Tupper shot her a warning look.

Rushing forward to try to push Graven back outside, the boy scolded, "You be nice, too." Then glancing to Torio, he said, "Sorry! I won't let him hurt you."

"He's a guardian. Let him guard," the Grif replied, fearlessly reaching out to scratch the tiger under his chin. Starstone fangs clicked as Graven snapped at his fingers. "Reminds me of my pet lion. All snarl and no bite. But, what's this? He's guarding *you*?"

"You can tell?" Tupper asked.

Freydolf cleared his throat. "Graven became attached to the lad."

"*Strongly* attached," Torio remarked, his gaze resting on the young Flox.

"Speaking of attachments, "Ulrica interrupted. "I've met all the merchants attached to the red mountain. You're not one of them."

"Quite true," the Grif readily admitted. "I'm not employed by the redstone Keeper."

"Does *any* Keeper claim you?" she asked sharply.

"I have always valued my independence," Torio said with an easygoing smile. "My journey is as much for personal enrichment as for trade. With my arrival here, I have set foot on *all* the magical mountains."

Freydolf eyed him closely. "You have a strong affinity for stone."

Torio's expression became studiously neutral. "You could

say that. Hardly strange for someone in my line of work."

The Keeper grunted, and Tupper asked, "Morven is your last mountain?"

"Put it off as long as you could?" Ulrica snipped in an undertone.

Thankfully, Torio seemed entirely amused by the woman's hostility. Bowing graciously, the Grif said, "If I had known what awaited me here, I would have flown to the Moonlit Mountain with greater haste. Let us instead say that I left the best for last."

Freydolf chivvied his sister back into the kitchen, promising refreshments, so Tupper was the only one close enough to catch the traveler's next words. Although they were softer than a sigh, the boy was certain he'd heard them aright.

Torio had murmured, "Last chance."

They gathered in the kitchen, and Torio made himself right at home in Aurelius's usual chair. "You don't get many visitors, Master Freydolf?"

"Nay, you're the first merchant to brave the rumors in nearly a decade." With a small shrug, he said, "It's quiet here."

Torio drained his teacup. "The rumors about your mountain are incredible. Since few have seen the Statuary for themselves, its glories have become the stuff of legends."

Tupper poured more tea and pushed a plate of sliced peaches closer to the Grif. Ulrica wasn't serving anything but dark looks and sour remarks, so the niceties fell to him.

Freydolf winced. "Dare I ask what you've heard?"

The merchant hesitated. "Well, for instance, if I remember correctly, it's said that the heart of your mountain is guarded by a terrible dragon."

"Thrall is no myth. Would you like to see the Cavern?"

"I would welcome a tour, but does a Keeper have time for such things? I have no wish to take you from your work!"

"Go," Tupper urged, shooing them with one hand. "It will give me time to clean his room."

Torio's eyebrows arched. "The master bends to his servant's will?"

"Brother, actually," Freydolf said. "And if Tupper wants us out from underfoot, then we'll go."

The merchant's eyes glittered with interest. "What a lovely muddle. I *wondered* why your ties were tangled!"

Freydolf explained, "We're bond-brothers in the Pred tradition."

"I gave him my name," Tupper supplied.

Torio peered at them in disbelief. "You don't know?"

"Know what?" Frey asked.

The Grif beckoned to Tupper, his taloned fingers crooking insistently. "What's around your neck? Show me what you're keeping close to your heart."

Tupper pulled out his money cord, displaying a small row of coins divided by two beads and his precious master key.

"That key," Torio said with authority.

"Snick," the boy said, his fingers closing protectively around it.

"If it bears a name, I assume it bears its maker's mark?"

"Aye, it's a guardian of sorts," Freydolf confirmed.

"And you bound it to the boy?"

"*Do* get to your point," Ulrica snapped.

Frey sighed at his sister, then answered, "Aye. The stone came to him, so I bound the key to him."

"*Came* to him?" Torio asked. He switched to Terse then, and Ulrica was dragged in to help clarify details on what had happened.

Tupper didn't really mind being left out since it was interesting to hear people speaking in another language. Sharp sounds. Crisp words. Jagged tones. Maybe if he kept practicing, he could speak to Torio in his own language. And Brand. Surely his redstone friend knew Terse. But did that mean he'd had to learn Verit? Were languages a problem for statues who were shipped overseas?

He frowned worriedly. Was poor Dart being left out because he lived in a Terse-speaking country? Or did the blue dragon know Terse because Frey knew Terse. *That* must be why Carden needed to learn all the languages. Tupper was quite pleased to have figured it out on his own.

Freydolf sat back in his chair, a dumbfounded expression on his face. "At the time ... I remember now. He was so overwhelmed. *Big*, he said. The bond was big."

Torio tapped the side of his nose and said, "It's been right in front of you all along."

"So you *can* be mercenary," praised Ulrica. "Your lambkin sussed out a thin trail of ambition wending through the thick forest of your passivity."

"Nay! I never would have done such a thing on purpose."

"If you *must* lay blame, look to Morven," Torio said. "She's the greedy one."

Tupper blinked, still out of the loop even though they were back to conversing in Verit. "What happened?"

Freydolf rubbed his chin, then messed up his dark hair. "And you were *crying* and couldn't stop," he recalled mournfully. "Tears. Of course there would be tears."

The boy slid off his chair and leaned into the distraught Pred's side. "I don't understand."

Ulrica intervened. "Whether he admits to it or not, this Grif has an unusually strong affinity. He can sense the potency of stones, the ties that bind, the quality of statues." With a slight curl of her lip, she added, "All the marks of a potential, wasted on a dusty peddler."

"I've no interest in breaking my back cutting dull stone in some Keeper's quarry," Torio smoothly countered. "Wandering suits me."

"You're a vagrant."

"Quite true, but beside the point," the Grif replied, his gaze slanting toward Tupper. "*You* have formed several magical bonds."

Nodding, Tupper listed, "Olexi, Rimbles, Graven, Snick."

"Aye, but I accidentally forged a deeper one," Frey confessed, his dark eyes pleading for understanding. "When I woke Snick,

I thought I was binding the key to you."

"You did."

"Aye, he's yours. But Morven meddled."

Tupper waited patiently. Freydolf often took his time choosing words he could understand.

The man's arm slid around his shoulders. "You started hearing her voice after that."

"Yes."

Torio whistled again at this juicy tidbit.

Frey gently ruffled Tupper's curls. "When I tied you to your key, Morven tied herself to you."

"And that makes you sad?" Tupper checked.

Freydolf lowered his eyes. "It probably means you *can't* leave."

The boy shook his head. "But you promised I could stay."

Ulrica laughed. Freydolf hid his face behind his hand. For his part, Torio gazed steadily at the young Flox and asked, "You wanted to stay?"

Tupper nodded adamantly.

The Grif's eyes gleamed. "Does the mountain *also* bend to the servant's will?"

Tupper didn't really understand. Why should he be sad to stay in the very place he wanted to belong? Even Freydolf seemed mixed up about the whole thing. Before leaving with Torio for a tour of the Cavern, the Pred had pulled the boy into a hug and acted like he never wanted to let go, whispering apologies all the while. Tupper planned to set him straight later. Worrying over something so silly was sure to make the statues uneasy, and he wasn't about to let that happen.

To Rimbles, he said, "Nothing's changed, so why should we?"

Lugging a bucket of soapy water up a narrow set of stairs, Tupper climbed to the room he'd chosen for Torio. After much discussion, the merchant had accepted Freydolf's hospitality, but only if they would give him a humble berth, befitting a man of his lowly station, preferably near the stables. The boy thought it was nice that the Grif wanted to stay close to his horses.

This room was over the stables, a small square with four walls—one for the door, one for the window, one for a fireplace, and the last taken up by a long, narrow sleeping niche. Throwing open faded red shutters, Tupper chased spiders out of the corners, then set to scouring the mosaic floor, which was decorated in a zig-zag pattern with redstone, brownstone, and sunstone triangles.

Rimbles chased soap bubbles, and Haimish hovered just outside the open door, a hopeful expression on his face. Tupper promised, "Once I'm done, we'll go find a washstand, a table, and a chair. And we'll need a lamp. And a basin and pitcher."

Haimish nodded, his tail swaying. The brownstone statue was happiest when he was helpful. Tupper could understand.

Even though the room was small, it took hours to finish readying the space for their guest. The afternoon was more than half gone by the time Tupper brought up cushions and blankets for Torio's bed and added fresh water to the pitcher. Handing his bucket to Haimish, he said, "Make sure the trough is filled. It's time to get the horses."

The merchant's two stallions were gentle old things. Bigger than their local horses, they were definitely built for pulling heavy loads. One was black from tip to tail, and the other was a deep, dark brown. Tupper had tethered them amidst the trees just off the quarry road since the Statuary offered no decent pasture, but he wanted to bring them back before starting dinner.

He poked his head into the stable to make sure everything was in order, and his gaze fell on the merchant's rig. Torio had backed it into one of the empty stalls. Its mysterious load was still lashed into place by ropes, and fear prickled across Tupper's skin an instant before the babble started anew.

Although he mostly wanted to run, he stood still and listened hard, trying to make sense of the raw, keening cries.

To his surprise, Morven responded. The Gray Mountain's voice echoed in Tupper's mind, singing softly, as if to a child waking from a bad dream.

He'd been frightened, but maybe it was really the other way around. It wasn't until he entered the stable that the rock cried out. "Did I scare you?"

Tupper climbed up onto the wagon wheel in order to reach the knotted ropes that kept the coarse canvas tarp in place. Humming along with the mountain, he began to croon, "There, there. Don't cry."

Over and over, he repeated little assurances. Finally freeing the corner, he reached under the covering, and his fingertips met a silky surface. Pushing the canvas up farther, he peeked underneath ... blinked ... and smiled.

"Pretty, pretty," he murmured. "Don't cry, pretty lady."

The stone's voice wavered, and the mountain's thrum continued. Peace and welcome. Tupper nodded and offered his own greeting, "Welcome to the Statuary. I'm Tupper." Then, he climbed right up on top of the block, which was big enough to fill the entire wagon. In a low voice, he continued, "Torio isn't far, so don't fret. He's with Freydolf, Morven's Keeper. He's safe. You're safe. Don't cry."

He patted the stone, telling her about the nice room upstairs and the good horses waiting in the woods. And she listened. Her frantic chattering ebbed into silence, and Tupper laid his cheek against the tiny patch of exposed stone, promising her that Frey was happy about her merchant's visit.

She whimpered.

Tupper listened closely, but there were no words. All she did was sigh and slip back into something like sleep. Maybe that was best. She'd probably had a very long journey, because stone like this didn't come from their continent. Or any of the others, for that matter.

"But here you are." Trailing his fingers across the glossy, jet-black rock, he smiled. "Won't Frey be surprised?"

A shadow fell across the door, and Tupper turned in time to see several emotions flicker across Torio's face—shock, indignation, and a darkening rage that made his blue eyes blaze. But just as quickly, his stormy expression dulled into resignation, and the Grif sagged wearily against the door frame, muttering imprecations in Terse.

Tupper held a finger to his lips, hopped down, tucked in the black stone, then waved for Torio to follow him outside.

The merchant trailed after, his back ramrod straight and his hands clenched at his sides. "You found out," he said in a cheerful tone that fell flat.

"Yes." Taking the man's arm, Tupper led him along the road. "She's very noisy."

Torio searched his face. "Everyone else has panicked."

He nodded. "I *was* scared. At first."

Torio peered perplexedly past his beaky nose. "How did you get her to stop?"

"You can hear her?"

"Of course I can hear her," the Grif said moodily. "That's how this whole thing started!"

As they neared the place where he'd left the horses, Tupper answered, "She stopped crying after I told her she was pretty."

"Is *that* what you think?"

"Yes."

The man muttered, "The others called her accursed."

Tupper frowned and asked, "Didn't they listen?"

"To what? She only spouts gibberish."

The young Flox tutted. "Even when you and the others are speaking in Terse, I can tell if you're happy or angry or surprised. Words don't matter for that."

Torio's smile twisted wryly. "I'll admit, she's moody enough. I've not had a moment's peace in six years."

They reached the bend in the road where the stallions waited, and Tupper clucked his tongue as he approached the pair. Torio held out his hand to the nearest, muttering a Terse greeting while the boy loosed the rope wrapped around a slender tree. The Grif accepted the brown's lead while Tupper ducked under the big, black horse to untie him.

Back on the road, Tupper gazed up into Torio's face and bluntly asked, "What about now?"

"Now?"

"Yes." Tupper tipped his head to one side and said, "This is a peaceful place. Don't you think?"

Torio's expression hardened. "It *won't* be once your master finds out about her."

"Why?"

"Let's just say there's sufficient precedent."

Tupper shook his head. "Say it again so I can understand."

"Simple-minded bit of fluff, are you?" teased the Grif.

"Maybe. Probably. You know more Verit than I do."

With a short laugh, Torio said, "I can be clear as the skies over Drom's desert. Here's the truth. I've visited *every* mountain, and I've shown her to *every* other Keeper. It's *always* the same, and it's *always* bad." Without any of his usual smiles and sparkles, the Grif said, "Your Pred brother will undoubtedly banish me."

"No." Tupper smiled a little before repeating, "No. Frey could never banish anyone."

"Then his sister will murder me."

He had to think that one over. "Maybe, but not because of your black stone. And I'm pretty sure I can stop her."

Torio's lips quirked. "So you have influence over *her* as well?"

"Yes."

The man walked on, and for a long while, the only sound was the *clip-clop* of hooves on cobblestones. It was hard to figure out what Torio wanted to do. Merchants usually sold magical stones, but this man had traveled the whole world with his. Six years was even longer than he'd been with Frey or Olexi or Rimbles. Maybe Torio cared what happened to her. Tupper nodded to himself, then said, "She didn't cry when you came into the stables."

Torio hummed an affirmative.

"You've kept her close. Kept her safe. That's nice."

"Seems more like madness, given how things turned out."

Tupper patted the man's arm. "You did good."

With a sidelong look, Torio haggled, "Will you be good and keep her a secret for me?"

"Why?"

The Grif didn't answer right away, but at the top of the rise, his steps slowed to a stop. He gazed hungrily at the sprawl of buildings that made up the Statuary. "I want some peace."

"Then stay," Tupper invited.

Torio accepted with a flourishing bow. "I shall, young master ... for now."

23

Freeloader

Brand slipped his arm around Tupper's waist, tucking the young Flox up against his side. While his manner toward Torio was polite, the redstone warrior asserted his rightful place. The merchant whistled. "I see you've earned the regard of one of my homelanders!"

"Me and Brand are friends."

"So I see." Torio straightened to his full height as he and the fire-bearer sized each other up.

They were both Grif, but they were hardly mirror images of each other. Without his hat on, the merchant lacked feathers. He was also a finger or two taller than the statue. As far as Tupper could tell, Torio was unarmed, but Brand's sword was prominently displayed at his waist. However, some things were alike. Torio's wide sleeves were styled to concertina in fancy pleats, much like the pleated kilt that swished to the statue's knees. And there were other similarities—lean face, narrow chin, and thin eyebrows with a quizzical arch. Even so, their personalities were an ocean apart.

Executing a bow, Torio generously declared, "He's a handsome enough relic."

The statue stood his ground and smiled thinly.

Tupper wasn't sure what to make of the merchant's compliment. "Relic?"

"That armor hasn't been used by our people in more than a thousand years," Torio explained, circling the boy and statue. "The feathered capes are still in vogue, at least for formal occasions."

"Do you have one?"

"Not I. I hardly have need of such extravagances."

"You have a fancy hat."

"Quite true!" he admitted as they started down the stairs. "But it's only elaborate compared to Flox hats. My plumage is common as curls in Grif territories. You're the peculiar ones! I can hardly believe you walk around with what looks like a bird's nest upon your heads."

"I could make you a straw hat," Tupper offered.

"What for?"

"To keep the weather off."

Torio snorted, but Tupper thought he looked pleased. The hat would be his next bathtime weaving project.

While he led the way along the colonnade toward the passage leading to the Cavern, Torio said something to Brand in his native tongue. The fire-bearer inclined his head but kept walking.

Tupper asked, "What did you say?"

"Only reassuring your friend that I mean well," the merchant replied disingenuously.

Nodding, Tupper quietly confessed, "I'm learning Terse."

"Oooh?" Torio inquired with a grin. "Come, now! Show off your skills!"

"I'm not very good."

"My Skrit is abysmal, so I'm in no position to mock your efforts," he promised.

So Tupper took a deep breath and gravely counted to ten, then named all the colors he could remember. Torio didn't laugh, nor did he throw peas or pebbles before correcting his pronunciation. He beamed under his compliments, then said, "Your Verit is very good."

"Probably because I spent some years in Drom," he explained.

"Aurelius is in the Drom capital," Tupper shared. "Maybe you passed him on your way here."

Torio swung wide the doors to the Cavern. "It's possible. So where are we bound?"

Tupper struck out toward the starstone gallery. "Do you like lions?"

The Grif chuckled. "Picked up on that, did you?"

"Yes."

"We keep them as pets."

Tupper nodded, then asked, "Are they as big as Graven?"

His companion snorted. "I should hope not! Don't you know what a lion looks like?"

"Yes. But things here are not always the same size as the things they look like," Tupper explained, following twist after turn and running lightly up stairs and down. "My lions are too big for pets. Probably."

"Yours?"

The boy nodded. "They're my friends."

"Are they now? You seem to have many."

"Yes."

They reached the end of the gallery, where the round passage opened into a spacious chamber with an expansive view. Two enormous moonstone warriors stood guard on either end of the room, spears braced in still hands, but the matching sunstone lions were on the prowl.

"These are vastly bigger than their living counterparts!" Torio exclaimed, holding out a hand to the ferocious-looking feline that paced over to investigate his visitors.

"I thought so."

He walked over to the second lion, who sprawled lazily in the sun. Rimbles climbed up between the big male's paws, and he nosed her before lifting his head and shaking out his mane.

Tupper said, "Up, please."

The statue cooperated, revealing a hidden door that led straight down through his pedestal. Torio asked, "A door in the floor? Where does it go?"

"Down."

"Down *where*."

"Do you want to see?" Tupper asked, a small smile playing across his lips.

The Grif regarded him closely. "Planning to lock me in some murky dungeon?"

"No."

"Is the space crawling with vermin?"

Tupper took hold of the handle and heaved upward, revealing nothing but darkness below. "After you."

Torio eyed the square suspiciously. "Any chance I can convince *you* to go first?"

"I've already been below," he replied, using his best bartering face. "Are you afraid?"

"Are you calling my courage into question?" the man blustered.

Without batting an eye, Tupper returned, "If you have any, I'd like to see it."

Tupper only felt a tiny bit bad when Torio broke down and slowly descended the rungs into darkness. He counted to ten before calling out, "Are you at the bottom?"

"Yes, yes. I'm in the belly of the beast." The man complained, "It's darker than the fifth level of catacombs under the Dapple Mountain. Have mercy and lower a light!"

"Coming!" Tupper called. He stopped halfway down the ladder and lifted a hand. Brand held his gaze for a long moment, clearly reluctant to relinquish the flame that kept him awake. Nodding, the boy produced a squat candle from one pocket. The redstone warrior lit it, then carefully passed it down.

Sheltering the flickering flame with his body, Tupper whispered, "Don't worry. I'll be fine." Then, he had to tell Rimbles the very same thing, for she was pacing the rim. She hated it when she couldn't get to him. "Wait there," he urged. "We'll be right back."

"Well?" Torio demanded, still in the dark.

"Sorry. Reach up? Here's a candle." The transfer was made, and the Grif held aloft the meager light.

A squawk of surprise was followed by a slew of Terse.

Tupper bit his lip to keep from laughing. Hopping down, he stood next to the awestruck man and asked, "Do you like it?"

Torio turned in the small space, offering a long, soft whistle. In the dancing light of their antic flame, lavender crystal came to life. Hundreds of faceted flowers caught the glow and scattered it. "Why is something this incredible hidden away in a hole in the ground?"

"There are lots of places like this," Tupper said. "I think the sculptors hid their best stuff so other people could find it."

"You like treasure hunting, I take it?" Torio shook his head wonderingly. "This shade of crystal is rare."

"I like it best," the boy admitted.

"Playing favorites?" the man teased.

"Maybe."

"So did your Pred brother first bring you here to see the grandeur?"

"No," Tupper replied. "I found it myself."

Torio smirked. "Was he surprised that you uncovered such a trove?"

"No. He doesn't know about it."

"You didn't tell him?"

"No."

The merchant turned in another circle, admiring the dazzling display. "Whyever not?"

"Sometimes it's good to have a secret."

Torio's gaze slanted his way. "Then why did you show me?"

"Sometimes it's good to share a secret."

One week turned into two, and two became four. Despite Ulrica's frequent and pointed inquiries as to the date of Torio's departure, the Grif cheerfully loitered about the Statuary. Freydolf was tempted to believe the man stayed on simply to annoy her. Torio certainly enjoyed toying with Ulrica's temper; he apparently liked dangerous games.

She rarely joined them in the evenings, when they lingered in the balcony over books, games, and gossip. Perhaps because it made her miss Aurelius all the more. Freydolf was yanked from his musings when Tupper abruptly announced, "I'm going to bed."

"Already?" Frey asked, glancing into his goblet. He hadn't even needed a refill, which meant it was early yet. "Feeling all right, lambkin?"

The lad was backing steadily toward the stairway. "Yes. I'm fine. Good night."

"Don't forget your wee grazer," Torio said, turning loose the small, white ram Tupper had left on a tabletop.

"Yes. Sorry. Good night," he repeated, then scuttled away, guardian in hand.

There was an awkward lull which Frey interrupted to say, "That's the fifth time, surely."

"Hmm?" inquired the Grif, his gaze fixed upon the neat row of candles on the low table where his stockinged feet were propped.

"My servant left us alone again."

"I thought he was your brother," Torio replied lightly.

Freydolf had played enough of these games with Aurelius to recognize a diversionary tactic. Something was amiss, and the Grif was at the heart of it. "Tupper has lived here since he was a newly-nubbed lad of ten, and he'd fall asleep in his cups before willingly taking to his bed. He's greedy for stories, and yours are good."

"You're too kind!"

Not to be diverted, Frey asked, "Why do you suppose he keeps slipping away early?"

"I hardly know the young master's mind."

"Oh?"

Torio uncrossed and re-crossed his ankles. "Perhaps he's simply tired. Your Flox brother spent all afternoon proving he can out-fish me without so much as a pole. It made a tasty feast at dinner, don't you think?"

Trying to change the subject again. Freydolf stared hard at the Grif who wouldn't meet his gaze. "Unless I miss my guess, he's been leaving you an opening."

"Is that what you think?"

"Aye. Is there something you need to speak with me about?"

The Grif stared into his goblet and muttered something in Terse.

Freydolf smiled. "Pushy? Aye, he holds considerable sway over those he cares for, and it looks as if he's decided *you* need mothering as well."

"Without a word, he's pressuring me."

"About ...?"

"Let's just say he's eager for me to display my wares."

"You have something to sell?"

"I am a merchant."

The oblique admission only solidified Frey's conviction that the man was harboring some secret ... to which Tupper had become privy. "Aye, but now's not the time for such things. Let's put off our dealings until tomorrow."

Relief flashed across the Grif's face, and he drank deeply, then clung tightly to his cup. With a forced smile, Torio asked, "Have you ever heard the story of how the Grif lost their feathers?"

"Nay," Freydolf replied, letting the other man divert him this time. "Is there such a tale?"

"A legend, more like!" exclaimed Torio, launching into its telling.

Freydolf listened well and laughed often, but all the while

he pondered the paradox this man represented. Never in his life had he met a merchant so reluctant to make a sale.

The Keeper had already woken when Tupper tiptoed back into the workshop with a cheeky monkey perched atop his head, her tail wrapped around one of his horns for balance. "It's late," the sculptor gruffly accused. "You've let me stay abed longer than usual."

"Yes."

"Where have you been?"

"The stable."

The man propped himself on his elbows. "Tending the horses?"

Tupper hesitated for a moment but nodded once. "I found a nice place in the shade for them. Today will be hot."

Frey had a strong sense that Tupper was saying less than he could have.

"Are you hungry?" the lad asked.

"Famished," the Pred admitted with a grin. His feet hit the floor with a *thud*, and he reached up in time to catch Nott, who flung herself at her creator. The little guardian scampered up his arm and ducked under the loose curtain of his hair, then reached around to tap his nose. Frey rumbled, "And good morning to you, my bit of mischief."

Just then, there came the rattle of wheels upon the cobblestones, and they traded a glance. Tupper asked, "Are you expecting …?"

At the same time, Freydolf asked, "Do you think it could be …?"

The door slammed open and shut, and Ulrica stormed in, looking out of sorts and waddling badly.

"Is Aurel–?"

"Nay!" she spat. "Just that bearded old goat and your precious apprentice."

Freydolf grimaced. His sister had probably gotten her hopes up.

"Do you want breakfast, Ulrica?" Tupper offered.

"I'll find something," she grumbled, disappearing into the kitchen.

"Let me help," the lad offered, hurrying after her.

Frey followed and leaned against the door frame, looking on as Tupper lured the woman to the table by placing a jar of her favorite pickled peppers at its center. She lowered herself slowly to a chair, eyes brightening when the boy added a plate of pungent cheese and a jar of plum preserves to the offerings. Ulrica was nearing her time, and her restlessness was becoming contagious.

"How are you faring, little sister?" asked Freydolf.

She bared her teeth. "I'm not poised to soil your clean floor with birthing fluids, if that's what you're getting at. However, if *that man* delays another week, I'll shred his winter wardrobe and bury his favorite boots."

"Don't do that," murmured Tupper, setting tea to steep. "They're nice boots."

"Then he has reason to make haste."

"He's not hurrying back for the boots," the lad reasoned. "It's *you* he misses."

Ulrica muttered sulkily in Skrit, punctuated by Prose, but she looked rather pleased. Frey shook his head in awe. Tupper had learned a thing or three from growing up with so many sisters.

Carden strolled into the kitchen then, a bouquet in one hand and a basket in the other. Presenting Ulrica with the flowers, he said, "From Dulcie." Then, he lifted the corner of the covering on the basket, displaying an assortment of breads and pastries. "These are a day old, but I hope they'll be welcomed. They're sent with compliments from Melina."

Ulrica's eyes widened, then took on the shine of delight. "If your wife were Pred, I'd carve out the heart of a bear and present it to her so we could feast upon it with ready fangs!"

The young man glanced uncertainly at Freydolf, who supplied, "A rite of sisterhood. Very solemn. Very messy."

"I *see*," Carden said. "I'll be sure to relay the sentiment to Melina on my next home day."

Tupper sidled up to Ulrica. "Do you cook it first? The bear's heart?"

The woman's brow quirked. "Naturally! Do you take me for some kind of barbarian?"

"Just checking," he replied in diplomatic tones.

Carden dropped to one knee beside Ulrica's chair. "My mother wants to know if it's time for her to pay a visit. Melina, too, is anxious to be here when you need her."

To Freydolf's surprise, his sister didn't snap. What's more, she gave the young man a straight answer—something he'd despaired of hearing.

"Nay, not yet. Another fortnight, certainly."

"Do you need company?" Carden asked. "Aggie is willing to come ahead of us if you want her."

Frey's heart lurched when Ulrica blinked several times, then whispered, "Aye."

Nodding, Carden turned enough to meet the sculptor's gaze. "I know you meant for me to help you with Phineas and Nerine today, but could we delay long enough for me to walk down into Hayward? I can collect Aggie directly."

Freydolf straightened. "Was that today?"

"Yes," his apprentice replied with the ghost of a smile. "Did you forget?"

"Aye." The sculptor rubbed the back of his neck. "To be honest, it slipped my mind. I haven't even begun sketching."

"Maybe that's good," Carden said. "I can see the whole process from the beginning."

With a sharp rap and a loud hail, Old Gruff's voice sounded from the entryway. "Where's Tupp? I brought his hayseed!"

"Here!" the boy answered, hurrying out to meet the quarryman. "It's good you found some this late."

"Ewert had a hand in it," the Flox confided.

Tupper nodded. "He usually does."

Gruff chuckled, then said, "Point me toward your fallow pasture. I've brought a plow."

Freydolf strode forward, hand extended. "What's this about a pasture?"

"It's for the cow," Tupper explained.

"We have a *cow*?"

"Soon," the lad answered, his eyes sparkling with ill-concealed excitement.

Carden ushered Gruff into the kitchen to join them for tea, but Freydolf hung back to ask, "Where's Torio this morning? He and I had business to discuss."

Tupper meandered toward the sculptor's bed, straightening the blankets and plumping pillows before saying, "Not sure. But not far."

He sighed deeply. "Do you know what he's hiding?"

"Yes."

"Should I be worried?" Freydolf pried.

The lad shook his head. Then hesitated. Then nodded. Skimming over as stealthily as a Pred, Tupper pressed a bundle into his hands and whispered, "Maybe about these."

With a start, Frey realized that all his guests had been too polite to point out that the Keeper was still in his nightshirt. Tupper had just handed him his pants.

24

To Each Their Own

That evening at dinner, Tupper set six places at the kitchen table. Fair curls were in the majority, for Aggie was tucked securely between her big brothers. The girl's blue eyes may have been a little wider than usual, for this was her first visit to the Statuary.

Tupper patted her hand, asking, "Did you eat enough? There's lots."

"Yes."

"Are you sure?"

She bumped him with her shoulder and tutted softly. "Yes, Tupp. Don't fuss."

"It's only natural for a brother to look out for his sister," Freydolf said with a sidelong glance at Ulrica.

The woman rolled her eyes expressively.

Carden calmly assured, "Don't forget, Tupp. Aggie's almost the same age you were when Master Freydolf hired you. She's quite capable."

The girl blushed under all the attention. "I'll do my best."

Torio watched the Pred siblings with a glint in his eye. "I'm feeling *completely* left out! You each have a Meadowsweet of your own!" His lament ended with a plea to Carden, "Pray tell, are there any spares lying around?"

Tupper nodded. "We could give you Farley."

"A fine idea," Ulrica blandly agreed. "Foist the rascal on this rabble. They deserve one another."

"A rascal, hmm? I think I *like* this brother of yours! Older or younger?"

"He's between me and Aggie," Tupper explained.

The merchant grinned lopsidedly. "To think! A Meadowsweet to call my own! I'd fit right in!"

Carden chuckled. "Farley would probably be delighted by the offer, but I'm not sure Mother can spare him."

"She could," Aggie said, slipping into haggling mode. "Mother already hired one worker and has two cousins spoken for in the spring. She would let him go if the wage was good."

Tupper gazed into the startled merchant's eyes. "Do you need a servant?"

Torio laughed weakly. "Is it a testament to the boy's irascibility that you're so eager to sell him off to the likes of me?"

"Count it as a tribute to Tupp's high opinion of you, sir," Carden said.

Freydolf assured, "The Meadowsweets look after their own."

"And that includes you?" Torio teased.

"By some miracle."

"I think it was magic," said Aggie.

Tupper shook his head. "No. It was one of Ulrica's peppers."

The woman stirred in her chair but refrained from comment. She'd been unusually subdued all evening, and Tupper suspected she was trying very hard not to scare Aggie. He appreciated the gesture, but it was silly. His little sister needed to get used to the Pred woman's ways sooner than later.

When the meal ended, Aggie helped him clear the table, and he showed her how the drain in the sink's stone basin worked. As soon as she took over the washing, Ulrica pulled him aside. "You should keep the girl in case she gets homesick. Let her sleep with you for a while."

"Agreed, but only if you'll watch over her bath," he bargained.

Ulrica hesitated. "Is that advisable?"

Tupper sighed and spoke out. "Aggie, you'll have your bath

with Missus Harrow. She and Aurelius have a necessary at their house, and it's the one you'll use most."

The girl gave Ulrica a searching look, then said, "Thank you."

The Pred's brows arched. "You don't mind?"

When Aggie shook her head, her long curls bounced.

Dark eyes flashed, and the woman asked, "Then ... will you let me play with your hair?"

"I don't mind." Aggie's gaze slid to the woman's abundant dark hair. "May I brush yours, too?"

Ulrica's lashes actually fluttered, and her fangs flashed in a fierce smile. Thrusting her hand out to the girl, she said, "Agreed!"

Aggie dried her hands on a dishtowel before accepting the woman's offer of peace. When Ulrica took advantage of her firm grip to tug the child along toward the door, the girl dragged her feet. "The dishes!"

"Leave them for the boy. They're his job. I'm yours!" With a superior smile for the males in the room, Ulrica haughtily announced, "I'll return her to you at a reasonable hour."

Once the front door slammed, Freydolf smirked and said, "It didn't take long for her to take charge."

Tupper nodded. "Yes. Aggie did good."

The last thing Torio expected to find when he left his borrowed quarters early the following morning was Freydolf sitting on his doorstep. Or rather *across* it.

His host leaned against the wall on one side of the narrow stairwell, his foot braced against the other, entirely blocking the way out. The Pred's posture was relaxed—arms folded, chin dropping onto his chest—but as soon as the door swung open, he lifted his shaggy head and regarded his long-term guest.

Torio's heart leapt into his throat, for the Keeper had him cornered. He'd had run out of time just as surely as he'd run out of places to go. "What brings you here so early?" he inquired lamely.

"We have business to discuss."

"Before breakfast?"

Freydolf's gaze sharpened in intensity. "Aye."

"There's no hurry."

The Keeper smiled grimly. "Perhaps not, but I've grown curious."

With little other option, Torio sat upon the mosaic tile and scraped together his scattered wits. Dredging up a smile, he chose his approach. "I've noticed you're comfortable with most, if not all, the magical stones. Even among Keepers, it's rare to find a man with such broad affinities. Indeed, it's said that there's nothing you cannot do!"

Freydolf waved off the flattery. "That goes too far, but it's true that I can sculpt any of the twelve. This should come as no surprise. As you pointed out earlier, I studied under Master Platt."

"Quite true. An uncanny coincidence."

The Pred's brows furrowed. "There's no accident when a mountain calls out to a man. Better to say that Morven was canny enough to seek what she needed."

Torio rubbed his nose and got on with it. "Word is, you're in the market for *any* stone, no matter the color."

"Aye, but sales are usually handled by my agent. We expect him back any day now."

"In that case, we could wait ...?"

"Nay. Show me," Freydolf commanded. He rose smoothly to his feet and gestured for Torio to precede him. "Show me what's in my stable."

With a wordless bow, Torio led the way to his wagon. Grasping the edge of the canvas, he fumbled his way into the old spiel. "I have something that might interest you. Something truly unique."

Freydolf stared past him with an expression of utter confusion. "Something powerful."

"Quite true." Taking a deep breath, he folded back the corner. "There's no denying that this stone has magic."

Freydolf frowned deeply. "Black?"

"You have a discerning eye." Torio pushed back more of the tarp. "Black as a starless night, through and through. Note the silky texture and sheen, which rivals jade!"

The Pred let his fingertips graze the stone's surface. "Impossible."

As the stone began her soft keening, the Grif grimaced. "The evidence is before you, sir. This isn't trickery."

"There's magic aplenty." In darkening tones, Freydolf asked, "*You're* the charlatan who's trying to convince the world there's a thirteenth mountain?"

"I see word has reached you even here."

"Aye, but the rumors failed to communicate the enormity of your crime."

Torio stiffened. "I beg your pardon?"

"Who cut this stone? Who removed it from its place?"

"I did."

"Do you realize what this is?"

"A new magical stone."

"Nay. This is no mere stone! Surely you can tell how much raw power it contains! How could you truncate something so precious? You greedy fool! Can't you see?" Freydolf seethed with righteous indignation as he growled out, "You didn't *discover* the thirteenth mountain! You *destroyed* it by cutting out its heart!"

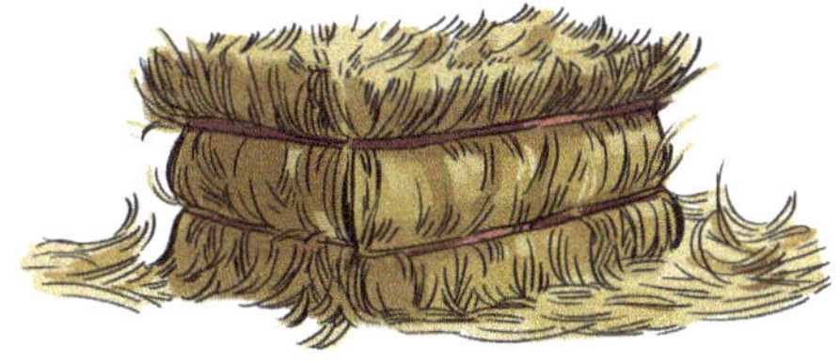

Tupper stumbled into the stable, still lacing his breeches. "What happened?" he demanded, rushing over to the wagon and clambering onto the exposed stone. The boy's hair was a wild mess, and his eyes brimmed with accusation. "Why is she crying?"

Freydolf left off pacing and rubbed his forehead. In utter

exasperation, he thrust his finger at the wagon. "This is the very black stone Aurelius told us about last spring!"

"I know."

"That unconscionable wretch Torio brought it here!"

"Her," Tupper corrected, patting the stone and making soothing noises.

"Aye, *her*," he conceded, with a pitying look at the stone. "His was a grave act ... nay, a terrible crime. That Grif tore the heart from a mountain! Unless it's swiftly returned, the mountain's magic will dwindle until there is naught but dull stone."

"It's too late for that," the lad said, still petting the inky rock. "Torio's had her for six years. Where is he?"

"Gone."

Tupper stilled. "Why?"

"He left." Gesturing to the stall, which was short one horse, he gruffly admitted, "I lost my temper."

"Why?"

"Because he's the worst kind of thief! He's practically a murderer! This poor, pitiable stone is all that's left of what could have been a majestic mountain!"

The lad stood up, bare feet braced upon bleak, black stone. "Did you listen?"

"To what?"

Freydolf was shocked to realize that Tupper was *angry*. And not with Torio.

"To him! To her! To his story! To her cries!"

Frey shook his head, a little frightened by the Flox's unprecedented fury. Stubbornly, he answered, "There's no excuse ...!"

"Wrong!"

He flinched, broad shoulders curling inward. Tupper had never shouted at him before, and the ringing note cut him more deeply than any of his father's railing or mother's disappointment. Freydolf stared up at his servant in abject dismay. "I don't understand."

"Because you didn't listen." There was no mistaking the dangerous light in Tupper's eyes nor the steel in his tone as he reached down and grabbed Freydolf's big hand. Placing it against the black rock, he demanded, "What is she?"

"The meager remains of a mountain that will never again know the touch of magic."

"Not what she was. Not what she cannot be. What she *is*."

Freydolf hesitated, caught between his own agitation and the crucible of magical upheaval roiling within the abandoned stone. He was obviously missing something, but he was equally sure of his initial assessment. "She *is* the heart of a mountain."

"Yes," Tupper acknowledged. "Yes, she is. And who did you drive away?"

"The one who stole her," he growled.

The lad shook his head.

"Torio *admitted* to cutting her from her mountain! He took her for himself."

Tupper rubbed at the base of his horns. "Yes, he did. And he kept her."

"He's a criminal!"

"*No*," the boy snapped. Pointing to the door, he rephrased his question. "Who is she crying for? *Listen* to her, Frey."

He placed both callused hands upon the rock, doing his best to obey the boy.

Tupper covered them with his own and held the man's gaze. In a much gentler voice, he prompted, "Who does she want?"

As realization dawned, Freydolf's stomach plunged, and his chest heaved. It made no sense, yet it was the only thing that made sense. This fragment of a lost mountain was cannier than he'd given her credit for. "She's calling for Torio. She wants her Keeper."

25

Known by Name

"**I**'m going!"

"Aye, go," Freydolf urged.

Although Torio's brown stallion pressed eagerly against the side of his stall, Tupper carried too many precious burdens to be satisfied with a horse for this chase. Regrets. Apologies. Explanations. Promises. The Grif needed to hear them all, but first he must be found. And quickly.

Rimbles was sleeping under Aggie's pillow because Tupper had promised she could wake the lynx, so his usual daytime companion wasn't afoot. Graven was, though. The tiger skulked right outside the stable door, tail lashing.

Tupper wrapped his arms around his guardian's neck. "Can you go fast?"

His tiger's silent roar was all boast, and as soon as the boy leapt onto his back, they streaked away. Tupper lay low over bunching shoulders, easily matching Graven's rippling stride. His knuckles whitened as the big feline proved that yes, he *could* go fast. In mere heartbeats, they crested the summit and plunged into the wooded southern slopes.

Leaps. Bounds. The lithesome statue flowed over and around every obstacle as his young passenger clung to his back.

"Find Torio! He's the one we're hunting!"

When they broke through the trees, Graven veered to the east, racing unerringly toward Drom. It didn't occur to Tupper until it was too late that they were out in broad daylight. Although it was early, farmers were already in their fields, and the countryside roads would soon be busy with traders.

As they hurtled past a gob-smacked cartman just outside Shepley, Tupper turned his face into the tiger's fur and hoped the old-timer wouldn't believe his eyes. "We should be more careful."

Graven had long wandered the continent, so perhaps he understood the value of caution. The guardian zoomed from copse to knoll and skirted Morven's southern villages with impressive stealth. They were cutting across the corner of a sheaf-dotted field along the easterly road when Tupper spotted a riderless black horse cropping grass in a ditch. Not far from him, a man hunched miserably beside a feather-fluttered hat.

Torio hadn't gotten far. All things considered, maybe he *couldn't.*

Sliding from the tiger's back, Tupper hurried to where the Grif huddled. Tapping the man's shoulder, he said, "Found you."

The Grif's eyes were red with tears and bright with fury. "You!" The man lunged for him, knocking him flat and kneeling over him. "You did this! It's all your fault, you horrible little bleater!"

As Torio pounded the ground on either side of Tupper's head with bruised and bloodied fists, the boy glanced worriedly at Graven, but the tiger lounged nearby, all smugness over the success of his hunt. It was probably a good sign that the tiger wasn't taking Torio seriously.

Giving the man's frustrated accusations some thought, Tupper said, "I don't think this is *my* fault."

"It is!" His face crumpled, and he repeated, "It *is* ... because you taught her my name."

Torio hid his face against the boy's chest, ragged sobs shaking his whole body. Taloned hands tore at the stubbled ground, yanked at sandy hair, and tried desperately to cover burning ears. The man cursed in Terse, spilling out six years of bitterness to a boy who didn't understand a word … but grasped the heart.

He patted the man's shoulders, and when Torio was reduced to sniffles and mutterings, Tupper said, "I did. I taught her your name."

Torio brokenly asked, "Why would you do such a thing?"

"She wanted to learn the word for you," he explained. "Because she loves you best."

The Grif sat back on his heels, dabbing at his nose. Tupper produced a handkerchief from one pocket, and though Torio glared, he accepted the square of cloth and honked into it.

"*Loves* me? She's a rock!"

"No. She's a mountain." After a little thought, Tupper clarified, "A very small mountain."

"Your Pred brother said I as good as killed her mountain."

"Did you?"

The Grif frowned deeply, and his gaze slipped out of focus. "It didn't seem so at the time."

Tupper was glad that Torio had calmed down. Folding his hands behind his head to make himself comfortable, he asked, "Where did you find her?"

"At sea," he said with a sigh. "There was a storm. We were off course. I could feel magic and convinced the captain to aim for it. We nearly ran aground."

"You found her on an island?"

"She was the island," said Torio. "An underwater mountain jutting out of a cold sea, shining like black glass, singing a siren's song that only I could hear."

Tupper scratched his nose to hide his smile. If Ulrica could get over hating Torio, she'd probably be giddy over his story. "Your pretty lady."

"The part I took was easy to quarry. There was already a wide crack." He looked down at his hands. "If I'd left her there, the waves would have eventually washed her to the bottom of the sea."

"You saved her."

"And doomed myself," he said harshly. "It almost cost my

life to get her, and it's cost everything I ever had to keep her."

"Don't worry. Freydolf finally listened, and he wants to help you." Tupper suggested, "You should tell your mountain not to worry, too. I can still hear her crying."

They both looked toward Morven, listening to the black stone's insistent calls, but another sound reached their ears.

Several things occurred to Tupper—they were in someone else's field, Torio still had him pinned to the ground, and there was a giant, varicolored tiger lounging in plain view of the road. However, those things faded in importance as the jangle of harnesses and beat of hooves passed on by. It was an elegant, high-wheeled carriage. It was drawn by six perfectly-matched blood bays. And the driver's seat was ominously empty.

Aurelius was back.

With a gasp, Tupper seized Torio's shirtfront with both hands and hauled him down just as two daggers thudded into the dirt beyond them, their jeweled hilts glittering in the morning sun.

The Grif's confusion turned to calculation, and he urged, "Stay down, young master. I won't let any harm co–"

His voice faltered as an arm snaked around from behind, laying a third blade across his throat.

"And who have we here?" Aurelius purred, hauling the Grif off Tupper. "You're a long way from your usual haunts, sprat."

"Yes." He scrambled to his feet. "Welcome home!"

"Did I make it back before Ulrica upended every bottle in my wine cellar?"

"Yes."

"My tunics?"

Tupper solemnly reported, "You're down by eight."

Aurelius grimaced. "What about my boots?"

"She threatened to bury them, so I hid them."

"A Flox after my own heart!" the man extolled. With all the important parts out of the way, the Pred turned his attention back to Torio. "Shall I slaughter this raggedy kidnapper with your birthday gift? Or shall I spare the Grif who refers to you as master?"

Tupper blinked. "That knife is for me?"

"Aye, and it has a fine edge," Aurelius boasted. "It's deucedly hard to find such craftsmanship anywhere outside Pred lands, but this is an exceptional hunting knife. You'll be equipped for gutting rabbit, buck, and bandit alike. Now ... which is he?"

"Thank you very much." Tupper studied the handle's decoration. "It's pretty."

Torio cleared his throat and tensely asked, "Tupper ...?"

The Flox straightened and met Aurelius's questioning gaze. "Torio's a Grif!"

"Aye, that's plain as the nose on his face."

"And he *didn't* kidnap me. I caught him. He mostly belongs to us now."

"Don't tell me you've gone and made *him* a Meadowsweet, too!" the Pred exclaimed, relinquishing his hold and whipping out a bit of lace-trimmed frippery in order to polish the bared blade.

"No, but we were thinking of giving him to Farley."

Torio massaged his throat and slowly stood, warily studying the other man. Aurelius smirked confidently. "How long has this Grif been lurking in these parts?"

"Since midsummer."

"And what did Ulrica make of him?"

Torio winced as Tupper bluntly reported, "It took her ten days to sheathe her knife, but her tongue is sharper than ever."

Inclining his head, the Pred passed along his gift to Tupper, then finally deigned to address the Grif directly. "I'm Aurelius Harrow, husband to Ulrica and agent for Freydolf, Keeper of Morven, the legendary Moonlit Mountain. And you are?"

The other man bent to pick up his hat and offered a flourishing bow. "Thank you for sparing me, sir. I'm called Torio."

"No, that's not right," Tupper scolded. "You should say it right."

With a bland smile, the Grif murmured, "I know my own name."

While Aurelius collected his daggers, Tupper pressed, "Is that all of it? Do you have a second name?"

"Kite."

Brightening, Tupper stepped up to the Pred and executed a small bow of his own. With great formality, he said, "Aurelius Harrow, this is Torio Kite, who has been granted sanctuary by Morven, Frey, and me. He's Keeper of the Black Mountain, and Frey wants to do business with him. So be nice."

"*Black* Mountain?" Aurelius echoed incredulously.

Tupper's chin came up, and he bartered hard for a little more respect for the beleaguered Grif. "He's in possession of the rarest magical stone known to all four continents. Very strong. Very beautiful. Very valuable."

"Did you say *Keeper*?" Torio whispered, for no one had thought to tell him yet.

"Yes," Tupper replied, pushing both men toward the spot where Graven waited. "And you belong with your mountain, so come home."

Aurelius balked. "You can't gull me into getting anywhere near that mosaic monstrosity!"

Graven bared his teeth.

Aurelius swore under his breath.

Torio chuffed the tiger's chin.

Tupper tugged the Pred's hand.

Aurelius muttered several more expletives, then hauled the boy over his shoulder and sprang lightly onto his nemesis's back. Tupper wriggled down to sit in front of the man.

With haughty dignity, Aurelius said, "I'll suffer with this galumphing scrapheap until he catches up to my carriage ... assuming he's capable of the feat. You may follow on your nag, Keeper."

Torio had just enough time for a sardonic smile before Graven surged away in eager pursuit of Aurelius's carriage.

Tupper leaned back against the Pred's ruffle-decked chest, letting go of Graven and trusting the man to keep him steady. Tilting his head back to see, he reached up and patted the tall man's smooth, brown cheek and said, "I missed you."

Aurelius's golden eyes glinted fiercely, for their wild ride suited his tastes. But his gaze warmed considerably as he replied, "I *wondered* if you'd get around to mentioning that, sprat."

26

Beginnings of a Village

Tupper's hasty search ended amidst the orphan stones. He found his master in their whispery chamber, curled up on his side. Setting his lantern on the floor, Tupper asked, "Did Morven scold you?"

"Aye, she's very disappointed in me. As are you."

"No." Tupper peered into eyes that were red from crying. "You listened. You changed your mind."

"Only after it was too late to take back my words."

Frey's voice was steady, but he sounded miserable. Giving the man's hunched shoulders a comforting pat, Tupper asked, "Is that why you're hiding?"

"How can I face my lambkin when he bares his fangs at me?"

"I don't have fangs."

The man snorted.

Tupper sighed. "I should have come sooner. I *would* have, but Ulrica was angry. Aurelius needed back-up."

The Keeper grunted, but that wasn't good enough.

Wrapping his arms as far as he could around his bond-brother, Tupper mumbled, "You're easier to talk to than your sister, but you don't listen any better."

"I heard you, lambkin. Your words still ring in my ears."

"No," he corrected. "Listen to the me that's here now. You

shouldn't hide from me."

"For all the good it did."

It occurred to the boy that his master hadn't done a very good job making himself scarce. This was Tupper's own chamber. Only the two of them shared its secret. Which meant Freydolf had made it easy.

"Yes. I found you." Pushing until the Pred sat up, Tupper asked, "Are you glad?"

Now that they were more or less eye-to-eye, Frey couldn't avoid his gaze. "Nay, lambkin. I'm ashamed. I made a terrible mistake."

Tupper nodded and quoted one of Old Gruff's sayings. "People do."

Another moody huff.

"I made mistakes today." Tupper counted them out on his fingers. "Our beds aren't made. I didn't sweep. The garden's not watered. And I forgot about the chickens. Aggie didn't though, so they're fine. But I spoke sharply to my master. *You* should scold *me* for running off without doing my work."

"Never."

"Does that mean you forgive me?"

The man's eyes slammed shut. "There's nothing to forgive, lambkin."

Tupper didn't understand. Something else was bothering Frey, and he needed to figure out what it was. Placing his hands on the Keeper's shoulder, he started with the obvious. "Morven's unhappy, which means you are, too."

"Aye."

"Then tell me in words I can understand," Tupper begged. "What's wrong?"

"Me." Freydolf scrubbed at his face. "How I behaved today ... it reminded me of my father."

"Are you like him?"

"My voice when I'm angry. My face when I scowl." His voice broke. "It's the same."

Tupper knew that Freydolf's father was mean enough to banish his son. Hadn't he taken away his name? Hadn't Ulrica run away from home? Even Aurelius had called Mister Rakefang scary. But didn't all that prove that Frey *wasn't* like his father?

"I'm already mother and brother. I'm not sure I'm good enough to be father, too. But I'll try. If you want."

"Oh, lambkin," groaned the big man, gathering him close.

As muffled sobs shook his bond-brother, Tupper held on tight. It was simple, really. Freydolf was having a bad day. The first one Tupper had ever witnessed. Maybe there had been others, back before they met. Had Frey endured them all alone?

Not this time. The boy tried to think of all the kinds of things he'd ever wanted to hear on bad days, and he fit them into each little lull. "I'm here. I'll stay. You're safe. You're you. It's okay. Promise."

A few days later, Freydolf still wasn't in a fit state to touch stone, so he abandoned his workshop in hopes of finding Tupper. The lad had been spending every spare minute getting ready for the arrival of Carden's family. A process that apparently required upending the contents of an entire block of quarters. Maybe he could make himself useful.

Adding so many new residents at once had more than tripled the list of goods they'd need to lay in before winter. There were extra storerooms to clear. Furniture to shift. And both a bakery and dairy to supply. That brought Frey up short. "Was *today* the day Aurelius planned to take the lad into Shepley?"

"No."

The Keeper turned to find Aggie sitting alone on a low bench tucked between two gray urns. Something about her expression held him there. "Is everything all right, Miss Aggie?"

She plucked at the hem of her sleeve. "I'm not sure."

Frey took a half step forward, then hesitated. Aggie didn't seem frightened, but he didn't want to loom. Lowering himself to the ground, he showed her his palms. "This is my mountain, and I'm responsible for everyone who lives here. If you're unsure of anything or unhappy in any way, tell me. I'll do what I can to make things right."

Aggie regarded him seriously, and Freydolf couldn't help smiling. She wasn't much more talkative than Tupper, such a difference from little Dulcie, whose constant chatter would soon be a part of normal life in the Statuary. Folding his hands together, Frey waited patiently for her answer.

The lass unburdened her heart with three words. "Pred are *strange*."

Freydolf chuckled, "Aye, to a Flox we must be. Has my sister confused you?"

"Over and over."

"Does she scare you?" he checked.

"Less than before. More than I like."

The girl's crisp tones reminded him a little of Tupper's mother, and Frey found her disapproval reassuring. Aggie wasn't looking for a way home. Having come up against their unusual clash of cultures, she was trying to take the same leap Tupper had made. But she needed help.

Freydolf asked, "What parts don't you understand?"

"Missus Harrow is particular about table settings and how I cut the carrots. She says I slice meat too thin, and my soup is bland. But when *she* spices things, it burns my mouth." After a little thought, Aggie added one more item to her list. "She uses angry words, but her eyes laugh."

"Sounds like you already know my little sister pretty well."

Aggie went back to pulling at her sleeve. "*Knowing* isn't the same as knowing what to do."

"Aye. I'll give what advice I can." Freydolf searched for simple words to help the girl. "You can tell when Ulrica's serious. She'll speak more softly than usual. If she's complaining loudly, it's probably nothing. But if she's truly displeased with your work, she'll teach you a new way."

"Like cutting meat into thick slabs."

"Aye. Very important for sinking in one's fangs."

"Oh. That makes sense," she murmured, eyeing the teeth his smile revealed.

Swinging legs that were too short to reach the ground, Aggie asked, "What should I do after my work is done?"

"Like now?"

She nodded.

"I'll be honest, Miss Aggie. I don't know the first thing about the pastimes of Flox girls."

"What do Pred girls do?"

Freydolf puffed out his cheeks and thought back. "Weapons care, combat classes, tracking practice, sparring sessions, and war games. Ulrica was also keen on sailing, hunting, and languages. And raiding the dress shops. But dancing most of all."

Aggie took her time before repeating, "Pred are strange."

"Aye," he conceded with a chuckle. "Let's see. Tupper is always making baskets in his spare time. Or exploring the galleries. And there are books and games in the balcony. You're always welcome."

"Thank you."

A thought occurred, and Freydolf said, "You aren't utterly tied to Ulrica. If she's given you that impression, I'll speak with her. Visit your brothers. Play with your nieces. Make yourself at home here."

She accepted that with a nod, then said, "Missus Harrow looks like she wants to hold me, but she's afraid to touch."

"Oh, lass. That's only respectful distance. You see, it's not in a Pred's nature to accept the embrace of strangers." Freydolf admitted, "When your brother first came to live here, he startled me more than once by crawling into my cot."

"Don't Pred children want to cuddle?"

"We do. Aurelius and Ulrica never withheld affection from their sons. But ... most are taught to fend off any kind of advance. Only those we trust are allowed under our guard."

"Did you like it when Tupper hugged you?"

The Keeper admitted, "Aye. Hugs mean trust, and I was glad to have your brother's."

Aggie asked, "May I hug you?"

Freydolf blinked. "Aye, lass. Any time you like."

Slipping from the bench the girl made herself comfortable in the sculptor's arms.

He ventured, "Are you homesick, Miss Aggie?"

"A little."

"Carden and his family will be here soon."

"I know," she replied. "That's good."

Frey rested his chin on top of Aggie's head. "Did we ask too much of you, bringing you onto my mountain?"

"Almost," she whispered. "But this makes it easier to be brave."

The lass clearly needed more affection than she was getting. "Be sure to tell your brothers when you're lonesome."

"Just did."

The man chuckled. "Aye. So you have."

She nestled against his shoulder, then asked, "If Tupper's your brother, is Missus Harrow my sister?"

"Ulrica never had a sister. Perhaps that would please her." Giving the matter more thought, Freydolf said, "I think she's hoping for a daughter. The baby, I mean. There's lore only passed down from mother to daughter, so she may feel left out, having only boys."

Aggie nodded. "Would it help if I hugged her first."

"Aye, teach her. Help her to learn Floxish ways."

"How?"

Freydolf smiled. "The only way to gain her trust may be to trust her. Not just with your life, but with your thoughts. Ask questions without worrying if they're impertinent. You won't offend her. They'll probably intrigue her. And give her hope."

"Be kin to become kin?" Aggie checked.

"That's the way, lass." Gently touching her abundance of curls, he asked, "Any other questions?"

"Yes." Peeping up at him, the girl asked, "Why does Mister Harrow have so many clothes?"

Frey laughed so hard, there were tears in his eyes, and by

the time he'd wiped them away, every one of his brooding thoughts were gone. His old life was worlds away. Father couldn't touch him here, in the safety of Morven's heights.

The familiar twitch was back in the master sculptor's fingers, and he grinned broadly. "Aurelius and his wardrobe are a mystery, even to me. But tell me, Miss Aggie ... do you have a favorite animal?"

Aggie's eyes took on a hopeful shine. "Why?"

"You should have a guardian statue of your own. Nay, two guardians! One for day, and one for night."

"Truly?"

"They'll be company for you. And keep an eye on you when we can't. And ... there isn't much else I can do to show you how glad I am you came. Thank you for watching over my sister for me."

The girl's smile was all sweetness. "I like babies."

"Aye, I suspect I do, too," Frey said. "So what kind of animal? Or any creature, really."

"How is a creature different from an animal?"

Freydolf explained, "There are many legendary creatures in Morven's galleries. They come from myths and stories."

"Like the mermaid in our courtyard?"

"What makes you think she's not real?"

Aggie's expression clouded. "She *can't* be. People don't have fins and scales."

"What about her Basq prince? He has scales."

"And pointy ears. But nice manners."

"Aye, as do most Basq. I've met a few. Scales are as common as curls on First Continent."

She shook her head. "Something ordinary, please. With soft fur."

"Aye, I can do that. Let's find your brother. I have a pretty piece of starstone already, but we'll see if he can find us something for daytime."

"Why Tupp?"

"Hasn't anyone mentioned it? He's a first-rate picker." Freydolf stood and offered a hand. When Aggie took it, he eyed her curiously. "Have you ever been tested for affinity?"

"What's that?"

The sculptor shook his head. "One thing at a time. How do you feel about ... bears?"

At the sound of his name, Tupper turned from the huge copper cauldron he'd just propped against some stairs to drain and dry. Nott sprang from the boy's shoulder and scampered up Freydolf's leg, forcing the man to let go of Aggie's hand in order to deal with her antics.

"What are you planning to cook in that vat?" Frey asked.

"It's for Melina's laundry room." Beckoning to Aggie, Tupper said, "I hope it's good. Do you think she'll like it?"

"Are there windows?" she asked.

"Lots. And two fireplaces. Good for when we're snow-stuck."

Stepping over Rimbles, who was basking on the sunny threshold, Tupper led his sister into a miniature colonnade. Basins for soaking, scrubbing, and rinsing lined a wall decorated by carvings of tropical foliage. Long windows with borders of green and blue glass scattered splotches of color on white tile floors. In addition to the fireplaces, a central fire ring showed where the big caldron belonged.

The boy pointed to hooks spaced at regular intervals just overhead. "Aurelius and I will look for clothesline in Shepley."

Freydolf strolled further into the room. "This must have been used by more than one family. A sort of communal laundry."

Nodding, Tupper said, "Lots of room for Carden's family to grow."

Aggie remarked, "If I wash diapers here with Melina, we can leave the Harrows' laundry for fancies."

"Good idea," the boy replied. "I'll find enough drying racks for three ... maybe four babies."

The Keeper blinked. "So many?"

Tupper shrugged. "Yona and two new babies. Unless there's twins. That'd make four."

Frey glanced around the spacious room with a measure of awe. "Aye. We're expanding quickly."

"Did you know this was here?"

"Nay. Whenever I explored, I didn't bother with these residential sections."

Nodding to the corner, Tupper said, "There's a laundress. She was glad when I told her a family is coming."

Freydolf strolled over to an alcove where a freshstone statue of a young woman with feathers for hair stood, cupped hands outstretched. "She's Keet!" the man exclaimed.

Tupper nudged Aggie. "Good job."

Aggie retorted, "I did ten jobs before breakfast. Which one do you mean?"

It was funny to hear one of Mother's sayings again. Tupper smiled and shook his head. "Morven is pleased with you."

"The mountain?"

"Yes." He pointed to Freydolf, who was searching for the maker's mark on the stone laundress. "You cheered up her Keeper."

Aggie shyly confided, "He cheered *me* up."

Tupper had been a little worried about how his sister was adjusting. He knew she was doing her best, but something was missing. Aggie still acted like a visitor instead of someone who belonged. Maybe Frey had explained things better than he could. Tupper whispered, "I like when you smile."

She wrinkled her nose at him.

That's how Tupper knew everything would be okay.

When Tupper led the way back outdoors, Freydolf said, "Can I beg a favor, lambkin? Do you know where that little bag of stones is? The ones I use for the affinity test?"

"Yes."

"Fetch it and meet us in the Barrens. We're going picking."

Tupper perked up. "You want to make something?"

Frey nodded. "For Miss Aggie."

"That's good. Right back." Pointing past them, he added, "You, too."

The Keeper chuckled when Aggie glanced over her shoulder and jumped. Graven blinked placidly at the girl, clearly pleased to have startled her.

"Come with me," Tupper said firmly.

Slinking past the others, his tiger accepted a ruffling of fur before allowing the boy to scramble up onto his shoulders. Together, they sprang away toward the workshop. Tupper's elation lent Graven speed, and the errand was accomplished in no time.

They caught up to Freydolf and Aggie in the Barrens along the edge of the outer courtyard. Aggie cuddled Rimbles while the Keeper explained the reason behind their colorful assortment of rubble. Tupper smiled when he recognized Frey's lilting recitation.

> **Blue for sweet waters;**
> **White for the brine.**
> **Gray under moonlight;**
> **Gold calls for wine.**

Skipping from stone to stone, Tupper held out the same pouch of stones that had been his introduction to Morven's Keeper. "They're here. They're ready."

"Aye. Thank you." Taking a seat atop a heap of redstone, Frey loosened ties and poured out his collection of baubles. "Come and see, Miss Aggie. These are some of my prettiest picks."

Aggie turned the lynx kitten loose and exclaimed softly over the Keeper's collection, which included jewel-like crystals, a sunstone pyramid, and a songstone disk. Tupper pondered the intensity of the gaze Frey fixed on his sister's face. No one had ever mentioned girls working with stone. Had any of the mountains ever called a lady Keeper?

"Do you have a favorite?" Freydolf asked lightly.

Aggie's fingertips grazed across sunstone and one of the smallest crystals. "Yellow's my favorite."

"Aye. Bright, cheerful stones." Pushing at the pile, he inquired, "Is that why you're so fond of Rimbles? Because she's your favorite color?"

"I love her because she loves my Tupp," Aggie corrected. "And I've liked yellow since I was little. I'm sorry, Master Freydolf. I don't think I have any magic in me."

The man grunted. "Not many hear a mountain's call, let alone a pebble's whisper."

Tupper asked, "Frey, what kind of stone are you looking for?"

"A daytime Guardian for Miss Aggie. Preferably sunstone since she's fond of the color." Shaking his trinkets back into their pouch, he added, "A big piece if possible. I want a guardian large enough to be of help if your sister finds herself in trouble."

"Sounds right," the boy murmured, picking his way over to the jumbled pile of sunstone scraps. When Aggie followed, he slowed down. "*Are* you in trouble?"

His sister shook her head. "Master Freydolf said to trust Missus Harrow so that she'll trust me."

"That's a good trade." Tupper circled around behind the sunstone heap before starting to climb.

In a softer voice, Aggie remarked, "Mister Harrow is back."

Tupper stopped and turned, searching her face. "That's good, too."

When his sister only nodded, he sat down and held out his hands. She was too big to sit on his lap anymore, but that didn't stop him from hauling her close.

"Tell me, Aggie."

"He's more than I can manage," she confessed, touching the braided trim on his tunic's pocket.

"You're nine, and he's ... Aurelius."

"Exactly." Aggie wriggled close and begged, "Advice?"

Tupper stared into space for so long that Freydolf made it to the top of the heap of buff stones first. Nott rode on the Pred's shoulder, her tail looped around the man's neck. Even though Tupper couldn't hear the words, he could tell Frey was talking to the little monkey. Their cheeky girl might get into trouble, but her maker was always sweet to her. And that gave Tupper an idea.

Holding Aggie's gaze, he quickly and quietly explained a thing or two about Pred. Not *everything*, since brothers were for back-up. But enough to give his sister the confidence that came with a little leverage.

Freydolf descended slowly, gaze roving. "Any luck?"

"Yes." Tupper kicked aside a layer of rubble, then knelt to pat a chisel-scuffed chunk of sunstone. "He likes Aggie. He's been howling for her since the test."

"Howling?" Frey muttered, pulling away more loose stones. By the time they freed the lopsided rock from the surrounding rubble, the sculptor was grinning fiercely. "Aye, I see what you mean. Miss Aggie, I do hope you can find room in your heart for a wolf. He's smitten."

27

Wolves Among Sheep

Aggie vastly preferred the Harrows' necessary to the one Tupper tended for his master. Her brother might not mind doing the wash by the light of lanterns, but she liked to see what she was doing. One by one, she folded open the shuttered doors surrounding the little building that housed their bathing room, letting in the morning light and breezes. On such a fine day, everything would dry quickly.

Filling her apron pockets with clothespins, she turned to the trunk in the corner. The contents were a gift Mister Harrow had brought back for his wife, who'd kept it to herself for several days. But after breakfast, Ulrica had goaded the man into moving the trunk here.

It was supposed to be filled with baby clothes made in the Drom capital. Aggie placed her hand on the trunk and wondered if she was in trouble.

Her new mistress had warned her against tampering with Aurelius's finery, which had special rules for washing. What if the baby clothes also had extravagant ruffles and ribbons? Or what if she was expected to wash silken diapers? It sounded ridiculous, but she'd *seen* the contents of her new master's wardrobe. His tastes were fancy.

Maybe she should try to get a message to Mother. The

Meadowsweet women were good at getting ready for babies. They could stitch up sensible things that were warm in winter and easy to wash. Would Missus Harrow mind if her baby used Floxish diapers?

Asking would have to wait. Her mistress was taking a nap. Mister Harrow had taken Ulrica along on a predawn hunt, which had improved the woman's mood more than three jars of spiced peppers. Pred were definitely still strange, but Aggie was glad the man was home. Watching how he handled his wife was already making it easier to catch on.

Curiosity mingling with dread, Aggie undid the trunk's latch and hoisted it open.

And stared.

Then smiled.

"We're the same after all," she whispered. Aurelius's gifts weren't too fancy or too frilly. She lifted out item after item, all brand new. All soft, warm, and sensible. Freydolf had called Aurelius a good father. This made it easier to believe.

"Why are you smiling?"

Aggie jumped at the sudden question. She hadn't heard Mister Harrow come in. Holding out a fur-lined blanket, she answered, "These are good. You chose well."

"Aye." With a wicked gleam in his eyes, Aurelius said, "You sound surprised."

"A little," she dared to admit.

The man didn't seem offended. "Babies are born into a home, where comfort comes first. The foibles of fashion can wait until he's ready to make his way in the world."

"He?"

"Or she." Holding her gaze, he announced, "Frey spoke to me."

"Oh?" she managed, her voice barely above a whisper.

Aurelius stepped closer, then dropped to one knee. "Are you afraid of me, Aggie?"

"Sometimes."

"Excellent! Now ... which of my actions make you uneasy?" When she didn't immediately answer, he added, "I cannot change what I am or who I am, but I can change my behavior out of consideration for you.”

Shaking her head, Aggie said, “I’m the servant. I should change.”

“Is that all you wish to be?”

She stalled again, thinking fast. Was this headed for a trade?

Mister Harrow asked, “Is that all Tupper is to his master?”

“No.”

“Aye. You’ve seen him with Frey. You know what they’ve forged.” With a tight smile, he said, “If such a thing could be bought, I’d pay any price to secure it for Ulrica.”

Aggie nodded to herself. Mister Harrow was a merchant, and he was definitely angling for something.

“My wife hasn’t been herself these past weeks.”

“Missus Harrow is better, now that you’re here,” Aggie assured.

The man reached for her hands, and she let him pull her closer. It felt like a test, and she faced it bravely.

“Why are you smiling?” Aurelius inquired lightly.

Aggie replied, “You need me; you have me. That’s a good bargain. But I think you want to trade for more.”

His eyes were gold, like a wolf’s. “Very good ... and very true. You have the upper hand, Miss Meadowsweet. My wife has always wanted something you’re in a position to give.”

“What are your terms?”

Aurelius shook his head. “I can’t barter for something beyond price, which puts me in a deucedly awkward position. Hear me out, Aggie.”

“I will.”

Big, lean hands enfolded hers, just as brown Freydolf’s, but very different. Tipped by manicured claws. Decorated by pretty rings. Soft and smelling like spice cake. To Aggie’s relief, Mister Harrow chose easier words than usual.

“Pred don’t normally allow strangers into their homes. Families take care of their own, but Ulrica and I left ours behind. Instead, we’ve taken you in, much like your family took in Frey.”

“I’m a Meadowsweet.”

“Aye, and a tribute to your family.”

His gaze was expectant. Was he waiting for her counter-offer? Aggie wasn't sure, so she asked outright. "Are you going to make me a Harrow?"

"You hardly look the part."

Aggie's eyes narrowed. He hadn't said *no*.

The Pred smirked. "I cannot give a straighter answer until I evaluate your level of commitment."

She sighed. "If you want my answer, ask a question I can understand."

"Aye, Miss Meadowsweet." Aurelius remained flawlessly polite. "I'm not asking you to abandon your family. I'm asking you to enter mine. Let us think of you as our own."

"I don't mind."

"You are generous to a fault, and too trusting by far. Keep your guard up, for my lady is Pred. Her mothering would bear no resemblance to anything you're accustomed to. Agreeing to this will have consequences."

Aggie recalled her conversation with Freydolf and ventured, "Weapons, tracking, and combat?"

Aurelius's fangs flashed. "So you *do* understand."

Her brows knit in concentration, for she *did*. Tupper was mothering Master Freydolf, but Ulrica would be mothering her. "I would be raised like a Pred?"

"Ulrica would insist upon it."

"And you?"

His brows lifted. "I'm consulting you in advance, to negotiate a peaceful accord."

"Missus Harrow doesn't know?"

"There are times when a woman doesn't understand her own feelings. Those are the times when men must be wise."

Aggie glanced back at the trunk filled with baby clothes.

"Why are you smiling?" Aurelius asked for the third time.

"Am I a gift for your lady?"

He cleared his throat. "Give as much as you're willing. Refuse anything that goes beyond your abilities."

Sensing her advantage, Aggie asked, "Will you agree to learn Floxish things?"

"Such as?"

"Birthdays. Festivals. Hugs."

Aurelius chuckled. "You ask much. Pred don't easily let down their guard."

"You'll get used to it," she promised.

The man gave in with good grace. "Proceed."

She reached up to wrap her arms around his neck. There were a great many ruffles, but Mister Harrow wasn't girly. He was strong, tall, and sneaky, three things he proved when her feet left the floor.

Once the upward rush ended, she was tucked into the crook of his arm. Snug and safe in Aurelius's clutches. "You ask much," he repeated. "But not too much. Unless you haven't finished naming your terms?"

Aggie liked this mountain, this man, this trade. But no one settled for a good deal if you could haggle for better. "You're my brother's brother's sister's husband. In Hayward that would make us family."

"Aye, but I'm not asking you to be my wife's brother's brother's sister."

She nodded. "You want a daughter."

"Something you're prepared to trade on." Aurelius asked, "What would you ask in return?"

"Only my right."

Mister Harrow frowned slightly. "And what's that?"

Aggie risked impudence. "Your fangs on a ribbon."

With a dark chuckle, Aurelius patted her cheek. "You haggle like a Flox."

"Will I hunt like a Pred?"

"Aye," he pledged. "And when you present me with your first kill, taken in the Pred tradition, I will consider you the first Harrow with blue eyes. But fair warning, Miss Meadowsweet. You'll have to strike your own bargain with Ulrica."

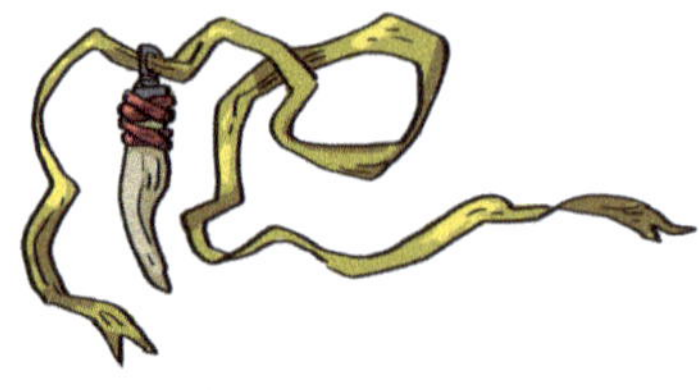

"Wolves among the sheep," Torio remarked blandly. "Usually a much less favorable arrangement for the flock."

"We're not sheep," Tupper said seriously. "And Pred aren't wolves."

"That may be true, young master," the Grif replied. "But this remains a miraculous reversal."

Carden and his family were expected, so a group from up top were strolling down the eastern trail, eager to welcome them home for good. Keeper and servant had been joined by Aurelius and Torio, whose conversation zipped back and forth so fast, it was hard for Tupper to keep up.

"Do Flox migrate?" Torio inquired.

Aurelius swirled one hand. "From village to quarry and back again, regular as you please."

Tupper thought that was going too far. "We mostly stay put."

Using his nose to point at the village below their vantage, Torio warned, "From thence comes what could be the first wave of a full-scale invasion."

"Let them come. We've plenty of room for more," Frey replied, lifting an arm in greeting as Carden rounded the bend.

"You're outnumbered," Torio said, tones gently mocking.

"Ambush is always an option," returned Aurelius.

Freydolf rolled his eyes. "This isn't an invasion."

"That's dazzlingly obvious," his brother-in-law assured.

Tupper belatedly added, "We're *all* outnumbered. By statues."

Aurelius reached over to flick his horn. "In that respect, the Statuary lives up to its name. And at your insistence, they have their representatives."

Brand and Haimish were part of the welcoming committee. Even if the two statues couldn't say how excited they were, Tupper knew the truth. The redstone Grif and brownstone Pred gazed down the trail just as eagerly as the rest of them. More Meadowsweets were coming to live on the Moonlit Mountain, and that meant holding hands and helping out.

Torio watched from under the broad brim of his hat. "Here comes their banner-bearer."

Dulcie danced ahead of her parents, as sure of the way as she was of her welcome. "Unca Doff! Unca Tupp! Unca Ree!" she called, curls bouncing, hair ribbons streaming.

"Be wary, Harrow. Something that small could slip past your defenses."

"And into my care," drawled Aurelius, making it clear whose protection she was under. He swung the girl up and crooned, "Have you come to live with me and your Auntie Ree?"

The girl giggled. "Not *me*! Aggie's yours, and I live with Papa and Mama and Yona. Do you have a baby yet?"

"Not yet, sprite."

Dulcie switched her attention to Torio. "*Feathers*! Are you Unca Doff's new friend?"

"I am in his custody for the time being."

Tupper stepped in to do a better job. "Mister Kite is a Keeper, Dulcie. Just like your Unca Doff."

She looked from face to face, then addressed Torio. "Unca Kite, I have a bunny."

The man's lips twitched, but he replied seriously. "You are fortunate. All I have is a rock."

"My bunny's a rock!" Dulcie exclaimed, pulling a wriggling dawnstone guardian from her pocket. "See?"

"A blushing bounder to keep you company!" Torio leaned close to inspect her pet, earning a wee thump on the nose for his trouble. "I recognize your uncle's handiwork. You must treasure his gift."

"Do you love your rock, too?" she asked sweetly.

Torio straightened quickly, then swept off his hat to bow to the girl's parents. "More Meadowsweets. I'm enchanted to finally meet Carden's lady fair!"

Tupper was watching Melina closely. His sister-in-law was walking much slower than usual. Her face was too pale, and her smile was strained. Maybe it was because she was in the early stages of pregnancy. Or maybe saying goodbye to Hayward had been more difficult than expected. Hurrying forward, Tupper stole Yona from her arms, saying, "Let us."

"Thank you, Tupp," Melina murmured.

Turning to Haimish, he said, "This is Yona. She needs your help."

The brownstone man's eyes weren't the only ones that widened.

Tupper thought he understood why. Unlike Brand, Haimish's maker hadn't given his creation a father's experiences. But Freydolf was gentle and good, and he'd learned quickly about babies once he had the chance. "Don't worry. Frey likes babies, so you should, too."

Haimish glanced at his sculptor, but Freydolf didn't jump in to correct Tupper. The brownstone guardian looked to Melina next. With a weary smile, she said, "Please, Haimish. She wants to be held, and I haven't the strength."

The statue offered his hands in a show of willingness, and Tupper gave him a quick lesson. Cradling Yona in the crook of his arm, he explained, "Like this. Or upright." Propping his niece against his shoulder, he patted her back. "The rest, she'll try to tell you herself. You'll understand because babies are feelings."

Tupper pretended not to notice how many people were holding their breath when he transferred the baby. This would help lots.

With a tentative wag of his tail, Haimish accepted the care of Carden and Melina's second daughter.

Torio did a double-take and demanded, "What did the young master do to that statue?"

"Gave him the baby," Freydolf replied indulgently. "That's little Yona."

"You can't see it?"

"See ...?" asked the Keeper, his gaze sharpening. "What do you see?"

"Never mind," sighed Torio.

Like most sculptors, Freydolf only had eyes for rocks. Being able to see the shape of a statue still hidden within stone was a rare gift, but it was much different than seeing magic itself. At a glance, Torio could see that Haimish's heart belonged to Freydolf. But at Tupper's coaxing, a slender thread had looped and knotted, forming a secondary attachment. One that was already gaining strength.

He sidled up to the stone Pred. Yona stared into Haimish's face, her tiny hand wrapped around one claw-tipped finger. The stone guardian didn't turn away at Torio's approach, a sure sign that the Grif had already been marked as a friend of the family. "Thank you for your trust."

Haimish's tail swayed in time to the contented pulse of the magic that sustained his life.

"The young master made you happy with this new task."

The statue inclined his head.

When Freydolf tucked Melina's arm through his and supported her along the upward trail, Torio stuck with Haimish. Following along, he kept half an eye on the stone guardian while shamelessly eavesdropping.

"Please, Melina. Anything you need," the Keeper urged. "What I cannot give, Aurelius can find."

"Anything," confirmed the merchant.

Freydolf cleared his throat. "I don't know if the lad mentioned it, but Tupper gave me a bakery for my birthday."

The young woman laughed outright. "A *bakery*?"

"Aye. He found it in one of the residential blocks, not far from your laundry. He cleaned them both up, so they're ready to use." Rubbing the back of his neck, Freydolf added, "I'd be honored if you'd consider them your own."

"There's an oven? Well, of course there *would* be ovens," she murmured. "There must have been hundreds living up here at one time."

"Aye. It's nearly as large as the one your father and uncle are using. Aurelius already placed an order for additional firewood, but let him know what else you need."

Melina gripped the Pred's arm more tightly. "I can bake for you!"

"Aye. I confess, I relish the thought."

Aurelius slyly said, "He's more excited about your bread than he is about your husband's affinity."

Carden chuckled. "So it's Melina you've all been after."

Torio eyed the young man. Carden Meadowsweet's soft smile suggested that he knew the truth. Even if the Flox was oblivious to the bursts of magic exploding around his ankles as he climbed, he knew this mountain wanted him. Steady. Serene. He was taking Morven's call in stride.

Freydolf stopped in his tracks. "Nay, I wouldn't ...! To take you and yours from them who love you? Not for all the bread in ...!"

Melina patted the Keeper's arm. "Master Freydolf, you have been generous beyond compare. You shall have bread and cakes and pies. All you can eat."

Torio shook his head at the cozy interplay. A sheep in wolf's guise, and sheep with the hearts of lions. If Tupper kept on as he'd begun, the galleries would soon be overrun by Meadowsweets and defended by Harrows.

28

Future Prospects

A few days later, Freydolf and Carden rolled heavy stone basins along the cobblestone road leading up to the Harrows' home. They set up the squat cylinders as close to their courtyard's fountain as possible and were splashed for their efforts. Torio wasn't surprised when neither man complained.

"Thank you, Nerine," Carden murmured, dipping his hands into tepid water and patting flushed cheeks.

"Aye," grunted the Keeper, who stepped right into the water to cool his feet. "It's hot enough to make sunstone shimmer."

"I'll bring your boots," offered Aggie, darting off toward the workshop.

On her way out, she passed Tupper, who maneuvered a cart heaped with blackened rocks. "No, no," he called, shaking his head at Dulcie. "Stay with your mama. These are hot."

"Yes, Unca Tupp," the girl promised, clambering back up onto the bench she shared with Melina and Ulrica.

Torio lounged in a patch of shade just inside the gate. "Your Basq prince should feel right at home in this weather," he remarked.

"Aye. Their homeland's heavy air would be unbearable if it weren't for the sea breezes that stir them." Aurelius shielded his eyes to peer at the heights. "How long do these Floxish doldrums last?"

"Until the storm breaks," Carden replied, carefully shoveling hot rocks into the basins. "Can't you feel it building?"

"Yes," Tupper sighed, pulling tarps into place. "It'll be a bad one, but rain would be good for the pasture."

"I'm glad the skies were clear last night," Melina remarked. "For Nerine's sake."

Torio's gaze slid to the blue mermaid, who'd experienced her first glimpse of stars the night before. Freydolf had added his mark and a starstone shell to her accessories, and the bond between blue and white stone held true.

A gentle fizz of anticipatory magic surrounded the invisible ties that bound her to Phineas. Torio would have been more comfortable blaming the connection on the fact that Freydolf had harvested the starstone directly from the white prince. Just as the blue shell that now graced Phineas's turban had once been part of the mermaid. But the Grif knew better. The bond had already been there. Could magical stone form connections on its own?

Aggie returned with Freydolf's boots, and while the sculptor sat to put them on, Torio eased to his side. "Are both of these statues masterworks?"

"Aye. Carved by former Keepers."

"Contemporaries?"

"Nay," Freydolf replied. "Phineas is older by many a century. But the Keeper who created Nerine was from First Continent."

Torio's brows arched. "Was he ...?"

"Aye. He was Basq." Frey stood, then followed Aurelius's example and peeled out of his tunic. "And she is his masterpiece. Small by some standards, but he died young."

"Do you think she remembers him?"

"I could never forget one of my statues, especially one I called by name." With a small shrug, the Pred added, "I like to think they'd never forget me."

"Sculptors find immortality in the hearts of their guardians?" Torio asked lightly.

"And Keepers in the mountains that call them," Freydolf returned evenly.

The Grif had been shying away from the idea for longer than he cared to admit, but it faced him squarely here. "But that bond is preservation. Not *love*, surely."

Freydolf lowered his voice. "Is it such a terrible thing to learn you are loved?"

"It was bad enough to be lashed to a chunk of screeching madness," Torio muttered. "I didn't ask for a Keeper's title, nor a life's servitude to the whims of an increasingly jealous anchor."

Concern flitted across the Pred's features. "Historically, most Keepers do take wives."

"Like Carden?"

"He's a prospective. It's too early to know if he'll be my successor, but aye. Most of Morven's Keepers were family men."

"And she wasn't jealous?"

Rubbing at the back of his neck, the Pred muttered, "I have no way of knowing. My predecessor was a bachelor, and I'll never marry."

"By choice?" Torio pried.

"By default. But you ... are you concerned about future prospects?"

"I'm a wanderer. I never planned to settle down."

Freydolf hesitated. "If I gave her form, perhaps she could travel with you."

"A roving mountain for a wandering Keeper?"

"Aye," he chuckled. "Assuming I can figure out what wakes black stone."

Ulrica interrupted in sharp tones. "Haven't you *better* things to do than natter with vagabonds?"

Nerine added force to her complaint with an insistent slap and splash.

"Only a few more minutes," the Pred promised. "We're almost ready to wake your prince."

"Everything's ready," Tupper corrected. He opened the folds of the make-shift tent, allowing a puff of steam to billow out.

With a gentle touch to Torio's arm that was a completely Floxish gesture, Frey excused himself. Moments later, the concealing curtains dropped away to reveal the Keeper clasping hands with Phineas. The Basq's gaze was fixed on the blue sky above. Frey murmured some form of encouragement, and the prince turned to Nerine, then knelt before her in the pool.

She smiled and reached up to touch the blue scallop decorating Phineas's turban. Thanks to the delicate ornament—and their Keeper's skill—the pair were able to overcome a formidable gulf. Nerine's fingers trailed down Phineas's cheek, and he covered her hand with his own.

Ulrica sighed and dabbed at tears. "Aye. They're well matched."

Freydolf returned to Torio's side, and the Grif lapsed into Terse. "Is that my future?"

"Would you welcome such a future?"

With an uneasy shrug, the Grif admitted, "Not by choice."

Frey's dark eyes sparkled. "By default, then?"

Groaning softly, Torio conceded. "I cannot walk away, so I'd be grateful if you can find a way for us to walk together."

"Aye," the Pred easily agreed, offering his hand to seal the pact. "Somehow."

Torio quietly stalked the various statues of Morven, trying to unravel the twists and turns that magic took in order to please Morven and her young master. He was hovering just outside the entrance to the Harrows' courtyard when a small dagger glanced off stone a handsbreadth from his nose.

Leaping backward with a Terse oath, he glared at Ulrica. "Unruffle your feathers, woman! I meant no harm."

The Pred waddled past, glowering haughtily. "And you are unharmed."

"Not all injury is physical!"

"Unruffle *your* feathers and fly, Grif. Or the next wound won't be to your sensibilities."

Opting for diplomatic withdrawal, Torio seized upon a telltale thread and followed the magical tracery to the bakery where Melina Meadowsweet presided. There he found Tupper sitting in the corner, an ankle crossed over his opposite knee as he minded baby Yona.

Carden stood at the oversized table in the center of the room, adding a coat of wax to a carved wooden cradle. Melina left off reading aloud from a fat book and smiled. "Tea, Mister Kite?"

"Thank you, missus."

Choosing the stool closest to Tupper's, Torio said, "So Haimish *will* relinquish the child."

"Yes." The boy smiled at the wee girl, who gummed his finger and blew bubbles. "Taking turns is only fair. And there are things Yona must learn."

"From books?" Torio asked, including Carden and Melina in his question.

Tupper's elder brother chuckled. "The books are for me. But Tupper's lore is easier to understand."

"Speaking of turns, let's have more of Uncle Tupp's lessons," Melina said as she set the teapot on the table and went for a cup. "I've had enough of battle and siege for one morning."

Torio looked more closely at the old record. "Morven's history?" he guessed.

"In excruciating detail," sighed the young woman. "It seems the eighth Keeper was a strategist. Go on, Tupp."

Addressing himself to Yona, Tupper launched into a lecture of sorts. "Haimish is strong, and he's kind. Don't mind if he's quiet. It's not a mad quiet or a sad quiet. Just the nice kind of quiet that comes from stone."

Melina pushed a plate of sliced bread closer to Torio, who reached for the accompanying pot of soft cheese. He chewed thoughtfully. Even though the baby couldn't have understood, Tupper's lesson continued. Perhaps for her parents' sake.

"Spicy smells after sunrise will wake him. And he likes

wind. If his hands are cold, let him stand by the fire or soak in the sun."

"Wind?" asked Torio.

"Brownstone likes it," the boy assured, holding Yona's gaze. "And if you want Haimish to hold you at night, you'll need to show him the sunset."

"Last light on a clear night," Carden murmured. "But we're on our own if there are clouds?"

"Yes." Tickling the baby's cheek, Tupper went on. "Haimish's eyes are kind because he's kind. And he's kind because your Unca Doff is kind. Smile at him when you're happy. Cry with him when you're sad. Tell him your secrets, and they'll be safe."

The brownstone man returned then, a water pail in each hand. He carefully filled the big jar in the corner, then presented his hands to Tupper, who nodded. "Look, Yona, here's your guardian. Haimish is back," he crooned, relinquishing the girl. "He's happy when you're happy."

Torio could see that the statue's heart was laced to Yona's, neat as you please. And with every thought, touch, and word, Tupper encouraged the bond. In Terse, the Grif muttered to himself, and at Carden's questioning glance, Torio offered, "The young master is a mysterious one."

Carden chuckled, and Tupper countered, "You have more secrets than me."

The shrewdness was back in the boy's gaze, and Torio straightened unconsciously. "And even more stories yet to tell," he offered.

"Not this time. Come with me." When Carden cleared this throat, Tupper added, "Please."

"Command me, and I will go. The farther, the better."

Tupper shook his head. "We'll go into Hayward. It's time for you to meet Farley."

"Your oft-maligned younger brother?"

"Yes. If you hire him, he'll lead the new cow home."

"And if I don't?" inquired Torio.

After a thoughtful pause, Tupper replied, "You'll have to lead the cow home."

"Your village is cautious of strangers," Torio remarked as he trailed after Tupper into the woods beyond Hayward.

"Yes."

"Don't they welcome your Pred brother? He and his sister attended your festival."

"No." Tupper ducked under the branches of a drooping pine. "But we vouch for them. Us and Old Gruff. That helps some."

"I do hope they realized I'm not Pred."

"Maybe." The lad skirted a stand of saplings, leading his companion deeper into the forest. "You're too fair to be Pred. But too tall to be Flox."

"And too many feathers to be anything but foreign?" inquired the Grif.

"Yes." Tupper stopped and faced him. "Sorry."

"I felt like a Grif among Pika back there."

"Flox are like Pika?"

"Small of stature. Lithe of frame." Nodding, Torio said, "If you'll pardon the traditional slurs, bleaters *are* like bounders, but with shorter ears."

Tupper turned his back and kept walking, but much slower. "Why are Pika afraid of Grif?"

"Our histories mingle in regrettable ways." When the boy reached up to rub the base of his horns, Torio chose simpler words. "In days long since gone, the Grif were as rude as the Pred. But we learned to appreciate the Pika, and they were gracious enough to accept what apologies we could offer."

"They sound nice."

"Pika aren't so bad. If your tastes run to long ears and tufty tails."

Swiveling, Tupper asked, "Tails?"

Torio jerked a thumb over his shoulder. "Right where a tail should be."

"Truly? There are men with tails?"

"And women." The Grif asked, "Did you think the world lacking in wonders?"

Tupper confessed, "I want to meet a Pika."

"You're not satisfied with a Grif for company?"

With a small smile, the boy asked, "Do you feel unwanted?"

"*You* are a gracious host and a stalwart guide," Torio proclaimed. "Even if certain womenfolk snarl and sharpen their blades, *you* trust me enough to sell me your brother. What more can a wandering stone merchant ask?"

"I'll talk to Ulrica. Again." Tupper added, "And if you need help, ask."

"Aren't your hands full with your bond brother?"

The boy nodded. "That's why you get Farley. If he takes you. I think he will."

"How much farther before we locate our quarry?"

"If Farley's checking traps like Mother said, there are two places to check."

"Wouldn't it have been faster by catamount?"

"Probably. But this is better. Fewer choices mean shorter haggles."

The Grif laughed. "Is *that* why the lynx kit is nowhere to be seen? You kept her under wraps to narrow the field to you and me?"

"No. It's him and me. And you'll pick him."

"Am I being dragged into some convoluted bout of sibling rivalry?"

"Say it again?"

"Does your brother envy you?"

"Yes. But mostly no." He explained, "Farley likes my tiger, the red hounds, and our dragon, but he doesn't like to sweep. He'd skip baths and let the lettuce bolt."

"Terrible crimes, to be sure."

Tupper nodded. "Frey needs a mother, but Farley's still a boy."

Torio blandly inquired, "Isn't he the same age you were when your Pred brother hired you?"

"Yes."

"Weren't *you* also a boy?"

Tupper stopped walking in order to think that over. Finally, he answered, "Yes. But I was a different boy."

"And what kind of boy is Farley?"

With an assessing gaze, the lad replied, "Your kind, I think. Show off your talons. Speak in Terse. Be tall and grand and strange."

"What good will that do?"

"Lots. Probably." Tupper backtracked in order to catch Torio's hand. "Impress him if you can. But it has to be a good trade, or he won't come up top. Even though it's what he wants most."

Torio leaned down and whispered, "To claim a Meadowsweet for my very own, I shall be tall and grand and strange. Young Farley *will* be impressed by me, but only because he hasn't the sense to be impressed by you."

Tupper hadn't meant to sneak up on his younger brother, but his Pred training held true. Farley was sitting beside a lumpy pack, staring into the stream without seeing anything. Canteen, baskets, bedroll, tarp, walking stick—why would he bring them here?

Stepping into the open, Tupper asked, "Is that your pillowcase?"

Farley scrambled to his feet and tried to shield his provisions from view. "What're *you* doing here?"

"Looking for you." Circling around to check the pile, he asked, "Why's your cloak here? And Father's compass?"

Rolling his eyes, Farley retorted, "Thick as ever, Tupp. Maybe I'm doing laundry."

"Without soap?" Tupper challenged. Something was very wrong.

A short burst of Terse accompanied Torio's emergence from the trees. The man swept off his hat and bowed low, blue eyes glittering as he sized up his prey. Then in the language of his homeland, he daringly announced, "You're a brat, and a miserable one at that, but I see more than you know, and I can help. If you're smart, you'll snatch at this chance. If you're perceptive, you'll realize your brother made it for you."

Farley's chest puffed out as he tried to hide his surprise. "Hey, mister. Are you the Grif merchant Ewert was talking about?"

Switching to Verit, Torio replied, "I'm pleased that word of my wanderings has reached you. I am Torio Kite."

The younger boy's eyes narrowed speculatively. "Could you teach me to talk like that?"

"Are *you* clever?" The slight emphasis that implied Tupper's lack of appropriate wits put a shine in the boy's eyes. And stirred Torio's sympathies.

Farley looked him up and down before asking, "What are you selling?"

"What would you barter for, given the chance?"

"A horse."

Not a surprise, given the boy's obvious intentions. Pointing with a taloned finger toward the stream, Torio politely inquired, "Even though you already have one?"

A tiny freshstone stallion trotted out of the shallows, shaking out his mane and pawing at the ground.

Dropping into a crouch, Tupper spoke to the little guardian in low tones. Torio saw the effects his words had—praising his loyalty, boosting his confidence, binding the statue more firmly to his younger brother. But Farley misunderstood.

The boy barged in, snatching up the guardian and glaring with a ferocity that was fueled by understandable frustration.

Tupper seemed puzzled by this turn of events.

With a thin smile, Torio clarified matters. "I'm sorry to learn you're leaving."

"He is?" The older boy looked between his sibling and the small pile of luggage. "Farley, are you running away?"

"Butt out," he grumbled.

"No." Stepping closer, Tupper demanded, "Why would you do that to Mother?"

Farley's jaw clamped shut, and Torio stepped in. "You mentioned traps, Tupper. Go, check them."

Relief flashed in the lad's eyes, and he vanished upstream without a sound.

Torio addressed Farley. "How set are you on this course of action?"

"Why do you care?" retorted the boy.

"On Tupper's advisement, I'd hoped to secure the services of a young man of unparalleled intelligence and considerable ...."

Farley didn't let him finish. "You say I'm smart, but you treat me like an idiot. My brother never said those things. Tupp doesn't know the words."

"But you do?"

"Melina and me traded," he revealed with a trace of pride. "So long as I helped with the babies, she let me listen in while she read to Carden in the evenings. It was a good trade. While it lasted."

"Tupper took them away from you?"

Farley snorted. "I'm not stupid, and neither was Carden. Tupp brokered a good trade for all the Meadowsweets." Ticking off his fingers, he listed, "Freydolf gets an apprentice. Carden gets a mountain. Ewert gets a house. And Aggie gets her precious Tupp."

"And you?"

"They don't need me, and they don't want me." Farley complained, "Ever since Tupp adopted that Pred, they act like he's something special. But he's *Tupper*. It doesn't make sense."

Torio tapped the side of his nose. "So you are investigating other options."

"I wanna see the stuff in those books. Other places. Other people."

"Like me."

"Yeah," he muttered, staring hard. "Guess you're proof that the books weren't lying."

"I meant that you are like me. One born to wander. A seeker of new sights. An explorer of strange territories."

Farley affected boredom, and Torio preened inwardly. Progress. Finally.

The boy demanded, "If that's so, how come you're here instead of out there?"

"Morven is unique among the twelve mountains. She welcomed me and mine, and her Keeper granted us sanctuary." Torio coyly added, "When my journeys resume, this is the nest to which I'll return."

"I thought you were alone."

"Not entirely. I have two horses."

"And Frey has a cow," said Tupper, who carried a stringer of fish.

Farley folded his arms over his chest. "I won't work for you."

"Freydolf is my master. Torio is yours." Tupper added a well-timed afterthought. "We *both* serve Keepers."

"What's the purse?"

"Same as mine, unless you'll take over the new dairy. Aurelius will surrender coin for butter and cheese."

"I'll earn more gold than you?"

"Probably."

The boy thrust out his hand. "Deal."

Tupper stepped aside, allowing Torio the final shake.

Farley clung to the man's hand and brazenly announced, "When you go, I'm going with you."

"Are you certain that's a bargain you want to make?"

Farley glanced at the brother who'd arranged for his placement.

Tupper gravely said, "That would be good."

With an impudent grin, Torio's new servant asked, "When can I start?"

Tupper held out the string of skimmers. "Since you're already packed, you can bring these to Mother and tell her goodbye."

With a whoop, Farley nabbed the stringer and sprinted off toward home.

Torio gazed after him. "That went well."

"Mostly. Sorry."

When Tupper bent to collect his brother's abandoned luggage, Torio touched his shoulder. "Let me."

"But this is backward. And a bad start." Tupper's frown deepened.

"This is a better start than the one he would have made if we'd arrived tomorrow."

"Yes." Gazing after his brother, Tupper said, "He does his best when it matters."

"I'm touched by young Farley's enthusiasm and untouched by his neglect." Torio shouldered the boy's paltry belongings. "Your brother is *my* servant. Let me take responsibility for him in my own way."

"That would be good," Tupper repeated, relaxing enough to smile. "Be brave and do your best."

29

Accord

Aggie slipped into the Harrows' kitchen through the back door and stood still, waiting for her eyes to adjust. Having Farley up top definitely made an evening in Freydolf's balcony noisier. Her newly-arrived brother had praised her starstone bear, pulled her curls, and pouted when the Keeper wouldn't leave off sculpting her sunstone wolf long enough to notice there was another Meadowsweet underfoot.

Tupper had tried to explain that when a statue was close to done, its hold on the sculptor grew stronger, but it wasn't much use. You couldn't tell Farley anything. Still, he was good at games and sweet to Carden's girls. He must have missed Dulcie and Yona almost as much as she had. Since his stunts kept their nieces in giggles, Aggie could forgive him for being *so* Farley.

Aggie's apron pocket wriggled, so she dipped in to rescue Near. The white bear nosed her palm, then nibbled her fingers. Tiptoeing over to the table, the girl turned her night guardian loose, then paused to listen. Even though she caught no unusual sounds, that didn't mean much. Especially where Mister and Missus Harrow were concerned.

Crossing to the sideboard, Aggie lit two candles and set

them where they would cast tattle-tale shadows. Taking a third, she perched on a high stool and opened one of Ulrica's best kitchen books to read through her pickling recipes. If someone tried to sneak up, the girl was as ready as she could be.

Aggie was pondering the possibility of cooked radishes as an accompaniment for breakfast when one of the candles wavered, and Near reared up on her back paws. Glancing up, the girl asked, "Are you hungry? I could make a snack."

Ulrica's dark eyes glittered as she eased into a chair. "Aye. Are there any more of those sugared nuts?"

"Lots." Slipping from her stool, she disappeared into the pantry. Even though Ulrica had taken a chair, Aggie glanced over her shoulder to be sure she wasn't followed. Sure enough, her mistress stood against the near wall, peering down her nose with a smug expression.

"You're quieter than whispers," Aggie remarked. "Did you want something else?"

"You learn fast," the lady drawled.

Had the woman been teaching her something? Aggie knew she was paying much closer attention to little things—drafts, noises, and the prickle of the hairs on the back of her neck. She minded her surroundings, kept an eye on shadows, and tried to step as lightly as her fierce mistress. All because of this Pred's little games. "I'm doing my best."

"I can help you do better," Missus Harrow proposed, holding up a loop of yellow ribbon and giving it a playful jounce. Bells twinkled. "I'll teach you."

"To do what?"

"To walk. To track. To hunt."

Aggie nodded. "In exchange for ...?"

"A place in this household," Ulrica replied loftily.

"That's not a fair trade," the Flox girl countered. "You give and give again."

"My offer is far from generous, girl."

Aggie turned back to the shelf and collected the tin of nuts, a box of sweets, and a jar of peppers. "Then we should discuss terms. Go sit, and I'll put the kettle on. Or would you rather have milk?"

"Aye, that would suit."

When Aggie returned to the table with a mug, Ulrica was playing with the little bear.

"She's fuzzy as a kitten," the woman remarked.

"Yes. I asked Freydolf for something soft enough to keep near."

"Near and dear." Ulrica chuckled when the cub turned a somersault on the table, then held up her front paws. "Clever girl," the woman praised, but her gaze rested on Aggie.

Taking her seat, Aggie asked, "What do you want, Missus Harrow?"

"A daughter." The woman gestured broadly as she explained, "I've borne four sons, which is all very nice for Aurelius. He gloated and doted on each one with an excess of paternal pride."

"Mother always said she was glad to have girls and boys in equal measure."

Ulrica took a slow drink, then sighed. "I have no complaints, but I also have no daughters. It's deucedly unfair, so I've made up my mind to take matters into my own hands."

"Your baby may be the girl you're hoping for," Aggie pointed out.

"Aye, but I want a hunting companion. Someone with whom to share the trick of snaring birds and the triumph of felling a buck." Her chin lifted rebelliously. "I've waited long enough."

"I understand, but you can't give and give again. It's a bad deal unless you let me give back."

Ulrica grumbled, "I'm willing to be generous."

Casting aside caution, Aggie circled the table and presented her hands to Ulrica. "To be fair, it has to be said differently."

"What would you propose?"

Aggie was grateful that Aurelius had talked to her first, for he'd given her time to think through this bargain. It was time to change the balance of her relationship with her mistress. Just as Tupp had done with Frey.

"Teach me to walk, and I'll follow in your footsteps. Teach

me to hunt, and I'll provide for our family. Teach me to fight, and I'll guard your children."

Ulrica's eyes widened, and she whispered Aggie's name.

Holding up a finger, the girl solemnly recited the rest. "I'll teach you our ways, so you'll feel more at home. I'll teach you to dance, so you'll remember happy days. I'll teach you to love me, so you'll know a daughter's love."

There were tears on Ulrica's cheeks when she pulled the girl close. Aggie kissed the woman's cheek, then rested her head on her shoulder. The bargain was fair as Flox, and their bond would be close as kin.

Subtlety had never been Ulrica's strong suit, so when the woman began passing along a mother's lore to Aggie, Aurelius noticed.

"My dear, why is Miss Aggie jingling through her tasks?"

Ulrica did a poor job of hiding a bowl of peas with the fullness of her sleeve. "Let me have my way. The girl is young enough to be teachable."

"I'll admit, she doesn't hop and patter like the sprat used to do."

"Clumsy," snipped Ulrica.

"Carefree," Aurelius countered.

Drawing herself up, she insisted, "The girl who looks after our baby should be capable of more than doing dishes and laundering diapers. I shall provide her with the skills to defend our child."

Aurelius knelt beside his wife's chair and gazed up into her face. "And you love her."

"Is that what you think?" she retorted haughtily.

"Aye. I have considerable experience in slipping under your formidable guard." Rising higher, he rested his cheek against hers in order to murmur in her ear. "Your best ferocity has always belonged to your brother, your children, and *me*."

"Presumption can be dangerous," she muttered.

"Persuasion can be delicious," he reminded.

Dark eyes flashed. "Pontification."

Aurelius kissed his wife. "Placation."

Fidgeting in her seat, Ulrica's tones turned petulant. "Don't oppose me in this."

"Oppose you?" He smiled as he threaded his fingers into her hair. "Haven't we been allies from the very start?"

With a soft growl, Ulrica relaxed into her husband's embrace. "Schemer."

"Rebel."

She smiled softly. "Conniver."

Aurelius's fangs flashed. "Colluder."

Ulrica knew full well that it was better to plot with her husband than against him. Accepting his support, she admitted, "Aggie and I have reached an accord. She will be magnificent."

"You are swift as a thrown blade once your mind is made up. But why fend with one dagger when you have two?" Resting his hand on her stomach, Aurelius said, "If you wish to continue as you have begun, let us proceed together. Take Miss Meadowsweet to your heart as a daughter, and I will do the same."

Leaning back to search her husband's eyes, Ulrica asked, "You are with me, even in this?"

"My dear, I have been with you in everything."

"Two hunters. One hunt."

Aurelius pulled her hands into his and kissed her knuckles before reciting the final part of their people's marriage vows. "In life. To death."

Tupper counted all his fingers twice, then sat on his bucket to think. Yona was too young, but even so, there would be enough Meadowsweets and Harrows at dinner that they needed more plates and bowls than he had. "And Torio makes eleven."

"What's that, Tupp?" asked Melina, who was arranging flowers in empty canning jars.

"Do you have enough spoons?"

The young woman laughed. "Not nearly. But if you bring yours, Missus Harrow can make up the difference."

Rubbing at the base of one aching horn, Tupper said, "There's more in storage. Lots. And bowls, too. If you want."

Melina peered around the bakery, then the long table. "That's a good idea, Tupp. If we kept enough dishes here for everyone, this could become our gathering place. A village dining hall with room for one and all."

Tupper nodded. "Frey likes it when everyone is together."

"Speaking of sticking together … why did you stay back?"

Aurelius and Carden had left earlier with Farley to fetch Merona Meadowsweet. Ulrica's time was close enough to bring her up top, and the Harrows had insisted on doing so in fine style. The carriage ride would give the men time to explain about magic and mountains. And there would be no chance for her to accidentally meet a statue. Aurelius would drive his carriage right to the bakery's stairs in time for a late lunch.

"It's better this way." Tupper stood and backed toward the door. "I'll find bowls and things."

Maybe it was selfish, but he didn't plan to spend too much time in his mother's line of sight. After so many weeks, he knew his curls were long past due for a trim.

As the carriage clattered to a stop on the cobbles below the bakery, Ulrica swept inside and scowled down at the Grif already seated at the table. "Are you still here?"

"Good of you to notice," Torio replied, all cheek and cheer.

"Wretched buzzard," the woman muttered.

Tupper hurriedly took her arm. "Your seat is here, next to Dulcie."

Ulrica's baleful expression softened. "Did you save a place for Auntie Ree?"

The little girl thumped the plump cushion of a chair on the opposite side of the table from the Grif's "All for you and baby Ree!"

"Aye, child," the woman murmured, lowering herself gracefully despite her bulk.

Tupper sighed in relief and turned to the door as Carden escorted his mother inside.

"And this is the Statuary's bakery, where Melina works her magic."

"Oh, Carden," the young woman said with a laugh, stepping forward to embrace her mother-in-law. "We're so happy you can be here."

"Gramma! Gramma!" exclaimed Dulcie, bouncing over for her hug. "Are you going to live with us?"

"For a time," Merona confirmed. Crossing to Ulrica, she said, "Your time is close?"

"Would that I could wrest this child from my body by want alone," the Pred snapped.

"Sounds about right," Merona said with a laugh. "Long walks and certain herbs are believed to hurry things along."

"Aye. Ply me with your home remedies, and distract me with your good company," Ulrica said more gratefully. "You bring wind to my sails."

At Merona's puzzled glance, Freydolf supplied, "A compliment, marm. You are most welcome."

Carden escorted his mother to a chair, and once they were all seated, the woman glanced around. "But where is little Yona."

Melina smiled softly. "Haimish has her."

"Who?"

"I suppose you'd call him ... a friend." Melina looked between Freydolf and Tupper. "Will you make the introductions?"

"Aye. I'll bring him," Freydolf said, quickly exiting.

All eyes swung to Tupper, who stood, then sat. "They told you about Morven? And statues?"

Merona smiled in the all-wise way of mothers. "Did you know that my eldest granddaughter recently become a *very* early riser, lest she miss dawn's light."

Dulcie guiltily ducked her head.

"And once my youngest son came into his nubs, he suddenly learned to love baths."

Farley slouched in his chair, gaze fixed on the ceiling.

"Oh," Tupper breathed. "They tattled. That makes this easier."

Merona tutted. "I've had enough hints and promises to nettle my curiosity. Show me this wondrous magic Master Freydolf works."

At Tupper's glance, Aggie darted over to the upturned bucket in the corner. She lifted it to reveal Rimbles, who remained stone still. "This is Tupp's kitten," Aggie explained. "Her name's Rimbles, and she needs sunshine to wake."

Turning in her chair, Merona asked, "Wake?"

"Like this," Aggie replied, pushing the golden statue into the nearest sunspot.

With a sideways spring, the little lynx's fur puffed out. Rimbles peered around the room with wide eyes, then scampered across the floor, leaping into Tupper's waiting arms.

"Quick as life," breathed Merona, who glanced down when Dulcie tugged her sleeve.

"This is Bunny!" the girl exclaimed, happily offering her pet for closer inspection.

Farley leaned over to set his blue horse in his mother's empty soup bowl. "And this is Tap." Sloshing in some water from the closest jar of flowers, he woke the stallion. "He likes water."

Tupper crouched beside her chair, cradling Rimbles to his chest. "They're our guardians. Frey's gifts."

"Why ... they're alive!" Merona exclaimed.

Freydolf reentered the room then, leading Haimish. "Aye, marm. That's the way of things on my mountain. A good many statues are like these. Touched by magic. Marked by a master. Alive."

The woman gasped at the sight of her grandchild in the arms of a stone man. Tupper quickly explained, "That's Haimish. He's good. Freydolf made him, so he's ... good."

Melina interjected, "Haimish has been a great help. Yona's very attached to him."

Merona shook her head. "How is this possible? You made him, Master Freydolf?"

"Aye, and we're prepared to show you how."

He beckoned to Aurelius, who sidled up to a cupboard and withdrew a weighty bundle from within. "What have we here? This lump's deucedly heavy."

"Miss Aggie's been waiting patiently ...."

Freydolf didn't have the chance to finish, for Aggie gave a glad cry and rushed forward as Aurelius unveiled another sunstone statue. The young wolf was much larger than Rimbles, perhaps half the size of Dag. He was the picture of patience, with muzzle resting on his paws and soulful eyes upraised. Aggie giggled, "He looks like he's begging."

"At your feet," Aurelius replied smugly.

"Aye, he's an impatient one," Freydolf added. "If you've a name, we'll wake him after lunch."

"I already picked." Aggie hugged the stone wolf and smiled sweetly. "His name's Zev."

Freydolf leaned in the frame of his workshop's door within a door, eating a peach. The day was fine, and the view was excellent. Mostly because Aggie had gone to Tupper for help.

Side by side, the siblings moved through the steps of one of the Flox's slow, strolling folk dances. Rimbles and Zev trailed after, capering through a crazy dance of their own. Even from this distance, Frey could tell Tupper was humming, but that was the only sound the siblings made. No bells jingled.

"Aggie's improving quickly."

"Aye," Aurelius replied, caught in the act of sneaking up. "The lass is quick on the scent."

Frey glanced at the loaf of bread tucked under his brother-in-law's arm and the plate of cheese tarts in his hand. "Feeling peckish?"

"Kite and I want to borrow the balcony for a game. A long one."

"Seeking sanctuary?"

"My lovely wife prefers the company of women these days."

Frey chuckled. "So she's spurned you?"

Aurelius affected unconcern. "Her mood will swing in my favor again before long. In the meantime, Missus Meadowsweet has her well in hand."

At a bright jingling of bells, Frey's gaze snapped to the siblings, who paused in their promenade to peer at the true culprit. Torio ambled out of the door to the lower colonnade with a bottle of wine under one arm and Dulcie by the hand. The little girl's every step sent up cheery peals. Catching sight of her Unca Tupp, she let go of her Unca Kite and skipped over to join the dance.

Snorting, Frey asked, "Isn't our little miss noisy enough? Who gave her bells?"

The Grif grinned. "One pretty pout, and Harrow buckled like a shoe."

"Such a little thing to ask," grumbled Aurelius. "And look at how happy she is."

"Oh, aye. Pure bliss," Freydolf agreed, shooing the men inside. He finished his peach, then meandered back inside. Taking up a sketchbook, he doodled a scalloped border that would make a good lesson for Carden. Then a feathered wreath. His next scrawl turned into an alphabet—good for training his apprentice *and* for teaching his girls their letters.

Satisfied with these rough plans, Freydolf peered around the room, wondering which of the waiting commissions he should tackle first.

Tupper's bed caught his attention, and Frey recalled the chunk of dapple the lad had been nurturing since spring. Frey knew for a fact that the boy often slept with the rock in his hand. And brought it outside on misty mornings.

Freydolf checked under Tupper's pillow and found the rock. To his amazement, the stone responded to his touch. He caressed the bit of dapple and asked, "Did he put you there? Or wake you up?"

Shyness. Or perhaps a loss for words.

With gentler tones, the Keeper tried to draw out the whisper of personality that stirred in the heart of this forlorn stone. "I know how it is, feeling the lad's touch. He gave me hope, too. Changed my life."

Weak and wary, the dapple's magic stirred in agreement.

"Aye, that's the way," Frey encouraged. "Would you like to stay close to the one who made your heart beat? I can give that to you. I can give you to him."

Breathless befuddlement.

The Keeper smiled. "You can spend more time with him before you decide. Or .... I don't know *all* the lad's secrets, but I know a few. For instance, he likes frogs. Thinks they're cute."

Stone swayed.

"There now," Freydolf said approvingly. "You have something to aspire to, and it will please him. Bear with me, and on a dewy morning, I'll be able to introduce you to a boy whose miracles are small and wonderful." Tucking the bit of dapple back under the lad's pillow, he whispered, "You'll belong to Tupper. Just like everyone else on this mountain."

The door slammed, and Frey straightened guiltily as his sister stormed into the room.

"Heart of a lion, he claims! Yet I grow weary of his roaring! Only cowards pace to and fro, boasting of their heart!"

"Calm down, Ulrica," Freydolf urged, shooting a worried look toward the balcony. "Let's take a stroll through the galleries. The cool and quiet will do you good, and you can tell me why you're upset."

He hustled the peevish woman out and down the nearest stairway, lit a lantern, then tucked her arm securely through his own. "Why aren't you with Missus Meadowsweet?"

"She insisted on a nap. I escaped."

Freydolf chuckled. "Should you be skipping along rooftops in your condition?"

The woman offered a haughty sniff.

"And what does any of this have to do with Torio?" he prompted.

"His beak offends me, and that cannot be healthy for the child I carry." She scowled and continued, "He smiles too often, flatters too well, lingers too long. The man could be a threat, and I would see him banished ...!"

He jerked to a stop, and Ulrica paled.

"Freydolf. *Brother*. I am sorry!"

Turning to his sister, Frey clasped her hands. "Torio wants peace. His only wish is sanctuary." In a voice rough with emotion, the banished Pred continued, "A whole world has rejected him. Let me harbor a weary man."

Ulrica grumbled, "He's a sarcastic, prattling tease."

"Aye, easily as impudent as your beloved husband." At his sister's growl, he slipped his arms around her and casually announced, "Torio has a lady of his own, you know. Tupper thinks you'll like their story. It's very romantic."

"Unlikely."

"A destined match between a pretty lady and the only man who could hear her heart's cry."

Ulrica snorted. "And where is this lady?"

"Imprisoned in stone."

His sister leaned back to search his face. "You're teasing."

"Nay. Torio is many things, including a thief of hearts." Waggling his brows, Freydolf set her a challenge. "If you can settle your differences, you'd be free to plague him for details. Wrest the secret from his grasp and ally yourself to his lady. That will be his downfall just as surely as you were Aurelius's."

Interest gleamed in the woman's eyes, and Frey smiled in satisfaction. The deed was done, and Torio's fate was neatly sealed. Ulrica wouldn't rest until she learned all, but in the process, they'd reach an accord.

Such was the price of peace.

Freydolf only hoped Torio would forgive him.

30

A New Star Shines

Aurelius enjoyed his morning at the local vintners. While Tupper hefted kegs of sweet cider and bushels of apples into the carriage, the merchant swapped stories and tasted cups. Their past year's barter had yielded several bottles of a delicate pear cordial, which the farmer counted dear. But Aurelius had come prepared with a selection of wine bottles from his private store.

"Blushing bubblies from Pika shores. Iceberry wines from the far north, where summers are short. And the buttery bite of Basq liqueurs, which refresh the soul on hot afternoons."

The foreign delicacies culminated in a challenge to replicate old Master Platt's spiced ale, which he described with such eloquence that Tupper had to step in and translate.

"From what Frey said, it might not be ale. More like hard cider. But with a different fruit."

The farmer tugged at his beard. "But Mister Harrow, if you can't produce this fruit, I can't produce your ale. Do you know what it might be?"

"Aye. Platt was a Drom, and that means melons!" From a breast pocket, Aurelius withdrew half a dozen seed packets. "Make a start with these next summer. Sandy soil. Full sun."

Satisfied with his take and buoyed by future prospects,

Aurelius vaulted onto the driver's seat and took up the reins. "Do we have room in the stow for Auntie Watercress's daughter-in-law's delectable soup and Granny Thistledown's inestimable sauce?"

"Yes," Tupper replied. "I put the apples in the hidden compartment to make sure we look hungry."

"Good lad," the merchant praised. "Be sure to spread word that the family's expanding."

"They know. I asked the Shepley ladies for diapers. That was before I knew Carden's were coming up top. The Hayward ladies are making some, too."

Aurelius snorted. "And I procured a sizable quantity in Drom."

With a small shrug, the lad said, "We'll have plenty, and babies do come."

"In their own sweet time."

Tupper patted his arm. "Any day now. That's what Mother said."

"She's been saying that for nigh unto a fortnight," Aurelius grumbled.

They rolled into Shepley, where Tupper began the process of gathering in the canned goods he'd already spoken for the previous spring. Auntie Watercress leaned on her cane in the shade of a big tree and brokered new deals. Two newlywed women offered jars of jelly, and a couple of young men from an outlying farm had come in special to show off their mother's cheeses.

The dickering went off without a hitch, but Aurelius wondered at the odd intensity in Tupper's gaze. "I'd swear those are the eyes of a tracker, looking for some hint of a trail," muttered the Pred.

But what prey?

Marmalade and syrups. Honey and squash. Potted herbs and laying hens. The lad considered each offering with his usual gravity, but Aurelius could have sworn that he was more interested in the women's progeny than in their provender.

When Tupper brought two heavy crocks of molasses back to the carriage, Aurelius was ready. "Why are you inspecting the young ladies of this fair village, sprat?"

"Because the ones in Hayward won't work."

"Your people are an industrious lot."

Tupper shook his head. "But not many are brave enough."

"For what?"

The lad gazed up at him with guileless eyes. "For me."

Aurelius's eyebrows rose. "Aren't you a little young to be stalking potentials?"

"How old were you when you found Ulrica?"

"Thirteen."

Tupper said, "I'm thirteen."

"So you are," Aurelius conceded. "It seems deucedly young from this side of things."

"Yes. But Ewert thinks it'll take a while to find a good match."

Eyes glinting as he considered the gathered womenfolk, Aurelius asked, "Do you favor golden curls, silver curls, buff curls ...?"

With a small sigh, Tupper said, "They're all the same."

Nodding to a young girl whose finery was a cut above her age-mates, Aurelius asked, "Is that one pretty?"

"It doesn't matter. She's afraid of me. And a wife should trust her husband."

Aurelius's amazement redoubled. Not just a girl, then. A wife. "Aye, sprat. You're right to be choosy."

"How did you know Ulrica was the person you were looking for?"

With a faint smirk, the Pred admitted, "Miss Ulrica Rakefang was peerless in both pedigree and prospects. I could do *no* better."

"That's good."

"Nay, it was terrible!" Aurelius countered. "For I was the youngest son in a large, lowborn family. But I fought my way to her side. Mostly because that's where she wanted me to be."

Some of the clouds cleared from the lad's expression. "She loved you."

"Naturally."

"And you loved her."

"Without reserve, without reprieve, without regret."

"So lots?"

"Aye, sprat. Lots."

"That would be good." In a softer voice, Tupper added, "That's what I'm looking for."

Torio was sitting in the shade of the arbor outside the laundry, minding little Yona while Haimish and Farley hauled water for Melina's washing. He murmured nonsense and whispered secrets to the solemn girl with downy curls.

"Making off with our children?"

"Hardly, Missus Harrow. I was asked to keep hold of this wee tuft lest a summer breeze carry her away." Glancing up at the looming Pred, he asked, "Are you here to steal her away?"

"Difficult as it is to pry her from Haimish's grasp ... nay. There is time to tame this child." Ulrica shifted her weight so that the bells at her ankles sounded softly. "Her heart shall be mine."

Torio started at the sound, and peered warily at the Pred. After weeks of baring her fangs, why make a covert offer of peace. "Did you need something?"

"Aye. Show me your lady."

The Grif laughed uncomfortably. "I have a rapscallion of a servant hereabouts, and there's *this* little miss. That is the extent of my current connections to any person ...."

"My brother calls you a thief of hearts," Ulrica replied coolly.

"Hardly a compliment." Torio didn't care for the new light in the woman's gaze. Her irritability and rudeness were easily countered, but her interest was a fearsome thing.

"Nay, Freydolf *smiled* when he said it. Which can only mean one thing."

Torio smiled thinly. "Do tell! I am in suspense."

Ulrica's dark eyes gleamed. "My husband talks of a stone's

rarity and rating, for he cannot see past the paperwork. Such is the lot of those born without affinity. But when my brother looks into the heart of a stone, he sees its future."

"None could deny Master Fr–" He closed his mouth on the platitude when the point of Ulrica's blade touched the underside of his chin. If Torio thought he'd be safe because he was holding a baby, he was badly mistaken.

Ignoring the child nestled in the crook of his arm, Ulrica declared, "Your future interests me."

"I'm pleased to know I have one."

Her blade skimmed his jaw, and she repeated, "Show me your lady."

Torio cast about for the thread of magic he needed. Holding the woman's gaze, the Grif raised his voice. "Haimish, if you please?"

The brownstone Pred exited the laundry, hands outspread in his customary offer of help.

Clearing his throat, Torio said, "I apologize for curtailing my usefulness, but Missus Harrow has need of me. Take Yona?"

Haimish strolled over, but instead of reaching for the baby, he folded his hands around Ulrica's blade. His smile was gentle, but the shake of his head was firm.

"Oh, aye," muttered the woman. "As long as the frowsy fool cooperates, I'll sheathe my blade."

Yona burbled a greeting for her guardian, whose tail wagged.

Breathing his thanks for Haimish's intervention, Torio stalked off in the direction of the stables. "I'm not harboring a woman, and there's no romance in a rock."

"Tell that to Nerine."

Torio lapsed to muttering in Terse, and inside the stables he loosened the ties to the black stone's coverings. "There. Satisfied?"

"Far from it."

When Ulrica's hand came in contact with the stone, the Grif winced. "Hush, you irrational lump. She cannot harm you. You're a rock."

The Pred eyed him curiously. "What happened?"

"Uproar."

"Is she frightened of me ... or frightened for you?"

Torio blinked. "Me?"

Ulrica rolled her eyes, then addressed herself to the stone. "Hush, beauty. If you think I mean this wretch harm, you aren't listening properly. And it's no use squalling at me; I'm a dullard. You'll only frazzle your lion-hearted fool further if you fuss."

To Torio's surprise, the black stone's cries tapered off. Perhaps because Morven was reinforcing Ulrica's words by wreathing the Pred in soft ribbons of magic. The mountain seemed fond of her Keeper's ferocious sister.

"Listen for her bells," the man said wearily. "Anything else is dramatic flair."

"Aye," Ulrica drawled, resting her hand on her belly. "Since there will be no riddance, good or otherwise, I aim to make peace with you and the man you chose."

Torio almost laughed. Instead of reaching an accord with him, Ulrica was allying herself with his mountain. Sly thing.

With the ghost of a smile, Ulrica continued, "My child will never remember a time without Flox for playmates, nor the offensive jut of this Grif's nose. I'm in my brother's keeping, and this is the shape life must take on his mountain." Rapping the glossy black stone with her knuckles, she added, "Trust my brother with your hopes. He's a romantic."

Horrified as he was by Ulrica's implications, Torio was grateful for the offer of peace. Maybe he could relax now. "Thank you, Missus Harrow."

She waved her hand dismissively. "My opinion has changed little, so don't cross my path too often."

Torio bowed low. "It would be my pl–"

Her grip on his shoulders stole his breath, but this was no attack. Ulrica leaned heavily on him, her knuckles whitening along with her face. Her gaze was turned inward, and her breath hissed between her teeth.

"Missus, are you ...?"

"Another word, and I'll tear out your throat."

"It might be the babe."

"I'm a mother four times over. Do you think me an imbecile?"

Torio sighed. "And this *would* be the day Harrow decided to restock the wine cellar."

Once Ulrica caught her breath, she roared, "Graven!"

Moments later, the mosaic tiger's muzzle appeared in the stable doors.

Drawing her blade, the Pred said, "Bring my husband at once, or the Grif dies!"

"*Or,*" the Grif quickly interjected. "I could fetch Harrow for you. He's far less likely to flee at the sight of me."

"I'd rather *you* bore the brunt of my displeasure until Aurelius returns."

"Leave off, woman. I'm neither your prey nor your persecutor. Give me leave, and I'll fetch the fool who willingly lashed his life to yours."

Freydolf skidded to a stop outside the door, eyes wide as he leaned through. "What's going on in here ... Sister?"

Ulrica shuddered as tension wracked her frame. Then her hand closed around Torio's throat, claws dangerously close to drawing blood. "Bring. Him."

"On my life," Torio swore. "He'll be here in time."

Tupper turned to stare up at Morven. "Aurelius?"

"Aye," he replied distractedly. The lad had discovered that Granny Thistledown's daughter-in-law's aunt made pepper jellies, and Aurelius had parted with gold in order to bring eight jars of the delicacy home to Ulrica.

"Aurelius," the boy repeated. "Graven's here."

The Pred whirled into a defensive crouch, blades in both hands, sending any lingering Flox maidens skittering. "Sorry, sprat."

Oblivious to his loss of an audience, Tupper strode toward the edge of town just as Torio staggered out of the shrubbery and signaled. "Ah, young master," he called. "Pardon my intrusion upon your foraging venture, but my life is forfeit if I don't fetch Harrow."

"Is it Ulrica?" Tupper asked.

Torio rubbed his throat with a rueful expression. "None other."

Aurelius caught up and briskly asked, "Well?"

"She sent me to bring you," Torio explained. "Go feather her nest."

"When did she start?" the Pred asked, glancing at his team. It would take time for the horses to pull such a heavy load up the switchback trail.

"Not even an hour since."

With an eye on the sky, Tupper asked, "Do Pred babies take as long as Flox babies?"

"Aye."

Torio shook his head. "She was most urgent. Take the tiger, and I'll drive your rig."

Aurelius hesitated. "What do you think, sprat? Under the circumstances, will your tiger permit an uphill blitz with me on his back?"

"Yes. Graven likes Ulrica. And babies."

"But not *me*."

Tupper's mouth twitched. "I think you're his favorite."

"Oh, aye," he drawled, stalking into the forest. "I'll leave the rest to you, Kite."

With the lad's help, Graven left off snubbing long enough to be coaxed, and Aurelius enjoyed his second ride aback the tiger. Sleek power. Silent grace. Truth be told, the Pred considered this statue the finest steed he'd ever mounted. Perfect for the wild hunts and armed races of his homeland. But Aurelius held his tongue—and fistfuls of soft fur—as Graven bounded up Morven's steep, forested slopes.

At the entrance to the Harrow courtyard, Tupper slid down from behind Aurelius and grabbed the tiger's collar. "Thank you for helping the new papa reach his baby."

"New? This is my fifth time standing guard over Ulrica's birthing." Aurelius scrutinized Freydolf, who sat before their bathhouse entrance, looking vaguely ill. "Are you meant to be my stand-in?"

"Aye. Somehow."

Aurelius crouched before his brother-in-law and cuffed his shoulder. "Show a little backbone, Frey. You won't convince anyone that you're a threat."

"*He'll* handle the fending," the Keeper replied, waving toward Phineas, who barred the doors to the bathing chamber, swords drawn.

Hand under his heart, Aurelius bowed. "My thanks, good guardian. I'll join your vigil."

Tupper slipped up behind Freydolf and patted his shoulder. "Where's Nerine?"

"Inside with the other ladies. Ulrica counts her as a sister, and the tub was convenient."

Aurelius shook his head and muttered, "Was there ever such a birth? Attended by Flox and a mermaid."

"And a mountain," said Tupper. "Morven's excited."

"*Two* mountains," Frey corrected. "Torio's has been in a whirl since Ulrica's labor began."

"I'll check on her," the lad offered, jogging past Carden and Farley on his way out.

"Hey, mister," the younger Meadowsweet demanded. "You gonna fight us if we try to get past the prince?"

Choosing to ignore the question, Aurelius announced, "I'm upholding my traditional role as an imminently expectant father. My presence allows Ulrica to focus on our child."

Dulcie flitted to Aurelius's side. "Can I help?"

"Your Auntie Ree is a formidable woman. She'll manage."

The girl's face scrunched. "What's that?"

Kneeling, Aurelius explained, "She's brave and beautiful, and she knows all about babies. We can trust her."

"Aggie gets to help, but Mama says I'm too little."

"Aye. When you're Aggie's age, your turn will come."

Dulcie went up on tiptoe. "Will Auntie Ree have another baby then?"

Carden chuckled, and Aurelius muttered, "Perish the thought."

"When will Auntie Ree bring us a baby?"

"Patience, sprite. Such things take time." Catching Carden's eye, he asked, "How do Flox fathers pass the time while waiting for their progeny to put in an appearance?"

"First-time fathers are hustled to Old Gruff, whose special reserve is said to steady the worst of the shakes. After that, we're left to entertain our restless children and answer increasingly delicate questions."

Freydolf beckoned to Dulcie. "I understand that on summer days, Nerine's fountain doubles as a wading pool."

The girl's eyes widened. "Can we, Papa?" she begged.

Carden's smile was grateful. "That's a fine idea."

Farley sidled up to Aurelius and bluntly pointed out, "Nobody here would attack Ulrica. No one's that stupid. She's scary."

"Aye."

"Want a water war?" the lad challenged. "Carden says you're good with a bucket."

As appealing as it sounded to dunk and douse Farley by turns, Aurelius replied, "Nay. I wouldn't dream of abandoning my post."

"Who'd want to hurt a lady and her baby?" Farley demanded skeptically.

Aurelius wasn't about to explain. Waving at the fountain, he ordered, "Entertain your nieces."

An hour later, Carden had retreated with Haimish to feed and diaper little Yona. Dulcie was still puddling in the fountain with her uncles. Freydolf held high a watering can from the garden, creating a sun-sparkled shower. Dag, Rimbles, and Zev stayed clear of all the water nonsense, but Nott fell in so many times, she finally stayed in. Tupper had retrieved a dozen small blue figurines for Dulcie to play with, and Farley was boasting about his stallion.

Rosy-fair skin and wet ringlets.

Chit-chat and low laughter.

They were diverted and diverting, but Aurelius's attention kept straying to the occasional sounds emanating from the bathhouse at his back. Splashes and snatches of conversation. He couldn't catch any words, but their tones were easy to read.

Merona's confidence mingled with Melina's attempts at encouragement.

Every so often, Aggie would ask questions.

But Ulrica was deucedly silent.

Normally, there were aunties and cousins streaming in and out, and any of them could have carried a message. Did his wife even know he'd arrived?

"I'm here, my dear," he muttered. Drawing his dagger, he used the flat of the blade and struck stone. Two beats. A pause. Two beats more. The wordless signal they used when hunting in tandem.

From within the chamber, two crisp raps sounded, followed by two more.

Aurelius smiled. "Two hearts, one beat. As ever."

Hooves clopped their way along cobbles, and Aurelius's carriage drew up to his gates. Torio leapt down and strolled into the courtyard, but his steps checked at the sight of Aurelius. "Why are you here?"

"I live here, Kite."

The Grif frowned. "I wouldn't have thought you would toy with my very existence."

Aurelius switched to Terse. "Talk sense, man."

With a disgusted noise, Torio strode up and took Aurelius by the arms. "You're a dullard, so I can forgive you for ignoring the mountain's prompts, but your wife's instructions were clear as the skies where eagles soar." Turning the Pred to face the entrance, Torio shoved. *"Bring him,* she said. And you shall be brought!"

Reluctant to injure the idiot who manhandled him past

Phineas, Aurelius found himself face to face with the Statuary's womenfolk. Both Merona and Melina looked shocked, and Nerine rose up defensively before them, arms widespread.

Torio raised his voice. "Lady, I fulfill my oath. Here is your mate, to feather your nest."

Aurelius rounded on him. "Nests and feathers. What does that *mean*? In plain Terse or Verit. I'll even take your answer in sketchy Skrit."

The man drew himself up. "If your customs differ, please excuse my trespass. But when Missus Harrow begged you brought, I naturally assumed ...." Torio rubbed his nose. "Grif fathers attend the births of their children. The mother delivers their child into his hands."

"Ah," Aurelius managed.

"On my life," Kite said in a clear voice. "I brought him in time. Keep him or cast him out, according to your good pleasure." Then he turned on his heel and left.

Aurelius didn't know what to expect from Ulrica. They'd certainly abandoned their share of traditions and strictures, but would she support this fresh audacity?

The Meadowsweet women kept their own counsel, awaiting Ulrica's verdict.

Nerine sank lower in the tub, allowing the man to meet his wife's gaze.

Aurelius lifted his hands in mute appeal.

"If you had a tail, would it be tucked?" Ulrica challenged.

"Aye. These Grif have strange ways."

Ulrica's chin lifted. "Afraid to bloody your hands?"

"Never. This family is ours to forge as *we* see fit. Do you want me here? Or gone."

"Never," she whispered, lifting her own hands in a show of willingness.

Aurelius needed no further urging to take his place at Ulrica's side.

When the long summer was finally fading, during the autumn festival's birth season by Pred reckoning, magic vibrated through the Statuary's galleries as Morven reveled in tears. A mother's pain. A father's pride. A newborn's hearty squall.

Everyone crowded around when Aurelius strolled from the birthing chamber with precious cargo.

"A son," he announced. "A son to bear the name Harrow."

Freydolf slipped his finger under the tiny hand that clutched the blanket's edge. Grinning broadly when hazy gold eyes blinked up at him, the Keeper rumbled, "Hello, nephew."

Tupper gasped, "He has *claws*."

"What did you *expect*, sprat?"

"This is my first Pred baby," the lad protested. Brushing soft auburn fuzz, he asked, "What will you call him?"

Aurelius's gaze swept all those gathered, including them in his son's naming. "A new branch is added to our tree. May he grow straight and strong. A new star shines in our sky. May he add glory to the name we bestow." In ringing tones, he boasted, "I have a son—Quintrell Harrow."

In the stables, the heart of a mountain eavesdropped on Morven's wordless song and struggled to learn its meaning. One person noticed her fitful echoes. A boy slipped into the stables and held his lantern high. Pressing his hand to the glossy surface that reflected his face, he remarked, "You're stronger than the others. Brighter."

Drawn by his confidence, she reached back the only way she knew how. Clumsy bursts of power and a soft keening.

Her visitor snickered. "Show off."

Intrigued by his fearlessness, she tried to hold him, but she didn't know the word for him. Her frustration turned to whimpers.

"Shush, or Tupp will find out," he grumbled. "And if you're looking for a name to call, mine's Farley. Farley Meadowsweet."

THIS ENDS BOOK TWO

Thank you for purchasing *Harrow*. I do hope the tale was to your liking. If so, I shall borrow from Flox tradition and say,

"THE TRADE IS GOOD; MAY OUR NEXT BE BETTER STILL."

C. J. MILBRANDT has always believed in miracles, especially small ones. A lifelong bookworm with a love for fairy tales, far-off lands, and fantasy worlds, CJ began spinning adventures of her own. Her family-friendly stories mingle humor and whimsy with a dash of danger and a touch of magic. Follow your curiosity to CJMilbrandt.com, where you'll find more stories and story art. CJ's books are also on GoodReads.

 Harrow began as a personal writing challenge. The entire Galleries of Stone trilogy was written on the fly, posted in three hundred and sixty-six daily installments during 2012. Completely crazy. Entirely satisfying.

GALLERIES OF STONE
Meadowsweet
Harrow
Rakefang

GALLERIES OF STONE
3
Rakefang
C. J. MILBRANDT

www.ingramcontent.com/pod-product-compliance
Lightning Source LLC
Chambersburg PA
CBHW061053100726
47911CB00012B/210